#UofJ3

PLAYING FOR KEEPS

PLAYING FOR KEEPS

#UofJ3

ALLEY CIZ

HOUSE OF CRAZY
PUBLISHING

Also by Alley Ciz

UofJ Series

Looking To Score

Game Changer

Playing For Keeps

Untitled #UofJ4- Add to TBR Releasing end of 2021

Savage Queen: A Royalty Crew U of J Spin-Off Novel- Preorder,
Releasing April 2021

BTU Alumni Series

Power Play (Jake and Jordan)

Tap Out (Gage and Rocky)

Sweet Victory (Vince and Holly)

Puck Performance (Jase and Melody)

Writing Dirty (Maddey and Dex)

BTU6- Coming 2021

**@UofJ411: House parties and handcuffs don't mix.
#IsThatBlood #DontMessWithTheFlock #Kaysonova**

The mighty Casanova has fallen.
Me: six foot five, two hundred and fifty pounds, collegiate
football player.
Protected by my pint-sized girlfriend.
Comical. Ridiculous. **BROKEN.**
She tackled my heart, but *they* want the rest of me.

Mason Nova is…MINE.
Gossips *love* drama. Anything to up their likes, especially
when *we're* the story.
Enough is **ENOUGH.**
I stopped hiding and paid the price…even have the *scars* to
prove it. It's time to control *my* narrative.
I'm taking a page from my boyfriend's playbook to prove he's
not the only one playing for keeps.

PLAYING FOR KEEPS is book 3 in the U of J Series and cannot be read as a stand-alone. It picks up right after the epic cliffhanger in GAME CHANGER threw you off of. Our rainbow-haired sass queen is out to prove her Caveman isn't the only alpha in their relationship to win their #HEA.

Playing For Keeps (#UofJ3)

Alley Ciz

Paperback ISBN: 978-1-950884-16-2

Ebook ISBN: 978-1-950884-15-5

Cover Designer: Julia Cabrera at Jersey Girl Designs

Cover Photographer: Wander Book Club Photography

Cover Models: Megan Napolitan & Wayne Skivington

Editing: Jessica Snyder Edits, C. Marie

Proofreading: Gem's Precise Proofreads; Dawn Black

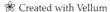 Created with Vellum

To my readers. For trusting me to shove them off cliffs and still coming back.
 # ILiveForYourShoutyCaps

Author Note

Dear Reader,

**PLAYING FOR KEEPS IS BOOK 3 in the U of J Series. You
must read book 1, LOOKING TO SCORE AND book 2,
GAME CHANGER, prior to this installment to follow the
story properly.**

#UofJ Series:

1. Looking To Score
2. Game Changer
3. Playing For Keeps

*If I'm new to you and you haven't read my BTU Alumni books
you're fine.
If you have met my other crazy squad of friends and Covenettes
there are a few cameos in here you might enjoy, with a tiny time gap
between the two series.*

XOXO
Alley

IG Handles

CasaNova87: Mason 'Casanova' Nova (TE)
QB1McQueen7: Travis McQueen (QB)
CantCatchAnderson22: Alex Anderson (RB)
SackMasterSanders91: Kevin Sanders (DE)
LacesOutMitchell5: Noah Mitchell (K)
CheerGodJT: JT (James) Taylor
TheGreatestGrayson37: G (Grant) Grayson
ThirdBaseAdam16: Adam
CheerNinja: Rei
TheBarracksAtNJA: The Barracks
NJA_Admirals: The Admirals
TightestEndParker85: Liam Parker

Nicknames

Mason Nova: Casanova / Mase
Kayla Dennings: Kay / PF / Smalls / Short Stack
E (Eric) Dennings
CK (Chris) Kent
Em (Emma) Logan
Q (Quinn)
JT (James) Taylor <CTG BFF- Cradle-To-Grave Best Friend Forever>
T (Tessa) Taylor
Pops (James) Taylor Sr.
G (Grant) Grayson
D (Dante) Grayson
Travis McQueen: Trav / QB1
Mama G- Mrs. Grayson
Papa G- Mr. Grayson
B (Ben) Turner

Playlist

- "I Won't Give Up"- Christina Grimmie
- "I'm Not Okay (I Promise)- My Chemical Romance
- "Youngblood"- 5 Seconds of Summer
- "Sit Still, Look Pretty"- Daya
- "Crazy Girl"- Eli Young Band
- "Castle"- Halsey
- "If I Can't Have You"- Shawn Mendes
- "Game Time"- Flo Rida
- "White Flag"- Bishop Briggs
- "Love On Top"- Beyonce
- "Classic"- MKTO
- "All We Do Is Win"- DJ Khalid
- "Lights Down Low"- MAX
- "Move"- Little Mix
- "Rumors"- Jake Miller
- "Burn It To The Ground"- Nickleback
- "Remember My Name"- Fort Minor
- "Don't Let Me Down"- The Chainsmokers
- "Amen"- Halestorm
- "Sucker"- Jonas Brothers
- "We Ready"- Archie Eversole

- "Glory"- The Score
- "The Bones"- Maren Morris feat Hozier
- 'Watch Me Burn"- Michele Morrone
- "Queen"- Loren Gray
- "I Don't Care"- Fall Out Boy
- "Superpower"- Adam Lambert
- "Headstrong"- Trapt
- "Keep On"- Kehlani
- "This Is How We Do It"- Montell Jordan

FIND PLAYLIST on Spotify.

#Chapter1

BLOOD.

The tremendous amount of blood has the edges of my vision going blurry as the ever-growing puddle of red continues to expand.

What the fuck just happened?

It's like I blacked out, only to awaken to a nightmare.

Kay is in a crumpled heap on the floor, and that motherfucking pool of crimson only gets larger.

Can I get a replay?

I run the tape back in my head, but the last thing I can remember is feeling Kay's hands pushing against my side.

Instinct finally kicks in and has me rushing to her side, yelling for someone to "CALL 911!" as I do. My knee cracks as I bend next to Kay's prone body.

My hands hover an inch over her, itching to touch her, to roll her and scoop her into my arms where I can keep her safe. I flex my fingers, spreading them out completely in indecision. Unsure how badly hurt she is, I can't risk moving her.

"Ambo's on the way," someone behind me confirms.

As scared as I am to touch her, I'm concerned about the amount of blood starting to stain her rainbow-colored curls. Head wounds bleed excessively, but I still need to address it.

The last thing we need added to this is Kay bleeding out before help can arrive. I whip my Hawks polo over my head and, with great care, press it to her temple.

How the hell did this happen? Why is she hurt?

With the gentlest of touches, I stroke the side of her face. The sight of a bruise already forming on her cheek has me biting the inside of mine hard enough that the coppery taste of blood coats my tongue. Rage floods my veins, pumping hot and fast through my body.

"Kay, baby." With light, steady pressure, I stretch my thumb to brush underneath the fringe of lashes on her unbruised cheek. "Come on, sweetheart, open those beautiful eyes of yours and show them to me."

Nothing.

No response.

Not even a flutter of her eyelashes or a twitch of her lids.

"Come on, Skittles." My forehead drops to hers. "I *need* you to open your eyes for me, baby."

She's so still. If it wasn't for the steady rise and fall of her chest, I would be afraid she was dead.

What can I do? How can I help her?

My muscles protest being crouched after hours of playing football. What I wouldn't give for Kay to lay into me about proper aftercare right now.

The shuffle of feet and a flurry of activity happens behind me, but every molecule of my being is still focused on my baby.

A hand touches the back of my bare shoulder, and I twist to see a navy blue shirt belonging to the male paramedic attempting to get close enough to Kay to exam her.

I know I should move, know they need space to work, but I *can't* bring myself to do it.

An authoritative command from the paramedic to do so has me reaching out to shove the table out of the way, stepping over Kay's body, and maintaining my close proximity while they get to work.

The smooth, barely textured material of a nitrile glove grips my hand with purpose, and I meet the confident *I got this* gaze of the EMT then release my hold on the shirt I used to stanch the blood flow of Kay's head wound.

"Can you tell us what happened?" He directs his question to me with a quick flick of his eyes up before dropping them to where he slowly peels the material away from Kay's head to inspect the injury site.

I wish I could say yes, wish I had the answer, but all I have are questions; I shake my head.

Trav makes his way over to my side, the unyielding clench of his jaw causing the bone to jut out as he takes in the efficient movements of Kay's vitals being taken and a c-collar being strapped around her small neck. His eyes darken in anger as they move to meet mine. I can tell by the strain around them that I'm not going to like what he has to say.

#Chapter2

"SHE WAS PUNCHED."

I blink.

Then blink again.

I must have heard that wrong. No way did Trav say someone hit her. *Right?*

There's a shuffle of feet, and one of the police officers—who must have arrived around the same time as the EMTs—moves in closer as the paramedic's head snaps up to me, an accusatory glare plastered across his face.

"The fuck you looking at?" I growl, annoyed as all fuck that he could even *think* I'm capable of harming a single hair on Kay's colorful head.

Above me, someone clears their throat, but I ignore it. That's not the point right now. No, that would be *who* the *fuck* punched my girl?

"Who?" I bark at Trav, jumping to my feet, itching for a fight. Someone thought they could put hands on what's mine? Time for that person to learn a lesson—a *very* painful one.

Trav looks from me to the officer whose hand dropped to his gun belt at the rage radiating off me before swinging back my way. His eyes harden and his chest expands with a deep inhalation before he says, "Liam Parker."

Fuck me! How could I forget about that douchemonkey and his little posse showing up to start shit?

Everything that got pushed aside in the wake of my worry for Kay comes flooding back.

The insults he slung.

The way he looked at what's mine like it was his.

I tried to keep Kay carefully behind me, but I remember her stepping in front of me then her arms wrapping around me.

Why didn't she stay behind me where she was safe?

But…

That doesn't explain how he was able to hit her.

You know what? None of that shit matters. Only this does.

Liam Parker hit Kay.

He put hands on her, and now she's unconscious and bleeding on the floor.

He's *dead*.

I whip my gaze around the room, searching for him, my hands curling into fists at my sides.

"He's not here." I spin around at Trav's statement; clearly the roaring inside my ears is making it impossible for me to hear him correctly. "He slipped out while everyone reacted to seeing Kay fly across the room."

The enamel on my teeth is at risk of wearing away from how I grind them. I want to say my best friend is exaggerating about what happened, but based on where Kay's body is and the blood on the corner of the table, there was definite force behind the hit she received.

"Just like the snake he is," Em says, pushing through the crowd of onlookers. I thought she went mama bear on me the first time she saw me after the breakup, but now she's full-on murderous. *Get in line, Em. Get. In. Line.*

As soon as I know Kay is okay, I'm going hunting.

#THE GRAM

#Chapter3

UOFJ411: I didn't do it. #ImInnocent

picture of two cop cars in front of the AK house

@Oamberwhereartthou: Have the Alphas ever had a party that the cops had to break up? #Untouchable

@Ofbooksandportkeys: Talk about a victory party. #WeKnowHowToParty

UofJ411: Drama at the AK house #PartyFoul #CasanovaWatch

picture of Kay being loaded into the back of an ambulance

@Lynnstifle: Oh, shit! Isn't that @CasaNova87 girl? #SomeoneCall911 #CasanovasGirl

@Madameizzy: Who has the deets? #NeedToKnowWhat-Happened #CasanovaWatch #CasanovasGirl

@Cheril2412: Anyone else think someone is about to die for this? #DontMessWithTheFlock #CasanovaWatch #CasanovasGirl

. . .

UofJ411: King watching over his queen #CasanovaWatch #Kaysonova

picture of Mason by Kay's side inside the ambulance

@Mimi_reads: Is it wrong to swoon over how he's not leaving her side? #IfItsWrongIDontWantToBeRight #CasanovaWatch #Kaysonova

@Miss_rae_mcnally: @CasaNova87 looks pissed AF here #IfLooksCouldKill #Kaysonova

#Chapter4

AFTER THE ARRIVAL of the first responders and the revelation that Liam *fucking* Parker is the cause of me being stuck in a living nightmare, it feels like someone pushes a button and everything happens in fast forward.

The police officers start questioning those who didn't scatter.

The EMTs finish their examination of Kay and load her onto a gurney.

I climb into the back of the ambulance, not once giving them the opportunity to deny me, while our friends and most of the party attendants not being questioned filter outside to watch the drama unfold, the former hustling to the parking lot behind the AK house to get into cars and follow us to University General Hospital.

Before the metal doors close, I see Grayson already on the phone calling E, and I shout out to Em to call JT as well. If the situation were reversed, I know Kay would be on the first flight to Kentucky.

The thin cushion on the bench seat does nothing to help absorb the bumps and potholes as we speed over the roads to U Gen.

I reach out and take one of Kay's small hands between

both of mine, smoothing a thumb across her knuckles. She looks so tiny and helpless, her skin a ghostly white to match the gauze now wrapped around her head in place of my polo.

"I love you, baby." It's a statement, a declaration, a whole-hearted promise.

U Gen is only minutes from campus since it's associated with the U of J's medical school, but each mile feels like thousands without Kay ever opening her eyes.

I pray to God, to my dad…*hell*, to whoever will listen that she will be alright. It's impossible to imagine a scenario where she isn't.

The rig comes to a stop, the doors are thrown open, people in white lab coats and red and maroon scrubs swarm in, waiting as I jump out and let the paramedics unload Kay, the wheels of the gurney hitting the asphalt with a loud *clunk!*

My sneakers pound against the tile floor as I rush to keep up with the flow of people hurrying inside the emergency room, the smell of antiseptic filling my nostrils as medical jargon and statistics about Kay's condition are volleyed between the EMTs and doctors.

My gut rolls and I have to swallow down bile at the thought of her having an injury so catastrophic it's considered a *condition*.

Two blue doors swing open as they push Kay into an open trauma room. I follow, almost certain I'm not supposed to, but I don't give a fuck. Wild horses couldn't drag me away.

Four-legged Equidae may not be able to stop me, but a dark-haired nurse in U of J-red scrubs has no problem keeping me from taking my place at Kay's side where I belong. "Stop right there, hotshot."

I glare down at the nurse, my gaze going to the palm splayed in the universal sign of her command then back to her face again. She can't be serious.

"You good, Vic?" one of the other nurses calls out, and I swear the edges of her lips curl in an *I dare you to try me* smile in response. She's tall—then again, most females seem tall when compared to the one being worked on a few feet away —but I could easily move her.

"Yeah." She nods, never taking her eyes off me. "I got this."

I narrow my eyes, adding every ounce of intimidation behind my glower. Her smile only grows until I can see a line of white from her teeth.

"If I can put a Kraken in his place on the reg, a little foot-ball player doesn't scare me." The humor behind her words washes over me, loosening some of the panic trying to strangle me like a noose. It probably helps that she referred to me as *little* when I can't ever recall being called that in my life.

"Now, Mr. Nova…" She glances over her shoulder to check the status of things, and I experience another stomach cramp at the sight of Kay's wound being flushed with saline when I follow her gaze. With the hospital's association with the school, it comes as no surprise she knows who I am. "Can you tell us what happened to Kayla?"

I swallow and have to work to clear the football-sized ball of emotion stuck in my throat before I can answer. It only gets worse when I see a doctor holding up a curved needle in preparation for stitching Kay's head wound closed.

"She was punched." I throw my arms up, holding my hands out to display my innocence. "It wasn't me," I rush to get out.

"Never thought that for a second." She places a comforting hand on my bicep, her blue eyes softening. Based on the paramedics' reactions earlier, that was the last thing I expected her to say, especially with such absolute certainty. "What about the gash?"

Again my eyes flip up to Kay, my foot rising to take a step closer of its own accord. As if anticipating it, the nurse—Vic-something—shifts with me, keeping me in place.

I have to shove my hands into the pockets of my jeans to

prevent myself from balling them into fists as I recall the details my friends filled me in on. I'm only one step inside the room, but it's obvious I'm not even supposed to be that close. I can't risk losing that small liberty due to someone thinking I'm threatening the staff when my fury is fully directed at one Liam Parker.

"She hit her head on a table when she fell." I have to pause and clear my throat once again. "I didn't want to risk moving her, but I tried to stop the bleeding with my shirt, and I touched her face *gently*, trying to get her to open her eyes but...*but*...she never did." My words come out rushed, breaking off at the end, the fear of what this could all mean getting the best of me.

Tears sting the backs of my eyes, but I blink them away, refusing to let them fall. I'm not afraid to cry, but I am afraid if I give in to the emotion, it'll be like confirming the worst-case scenario with the universe.

"We're taking her down to CT, Vicki," calls out someone I assume is a doctor based on the white lab coat, the bed Kay is lying on already in motion toward the doors opposite the ones I stand in front of.

"Thank you, Dr. Holloway. I'll stay with Mr. Nova until the results are back."

Just like before, she shifts with me when I attempt to follow. I appreciate her for offering to wait with me—really, I do—but how can she expect me to stay behind when that's my heart they're taking away?

Please be okay, baby.

At nurse Vicki's suggestion, we make a pit stop at the bathroom so I can wash the blood—Kay's blood—off my hands. As I watch the crimson-tinted water swirl around the drain, my veins burn with the need for vengeance.

The only thing powerful enough to keep me from chasing down Liam Parker right this moment is the necessity of being here for Kay in any way possible.

Psst! Over here. My inner coach chimes in for the first time in a while. *We should figure out where they do the testing and go get our girl.*

Now that's a play I can get on board with.

I crumple the rough paper towel in my hands and toss it into the garbage, ready to follow through on my new plan, but I stop short in the doorway to the bathroom at the knowing look nurse Vicki sends my way.

"You alpha men are all the same," she says on a laugh, dropping her crossed arms and pushing off of the wall she was leaning against to step to my side.

"What do you mean?" I feign ignorance, which earns me another laugh. I don't know what I expected from the emergency room staff, but she was not it.

"Aw, you're trying to play dumb...cute." Her hand is cool when she pats me on the back, reminding me I'm still shirtless. She increases the pressure of her touch, steering us through the emergency department and out toward the waiting room. "Now, before you go trying to pull out those dimples the world knows you have"—she circles a finger in front of my face while I think, *Yeah, thanks for that, Instagram* —"just know those don't work on me either. *And*...don't try to say that wasn't your next move. Like I said"—she nods to herself—"I know alpha men."

For the first time since Liam Parker crashed the AK victory party, I feel my own lips tug upward.

The automatic doors *whoosh* open, and it feels like every person waiting turns to look. To be fair, the majority of them are people I know.

There's a cluster of my teammates huddled together on one side of the room, the camaraderie of the team proving its strength as they lend their support while a set of officers take their statements.

Across the room, Kev leans against the wall, his arms folded over his broad chest, standing guard as Trav and Grayson do their best to wear a groove in the floor in front of where CK looks to be trying—and failing—to comfort Em and Quinn—*Are they upset or pissed off?* Bailey, who I'm surprised to see, doesn't seem as concerned as she scrolls through something on her phone.

Em's the first to spot me, jumping up and almost knocking over the coffees Noah and Alex are passing out in her rush to get to me.

The floodgates open and nurse Vicki and I are swarmed, questions flying and tripping over one another in the quest for information.

If I had expected nurse Vicki to be bothered, I would have been disappointed. Nope, instead I swear she's amused by the spectacle despite it taking *forever* to quiet everyone enough to relay the little information I have.

More than a dozen variations of *How's Kay?* come at me. If only I knew how to answer them.

Chapter5

CHAOS.

Pure and utter chaos.

You know the phrase *too many cooks in the kitchen*? Yeah, well the same concept could be applied to loved ones in the waiting room. Nothing, I mean *nothing* is getting accomplished. Everyone talks and shouts over the other, and I can't get a word in edgewise. Kay will be done with her tests before I can tell these crazies that's what's happening.

"Oh my god, Mase." Bette's breaths are coming out in pants as if she was running as she pushes her way to my side.

Arms wrap around my middle, and I return her embrace and exchange a dude nod with E over her head. *How are they here already?* So much has happened, but a quick glance at the clock on the opposite wall confirms it's only been about an hour since Grayson called them.

"How's Kay?" E asks at the same time I ask, "How did you get here so fast?"

I honestly have no idea why this information is important to me. Maybe I just need to distract myself with anything that isn't my ever-growing worry for Kay; who knows.

"We took a helicopter." E slashes a hand through the air. "That doesn't matter. How's my sister? Where is she?"

"They took her for tests." This time I give in and let my hands curl into fists, my knuckles straining with the effort. "They're concerned she might have a bleed in her brain because she was still unconscious."

"*Ohmygod.*" Bette's hands fly up to cover her mouth, tears springing to her eyes. E reaches for her and tucks her against his side while she tries to hold it together.

"The doctors should be up shortly with the results. The tests themselves don't take too long, and they would have moved Kayla to the front of the line," nurse Vicki informs us all.

The group lets out a breath as a whole. Not much longer for an update.

Whether it will be good or bad is the real question.

A throat clearing brings our attention around to the two officers I saw speaking with my teammates. They introduce themselves, and I realize they aren't the same ones I remember seeing at the AK house. To be honest, it was such chaos they could have been there and I might not have seen them.

They start to explain what they've been doing since arriving on the scene earlier this evening, but before they can start to get our statements, Dr. Holloway returns. When his dark eyes land on our group, I recognize him immediately.

"Family of Kayla Dennings?"

E and I step forward simultaneously.

"Is my sister okay?" E's voice wavers on the question.

"Her scans came back clear, no bleed in the brain, but she will feel the lingering effects of her concussion for a few days."

My entire body sags in relief, Bette fitting herself under my arm the only thing keeping me from collapsing to the floor completely.

"The gash on her head took five stitches to close, but it's

close to her hairline, which should minimize any appearance of a scar."

Stitches—she needed fucking stitches because of that asshat.

"Due to the contusions Kayla suffered from her fall and the one on her face where the punch impacted, we also took a number of x-rays."

Nails dig into my forearm from the bracing hold Bette takes on me, but I don't flinch. My rage surges with each reminder of all the ways Kay was hurt and serves as a balm to everything else.

"Kayla isn't in any serious danger. However…" The somberness in the doctor's tone has my back straightening in attention. "She will require surgery to properly reset the fracture in her cheekbone."

It was bad enough knowing that motherfucker put hands on a woman—*my* woman—but to literally break a part of her…homicidal is too tame a word to describe the feelings ripping through my system.

"When will her surgery be?" Bette asks.

"Within the hour," Dr. Holloway confirms.

"Will you be doing it?"

"No." The doctor shakes his head. "One of our plastic surgeons, Dr. Nikols, will be performing the surgery." He lifts his arm to check his watch. "She should be down shortly to discuss the procedure and recovery with you all and Kayla."

That gets my attention. Does that mean…

"Is she awake?" It's impossible to keep the hope from bleeding into my words.

"Yes." He nods. "She regained consciousness during her tests. She's a little groggy from the pain medicine we administered and the concussion, but she's been asking for you."

What the fuck? He waits until *now* to tell me this? What the hell are we standing around here for? I knew I should have chased after them earlier.

A familiar chuckle reaches my ears, and I can tell nurse Vicki has once again read my mind. "Slow your roll, hotshot." Her slim fingers circle my wrist, halting my movements. "You can't all go back there."

Dr. Holloway takes a moment to look over the crowd standing before him, and from the widening of his eyes, you can tell he's shocked by the sheer number of people. "Yes, that is correct. I can only allow four of you in to see her for now."

"I'm the fourth." Tessa Taylor, having arrived at some point during the pandemonium of questions, jumps forward, linking a hand with E's and shooting an apology over her shoulder to Grayson. Not one person here would deny that E, Bette, and I would be the other three.

"I'm aware Kayla sustained her injuries from an assault." Dr. Holloway speaks to the group as a whole but gives the bulk of his attention to the two officers. "Given the severity of those injuries and the resulting concussion and pain medicine administered, now is not the best time to get a statement."

"Understood." The officers are quick to nod their acceptance. "We will still need to speak with both Ms. Dennings and Mr. Nova eventually, but that can wait. With video taken of the incident and statements from witnesses at the scene, we have enough to proceed with bringing up charges should her family wish to do so."

"You're goddamn right we do," E fumes. "Throw the whole fucking book at that son of a bitch."

Bette runs a hand over E's back to calm him. This is not the time or place for him to lose it, not that I'm doing any better at the moment.

"Listen…" E says after taking a deep calming breath. "I'll give you whatever you need from me, just let me check on my sister first. After that I'm all yours."

Details sorted, Dr. Holloway informs nurse Vicki where we can find Kay, and we follow her back through the emergency room, past various bays and beds filled with other patients being treated, until we come to one toward the back.

I stare at the white curtain in front of me as if by doing so hard enough, I can see through it. The metal rings clink and clang as nurse Vicki pulls it aside, and I suck in a breath at what's revealed.

Kay looks even smaller and more fragile than I've ever seen her, lying propped up in the hospital bed. Her blonde curls are in disarray across the pillows supporting her, the usually vibrant rainbow highlights almost appearing muted by the gravity of the situation.

There's a faint hint of orange peeking out from under the dressing covering her temple left over from the betadine solution used to clean her wound, and the bruise on her cheek is more prominent than it was half an hour ago. The center is a garish yellow ringed by red, and the outer layer is a deep purple. My molars grind knowing underneath the baseball-sized bruise lies a broken bone.

"Oh, Kay," Bette coos, walking slowly to her side, dragging E with her since their hands are clasped together tightly.

Kay stirs at the sound of her sister-in-law's voice, but her eyes remain closed.

Tessa hangs back at the foot of the bed while I make my way up Kay's right side. Carefully, I slip a finger under the edge of her hospital gown, lifting it to see how bad her injuries are. I mutter more than a few choice curses at the mottled pattern of discoloration decorating her ivory skin. Seeing her hurt like this breaks a part of me.

"Kay?" I brush a knuckle over the curve of her uninjured cheek. "Can you open up for me, baby?" I ghost a fingertip over her closed lashes.

"You—" She coughs. "You talking dirty to me, Caveman?"

The relief of hearing her voice is enough to have my legs give out, and I have to catch myself on the hard railing of her bed. "Fuck, baby." I lock my knees so I don't eat it and bend over to rest my forehead to hers, one of my hands going around to cup the back of her neck. Everything and everyone fades away as I pause to breathe her in. It doesn't matter that her peppermint and vanilla is masked by antiseptic; all that does matter is that she's here, she's awake, and she seems to be alright.

"There's my girl," I say when I finally get a glimpse of her gray eyes.

"Why are you naked?" Kay asks, her gaze moving down my neck to my bare torso.

A deep chuckle rumbles from inside my chest. "I have pants on."

"Pity," she whispers before her eyes fall closed again.

Just seeing her awake was staggering, but hearing her usual brand of sass has me close to tears. I swallow down the emotion and place a kiss on her forehead.

"Why *are* you shirtless?" E asks, the stress lines on his face already easing. "Don't you have any self-respect, man?"

I raise my tatted arm, making the ink dance with a flex. "Jelly, old man?" I tease back, latching onto a rare moment of levity in the heavy.

"I'll show you an old man." E brings his arms down in front of him, doing his best impression of a bodybuilder, twisting his face and grunting for added effect.

"I can't even with you two." Bette rolls her eyes in a very Kay-like fashion.

"You're not going to hear any complaints from me." Tessa eyes me with a shrug, giving me a wink when I look her way.

Soft laughter comes from Kay, her hand squeezing mine as she comes back to the moment.

"You"—E swings an arm around to point at Tessa—"are *too* young to be noticing boys."

Another laugh from Kay, but this one is followed by a groan and a mutter about not rolling her eyes.

"I'm sixteen, not *six*, E." Tessa puts a hand on her hip and cocks it, punctuating her statement in true teenage fashion.

"Is he even allowed to be in here like that?" E waves a hand at me but directs his question to nurse Vicki. By the time she finishes checking the fluid levels on the IV, Kay has fallen back asleep.

"I'm not sure I'm the best person to ask. From what my daughter-in-law tells me, my son struggles to keep his clothes on...even inside her work kitchen." With that parting shot, she pats me on the shoulder again, the slap of skin on skin only emphasizing my nakedness, before taking her leave.

E steps out, saying he needs to make a phone call before talking to the police, and I turn my attention back to Kay. I don't care that she wasn't awake for long; getting a few moments with her conscious is enough for now.

Chapter6

WATCHING Dr. Nikols and her team wheel Kay away for surgery is one of the hardest things I've ever had to do. Hell, I feel like that's been the theme of the night, but I can't protect her if she's not with me, and I loathe that.

Nurse Vicki arrives at the same time as the surgical team, and with her is one Jordan Donovan.

"And you thought my kids kept you on your toes," Vicki says to Jordan, a comfortable air of familial affection between them.

"Please, Mama Steele"—Jordan waves off the comment —"*half* the shit Vince gets into is because of my wombmate." Shrewd hazel eyes track from me to E. "Plus, a little bit of football drama might be a nice change."

I get the impression there's something I'm missing, but I don't have the brain capacity to handle it with everything else going on.

"For someone I pay to help manage my public profile, you sure do give me a lot of shit, Donovan," E says as he and Bette exchange hugs hello with the PR dynamo. Jordan Donovan is nothing like you would expect given her cut-throat reputation when it comes to her clients. For starters, most of the "suits" in the sports business always come dressed the part—i.e. in a

suit or such—not leggings and an oversized New Jersey Bliz-
zards hoodie.

"I may talk shit"—Jordan splays a hand over the yeti
printed on her chest—"but I was able to convince Mama
Steele to use her pull here to get Kay into one of the bigger
rooms with a couch and a large recliner. You can thank me for
having   a   more   comfortable   place   to   sit,
sleep…*whatever*…later."

Bette turns, burying her face against E's side to smother
her laughter, but her bouncing shoulders give her away. Tessa
has no such qualms and is bent over with her arms banded
across her stomach.

I carry the surprising good humor with me while I take
care of the unpleasant task of giving my statement to the
waiting police officers. Hopefully, I can keep them from
seeing the malice simmering beneath my surface.

The time I spent talking to the police was a lot shorter than I
would have expected. Thankfully they meant it when they
said they had enough evidence from others, because I wasn't
much help, seeing as I'm not completely clear on what went
down. Most of what I gave was backstory about what led up
to tonight.

As soon as I'm done, nurse Vicki—or Mama Steele, as
Jordan refers to her—escorts us and what she says is "half the
U of J campus" to the surgical waiting room on the fourth
floor. It's a lot nicer than the one for the emergency department. The ceilings are two stories high, and the couches and
cushioned seats are done in a homey tan and gray color
scheme.

This late at night—or early in the morning, depending on
how you look at it—there's only one other couple besides our

group in the space. Other than looking our way when we first clomp in, they don't pay us much mind.

Much to the hospital staff's relief, a quick thank you to my teammates was all it took to cut our numbers down to sixteen people. It doesn't seem like much, but you notice when the original group was upward of two dozen.

"Okay…" From her giant purse, Jordan pulls out an iPad, ready to jump right into the issue at hand. "Tell me everything that happened, and don't leave anything out."

Furniture is moved and repositioned into a makeshift circle in front of where E, Bette, Jordan, Tessa, and I sit. Em climbs onto Grayson's lap, the two sharing a look as Em pockets her phone. Since Thanksgiving a few days ago, I've noticed CK hasn't been as distant with Quinn, going as far as letting her sit in his lap now and looping an arm around her middle.

Trav settles himself across from me, the way his legs bounce giving away his own pent-up anger, while Noah, Alex, and Bailey round out the remaining open chairs.

Savvy, who arrived with Tessa, comes around, squeezing in with her friend, the two sharing some kind of silent communication. Carter and Wes have also hung around and remain standing, arms crossed behind those sitting, the former's jaw hardening any time his eyes shift to Em in Grayson's lap.

As a unit, we recount everything that transpired in the last eight hours or so, from Carter starting with what went down in the tunnels through Grayson ending with Kay taking a hit meant for me.

"I had a feeling something happened before the game based on how aggressively you all played tonight," E says with a nod of approval.

"My guys and I had a message to deliver," Kev says proudly, his pacing coming to a halt, his hands curling over the back of Alex's chair. "Kay's a Hawk. You don't fuck with one of us."

We echo his statement with automatic hawk cries, and E stretches out a fist to bump with a "Respect."

"Why punch Kay though?" Jordan looks up, continuing to tap out something on her phone. "If his goal was to goad you into a fight, why pivot and hurt her?"

Because the motherfucker has a death wish, my inner coach surmises.

CK leans around Quinn to speak. "She wasn't his intended target."

"Explain," E says with authority. I may have been nervous to face off with him when I was trying to win Kay back, but this? I think I'm finally getting to see his true scary-overprotective-brother side. Not gonna lie, I think it's fiercer than his persona on the gridiron.

CK's eyes find and hold mine, answering E but speaking to me. "Liam was slinging his typical bully-type shit, so when you turned to make sure Kay was okay, you didn't see him lunge for you. Kay saw and tried to push you out of the way."

"What the hell was she thinking?" I say through gritted teeth. She and I are going to be having some words later.

You need to check your girl, Nova.

Not helping, I snap back at my inner coach, though I hate that he's right. Because, really…what was she thinking? Trying to get between me and a punch? I'm twice her size.

I rip my hat from my head and run a hand through my hair in frustration. I swear there are times I think she forgets how tiny she actually is.

"No, that's not the right question to ask." Savvy chimes in, sharing a conspiratorial smirk with Wes. "What we should be asking is, if Mase was his intended target, where the hell was he aiming for with his punch that he hit Kay in the face? She comes up to here"—I startle from a hand slapping against my breastbone—"on him."

The logistics don't matter to me. Knowing Kay was hurt trying to protect me when it's supposed to be the other way around is what's unacceptable.

#Chapter7

UOFJ411: Update on #Kaysonova

 picture of Kay lying in a hospital bed

 @Msteresaap: She needed to be admitted? #HowBadIs-SheHurt #CasanovasGirl

 @Mylifethroughfiction: Holy shit! Look at the bruise on her face! #HumanPunchingBag #CasanovasGirl

 @Notnow.imreading: We NEED to know what happened. #ISmellDrama #CasanovaWatch #Kaysonova

Chapter8

GRAYSON and I fall into step as Dr. Nikols leads us down a stark taupe hallway past a handful of closed doors before coming to a stop in front of one labeled *Recovery #5*.

"Kayla won't be here long. We'll move her as soon as she regains consciousness and seems cognizant of her surroundings. It's important to note that she may not remember much from any of her interactions as she's coming out of anesthesia," Dr. Nikols explains.

Both Grayson and I nod our understanding, each of us using the automatic hand sanitizer dispenser bolted to the wall outside the room.

I step across the threshold and stop—*fuck!* Grayson bumps into my back at my abruptness, our athletic reflexes the only thing keeping us from crashing to the floor in a pile of limbs.

The sight before me slays me. My breaths stutter in my lungs, my heart pushes against my ribcage, and blood roars between my ears.

Kay lies in a hospital bed—a sight I'm pissed is becoming all too familiar—arms resting on top of a white blanket tucked around her waist, IV taped to the back of her right hand, heart rate monitor clipped to the end of her pointer finger—her now ringless finger.

An oxygen tube is tucked inside her nose, the clear plastic following the curve of the bruise on her cheek then hooking over her ears. I wish they were able to wash her hair because her bloody curls look stiff where they're fanned out on the pillow.

My gaze shifts to the screen next to the bed, focusing on the steady stream of peaks proving she is here, alive, and will be okay.

My need to reaffirm these facts with the physical, to feel the brush of her soft skin on mine, her pulse under my fingertips has me taking the open chair by the bed and carefully slipping my hand under hers. My thumb traces the edges of the tape securing her IV while Grayson pulls up his own chair across from me and takes Kay's other hand in his.

Neither of us speak, the only sounds in the room the constant flow of oxygen and the even beeps of Kay's heart rate.

Beep. Beep. Beep.

My breathing syncs with each slow inhalation and exhalation of Kay's.

A wave of exhaustion rolls over me as the adrenaline from the night starts to wane and my head falls to the bed. Inside my pocket, I can feel my phone vibrate. Normally I would ignore it, but given the events of the evening, my gut tells me I should check it.

As much as we all wish otherwise, I'm sure the story of what happened tonight has gotten out, though whether or not the facts being circulated are correct is another issue altogether. Gossips *love* drama. Anything to up their likes and shares on social media.

This?

School's star tight end's girlfriend gets taken away in an ambulance after a Hawks victory party—it's like catnip to them.

Plus there's also the chance—albeit a slim one since it's the middle of the night—my family has found out what happened and could be reaching out.

I press my thumb to the button to unlock my phone and pull up UofJ411's Instagram. Sure enough, there are pictures documenting our departure from the Alpha house.

Grayson lets out a snort, and when I look up, his own thumb is swiping along the screen of his phone. I know he must be seeing the same thing as me.

I scroll and scroll, the red low battery icon ignored, not stopping to double-tap a like or comment.

Then…

I see the most recent post.

My hyperawareness of all things Kay is the only reason I'm able to detect the faint twitch against my palm as I reel with thoughts of how somebody was able to get a picture of her in here.

The nurse standing by swoops in to check all of Kay's vitals, and as much as it pains me to do so, I motion to Grayson that I'm stepping out. It won't be long before Kay is moved into a regular room, and it looks like we have a whole new set of issues to deal with.

E is not going to react well to this at all. He's been more— if that's even possible—adamant about keeping Kay out of the public eye than Kay is about our trending hashtags.

The way E's pulling at his hair while he talks to Jordan when I make it back to the waiting room tells me he already knows about the pictures. It's probably also why nurse Vicki has made a reappearance.

"Bruh…where's your shirt?" JT's question has me noticing him for the first time as I join their circle of people. Guess he arrived while I was with Kay.

"Romeo here is trying to get the nurses to like him by showing off a little skin." E hooks a thumb in my direction only to get a backhand to the chest from Bette.

"Don't be an asshole, Eric," Bette admonishes.

"Oh-ho-ho," JT chortles. "Watch out, old man—it never ends well for you when she calls you Eric."

There's more eye rolling—Kay's proclivity is becoming a damn epidemic in our group—but respect and gratitude shine in JT's eyes, telling me someone told him the real reason I'm shirtless and he's giving me shit because that's what guys do when we can't handle serious emotions.

"Thanks, man," I tell him when he hands me a shirt from his duffle bag that sits on one of the chairs. I pull the white cotton over my head; it's a bit snug, but it fits.

Joke time over, E falls back into the conversation he was having with nurse Vicki and Jordan. "So do you think it's possible to get a room in...fuck...I don't know..." E runs another hand through his hair, the already disheveled strands becoming wilder. "A more secure wing or something?"

"Eric..." Nurse Vicki gives his shoulder a squeeze.

"I know." E lets out a heavy sigh, his head falling forward, his chin tucking into his chest. "I worry with the press coverage from after the game and what I'm sure is getting spun from all this"—he circles a finger in the air, indicating the hospital and the reasons that brought us here—"these new pictures will bring out all the vultures."

Is that a real possibility? Could this grow to something more than campus fodder?

Somewhere in the distance, the elevator dings, and then B bursts into the room, his sneakers making a nails-on-a-chalkboard-type squeal as he pulls up short.

"B?" E's eyes bug out and his brows hit his hairline at the sight of Ben Turner, the Crabs' quarterback. "What are you doing here?"

"What the fuck?" B squares off against his best friend, his hands braced on his hips. "You think I wouldn't want to come too?"

"The game." E doesn't say it, but his tone gives off the implied *duh*.

"You think *that's* what's important here?" B tosses his arms up.

"There's *no* way you got approval to miss the game too."

"Fuck that." B smacks E's chest, the sound reverberating through the room, every set of eyes bouncing between the two of them, watching in rapt attention. "I'll take the fine. Our girl needs us more. Family sticks together."

All the defiance drains out of E at the reminder of their mismatched family unit.

"Like, I'm seriously pissed at you, bro. You text me asking me to take care of Herkie because Kay's in the hospital and you have to leave for Jersey. What. The. Actual. Fuck?"

"Where is my dog?" E asks defensively.

"Don't take that tone with me." B sticks a finger in E's face, sounding scarily like Bette. "I picked him up and dropped him off at your house here before coming here."

"*You*"—E pokes B, his finger bending back with the force —"let my"—he hooks his thumb back at himself—"*dog* in your"—his hand reverses direction again—"*Ferrari*?" E's jaw drops, and Bette slips a finger under it to pick it up off the floor.

"Hell no." B tosses his head back with a laugh. "When I grabbed him, I availed myself to your Escalade too." He reaches into his pocket, twirling the keyring around his finger. "Figured you need something to drive, and it has enough room to fit everyone, both the two- and four-legged variety."

"Thanks B." Bette frees herself from under E's arm to finally give him a proper hug hello, shooting her scowling-again husband a *Be nice* glare.

"Oh-kay." JT claps his hands, shouldering his way in, clearly used to the way these two interact. "Now that that's out of the way, can we bring the focus back to Kay?"

"Whoa. Dude." E falls back a couple of steps. "Don't call her Kay. Freaks me out when you do."

JT chuckles. "She says the same thing."

"True story," Tessa agrees from somewhere behind me.

"Man…" E pulls B into a headlock, noogie-ing him. "Kay is going to give you so much shit for being here."

"Me?" B threads an arm between them and delivers a purple nurple to set himself free. "Wait until she realizes what *you* being here is going to do to her fantasy score for the week."

"Why am I even friends with you?" E rubs at his sore nipple.

Around us, the hospital slowly starts to show more signs of life, dayshift nurses checking in, a cluster of doctors gathering around the nurses' station to prep for morning rounds while E and B continue to bicker like an old married couple.

Arms stretched overhead with a yawn, Grayson makes his way back to the group, informing us that Kay is officially being moved to her private room. The puffy bags forming under his eyes and the barest lightening of the sky outside the windows drive home how late—or early—the hour is.

"Okay, listen." Jordan motions for everyone to gather round. "Today is going to be a long one. We still have a brief window of time for ourselves, but after that, things are going to happen fast." My earlier fatigue starts to creep back in, making my bones feel heavy as I think how right she is. "Why don't you guys head home and grab a couple of hours of shut-eye?"

A communal negative sounds out, causing Jordan and nurse Vicki to share some kind of silent communication before the stern healthcare professional takes the reins.

"Look…it's admirable how you all have hung around to support your friend, but there aren't enough strings in the world for me to pull to let *all* of you stay." She holds up a hand, cutting off the rebuttals sure to come her way. "Eight"—she pauses for emphasis—"eight can stay, and *that's* pushing it. The rest of you can come back when visiting hours officially start at nine o'clock."

For a group who was generally keeping its volume down out of respect for our surroundings, we sure fail now as people start jockeying for the right to be one of those allowed to stay.

The Royals were an easy sell, but getting Tessa to agree to leave with them took a Herculean effort on JT's part. It was only Herkie needing someone to be there to feed him breakfast that convinced her.

I had a similar issue with the guys, especially Trav, but he was driving Quinn and Bailey back to campus. Plus, I need people to talk to Coach Knight about what *actually* happened before it gets spun out of control.

Chapter9

BEEP.

Beep.

Beep.

What's that beeping?

Ugh. God my head hurts.

Beep.

Beep.

Beep.

Oh, wait…

I'm in the hospital. That's good.

Whatever the doctors gave me earlier has helped take the pounding inside my skull down to a dull throb, but still…it doesn't tickle.

"Babe, I need your phone."

"What? Why?"

"You're the league commissioner—you can go in and edit Kay's lineup."

"Why would I do that?"

My brain is still fuzzy and floaty. I'm not sure if the voices I'm hearing are in my head or real. I'm leaning toward real because two of them are male and my inner cheerleader is the only one I typically have speaking and, more often than not,

shouting at me internally. Either way, they are pretty entertaining.

"Your husband is scared of his little sister."

*"And you're just jealous she drafted Dennings from New
England as quarterback over you."*

"Yeah, yeah. Whatever."

"Babe…" There's a sigh. *"If you want the chance of us having a
baby, you need to change the lineup. Otherwise Kay will have my
balls."*

I try to open my eyes, but my lids feel like my eyeshadow
was mixed with lead and they weigh a million pounds.

"Mase, take this seat."

"I'm good with this."

Familiarity slips under my palm and washes over me with
a gentle squeeze. I will my muscles to return the gesture.
Unable to manage such a simple task, I give myself over to
the haze of my painkillers and fall back asleep.

I'm not sure how much time has passed when I come to
again. My body feels like it's been hit by a bus, and when I
blink my eyes open, I have to squint against the light, grateful
at least the one directly above me is turned off.

The earlier conversations have quieted, the only sound the
faint strains of an old rerun of *Friends* on the television
mounted on the wall.

My vision clears and the room comes into focus. The first
thing I take note of is its size. I get the impression strings were
pulled to arrange it, as well as the number of people sleeping
scattered around it.

There's a full-sized couch under a wide window where
Bette is currently cuddled up with E, and B is knocked out
next to them, his head resting on his arms folded over the
armrest.

A small round-top table sits in the corner, a variety of hoodies and such serving as makeshift pillows for G, Em, and CK.

Soft snores bring my attention to the right, my head swimming when I move too fast at the sound. Spots dance in my vision and nausea rolls from my gut up into my throat. I breathe through the worst of it, inhaling through my nose and exhaling out my mouth.

When I'm no longer in danger of tossing my cookies like a basket toss, I can't help but smirk at JT—not even going to question my cradle-to-grave bestie being here—passed out in a recliner-style chair.

Too bad you don't know where your phone is because look at that photo op. *points repeatedly* You could kayak down that river of drool.

I roll my lips in to hold the laugh my inner cheerleader is trying to get out of me. She may have jokes, but it doesn't take away from how it feels to be surrounded by these people, my mishmash of a family.

My heart does a toe touch inside my chest when I look down at the weight causing the mattress to dip.

Mase.

My left hand is sandwiched between both of his, making it look like a toddler's compared to his baseball-glove-sized mitts. His face is turned in my direction, as if even in sleep he was unable to look away.

Mentally I curse out Liam *fucking* Parker for the dark, bruise-like circles I see under Mase's long, envy-inducing eyelashes. Though sparse, in every flash of memory I have of being here, he's been by my side. It's wrong. He should be in bed, recovering after a hard game, not running himself to the brink of exhaustion worrying over me.

That's just who he is—my boyfriend, my protector, my Caveman.

Not gonna lie, his Neanderthal tendencies do make me all

swoony at times—don't judge me—but the issue at hand is when those protective instincts cause him to have blinders to everything that isn't me. They're the reason he didn't see Liam go after him because he was too busy checking on me when I was fine.

Hold up! *makes T with hands* Can we take a second to wonder how the douchemonkey even got into the Alpha house?

Miss IC has a point, but my mind is too muddled to make the math compute on that issue.

So what's a girl to do when she falls in love with an alpha man with zero sense of self-preservation? I'll tell you: you pull a page right out of his own damn book—though the way my face feels like I took a frying pan to it has me rethinking that strategy.

Except...

The longer I look at Mase...

I can't say I wouldn't do it again.

His standard ball cap must have dislodged from sleep and is resting somewhere by my knee. His dark espresso-colored locks are disheveled, and I can't help but reach out to run my fingers through it.

Though my touch is featherlight, he stirs under it, his hands reflexively squeezing around mine. I'm about to snatch my hand away from his head when those same eyelashes I was coveting minutes ago lift and I get a peek at my favorite shade of green.

"Hey." I whisper so softly it's more mouthing the word than speech.

It takes a few seconds for the veil of sleep to clear and the realization that I'm awake to set in. When it does, he jack-knifes in his chair, causing my hand to fall from his hair and a pout to form on my lips.

"You're awake." His whisper-shout is full of disbelief.

"I'm awake," I agree. "I didn't mean to wake you."

A frown pulls at his brow, a V forming between them as

his eyes dart around, his lips twisting to the side like he did something wrong. "I shouldn't have fallen asleep."

"Are you crazy?" An amused lilt enters my voice. "You needed sleep." I scan his tired but handsome face and sigh. Even exhausted, he really is too gorgeous for words. "You still do if these bags are any indication." I run a finger over the puffy skin.

Rough callouses brush along my knuckles as he cups the back of my hand, holding it against his cheek, nuzzling into my touch.

"Is that your subtle way of telling me I look like shit, babe?"

"No." I fight another smirk. "I'm just saying they are big enough to fit the entire contents of my backpack."

His lips twitch at the reference to my infamous school bag. The guys have taken to teasing me that it weighs more than I do.

"How are you feeling?" His gaze runs over me, taking note of my injuries. I can only imagine the Halloween-ready sight he sees.

"Like I was used as a tackle dummy." My joke falls flat, as do his eyes, which darken from a beautiful seafoam green to the color of pine trees.

"You know I'm pissed at you, right?" His stern expression and flat tone clue me in to the fact that he's not kidding.

"At me?" I try to arch a brow, but it hurts too much. "Why are you mad at *me*?" The last word comes out as a squeak.

He doesn't answer. Instead his free hand comes up to run through his hair, the strands sticking out through the pinch of his fingers before he continues down to grip the back of his neck. *Damn, he is pissed.*

"What the *hell* were you *thinking*?" His hard stare pins me to the bed.

"Huh?" He's going to have to be a little more specific.

"I'm probably concussed, so speaking in riddles is not a good way to get answers."

His nostrils flare and his chest expands with a deep inhalation.

Boo. *pouts* He put a shirt on.

Not the time, I scold my inner cheerleader.

"I *mean*…in what world did you think it was a good idea to get between me and a punch. *Meant*. For. Me?"

How is this even a question?

"*Seriously?*" He has the audacity to only give me a simple nod. "You're always going on and on about how I'm yours and you protect what's yours. Well *dammit*—" I smack the bed with my free hand, my IV pulling against the tape securing it. I'm so damn frustrated I want to rip my hair out, but I don't dare; my head hurts enough without adding self-harm. "*You*"—I curl my fingers under his palm and poke him—"are *mine*. And *I*"—I ignore another pull of the tape to slap my chest—"protect what's mine *too*."

An amused chuckle comes from behind us as the rest of the room starts to wake.

"Careful," E warns.

Bette snickers. They may have only been my guardians for a few years, but they have always taken great pride in having been the ones to raise me through the last—and, according to them, most important—years of high school.

"I'll play nice," Mase tells my brother while keeping his focus solely on me, "but it doesn't change the fact that I can handle taking a punch better than she can."

"I wasn't going to let him hurt you," I argue, the volume of my voice rising with my anger, waking those who weren't already up.

Mase scoffs. He fucking scoffs. I so want to slap him right now.

"Baby…" He shakes his head. "He wouldn't have hurt me."

I make a noise in the back of my throat, causing his shoulders to bounce with suppressed laughter.

"Of course." I puff out a frustrated breath, barely withholding an eye roll. "How silly of me to think getting punched would hurt the *great* Mason Nova." I bring my palm to my forehead for a gentle facepalm.

The jerk has the audacity to laugh at me. "I'm not saying that, but..." He oh-so-gently cups the injured side of my face. "I am *literally* twice the size of you. The physics alone are on my side. And..."

My eyes drift closed as he trails his fingers down to curl around the back of my neck in a solid grip. His weight shifts, and I feel him push into the side of the hospital bed seconds before the intoxicating scent of his soap fills my senses above the strident smell of antiseptic.

"...based on how he hit *you* in your *face*, god only knows where he was aiming on me."

JT snorts, and now *he's* the one I want to smack.

As Mase pulls away to retake his seat, I reach up to wrap my fingers around his wrist as best I can, my thumb still a couple inches from touching the tips of the other digits. I rotate his hand until the knuckles are visible for inspection. They're not bruised, swollen, or cut up like I would expect.

"What are you doing?" He sounds amused as I trace each bump of his large metacarpals.

"You didn't fight him?" I jerk my gaze to his, a slash of pain streaking across my temples.

"Oh, I wanted to." This time his deep chuckle has all my girly bits standing at attention as he twists to link our fingers. "I was just more concerned with stopping the blood coming out of your head." The strain in his voice tells me how hard the memory hits him.

I bring my hand up to the small square bandage now covering the stitches that were required to hold the torn skin together.

"What do you think happened to my shirt earlier?" he asks, one of his dimples popping out with his smirk.

I don't know if I should be thankful or not that my injuries were catastrophic enough to make me an unquestionable priority, but all I feel is an overwhelming amount of guilt.

This whole thing is my fault. I should have stayed away, if not because of the drama I could bring down on Mase myself then to keep Liam away. From the first time Liam tried to use me on his Instagram to incite beef with Mason, I knew he viewed me as my boyfriend's weak spot. The way each of his jabs and barbs outside the locker room before the game and at the Alpha house were centered around me only further proved it.

What I can't figure out is how Liam could think a fight between them wouldn't also hurt his draft stock come April.

There's also how he plans on using Chrissy/Tina…

"Hey." Mase pinches my chin to lift my gaze back to his, those green eyes reading me down to my soul. "What's going on in that beautiful head of yours?"

"I'm sorry," I blurt out.

"For what?"

"For bringing"—I flail my hands in the air—"all…*this* on you." Without giving him a chance to comment, I barrel on, the rest coming out like word vomit. "What if you did fight him? What if that happened and it got out and made you ineligible for the draft? Don't say that can't happen because we both know it could. What if I cost you everything you've worked for? How would you ever be able to forgive me if I was the reason you didn't get to have your dream?"

I hiccup out a sob, the heart rate monitor beeping wildly with my increased stress.

An acutely unpleasant screech hurts my ears as Mase abruptly stands again. His movements are jerky, but when he cups my face between his large hands, it's like I'm a piece of fragile glass. "*You*." He stares *directly* into my eyes. "Are.

Everything." The breath gets stuck in my lungs. "All that other stuff is just gravy."

Tears leak from my eyes, and the flow only grows stronger when he thumbs them away.

"Mase." Emotion cracks my voice.

"I know, baby." His lips graze mine for a far-too-brief kiss.

"Ugh. Gag me." JT groans. "Are they *always* this…*cutesy*?"

"Pretty much," CK answers.

"Be grateful you go to school so far away," G adds.

The door to the room is pushed open, cutting off whatever shit-talking comment E starts to say, and I've never been happier to be poked and prodded by a nurse checking my vitals.

Chapter10

I HANG BACK with JT while the nurse does her examination. Fuck it's painful to look at Kay with her beautiful face swollen and discolored by all the bruising. All my baser instincts are screaming at me, and I know they won't be satisfied until Liam Parker meets a similar fate. If Kay wasn't currently lying in a hospital bed, I'd be running out to find him and beat his ass until not even his mom would recognize him.

The soft snick of the door opening has everyone turning to see Dr. Nikols enter the room. She gives a cursory nod before swiftly moving to Kay's bedside, following up with both her and the nurse.

Dr. Nikols pulls a penlight out of her lab coat's pocket, and my teeth grind when I see Kay wince at the brightness. I know from experience how painful having a concussion can be, and I'm sure the rest of her isn't faring much better given the hits it took.

I'll never admit it to her, but her worrying over me and her attempt—no matter how misguided—to protect me only makes me love her more. However, it doesn't take away from how annoyed I am that she would literally put herself in harm's way to do it.

Me.

Six foot five.

Two hundred and fifty pounds.

Collegiate football player.

Protected by his girlfriend who isn't even five feet tall.

Comical.

Ridiculous.

But completely mine.

"How are you feeling, Kayla?" Dr. Nikols asks.

"I've been better." Kay's expression twists as the doctor gently inspects her recently reset cheekbone.

"I bet." A small smile tugs at Dr. Nikols' lips. "Any nausea?"

"Only when I first woke up," Kay answers. "As far as concussions go, this one's not that bad."

"You've had concussions in the past?"

Kay starts to nod only to cut it off with a pained breath sucked through her teeth. "I was a competitive cheerleader."

Understanding dawns on the doctor's face. "Ah, yes. I've fixed quite a few broken noses from the sport."

"One injury you've never had, PF." JT laughs around the *pfff* pronunciation of Kay's nickname.

"Yeah, congrats, bro." E snorts. "That's *one* injury you didn't check off when failing to catch her," he says sarcastically.

"Aww." JT folds his hands over his heart and flutters his eyelashes. "Don't knock my catching skills because they're better than yours, E."

"Says the cheerleader to the professional football player."

"Says the person who catches a ball to the one who catches people."

"Will you two idiots behave?" Bette slaps E on the chest with the back of her hand. "This nice doctor is going to think we surround Kay with animals."

Across the room, Grayson and CK do their best to smother their laughter while Em and B let their guffaws fly free.

Dr. Nikols shakes her head, but with the way she rolls her lips in as if to hide another smile, you can tell she's amused by the antics. She writes something on Kay's chart and turns her attention to Bette, who has moved to hover next to the bed.

"When can we take her home?" Bette asks the question we are all anxious to have the answer to.

"Everything seems to be tracking nicely." Dr. Nikols closes Kay's chart. "As long as her vitals remain stable, I don't see why she couldn't be discharged tomorrow."

I let out the breath I didn't realize I was holding.

"Thank you, doctor." Bette reaches out to shake her hand.

"You're very welcome." She casts a look around the room. "Try to keep it down in here, okay?"

We're all quick to agree before she takes her leave. We appreciate them turning a blind eye to us breaking their protocols, and there's no way any of us will risk losing the leeway we've been given.

It isn't long after the doctor's departure that the door to the room is once again pushed open, bringing the re-arrival of Jordan Donovan with it. Gone is the casual but in charge publicist who spent the middle of the night troubleshooting in a hoodie and leggings. No, this version—the one dressed in straight-legged black leather pants, strappy pointed spike heels, a white silk blouse with a black skinny tie, the knot hanging loosely down by her chest, and a fitted black suit jacket—is the famed PR powerhouse.

"Oh good"—she glances around the room, setting her bag on the floor, not caring about the designer label, and taking a seat on the arm of the couch closest to Kay—"you're all up."

"Kind of hard to sleep through people poking and prodding you," Kay says dryly.

A ghost of a smile forms on Jordan's lips as she pulls out her trusty iPad. "How are you feeling?"

"I'll live."

"You fucking better," I mutter as I grind my teeth.

Kay groans when she attempts to roll her eyes. "Chill, Caveman." She lifts her arm, holding out a hand to me. "Come here."

My eyes narrow at how callously she brushes off what happened to her, like I didn't spend the most painful, most stressful couple of hours of my existence wondering if she *would* live.

Blood—*fuck*, I can't get the vision of it out of my head. I swear I still feel the sting of every time I begged her to open her eyes without getting a response.

"Mase." She wiggles her fingers, my feet already closing the distance between us, unable to ignore the plea in her voice.

I weave my fingers between hers and squeeze, probably harder than I should. I whisper an apology while trying to shake off the last of those dark thoughts. It's hard. My life before Kay came into it pales in comparison to these past few months with her. Who would want to lose that?

Her thumb moves to trace figure eights down the length of mine. Even concussed, she's still able to read my mood enough to know to soothe me. I lift her hand and kiss the back of it.

"You up for hearing plans A through"—Jordan tilts her head from side to side like she's trying to calculate something —"H?"

"H?" I ask.

"Give or take." She nods. "Before my partner Skye got on a plane to come here from Chicago, I think we were able to come up with eight scenarios."

"Skye's flying in?" E shifts to lean forward, bracing his elbows on his spread knees.

"Yup." Jordan shifts her attention to him. "My gut tells me we're going to need all hands on deck for this."

"Shit." Kay curses beside me, and this time I'm the one soothing her with a stroke of my thumb.

"We're dealing with too many variables to be able to predict how this will play out. If we can at least get the broad strokes worked out for all the different what-ifs, it'll make it easier to deal with them if they come to fruition," Jordan explains to the room. The ease and confidence with which she speaks makes it clear to see why people seek her out for representation. Hell, Brantley would sell a kidney to have her represent me when I go pro.

"First things first"—Jordan swipes along the iPad's screen and turns it to face Kay and me—"I'm sorry to say it, Kay, but I think your days of hiding have come to an end."

On the screen is *ESPN*'s website, opened to an article titled: *U of J's Mason Nova scores more than touchdowns in last night's win over Penn State*.

Above the link for the article is a shot of me kissing Kay after the game. Seeing the picture in all it's high-pixel glory fills me with an immense sense of satisfaction. In bold red lettering, my name and number are clearly visible stamped across Kay's back for all the world to see. If that isn't enough to show she is mine, the way the two of us are wrapped around each other does. My arm is curled around her underneath the white outline of the large #87, my helmet hanging just so, making it look like Kay's delectable ass is sitting on it. The grip of my other hand on her thigh is all possession, the quality of the lens used to take the shot high enough to pick up the whitening of my knuckles.

Fuck I love this picture. There's a reason I set it as the background on my phone.

My favorite part about it—and I mean my *absolute* favorite —is how equally clearly my girl is claiming me right back.

Her legs are wrapped around my hips, her feet hooked together at the ankles, keeping us locked together. Her arms mirror the hold around my neck, the black of her nail polish covering the smear of eye black on my cheek with her hand spread along the side of my face, the other cupping the back of my head with a proprietorial hold on my hair.

Hottest. Fucking. Thing. Ever.

I remember the sting of my scalp as she tugged on my hair with each squeeze of her legs, bobbing slightly on my body… the mingling of our breaths, the salty taste of my sweat, and the lingering sweetness from her coffee each time our tongues stroked each other.

This picture is a physical manifestation of the adrenaline from what happened both before the game and during and what we were feeling because of it. With one kiss, we each owned the other—wholly.

"*Dayumn.*" JT blows out a dramatic whistle, having stood to look at the screen over my shoulder. "That kiss is almost not suitable for public." He waves a hand over the iPad. "I feel like there should be a black censor block on top of you two."

"Shut up." Pink stains Kay's cheeks in an adorable blush, but JT only laughs. "Why is this even the article?"

"Because…" I pass the iPad back to Jordan when she gestures for it. "Stuff like this? It's clickbait gold. Romantic pictures like this get picked up by the BuzzFeeds, Reddits, and Tumblrs of the world and pull in the non-sports-minded readership. I can almost guaran-damn-tee you this picture will be pinned and repinned on countless Pinterest boards. You two"—she circles her finger in front of Kay and me—"are what we *in the biz*"—the tilt of her lips only adds to the sarcasm in the coined phrase—"like to call *media darlings*."

#Chapter11

UGH. Media darlings. *Awesome.* Oh you heard that sarcasm, did you?

I don't know what makes me want to groan more, those two words or the proud dimples peeking out from Mason's cheeks.

"Is this where you tell me to steer into the skid and take a page out of your book?" I ask Jordan. As a sister to not one but two top players in the NHL and the wife to another, she has mastered the art of her own public profile. The follower count of her TheMrsDonovan Instagram account is close to those of the athletes she manages.

The beeps from the heart rate monitor pick up speed, and I glare at it for giving away the anxiety building inside me.

"That's kind of an extreme flip from your stance now," Jordan acknowledges. "No need to go from zero to a hundred. Honestly…what you've been doing this last week with Mason slowly integrating you into the content he posts is enough to help satisfy some of the curiosity of those who use the CasanovasGirl hashtag."

I sag back against the pillows propping me up, the beeping easing with my long breath out. *Shit!* If Jordan only knew how close to throwing up I came when I told Mase to post that selfie of us in my *I like the game but I LOVE the player* shirt. Still...Liam pushed me to my breaking point with his taunts about who I would root for at the game. I'd had enough and did the only thing I could think of to shut him— and anyone else who dared prattle on with the bullshit about me being a Penn State spy—up.

My temple and cheekbone simultaneously ache at the thought of the person who bestowed these injuries on me. I wish I knew what he could have possibly been thinking. If he was hoping Mase getting into a fight would make him look bad, like he was a hotheaded player who couldn't control himself, that plan was certainly flawed. Being the one trying to start the fight himself would have made Liam look just as bad.

Liam's taunts about my past tainting Mason's reputation and paying off Chrissy/Tina to spew her vile bullshit were much more significant and could legitimately cause Mason to be seen as a less desirable draft pick. Hell...if that bitch does go through with what she threatened, there is potential there for it to make Mase completely undraftable in the eyes of the teams.

Now that the game is over and I don't have to worry about my current boyfriend committing homicide against my ex-boyfriend, I need to tell him. Actually, I should tell Jordan too to see if there's any way we could put a stop to that bitch's scheme before it gets the chance to come to light.

"We can circle back to all that later." Jordan's sure voice snaps me from my musings. "I want to talk about the possible next steps and potential new stories that could develop as things unfold."

That prickly, bugs crawling under my skin feeling travels up my arms. I hate this, hate how my private life doesn't get to stay...private. But as I lift my gaze to the man sitting beside me, bags under his eyes, sleep-rumpled hair now hidden beneath his ball cap, hand holding mine, I realize losing some of the anonymity I clung to as a means of survival is a price I'm willing to pay if I get to have Mason Nova in my life.

I love him.

Yeah you do, my inner cheerleader singsongs smugly in my ear. She's had a lady boner for Mase from the beginning.

Me? I fought him. Fought letting his type back into my life. Fought the big scary feelings I felt for him as hard as I could, but the man was too damn stubborn to listen.

Now it's the thought of losing him that scares the shit out of me.

He said I'm the only thing that matters to him. He made it sound like I mean more to him than football. Here's hoping that's still true after I finally come clean. It's time. He needs to know all the details of my past if we're going to have a future.

"Here's what we know…" As if knowing I need an anchor, Mase gives my hand a gentle squeeze when Jordan starts again. "An arrest warrant has been issued for Liam, and officers will be executing it this morning."

"That quickly?" Bette asks, linking her hand with E's.

"Yes. With Penn State due to check out of their hotel, it makes this exponentially easier if they can get him before he crosses back over state lines," Jordan explains.

"How big of a story do you think his arrest will be?" I voice one of my bigger fears.

"Unless there's a leak, it shouldn't even be a passing comment. These bigger schools don't like unfavorable stories out there if they can help it."

"It's true," E agrees with a nod, the tightness of his jaw giving away his frustration with this situation. "Unless approached directly, Penn won't issue a formal statement. The closest they'll come to saying anything is if they suspend him from whatever small bowl game the Nittany Lions get selected to play."

"Do you really think they would suspend him?" My voice comes out a lot smaller than I would like.

"If E has anything to say about it, you know they will." A conspiratorial smirk graces JT's face as he takes the open chair near CK.

"Fucking A." E reaches out a fist to bump. "I may not have been able to get that asshat's scholarship pulled four years ago, but you bet my sweet ass I'll be making a phone call to Coach Daniels to remind him of his own beliefs on violence toward women."

"Bruh." B snorts, running a hand over his face.

"What?" E eyes his best friend.

"The phrase is 'you bet *your* sweet ass', not *my*."

"One"—E makes a fist and extends his forefinger —"that's"—he swings his finger around to point at me—"my sister. I'm *not* going to comment on her ass. And two"—he extends his middle finger, wiggling them both inches in front of B's nose—"you're just jelly my ass is better than yours."

"Lies!" B shouts, shooting up from the couch and cupping his butt in both hands.

"Do we need to do a side-by-side comparison and put it up for a vote on our IG stories again?" E asks, finding a way to brag about his win as *Best Crabs Ass* from years ago.

"Bring it, Dennings. I've been doing my squats. Your ass is grass this time." B cocks a hip to spank himself in front of E's face.

"Are they always like this?" Mase asks, his light eyes sparkling with his first true hint of amusement since I was admitted. It takes me a moment to look away from the captivating sight to where B is now twerking.

"Pretty much. It's actually a miracle E was able to lock himself in as one of Jordan's first non-hockey-playing athletes with the company he keeps."

Jordan barks out a laugh. "Puh-lease. At least they argue with real-life people. Do you have any idea how often I have to listen to my brother argue about having a better ass than a fictional character during book club?"

"Oh my god." Bette chokes on a laugh. "You *have* to be talking about Jase. I live for Lyle's stories about your squad's book club."

I have to agree. I love when I'm around for Lyle's—the most fabulous barista in existence—hair appointments. I could *so* go for a coffee from his coffee shop, Espresso Patronum, right now too.

I honestly think, outside of Jordan's business partner Skye, there's no one more suited to handle our family's dynamics than Jordan. She comes from her own mashed-up crew with the similar belief that you don't have to be related by blood to be considered family.

"Best ass title aside…" I'm jealous of how easily Jordan schools her features. "We shouldn't have to worry about Penn. U of J, though…" Her words trail off as she refers to the iPad again. "Have you heard anything from your coach at all?" she asks Mase.

The bed dips as he shifts to pull his phone from his pocket. "It's dead." The screen remains dark when he presses the side button. "I remember it being low earlier from all the notifications." He tosses it down next to me. "What makes you think Coach Knight would be reaching out?"

Jordan pulls up the UofJ411 page, and post after post scrolls by with the drag of her finger, each one a snapshot of something I missed while unconscious.

"I know when I swam for BTU, our athletic director would have alerts set up to stay informed on anything related to Titan athletes. I imagine it's the same for the Hawks, *especially* with you having a consistently trending hashtag."

A flash of guilt streaks across Mason's features, and this time I'm the one giving his hand a squeeze. This isn't on him. It is 100% me. I used my determination to avoid all things social media as an excuse to not take him back when we broke up. I spent weeks wallowing in my heartbreak, too afraid to give us a shot, all on the chance that Mase would think I wasn't good enough for him.

While I still hate the intrusive questioning of #Casanova-Watch and #CasanovasGirl, I hope having Mase create a hashtag out of our ship name Kaysonova will help prove I won't let social media run me off. I also want him to know how proud I am to call him mine.

I just hope he can still say the same about me and won't—as Liam insinuated—think I *am* my mother's daughter when I spill the last of my secrets.

#Chapter12

MOST PEOPLE WILL ALLUDE to going to plan B when A doesn't work as a figure of speech. The same can't be said for Jordan Donovan. When she says she has thought through the first third of the alphabet, she damn well means it.

Holy hell, she's sketched out a response to scenarios I didn't even think were a possibility.

Kay lets out her ninth yawn, last night's events clearly still taking their toll on her body. I'm shocked my little anti-morning person hasn't made a demand for coffee. Then again, having experience with concussions, she knows caffeine is one of the things you should avoid. I wonder if I have to worry about her doing me physical harm if I get a cup for myself.

My stomach rumbles, reminding me it's been hours since I put anything substantial in it. As if it set off a chain reaction, everyone else's follows suit.

Bette, taking on her mom role, pushes to her feet, arms rising overhead in a stretch and offering to grab breakfast sandwiches from the hospital's cafeteria.

"I'll go with you," Em says through her own yawn. "Do you think I could convince one of the nice nurses to hook me up to an IV drip of coffee?"

"Don't even think about it." Bette spins and points the mom finger at Kay, who blinks innocently.

"Not as fun when the shoe is on the other foot, is it, Squirt?" E shoots a finger gun Kay's way, exaggerated sound effect included.

"Don't act like you were an angel with your concussion at the beginning of the season, Eric," Bette counters.

"I love when she hits him with an *Eric*," JT stage-whispers to B.

"Oh yeah, crack that whip, B Boss." B mimes cracking said whip, adding a *woopah* at the end for good measure.

"Children…the lot of you." Though tired, there's a smile tugging at the edges of Bette's lips as she and Em make their way to the door once again. Before they reach it, though, it swings open, letting in my motley crew with a looking-far-too-awake Trav leading the charge.

The smells of grease, eggs, and coffee follow in the wake of my teammates, and it's then I notice each has a white paper bakery bag or cardboard coffee carrier in his hands.

"Damn, Short Stack." Trav whistles through his teeth as he comes to a stop at the foot of Kay's hospital bed.

"Is that your charming way of telling me I look like shit, QB1?"

"No way, babe." My jaw tightens at my best friend's blatant attempt to fuck with me by flirting with her, especially when he moves in to drop a soft kiss to the crown of her head. "You're still too pretty for this asshole." He hooks a thumb my way, and I flip him the bird.

"Move your ass, McQueen." Alex hip-checks him out of the way.

"For reals…" Noah does the same to Alex as soon as he pulls away from giving Kay a hug. "Stop hogging all the attention."

"Always acting like he's her favorite because he's Nova's best friend," Kev adds.

Quinn pushes her way through the idiots sharing a three-way exploding fist bump, and hands Kay one of the paper bags. "Wasn't sure what you're cleared to eat, so I got you—"

"*We,*" a quartet of football players corrects.

"—a bunch of soft options," Quinn continues, ignoring the guys completely. "There's a yogurt, a banana, some apple sauce, and a blueberry muffin in here. I figure you eat what you can now and the rest will keep if you want it later."

"Thanks Q," Kay says around another yawn, fading fast.

Noticing a bottle of orange juice—Kay's second-favorite morning beverage—amongst the coffees on the carrier, I get up to grab it, my palm gliding across the condensation collecting on the plastic and twisting to crack the seal.

"Hey!" Trav holds his arms out in a *What about me?* gesture, doing his best to play up being hurt. "Where's our thank you?"

"Aww…" Em drags out the word playfully as Quinn squeezes onto the chair with her. "I think someone's looking to have their ego stroked."

"I'm not stroking *anything* on Trav," Kay deadpans.

I try to bite back my smile and fail miserably. When I first tried to get to know Kay, she was a ball-busting spitfire. To be fair, she still is. She can hurl insults as well as any guy in a locker room.

"What are you smiling about?" There's laughter dancing in Kay's gray eyes as she shifts her attention my way.

"You know I love when you give him shit."

"HA!" Grayson barks out a laugh, coffee spewing from his nose.

Em and Quinn screech, jumping up in an attempt to avoid the java spray while JT reaches out to slap Grayson between the shoulder blades as he works to clear his throat. Once he has himself under control, he says, "I love how you sit there acting like you're immune, Nova."

That has the older people in the room sitting up to take notice.

"*Ooo.*" Jordan lowers her iPad to the tops of her thighs, bracing her elbows on her knees and leaning in closer. "Do share with the class."

The back of my neck prickles, and for some reason, my cheeks heat as all the attention turns my way.

Delicate fingers start to trace the black designs inked onto my arm, and I drop a hand over them, stroking across the now bare skin where my ring usually rests. It's only been a few weeks that I've had the honor of being one of the birthstone bands Kay wears to represent those who mean the most to her, but I hate that it's absent now. Yet another thing I can blame Liam Parker for.

"I feel like there are too many good ones to choose from." Noah taps the tip of his chin in thought.

Flashes of the playful insults, the digs taken in jest, and, at the very beginning, the blatant dismissal of me dance through my memory. Inside my pants, my dick twitches, and like many times before, I wonder what is wrong with me that that side of my girlfriend gets my engine going.

"Remember how many times he failed at getting her to agree to go on a date with him?" Trav asks the room at large.

It's true. Kay did her best to try to make it impossible for me to crack her shell. Even after I finally got her to acknowledge my existence and engage in conversation with me, she made me *work* to get her to say yes to a date. Good thing I'm a determined-as-hell guy who doesn't know the definition of quitting.

"My favorite was when she called him herpes," Em says with a shit-eating grin.

"*Noooo.*" Jordan's jaw hinges open.

"Yup. Thought the Hawks were going to need to start their second-string quarterback with the way Trav choked on his water when she said it."

I hate Trav a tiny bit for the way he's cackling behind me. If I didn't have to worry it would jostle Kay's hospital bed, I would swing my arm back and nut-check him to shut him up. That particular urge only grows at his breathy "Good times."

Instead of risking causing my girl discomfort, I crane my neck to send my best friend a glare promising a painful payback at the first opportunity.

"Alright, Caveman." Trav snickers around Kay's nickname for me before composing himself. "Before you get your panties in a twist more than they already are"—he lifts a duffle I didn't realize he had with him—"I grabbed you a few things from your room."

That right there, thinking to do that, having my back without question...that's why I don't actually beat him up for his constant flirting toward my girl.

"We also swung by to talk to Coach like you asked, which was a good thing—man was losing his shit."

Looks like one of Jordan's theories is proving correct. I wonder if her suspicion about Coach Knight trying to reach out to me was right too.

"Hope you're prepared to run suicides all week, bruh," Noah cuts in.

Trav nods his agreement and confirms my earlier thought. "He's pissed you've been ignoring his calls."

I lift my dead phone from the bed and wave the dark screen for them to see. Again, without needing to be asked, Trav hands me his.

"He's doubtful we'll be able to keep this fully quiet given that photos of you and Kay in the ambulance are already circulating—"

Kay tenses and I reach for her hand again, lending my support in the only way I know how for now. I wish I could take her in my arms and shield her from everything going on around us, but I can't. The best I can do is stand beside her and help her weather the storm. There's not a force on this earth that could keep me from doing exactly that.

"—but he pretty much wants to tell you to answer 'No comment' if asked about anything regarding last night."

Another point for Jordan Donovan. Looks like I have a phone call to make.

Chapter 13

I'M BEYOND OVERWHELMED. The number of people scattered throughout my hospital room when I first woke up was staggering to realize, but now? *Holy crap.* It reminds me of the chaos inside The Barracks before a competition. If Pops were here, I'm sure he'd be making a crack about how we are breaking all sorts of fire codes. Good thing he's on shift at the firehouse.

The last thing I expected was for Trav and the guys to show up, though with how they've been acting, I'm sure I would offend them if I said so. Instead we act like it's normal for four hulking football players to be sitting on the floor, backs resting against the wall.

I'm also exhausted—damn exhausted. Each time my mouth stretches open for a yawn, a slash of pain radiates from my cheekbone.

Bette has told me at least six times to go back to sleep, but I've steadily refused. Instead, my increasingly heavy eyes remain locked on the door to my room. Mase stepped out over ten minutes ago to talk to Coach Knight, and he still hasn't returned.

Shouldn't he be back by now? It seems like he's been gone

way longer than a simple directive of 'No comment' should take.

That familiar anxiety bubbles in my gut, along with that constant feeling of *This is all my fault.*

Beep. Beep. Beep.

"Trav," I call out, ignoring the increasing beeps of the heart rate monitor.

He braces a hand on the ground and jumps to stand. "What's up, Short Stack?" He bends and rests his forearms on the high railing on the side of my bed.

I try to let the sight of his panty-dropping smile soothe me but fail.

"Tell me the truth." The crinkling sound of my stiff hair fills my ear as I attempt to shift to a more comfortable position. "Is Mase in trouble?"

"For what?" A wrinkle forms between Trav's brows.

"For yesterday." I flip a hand toward the still closed door.

I honestly can't imagine what Coach Knight thinks of me. First I crashed his locker room before his team's most important game of the season. Then I was the reason his captains almost got into a brawl.

"You're kidding me, right?" His blue eyes scan my face, looking for clues that I am indeed joking, but all he finds is stoic resolve. "Shit, Kay. You're serious?"

I can't help it. No matter how many times JT tells me I'm being melodramatic about fearing my past coming around and affecting the potential of Mason's career, I can't shake it. A lot of it probably feeds off the guilt of him not knowing all the details. Hopefully, coming clean will help.

There's also…

"When you and Mase found out about the whole Chrissy/Tina thing, who broke up with who?" I do my best to keep my voice low enough to keep our conversation private.

Trav rears back like I slapped him, the wide-eyed blinking he's doing giving away his shock.

Ooo, he was not expecting that to be your question. My inner cheerleader looks on with interest.

"Shit." Trav runs a hand over his head, mussing his blond hair before dragging it down to grip the back of his neck. His eyes dart around the room almost frantically, and though I know deep in my gut she was full of lies when she showed up at my door, I don't like the way a sliver of doubt sneaks in like smoke.

The urge to yawn—again—hits, but I bite it back. Doesn't matter, though; like Mase, Trav catches it, his blue eyes soften, and I see him cataloging my injuries yet again.

After one more glance backward, Trav moves in closer. With an elbow propped on the pillow next to my head, he brings his mouth close to my ear.

"Tina is not a time in my life I like to revisit," he admits, and I keep my gaze trained over his shoulder at the door that still refuses to budge. I can't recall a time I've ever heard Trav sound so serious, so solemn.

"I get it." Boy do it get it. Look at my ex.

"I know you do." I hear him swallow. "That's the reason why you—and only you—are the person I will do so for."

A lone tear falls down my cheek, but I don't dare interrupt the moment to wipe it away. Like Mase, QB1 rarely shows his soft underbelly for others to see, instead choosing to live behind a charming playboy mask. Trav may be a shameless flirt—especially in Mase's presence—but he's his ride or die. It doesn't matter if answering questions would be slicing open a vein; Trav wouldn't hesitate to take the knife to his own skin.

I know this to be true, and what he just said? It's his way of telling me the same is true for me. Another tear follows the first.

"Now is not the time though, because if my best friend comes in here and hears us talking about *her* when you're yawning every other second"—Trav pulls back and thumbs away the wet streak on my face—"he's going to kick my ass."

I fold my lips between my teeth, to hold back a sob or a smile, I'm not sure which.

"I know he's your Caveman." This time I give in to the urge to grin; there's too much laughter dancing in Trav's eyes as he says Mase's nickname not to. "But seeing you like this"—he waves a hand down my body propped up in the bed—"his control is on a razor wire. It's not going to take much to make him snap."

#THE GRAM

#Chapter14

UOFJ411: The calvary has arrived. I hope no one has money on the Crabs today. #StartingThatSecondString #CasanovasGirl

picture of E and B standing together in front of the nurses' station at U Gen

@Oamberwhereartthou: Wow! I know Eric Dennings is her brother, but Ben Turner is there too? #CanIGetAnAutograph

@Ofbooksandportkeys: Holy shit! @CasaNova87 girl is CONNECTED. #HowManyCrabsDoesSheKnow

@Raineydaybookreviewslorraine: Damn! We NEED an update on your girl @CasaNova87. It must be bad if these two are missing a game. #WhoCaresAboutHIPAA

UofJ411: Guess this Penn State alum isn't too broken up over his old team losing to the U of J last night #FutureLegendsOf-TheGirdiron #CasanovaWatch

picture of E and a bare-chested Mason with their heads bent close together in the hospital waiting room

@Redhatterbookblog: Damn! It should be illegal for @CasaNova87 to wear a shirt #LookAtThoseMuscles

@Reynereadsalot: Anyone else curious what they are talking about? #TellUsYourSecrets #CasanovaWatch #Kaysonova

#Chapter15

I'M TIRED AND FRUSTRATED, not a good combination on top of the way I still want to hunt down and beat the shit out of Liam Parker.

What was supposed to be a simple phone call with Coach Knight turned into an almost half-hour conversation detailing all the events of yesterday, starting at what happened before the game and ending with Kay's surgery. To say Coach isn't pleased would be putting it mildly.

'No comment' is the clear and decisive directive from both him and the school should anything come to light. It seems Kay isn't the only one worried about how quickly things could escalate if the rivalry angle gets played. For now, the story of what happened has been contained to only the handful of pictures posted on UofJ411's Instagram. God willing, it will stay that way.

There's a crick in my neck and my lower back spasms every so often, reminding me that the few hours of sleep I did manage to get were spent hunched over in a chair at Kay's bedside. It's not that I'm complaining, because I'm not. I'll be here with her until she's released. It's the only way to guarantee she will rest, because she sure was fighting doing so before I left.

Thankfully, Kay is sleeping by the time I make it back to her room. A little bit of the stress I've been carrying falls away upon seeing her lashes fanned over her cheeks and the wrinkle between her brows smoothed.

"Everything go alright with Coach?" Trav asks as I hand him back his phone.

"Yeah." My feet are heavy as they carry me back to the chair I've claimed as my own, my butt hitting the seat with a thump as I all but collapse into it.

"Livi texted me this morning."

I bite back a curse. For one, the hospital sure won't respond too kindly if *more* people show up. The twins love Kay, as does Mom. It wouldn't take much for them to convince her to bring them, and if they all come by, I run the risk of Brantley tagging along. I don't have the energy to deal with *that*.

"I told her Kay is fine, but we have to keep the number of visitors down." Trav looks over the room packed with more people than seats available and smirks. "She promised to update Moms."

"Thanks, man."

I scrub my hands over my face in an effort to rid myself of the lingering exhaustion. This whole situation is fucked. It feels like I'm walking a tightrope and one misstep is all it would take to have everything come tumbling down.

I did anything and everything I could think of to get Kay back in my life. Why do I feel like it's going to be an ongoing battle to convince her the only place she belongs is by my side?

"When the Crabs announced that both Eric Dennings and Ben Turner would be inactive today, it came as a shock."

"Oh shit." E's curse has me snapping out of the half-awake daze I'd started to fall into.

"G, turn it up," Bette instructs as my eyes blink the TV hanging on the wall into focus to see the Crabs' pregame show playing on it.

"With the news of Dennings' sister being in the hospital breaking, it now comes as no surprise he is missing today's game."

"She's going to freak when she hears they're talking about this in the pregame," JT says, leaning back in his chair.

"What about Ben Turner?"

As the broadcast switches back to the on-field reporter, the screen splits to show her side by side with a post from B's Instagram of him and E mugging it up for the camera at Thanksgiving the other day. Just as the tension in the room starts to ebb, the blood in my veins turns to ice.

It's not the new picture of the most famous bromance in the NFL that does it. No, it's both what they are doing in the shot and who posted it—UofJ411. *Sonofabitch!* How did they get a picture of them in the waiting room last night?

"It's common knowledge that the two players share a close bromance both on and off the field," the sideline reporter explains. "I know I wasn't surprised to see he would be with his friend in his time of need. Details of what led to the younger Dennings being hospitalized have not been confirmed, but one thing is for certain… the Crabs offense certainly has their work cut out for them today if they are going to pull off a win against Cincinnati."

Not one person says a word, the only sound coming from the furious tapping of Jordan Donovan's nail as it flies over the screen of her iPad.

"What did they mean by 'news breaking'?" Kay's voice, still slightly scratchy from being intubated from surgery, jerks everyone to attention. She was asleep, and I was *hoping* she'd stay that way and we would be able to come up with the best way to tell her about this.

#Chapter16

MY BACK ARCHES as I wiggle first to the left then to the right, trying to find a comfortable position. I've been sleeping in spurts throughout the day, but I wouldn't say any of it was restful.

Though I was touched beyond words by how many people wanted to be here to show their support, the increased stimuli of cramming so many bodies into one room wreaked havoc on my senses thanks to the effects of my concussion.

Bette stepped in and mommed the crap out of everyone, a nice change seeing as I'm usually the only one who gets to experience that type of treatment. Thanks to her logic, Trav and the guys didn't put up a fight—well, not a big one—when she convinced them to head back to campus. Thanks to the win against Penn State, the Hawks will be playing in the Big Ten conference championship this upcoming weekend. It's bad enough Mase will be missing practice tomorrow; we can't have all the captains absent if they want a shot at clenching a berth to a playoff bowl game.

G and the girls left for a similar reason, though they were more reluctant to go than the others.

I agreed to taking a week off from classes to recover from my injuries. It'll be a few days before I'm permitted screen time, making it an easy decision, and CK clinched the deal for me when he offered to gather anything I might need to help keep up with my coursework once I can read without the result being a pounding headache.

"What do you need, babe?" Mase asks when I attempt to beat one of my pillows into submission without much success.

I blow out a frustrated breath and lift my gaze to his. He's the only person who held steadfast in his resolve to not leave my side. To be fair, I think knowing Mase would be with me is the only reason E and B agreed to Jordan's suggestion of moving things to the offices at All Things Sports. With the press being aware of the reason behind them missing the game today—Baltimore losing to Cincinnati by two touchdowns—my brother has been even more adamant about figuring out the best way to get ahead of the story so we aren't blindsided like we were with all the media attention surrounding Dad's trial.

When JT said goodbye to me before Bette drove him to the airport for his flight back to Kentucky, he held on a little bit longer and whispered in my ear, "Be brave."

With my best friend's words echoing inside my head, I take a deep breath before following his advice.

"Will you lie down with me?" My voice is small as I make my request. Yes I want Mase next to me because it will help me sleep, but really I need his arms around me while I face one of my bigger fears—my truth.

Crinkles form at the edges of Mase's eyes as he once again catalogs my injuries. The movement of his throat as he works to swallow gives away how torn he is about giving in to my request. After a few seconds, he shakes his head. "I don't want to hurt you."

"You could never." My response is automatic.

His expression turns pained and he grips the back of his

neck, his bicep popping like a coconut and making me want to sink my teeth into it. What? I'm concussed, not dead.

"You can't put any pressure on your cheek." Mase makes another attempt to deny me, but I'm not having it.

"So lie on my right side." I lift my arm and pat the mattress twice.

"I don't want to pull on your IV."

This is one objection I can work with. I skim my fingers over the buttons of the bedrail until I come to the call button that will summon a nurse. In no time at all, a petite brunette arrives and makes quick work of switching my IV to my left arm.

"See?" I hold up my newly bandaged and IV-free right hand with a flourish. "Problem solved." I pat the mattress again and rub my hand in a circle for good measure. "Now get that very tight end of yours in this bed with me right now."

My punny compliment gets his lips to quirk enough for one of his dimples to pop out, but not enough for his feet to move.

"Please, Mase." I purse my lips into my best pout. "I'll sleep so much better in your arms." I'm not above using guilt as a motivator.

The maddening man makes me wait a full minute before he rounds the bed, toes off his sneakers, and gingerly lies down in the space I indicated. His tattooed arm snakes its way behind my neck and wraps around my shoulders. Fingers trail along the back of my arm, guiding me to fit against him. Shifting around, I find that sweet spot that is the hollow between his armpit and muscular chest and make myself at home.

Mindful of the needle stuck in it, I carefully drape my arm across his stomach. I slip my fingers under the hem of his t-shirt and slowly trace the grooves of his lickable abdominals.

The relieved sigh that escapes Mase tells me he needed to feel me in his arms as much as I needed to be in them.

I can't believe everything that's happened in less than twenty-four hours. Life as I knew it will never be the same. Goddamn Liam Parker.

Inhaling deeply, I try to take in as much of his familiar fresh soap scent as I can. It's faint, but it lingers enough to calm my nerves before spilling my most shameful secrets.

You are your mother's daughter. God I *hate* that I can't stop the thought from playing on repeat. I'm nothing like that woman, but the seed of doubt has been planted. Yet another gem from my scumbag ex.

"Remember when you told me nothing you learned about me could change how you feel about me?"

"*Mmm*," Mase hums in the back of his throat as he buries his nose into my hair. "I think I recall. I do seem to have a steel-trap mind for those moments I've had you pinned against walls."

My body flushes, it too able to recall them...but this is too important. I've chickened out too many times already to allow myself to be distracted.

"Did you mean it?"

Something in my tone must give away the gravity of the situation, because in the most feather-light way, a hand comes up to cup my broken cheek. "This"—behind my head, his fingers flex—"is the woman I love. Your past made *this* person."

Here goes nothing.

"My mom killed my dad."

Silence.

If we were anywhere but inside a sterile hospital, I'm sure we would be hearing crickets chirping.

Instead, there's the steady *drip-drip-drip* of my IV. Thankfully the nurse removed the clip from the heart rate monitor earlier, so there's no erratic beeping to go along with it.

I finally work up the nerve to lift my gaze from the even stitching at the collar of Mase's gray t-shirt to his face. I'm prepared for the worst, for the judgment I've come to expect.

Except…

It's not there.

"What?" Mase breathes the question out.

I repeat one of the hardest sentences for me to utter. "My mom killed my dad."

"I thought…" His Adam's apple bobs with a swallow. "I thought you said your dad was killed by a drunk driver."

It sends a bolt of pain through my cranium, but I nod instead of giving a verbal answer. This is difficult enough for me to talk about; I can't waste the precious few words I'm capable of getting out.

Memories of that night slam into me.

JT and I had successfully landed a standing full toss in our partner stunt routine, making us one of only a small handful of pairings to complete such a difficult stunt.

T and Savvy were losing their minds, having captured the whole thing on video.

Coach Kris practically had stars in her eyes as she watched us repeat it for the second time and immediately declared it was something to be added to our routine for Worlds.

When T sent E the video, he was so proud he risked getting in trouble during a team dinner to FaceTime with us. That might have been my favorite part. We were going to see the goober the next day when we all flew to Houston to see Penn State play in the national championship.

So when Pops showed up at The Barracks earlier than normal to pick us up, we all thought it was fortuitous timing. None of us noticed his red-rimmed eyes or how utterly crestfallen he looked until he had to shatter our world.

"My mom—" I cough around the title she lost the right to. "Was the drunk driver."

"Baby." Mase tightens his hold, moving me fractionally

closer to him. His eyes fall closed and his forehead drops gently to mine as if he can absorb my pain. "Is that why you don't talk about her? Because she got behind the wheel that night instead of your dad?"

I wish that were the reason. Too bad the truth isn't that simple.

"My parents weren't in the same car. *She* was driving the car that *hit* my dad's."

Bile churns its way up my esophagus. I thought I'd gotten over the sense of abandonment my mother's life choices gave me years ago. I was fine. I had amazing women fill the motherly role—women who *wanted* to fill it—through the years: Moms (Michelle, JT's mom), Coach Kris, Bette, even Mama G. Just because Patricia is my blood doesn't mean I need her in my life.

"I don't talk about her because when I was eight years old, she decided being a mom wasn't for her…at least until she *traded up*"—I spit every ounce of revulsion I feel into those two words—"to a new Hollywood husband who came with two kids in tow."

That was the part that hurt the most. E and I weren't good enough to stick around for, but our step-siblings—our almost-the-same-ages step-siblings—were.

The most humiliating part was when she did show up, I welcomed her back with open arms. Damn was I naive.

"For months, the press ate up every detail of the Dennings' family drama. And when…" My words trail off, unable to finish for fear he'll agree.

One long finger curls beneath my chin, tilting it up until I meet his light green eyes again. "And when?" Mase prompts.

I might as well tell him. It's not like he could want to murder Liam any more than he already does, right?

"And when Liam sent me that shirt"—Mason's grip on me borders on painful at the mention of my ex—"he included a note."

#Chapter17

MY MIND IS STILL REELING over everything Kay told me. As hard as I try, I can't seem to fall asleep. A quick glance confirms at least she's not suffering from the same problem. *Good.* She needs her rest if she's going to get better.

The quiet snick of the door has me looking up to see E, Bette, and B have returned. In the light spilling in from the hallway, I can read their surprise at finding me in bed with Kay.

I hesitated to climb in next to her, though not because I didn't want to—*god* did I want to. It was the fear of hurting her that brought on the reluctance, and I *never* want to be the one to bring my girl pain again.

When she turned those gray eyes my way, pleading, how the hell was I supposed to say no? Easy—I couldn't. Now I happily serve as her body pillow. Plus, selfishly, having her in my arms, feeling her body pressed to mine is the first real thing to reassure me she *is* okay.

"Has she been sleeping long?" Bette smooths a hand down Kay's head.

"About ten minutes," I answer, and her mouth twists into a frown.

"Has she been in a lot of pain?" E steps to his wife's side, repeating the same caring gesture. "I would have hoped she would get more rest without us here."

Understandable, and if Kay hadn't spent the bulk of the time finally filling me in, *letting* me in, I'd be more upset about her lack of sleep as well.

Keeping my voice low as not to disturb our patient, I tell them, "She told me about your mom."

Bette gasps, and E's nostrils flare as he falls back a step. A shield slams down behind his eyes, and an expression fiercer than the one when we told him about what happened with Liam takes over his face. A vein visibly pulses at his temple.

"If only that bitch understood the concept of *staying away* then life might have turned out different..." E audibly inhales, his shoulders rising, chest expanding with the action. "For *all* of us."

Sensing the same anger I am, Bette guides her hand down E's arm to link her fingers with his, the move bringing discernible change to the big man.

"E." Bette shakes her head. "Now's not the time."

"Listen to the missus, bro." B stretches out in the recliner JT spent the night in.

E takes his friend's advice and snuggles with his wife on the couch, each of us closing our eyes and giving in to our exhaustion.

I'm not sure how much time passes before I'm roused from sleep, this time by a nurse coming to check on Kay.

"It's against the rules to be in the bed, sir." She eyes me disapprovingly.

Kay lets out a whimper and starts to stir, anticipating the loss of my presence. I stroke a hand down her arm, silently reassuring her I'm not going anywhere. We haven't listened

to the rules since we got here; why start now? A small puff of
air dances across the skin of my throat as Kay resettles.

Giving the nurse my most charming smile—you don't get
the nickname Casanova without having buckets of charm—I
do my best to ease any of her concerns.

"I know it is, but you see…" I smile harder, bringing into
play the dimples Kay loves to tell me make girls stupid. "My
girl *begged* me."

I raise my brows and attempt to convey a *How was I
supposed to say no?* plea.

The nurse's frown only deepens.

*Oh no. *grips chin and shakes head in mock concern* Guess
you're not as Casanova-y as you thought.* I'm sure I've said it
before, but it bears repeating—my inner coach is a dick.

Afraid the nurse will follow through on kicking me out of
the bed, I make one last-ditch effort. "She said the only way
she would be able to sleep is if I held her, and I figured sleep
is what she needs most right now, correct?"

"Fine." She finally relents. "Make sure you're mindful of
her cheekbone. There can't be any pressure on it if it's going
to heal correctly."

My chest deflates as I blow out a breath of relief. "You
have my word."

I watch, doing my best to stay out of the way as monitors
are checked, fluid levels are assessed, and notes are made in
Kay's chart.

"I need to wake her to finish my evaluation." She tips her
head at Kay's sleeping form.

I nod my understanding. I may not know how long we've
been out, but I'm well aware concussion protocol mandates
these types of checks every few hours.

With a ghost of a touch, I run a finger down the side of
Kay's face. "Skittles, baby." I trace along her jaw. "Wake up,
sweetheart."

Kay stirs again, pushing deeper into me, her eyes scrunched tightly closed. "Too early," she mumbles.

A chuckle rumbles inside my chest. It may be evening, but with all the chaos, it seems my little anti-morning person is about to make an appearance.

"I promise you can go back to sleep as soon as this nice nurse"—I send a wink over my shoulder—"is done with you." I'm not above a little flattery and flirtation if it keeps me in the hospital staff's good graces.

I run a thumb along Kay's lower lip; it's chapped, and I bet she will be asking for that lip stuff girls love so much.

Storm clouds rage in her gray eyes as they lock onto me in accusation, like *I'm* the bad guy here. "Can't you let a girl sleep?" she grumbles.

I place a kiss to the tip of her upturned nose. "I thought you said you're a better patient than E?"

She curses under her breath. "Sometimes you suck." She shifts to sit up so the nurse can finish her examination.

This time my laughter isn't as quiet. God I love this girl. I swear we'll be old and gray and she'll still be giving me shit.

"You could always be the one to dump *his* punk ass this time, sis," E's voice calls out, all the activity waking the others in the room.

"But he's so cute." There's a mock whine behind Kay's words.

"That's half the reason I stay married to your brother," Bette jokes, and even the nurse joins in on the laughter.

#Chapter18

IT HASN'T EVEN BEEN a full thirty-six hours and I'm more than ready to be sprung from this joint—er, hospital.

I need a shower, or better yet, a nice long soak in the jacuzzi tub in the master bathroom at home in the worst way. Don't get me started on the catastrophe I call my hair.

On my numerous trips to the bathroom—and there were many thanks to all the intravenous fluids I was given—I managed to avoid looking at my reflection. I've put the task off as long as I possibly could.

*Stop being a chickenshit. *props hand on hip* How can you say your hair is a catastrophe without seeing what it looks like?*

My inner cheerleader is lucky it still hurts me to roll my eyes. I don't need to see it to know my assessment of the situation is correct. I can feel it, *hear* it any time it moves. Hair should not be something that is audible.

Hands braced on the counter, fingers curling over the rim and digging into the porcelain of the sink, I lift my gaze and gasp at my reflection.

Okay, you were right. You look like shit.

My usually country-music-star-worthy curls currently look like they are vying for the role of Merida if Disney were to do a live-action version of *Brave*, the blood staining one section only adding to the authenticity. There is *no way* I'm going to attempt to untangle this mess until it's loaded down with at least a gallon of conditioner. I can't even successfully pull it back into a ponytail.

That's not the worst of it. No, that honor goes to my pale complexion. I think I prefer the Disney princess goals of my hair as opposed to the could-be-Casper's-sister status my face is going for. Even my freaking freckles look bleached.

It's no wonder I've heard Mase's teeth grind any time he looks at me. The bruise on my left cheek is like a giant tie-dye beacon against my deathly pallor.

In an effort not to moon a room full of people, I moved like an octogenarian and slipped on the leggings Em brought me before I got out of bed. I don't care how much Mase was enjoying seeing my ass waving in the wind thanks to my highly fashionable hospital gown—I was over it.

With a deep breath, I peel the gown from my body and set it on the counter. Thankful Em had the foresight to grab one of my sports bras that zips closed in the front, I get the girls secured and carefully finish dressing in a black *Death Before Decaf* tee. A smile tugs at my lips—I'm surprised Em didn't try to steal this one for herself.

By the time I step out of the bathroom, the number of occupants in the room has grown by three. A brooding Carter King is holding up the wall with his leather-jacket-clad arms folded over his chest while he periodically casts a glare at G and Em talking with their heads bent close on the couch. Outside of giving him a chin tip in hello, I don't pay him much mind, instead sending my focus to the other two new arrivals: Jordan Donovan and her business partner Skye Masters. I remember Jordan mentioning something about Skye flying in to help manage everything, but her being *here* has my gut clenching.

"How are you feeling?" Jordan's bright grin should put my mind at ease, but it doesn't.

"Outside of feeling like I went a few rounds with Vince Steele?" I say, referring to the current UFC Light Heavyweight Champ. "Not too bad."

"Oof, don't say that too loud here—Vicki might overhear," Skye says, pointing to her ear with a manicured finger, a teasing smirk playing on her lips. I haven't had many interactions with the other half of ATS—Jordan mostly handles E's PR needs—but I can tell she's a ballbuster.

"Vicki?" *Who's Vicki?*

"The nurse from the ER?" Mase asks, holding out a hand to me as I pad my way across the room to him.

"Yeah." Jordan exchanges a look with Skye I can't get a read on, almost as if they're sharing a secret. "Vicki—or Mama *Steele*"—she emphasizes the last name—"is Vince's mom. It's because I put up with the ridiculousness her son and my wombmate get into that I was able to convince her to pull strings for you all to stay with Kay here."

Mase's jaw drops, and I poke a finger under it so he can stop looking like a fish. I've always found it entertaining whenever he makes comments about how nonchalant I am about being around E and his teammates. Jordan Donovan? She's the definition of blasé when it comes to famous connections.

"Aw…" Skye bends an elbow onto Jordan's shoulder, leaning into her. "It's cute you think being a star athlete is what got you preferential treatment."

"Don't be mean." Jordan taps Skye in the stomach with a playful backhand. "You know their status helps." She shrugs her free shoulder. "We just know how to leverage it better."

I pause and take a moment to study the hockey queen. She might have a point. Since she pointed out the whole media darling angle Mase and I have going for us, I wonder if maybe I should leverage it to use the press to my advantage for the first time ever.

Now's not the time, though. There's a palpable tension

hanging in the air that wasn't here when I went to change. I felt it when I first came out of the bathroom and saw the new arrivals. No more. I need to confront this head-on.

"What's wrong?" I ask the room, cutting to the chase.

"What makes you think there's anything wrong?" E evades.

"Oh...I don't know," I drawl sarcastically. "Maybe because you all stopped talking the second I opened the door. Or, you know"—I thrust an arm in the direction of Carter, ignoring the twinge from all my bruises—"the fact that King is randomly here."

"To be fair"—Carter smooths a hand over the black beanie on his head—"I was here when you were admitted."

"And I'm sure it was only because *my* sister was with *your* sister when she got the call about what happened."

There's a tiny twitch to his lips, so small you would miss it if you weren't paying close enough attention, before he shakes it off like it's irrelevant.

I let him have it and focus on my next point. "There's also the fact that not just Jordan is here, but Skye too. You spent most of yesterday at ATS—there's no more strategic planning that could *possibly* be done. If they are here, it means they are reacting to something."

Again, everyone looks at each other instead of answering me. It's annoying as hell.

"There's a bunch of press outside the hospital," E says through his teeth.

My head falls forward, and one of Mase's arms wraps behind my back to tuck me close to his side.

And the media circus begins.

Neither E nor B has made a statement since the pictures were leaked of them being here and confirming the reason why they missed yesterday's game. If the press is already circling for a simple comment, what the hell would they do if they learned the details of *how* I ended up here in the first place?

"So we've come up with a brilliant plan." B claps his hands and rubs them together.

"You only think it's brilliant because *you* came up with it." E proves he's my brother by rolling his eyes.

"Don't be salty, bruh." B taps E's cheeks before pinching them until E's lips pucker and pushes his face from side to side. "You just get that million-dollar smile of yours ready to distract the cameras so Little D can sneak off undetected."

That's their plan? I swing my gaze back to King by the door. "Yes, Dennings." He nods. "That's why I'm here. Your brother wants me for my *Speed Racer* skills."

"I'd say you're more *The Fast and the Furious* than anything else."

"Always the smartass," Mase whispers, a bolt of heat darting down my spine at the feel of his lips brushing along the shell of my ear. "I thought I was the only one you gave shit to."

"Do I detect a hint of jealousy, Caveman?" I tease.

"Nope." He nips at my ear. "I know you're mine."

I could never tell him because it would only encourage him, but I do love his possessive side at times.

"There's also—" G's words get cut off by Em smacking her hand over his mouth with a "Not the time." I eye her, curious, but she only gives me a shake of her head. I'll have to remember to ask her what that was all about later.

Jordan and Skye lay out the details of B's—hold on, let me mentally roll my eyes—*brilliant* plan. E and B will go out the front, drawing the attention of any of the vultures lying in wait. Just in case anyone is looking, Em will pretend—not all that hard, mind you—to be me with a hoodie shielding her face while Bette and G escort her to E's Escalade. It's not much, but it should hopefully buy us enough time for Mase and me to sneak out the employee entrance where King will be waiting for us with the Royals' Camaro.

Mase smirks, his dimples coming out to play as I accept the hoodie G brought with him from the AK house. Always wanting his name on me. He crouches in front of where I sit on the lowered hospital bed, his long fingers slipping inside the collar of the sweatshirt to free my trapped hair. His features soften as he looks at me adoringly, his thumbs coming up to stroke along my jaw.

I reach up and wrap my hands around his wrists as I catch another flash of guilt when he locks onto my cheek.

After a few more seconds, Mase lifts his backward ball cap from his head and places it on mine, this time with the bill facing front. I like how I can still feel his heat radiating from it. The hat should be too big on me, but my out-of-control hair helps keep it from being too loose.

With a small adjustment, he reaches back and pulls the hood of the sweatshirt over the top. Once satisfied I'm covered as best as can be, he places a kiss to the top of my head and holds out a hand for me to take. "Let's get you home, baby."

#Chapter19

KING HONKS the horn in goodbye as he backs out of the driveway of my family home after dropping Mase and me off. Mase keeps his stride slow and small to match mine as we make our way to the front door, and I cast a curious look in his direction when he opens it without needing a key. We beat E and Bette home; the door shouldn't be unlocked.

My unasked question gets answered as soon as we step inside and get hit with a delicious aroma wafting from the back of the house. I'd know the scent of Mama G's chicken and dumplings anywhere.

"Oh god," I moan. "I think I've gained five pounds just from the smell of your cooking," I tell her as we make it to the kitchen.

"Sugah." Mama G's southern twang washes over me as she rushes around the counter to take me into her arms in a gentle, but still fierce, hug. She is where her sons learned how to bear-hug. Seriously, best huggers *ever*.

"I'm fine, Mama G." I hold on a few seconds longer. "I promise."

"Hungry?" She doesn't wait for my response before pulling a plate from the appropriate cabinet.

"For your cooking?" The pressure of Mase's hand on my back has me continuing on to the living room. "Always."

I'm not surprised to see an episode of *Chopped* is playing on the flat-screen above the fireplace. Mama G loves her cooking shows, and it for sure shows in her culinary creations.

Mase helps me arrange a couple of throw pillows for support before settling a few cushions a ways down from me on the sectional and lifting my feet to remove my boots.

"*Yaassss!*" G's voice bellows seconds after the front door opens and closes again, his footsteps smacking against the tile floor as he runs down the hallway. "Chicken and dumplings." He lifts his mom into a spinning hug.

"Grant Samuel," she scolds. "There's no need for all that yelling." She pats him lovingly on the cheek as he beams down at her.

I love watching G with his mom. He turns into such a ball of mush for her. Physically, they are as much an example of opposites as him and me. Papa G definitely has the dominant genetics of the pairing because G is all tall height with dark hair and skin like him, where Mama G is all short, blonde, and pale skin like me.

"Ah," I mumble around my own forkful of G's favorite dish. "Now I see why you *really* came to help spring me from the hospital." I tap my temple. "Here I thought it was for me"—I flatten a hand over my heart—"but in reality it was so you could be here for Mama's cooking."

The others filter into the house as G and I continue to bicker over the merits of his bestie card. E and B greet Mama G in much the same way her son did while Bette takes a more subtle approach.

The boys go in on their dishes like they haven't eaten in weeks while I continue to consume mine like a reasonable person.

When I'm finished with my food, Mase takes the plate

from me to set it on the coffee table. Nothing like a home-cooked meal, and Mama G's chicken and dumplings are enough to have me feeling halfway human again.

"Hey Bette," I call over the back of the couch.

My sister-in-law disengages from where my brother has her pressed against the wall. I'm grossed out by the fact that he's probably whispering dirty nothings in her ear, but I want a niece or nephew badly enough not to voice that particular opinion.

"You doing okay? What can I get you?" She braces her elbows on top of the cushions, leaning into my space as her maternal instincts take over.

"I'm fine." I wave off her concern. "But"—I point to the riot of curls on my head—"can you help me wash all this? I'm not supposed to get the stitches wet yet and figured that particular task would be easier to accomplish if I had some assistance."

"Of course." She reaches out to gently smooth back one of the bloody curls. "Meet me upstairs."

Before I can follow Bette, Mase lifts me into his arms and carries me the whole way. I don't bother to fight him, much too comfortable in his hold.

"Nice," he comments when he steps inside the master bathroom.

It is nice, but nothing overly fancy: a glassed-in shower stall large enough for three to the right and a separate jacuzzi tub past it, a water closet in the corner, and a set of his-and-her sinks across from the tub. Bette's favorite feature though? The shampoo station E had installed.

Mase is lowering me into the padded seat in front of the adjustable sink when Bette returns from my own bathroom with my shampoo and conditioner.

"Mmm, peppermint." Mase pops the top on the conditioner, shooting me a wink.

"Merry Christmas," I tease, remembering his candy cane confession when we were down in Kentucky.

Bette instructs me to lean back then carefully wraps a rolled towel around my head, positioning it like one would a headband to help protect my stitches. It's okay if they get a little bit wet, but we'll do our best to keep them as dry as possible.

Mase stands by as Bette carefully works to clean the blood from my hair. The two of them carry on their own conversation while I let the sure strokes and kneading from Bette's strong fingers help chase away the last of my lingering headache. There really is nothing better than someone else washing your hair for you.

"Did you wanna soak for a little after this?"

I crack my lids open to look at the upside-down face of my sister-in-law. "Yes please." My eyes fall closed as warm water rinses the suds out of my curls.

"I got it." I feel the loss of Mase's body near mine as soon as he steps away to start the water seconds later.

"As hot as you can stand it, please," I request.

"Fine." I hear him adjust the taps. "But you're icing everything after."

I want to argue, but I don't because he's right. The heat will certainly help my sore muscles, but it won't do anything to help my bruises or the swelling I have going on.

A soft kiss presses itself to my unbroken cheekbone before I hear Mase whisper that he'll be right back.

Bette starts a second round of shampoo as the sound of Mason's retreating footsteps fades. "That boy really loves you."

"I love him too." My heart squeezes inside my chest. "He's...*everything*." I whisper the words as if afraid to test the universe by saying it too loud. We still have so much left to face if we're going to make it as couple; I don't want to add tempting fate to the list.

I expect Bette to comment, but she doesn't. When the silence continues to stretch, I open my eyes again to see she has one of those dreamy smiles she usually reserves for when she's looking at my brother on her face. Romantic Bette is such a sap. "From what I overheard at the hospital, I'd say he seems to think the same of you."

It's my turn to grin like a lovesick idiot at the memory of Mase's declaration while simultaneously laying into me for trying to protect him.

Mase returns as Bette's working the conditioner through my tangled strands. She does her best to finger-comb out the worst of my knots but opts to leave the conditioner to soak in to make it easier to work through later. Round and round she winds my hair into a bun and uses a clip to secure it on top of my head.

I sit up, regretting not removing my hoodie before Bette started. Oh well.

She wipes down the sink and gathers up the bottles of my toiletries. Then she moves in front of me and places a kiss to my forehead before turning to Mase. "Take care of our girl." He nods at the order.

Not wanting to risk losing my balance and busting my ass more, I remain seated to remove my socks and toss them in the direction of the hamper in the corner of the room.

Mase pulls two fluffy towels from the linen closet, hanging them on the rack, and places my cell phone within easy reach on the tub's ledge. "Call me if you need anything." I get another gentle kiss, this one to the crown of my head.

Not liking the way that sounds, I'm quick to grab him before he can get too far. "Stay."

His gaze goes from the almost desperate grip I have on his wrist then up to my face. His Adam's apple bobs with a swallow. I shouldn't find such a simple action sexy, but I can't help it. "Babe…"

"*Please?*"

He rubs at his ear, turning his head to look at the door to the bathroom. "You're hurt. As much as I like to think I'm a gentleman—"

I snort, and his eyes narrow. Gentleman my ass.

"—if I see you naked, I don't know if I'll be able to control myself."

There's the Caveman I love.

I bite my lip to restrain a victorious smile and mentally bump fists with my inner cheerleader at how the action has Mase's gaze locking onto my mouth.

"Join me." I take two small steps, my chest brushing against his. The seafoam color of his eyes darkens at my words, but he keeps his body ramrod straight, battling with himself over my request. Yes I can admit it's selfish, but I need this. I need to prove to both him and myself that—fractured cheekbone excluded—it's going to take a hell of a lot more than Liam *fucking* Parker to break me this time around. "Please."

"I don't want to hurt you." The gravelly edge to his voice tells me how pained he is by the possibility, but I'm shaking my head before he finishes saying the words.

Releasing my hold on him, I bend my elbows, pull my arms from the sleeves of my sweatshirt, and tuck them into my torso. I bring my hands up to the opening, spreading my fingers wide on either side of my neck, and stretch the thick cotton as far as I can as I ease it over my head.

"If you really don't want to hurt me…" I repeat the same process with my t-shirt. "Then get in the tub." I keep my gaze locked on his as I slowly lower the zipper of my sports bra and toss it onto the pile forming on the floor.

I hook my thumbs in the waistband of my leggings and start to push them down my legs. It's not the sexiest strip-tease, my movements slow and not at all fluid thanks to my concussion, but I let my now naked body do most of the work for me as I spin to face the tub. "I'll need help washing my back." I arch my spine enough to pop my ass out in his direction.

"You don't play fair, babe." He sucks in a breath as I step to him again, slipping my hands under the hem of his shirt, the muscles of his abdominals jumping under my touch. I love when they do that.

"Never said I do." I run my fingers along the edge of his boxer briefs, dipping under it. "Then again…" I pull my left hand free and hold it up close to his face. "Neither do you." I wiggle my fingers, making the light bounce off the peridot birthstone band once again adorning my left ring finger.

Those damn dimples flash as he circles the band, ignoring the other two on the hand. The jerk knows *exactly* what it did to me when he was trying to win me back. Only he could be cocky enough to add in the significance of the particular finger he sized it to.

When I think he's going to contradict me or offer another excuse for denying me, he instead surprises me by pulling his shirt over his head in that hot one-handed way guys do.

Inch by inch, warm olive skin is revealed to my hungry gaze. The black ink decorating his body only emphasizes each sinew of his forearm, each bulge of his biceps, the breadth of his chest, and each dip and cut of muscle down his side into his Adonis belt. Even in my concussed state, I can appreciate what a freaking work of art my man is.

He flings his hat to the side like a frisbee, rubbing a hand over his head and making his dark espresso-colored hair disheveled like after I've been grabbing on to it for dear life while he brings me to multiple orgasms.

Between that and the way he keeps his dilated eyes locked on mine as he pushes his joggers and briefs down his strong legs, my body flushes and I feel myself go wet.

Welp, I want him—concussion and injuries be damned.

Neither of us move, each staring at the other, both breathing heavily. The brick wall of his chest heaves with each inhalation, and my breasts jiggle with the force of my own.

I've long since lost any shyness I feel in my attraction to him, greedily taking in what's displayed in front of me. There's some slight bruising on his torso from the game, but nothing as prominent as what I'm sporting. I count each of the bumps of his eight-pack and follow the path of his happy trail to his already hard cock, those amazing V cuts bracketing it beautifully. It's really unfair for him to have those *and* a perfect set of dimples in his cheeks. Damn them both and their ability to turn me stupid.

"Skittles," he growls, and my nipples tighten to the point of pain. "Get your fine ass in the tub before I end up fucking you over the counter like I did in Kentucky."

If I thought I was wet before, it has nothing on how soaked I am now.

"Is that supposed to be a deterrent?" I tilt my head to the side. "Because that was some of the hottest sex we've *ever* had."

He points an aggressive finger at the jacuzzi. "Tub. Now."

Air hisses through my teeth as my toes hit the water, the temperature just this side of scalding. *Perfection.*

Mase does the same as he lowers himself behind me. "Damn, Skit. You taking a bath or boiling lobsters?"

I giggle at his exaggeration, settling myself between his spread legs and resting my back to his chest. My head lolls to the side, my uninjured cheek resting on a hard pec. I could stay like this forever.

Fingertips glide up my left arm, droplets of water left behind in their wake as the gentle touch continues to trace the line of my collarbone. Mase's large hand curls over the curve where my neck meets my shoulder before I feel the callouses on his thumb trace around the Peter Pan silhouettes tattoo behind my ear. "You never told me what these meant."

No, I didn't. The only time he asked about the tiny Disney

characters inked on my body was when we first started hanging out. I was able to play it off then by claiming it was too personal to share. In reality, I wouldn't have been able to explain it without having to reveal the truth about my mom.

All of that's changed now.

"It's a combination of a few things, but essentially it's in memory of JT's mom."

"In memory?"

"She passed away when JT and I were in middle school. Breast cancer."

"I'm sorry, baby." Mase grips my neck, his other arm wrapping around my middle and holding me a little bit tighter.

"Thanks." I don't need the condolences, but I appreciate them nonetheless. It's been years, so the pain of losing the main mother figure in my life has faded with time. Like Pops, Moms Taylor was always a surrogate parent; it's probably why when our biological mother abandoned us that first time, it didn't hit E and me as hard as it could have.

"She loved the story of Peter Pan. There are copies of every version and retelling of it stored on the bookshelves inside the Taylor home." Pops spent countless hours tracking down as many as he could, gifting her a new one for every anniversary or birthday.

"When it became clear she wasn't going to get better—" Time may have lessened the pain, but I still have to stop to swallow down a ball of emotion. "We all flew to London to see the famous statue." This time it's a laugh that interrupts. "I think there are legit five hundred pictures from that day alone with all the combinations of groupings we made."

"I think I remember seeing a few of them on the wall at E's."

I chuckle thinking of the ridiculousness of the pictures he used in making up the gallery walls around his home in Baltimore.

"E has a lot of pictures of Moms on display. It may have been years later, but I think part of the reason he loves Bette so much—even if it's unconsciously—is because she stepped into that mother role for me without even being asked."

The heavier conversation fades, nothing more needing to be said on why that would mean so much to us.

Behind me I feel Mase's muscles bunch and stretch as he reaches for something. A moment later there's the pop of a top, and the scent of vanilla fills the air. "*God.*" His teeth nip at my tattoo and he brings his arm around, the loofah held in his hand. "All your scents make me hungry." Lust coats his voice.

I want to agree, want to tell him the smell of him fresh from a shower is one of my favorites and I'm grateful I get to experience it twice a day because of his rigorous training schedule, but I'm incapable of speech. Every nerve and brain cell in my body is focused solely on the drag of the loofah, down my arm, back over my shoulder, and across my chest.

Back and forth. A dip down into the water before a new round of circles traces around my breasts.

His free hand comes up to aid in the washing, cupping and squeezing, his thumb smoothing away the suds clinging to my now fully erect nipples.

My back arches, none of my earlier soreness registering as pleasure from him pinching my buds between his thumb and forefinger fills me. The slight twist he gives them shoots a bolt of lust straight to my clit, my legs falling open of their own accord.

His hard-on pokes my lower back as he continues to tease me. I breathe in the thick fragrant air, my breasts full, heavy, and aching for…more.

Instead, they bob slightly in the water as Mase releases them and shifts me to sit forward, the loofah washing a path across my shoulder blades.

I tilt my chin and level him with side-eye.

"What?" An evil smirk tugs at one side of Mase's mouth. "You said you wanted help washing your back."

And he says you're the smartass? My inner cheerleader folds her arms in a huff.

"That was before you started teasing me."

Two can play this game. I place both my hands on his knees, angling them so my fingertips fall toward his inner thighs, and start to draw lazy, almost absentminded figure eights up and down his skin, inching higher with each pass.

"Who said I was a tease?" His hips buck forward as I run my thumb along the crease where his thigh meets his hip.

"Me." I cow-stretch, my ass brushing his erection with the subtle movement.

Water sloshes as an arm bands around my middle, tugging me until my back is suctioned to his front. In my peripheral vision, I watch the lavender loofah disappear under the surface of the water.

I hold my breath, anticipating it touching my pulsing center. Instead it runs down the length of my thigh, taking a slow trip down then up before dipping into the space between my legs. All I get is one quick brush over my clit before it's lifted to repeat the process down my other leg.

Mase cups a hand under one of my knees, bending my leg and placing my foot on the outside of his to spread me open. Again he ignores where I need him most, washing down my calf and over my foot.

Finally I feel the rough texture of the loofah press against my center, Mase using his fingers to part me enough to give him direct contact with my clit, each pass both too much and not enough. I swivel my hips in search of some relief, but he clamps his free hand over one of my hipbones, holding me in place.

I'm about ready to beg or lose my mind, not sure which.

He releases the loofah, the puff floating to the surface, then two fingers plunge inside me. A keening moan escapes my mouth and my back arches with an audible suction noise as I rise away.

"Fuck, baby," Mase moans, his breath blowing across my ear. "You're *soaked*." He scissors his fingers, setting off an orgasm so strong it has me seeing stars that have nothing to do with my concussion.

"Oh god." My body collapses against his as he continues to work me. The things he does to me, the way he makes me *feel* should be illegal. Lord knows I could never tell him though. His ego is big enough; no need to inflate it more than it already is.

Once I recover from my release and he's eased his fingers from the viselike grip my pussy has on them, I push to my knees and turn so we are face to face.

I pick up the loofah, add another dollop of body wash, and get to work washing his chest.

One would think being fresh out of the hospital, in recovery from reparative surgery, bruised, and concussed would mean sex is the last thing on my mind, but the feel of Mase's muscular body under my hands has all that fading away.

"Careful, baby." His eyes fall to the bruises mottling the right side of my torso. "I don't want you to hurt yourself."

"I'm fine." I spread my knees to straddle his hips.

I know to Mase, and probably most other people, it's crazy for me to be the one to protect him, but the thought of something hurting him drives me to the brink of insanity.

Stepping back from the situation, I can see that Mason could have easily taken Liam in a fight. He has a few inches and more than a dozen pounds on my ex, but in the moment, all I could think about was keeping him safe.

It's like my body needs to reaffirm he is okay, needs to make sure he really wasn't hurt the other night. I line up my entrance with his dick and thank the birth control pill gods as his tip slips inside easily. He was right—I'm so wet not even the water could wash it away.

"Kayla." The use of my full name is a whispered curse, a warning I don't heed as I continue to sink down until my still engorged clit is resting against his pubic bone. "*Fuck.*"

My hands go around his neck, my fingers locking together as I anchor myself to his body. His head tips back, our eyes locking, never breaking contact as I start to move.

Slowly.

Up and down.

In and out.

Mase's hands find purchase on my hips, not squeezing like he usually would, only cupping the joint as he lets me keep our pace slow.

My eyes telegraph every thought and feeling I have.

I love you.

I need you.

You're mine.

You're safe.

A part of me is afraid he's going to stop me in his own driving need to protect me, and I'm relieved when he doesn't.

Our pace remains unhurried yet intense.

Up and down.

In and out.

My hips rock back and forth, pulling off him until only the tip remains inside me before sinking back down completely.

To the tip.

Down to the hilt.

A swivel of my hips.

The brush of his pubic bone on my clit.

A mutual groan.

Over and over, our languid pace continues.

The pressure inside my body starts to build once more, and I know I'm on the verge of coming again. The tightening of his fingers on me is the only sign he's as close as I am.

Another figure-eight swivel of my hips and we explode together. It's not the most animalistic orgasm we've given each other, but it's not any less intense.

My hips still as we ride out our highs together. Mason's arms close around me, pulling me down to bury his face in my neck.

"Holy shit," he murmurs breathlessly against my skin.

My head bobs in agreement.

We stay this way, holding each other like we don't plan on ever letting go, until the water starts to cool around us. Finally I shift so we can finish getting clean.

I flip the lever to drain the water and reach for the removable shower head. I hand Mase the loofah and release the clip from my hair. As I start to unwind it from its bun, I feel his long fingers start to tenderly comb through the curls, rinsing the conditioner from them for me.

Once we're both clean, Mase holds my hand as I step out on the memory foam bath mat then he wraps one of the fluffy sky blue towels around my body, using the soft terrycloth to dry the water from my skin. After he's done, I return the favor, the two of us grinning at each other like idiots.

I wring my hair out over the tub as best I can before going to the linen closet to grab another towel since he used the other one.

I start rubbing at my long strands then the exhaustion of my ordeal hits me and I stumble to the side.

Mase is there with a steady hand on my elbow. "Come on, Skittles. Let's get you in bed."

"Round two already?" I try to wiggle my eyebrows, but like rolling my eyes, it hurts too much, and I stop after one lift.

He doesn't miss my wince and scoops me up into his arms yet again. I could make a comment about how I'm fully capable of walking down the hall to my room, but why would I? In his arms is my favorite place to be.

Chapter20

THE FACT that Kay doesn't fight me when I lift her into my arms bridal style is my first clue that she's more worn out than she lets on. My girl is pure sass even on her worst day; this docile version I'm holding is the biggest sign she needs sleep, and she needs it now.

Once inside her room, I place her down next to the bed, keeping my hands wrapped around her arms for a few extra seconds. Once I'm sure she's steady on her feet, I move to her dresser and start pulling open drawers until I find her clothes to sleep in.

Dropping a pair of well-worn black NJA sweatpants, a tank top, and a Henley—both in blue because we all know how she loves to match—onto the bed, I reach up and unwind the towel done up turban-style, causing Kay's long curls to tumble around her shoulders and down her back.

If the guys ever found out one of the first things—outside of her height, or lack thereof—I noticed about her was her hair, they would make me turn in my man card. Still, I can't help but twirl one of the waist-length curls around my finger, savoring the silky feel of the strands against my skin. The way the colorful combination of purple, pink, red, and black plays peekaboo through the golden mass of curls always has my fingers itching to sift through it to discover what other hues are hidden inside.

A small sigh escapes Kay's mouth as I play with her hair, but it's the goose bumps covering the bare skin of her shoulders and arms that have me blinking myself out of my trance.

Making sure my own towel is secure around my waist, I take a knee in front of Kay to help her into her sweats.

Oh how times have changed, huh, Nova? You used to be known for getting girls out *of their pants, not into them. Good thing this one is a keeper.*

My inner coach may live for giving me shit, but at least he understands what Kay means to me.

Unlike some…

The slide of Kay's hands bracing herself on me once again grounds me back in the present as I work the pants up her toned legs and underneath the terrycloth. Not removing her towel was a strategic move. If I'm going to keep the head on top of my shoulders currently being kneaded by Kay's fingers in charge and not the one in my pants, I can't risk seeing her fully naked again.

I'm only human, and a man at that. The struggle is real, people.

As if reading my mind, Kay pulls her tank top on over her towel. The bath, and maybe the two orgasms she had, seems to have helped with any stiffness the bruising she sustained on her torso caused her, because her movements aren't as jerky as they were earlier.

"Is your brother going to kick my ass if I go downstairs like this?" I point to the towel riding low on my hips. "Or do you think JT would mind if I borrowed more of his clothes?" They may only live a few blocks from each other, but they both have stuff for the other at their homes.

Gray eyes coast down my body, blatantly checking me out. See? I'm not the only one who does it. She's as hot for my body as I am for hers—one of the many reasons she is perfect for me.

"No need." She smooths down the Henley. "Yours are in the upper left."

"Huh?" Her lips quirk at my less-than-eloquent response.

"The top drawer on the left side of the dresser is filled with your clothes."

As much as she likes to give me shit for always trying to get my name on her by giving her my football shirts and hoodies, there's no way she's amassed enough to fill a drawer. Besides, even if she did, it would mean I would have to Donald Duck it because I've never given her boxers or pants to wear.

"Aw…" I loop my arms low on her hips, crossing my hands at the wrists and letting them hang loosely over the curve of her butt. "You gave me a drawer," I tease.

She gives me an *Of course, dumbass* eye roll, the move only bringing a mild grimace with it. "You're important to me. I wanted to make sure you felt at home here." The complete lack of humor in her deadpan delivery hits me in the squishy part of my heart I didn't even realize I had until I started dating her.

Oh, baby.

It isn't flashy, but like her including my birthstone band in her collection, this is one of her own ways of making a declaration about the seriousness of our relationship. When I slide the drawer open, I'm taken aback by how full it is. T-shirts, a hoodie—both not the ones I've given her—a few pairs of basketball shorts, joggers, boxer briefs, jeans, and socks round out the collection.

How?

"I asked Livi to bring me a bag of your stuff to practice one night," Kay says, answering my unvoiced question.

Herkie meanders in while I make quick work of dressing in gray sweats and a black *Property of U of J Football* tee. Liberating the wide-toothed comb from Kay's grasp, I take over brushing out the last of her tangles. Once done, I give her a gentle nudge and motion for her to get in bed.

Reaching for the painkillers and bottle of water Bette left on the bedside table, I uncap both and pass them to Kay. When she's done, I trade them out for the instant cold packs.

"Lie on my side," I suggest, patting the side she usually sleeps on for Herkie to jump up. She's less likely to roll over onto her broken cheekbone if she's cuddling her pup this way.

Squeezing the packs, I smack them against my thigh to finish activating them. Peeling down the comforter, I get two in position between her tank and Henley, arranging them where I know the worst of the bruising is.

The last pack gets wrapped in a hand towel before I gently place it over Kay's healing cheekbone. I note that the swelling has gone down considerably, but I won't be happy until I can no longer see the discoloration from what happened to her.

Her arm goes around Herkie's furry body as I tuck the covers in around her, hoping the blankets are enough to keep her from getting too chilled by the ice packs.

"Sleep, baby." I kiss her forehead and give Herkie an ear scratch and a "Good boy."

I'm closing the door behind me, making sure to leave it cracked in case the dog needs to leave, when I hear a whispered "Love you, Caveman."

A smile tugs my lips. "You too, Skittles."

"She good?" E asks the second I enter the kitchen.

"Yeah. She's down for the count." It's not surprising either. It's only the afternoon and this day has been packed with drama. First Kay finally gave her statement to the police about what happened. Then there was all the crap with the press at the hospital. It's enough to make me wish I was the one who crawled into bed with her, and I'm not the one with the concussion.

Actually…I could probably do with a workout to help burn off some of the anger coursing through my body. Crazy intense sex aside, seeing the full extent of Kay's injuries on display in the bathroom only made me wish I did go after Liam Parker the other night. She had to have hit the floor *hard* to be bruised to the extent she is.

The front door opens and slams as Tessa rushes into the house, her red hair flying behind her. She scans the people scattered throughout the kitchen and living room, a furrow forming between her brows.

"She's sleeping," G calls out, and she spins on her heel, her footsteps thundering up the stairs.

I move to follow, not wanting her to disturb Kay when she needs sleep, but a gentle hand on my forearm stops me. Dropping my chin, I see Bette shaking her head beside me. "They'll be fine. Tessa will just cuddle up with Kay."

Great. Now I'm jealous of a canine and a high schooler.

A few hours later, Tessa has made her way back downstairs— Kay thankfully remaining asleep—when Trav arrives, walking into the Dennings' home like he does so on the reg.

"Bruh…" Without warning, Trav tosses keys at me, and only the athletic instincts that allow me to catch the most unlikely of passes from him on the field have me doing the same now. "I think that King guy is planning the best way to steal your car."

Next to me, Tessa's fingers fly across the screen of her phone before she lifts it to her ear as I reach out a fist for my best friend to bump.

"Tell your brother he's too old to cream his pants over a car," Tessa says to who it's safe to assume is Savvy, and then E shouts, "TESSA!"

"Like you don't hear worse in the locker room." She

waves him off and tosses her phone on the cushion between us.

B, seated on a barstool at the counter eating yet another plate of Mrs. Grayson's cooking, snorts. "Pray you don't have any daughters, dude." He points his fork at E. "Your little sisters will give you enough gray hairs. I can only imagine any female offspring will have you going bald." He snorts again.

"Don't worry"—Bette tunnels her fingers into E's hair, the annoyance on his face melting away as his eyes close —"he isn't showing any signs of either of those things happening."

"Why are you such a smartass?" King asks Tessa as his sister strides over to her bestie.

"Runs in the family," Tessa, E, and Bette answer in unison.

Mrs. Grayson busies herself serving food to the newcomers, Trav placing a smacking kiss on her cheek when he's handed his, bringing a brilliant smile to her face. He really is shameless in his flirting. I don't know why I let him get to me so easily when he does it with Kay. I think "flirt" is one of the chromosomes in his DNA.

"Why are you here?" I ask.

"Came to bring you the Shelby," Trav mumbles with his mouth full. "Figured you'd be sleeping here tonight." He lifts a brow in question, and I nod in confirmation. "This way you don't have to worry about figuring out a ride, and I can hitch one back with M&M later."

Em's face twists in disgust, whether at the asinine nickname or the arm currently hooked around her neck in an almost chokehold to allow Trav to keep eating yet to be determined.

"M&M?" She twists herself free, and I notice King's features smooth out as she does.

Interesting.

"What?" Trav asks, cheeks puffed out with food. "No

good?" Em shakes her head, and Trav tilts his head in thought. "Should I stick with Jackie O then?"

"Jack—" Em's words cut off with a gasp, and she whirls on King. "Fuck you, Carter."

The doorbell rings, cutting them off before they can get into it.

Extracting himself from a situation he unwittingly started, Trav calls out that he's got it and hustles to answer the door.

I can't help but chuckle at how E mutters something about quarterbacks always making themselves at home.

"Can I help you?" we hear Trav ask.

"I thought she was dating that Nova boy? Isn't this the quarterback?" a feminine voice asks, and E's shoulders hit his ears.

"That's what they're saying, but maybe Liam's right and she really is jersey-chasing her way through the team. I wouldn't be surprised if that were the case," a male voice answers.

What the fuck?

"What the fuck?" E echoes my thought, and we're on the move, me jumping over the back of the couch.

"Excuse me," Trav cuts in, a bite entering his tone. "But who the *fuck* are you? And what the hell do you want?"

As we close the distance to the door, I can see Trav standing with his feet spread wide and arms folded across his chest, effectively blocking the doorway like a bouncer working the door at a club.

His outburst provokes a feminine gasp, but my inner coach and I are mentally high-fiving each other.

"How *dare* you speak to us that way?" Incredulity bleeds from the tone of whoever the man is.

"I'll talk to you however I damn well please." I don't have to see him to know Trav's wearing his *Fuck you very much* smile. "You show up at my family's home and insult my sister in front of me"—he shrugs his shoulders, the action seeming more intimidating since he doesn't uncross his arms —"there's not a fucking chance I'm going to be *polite*." He spits the word out like a curse.

I knew my best friend had grown close to my girl and that is why he is instinctively protective of her now, but if Kay were to hear Trav calling her his sister the way she does with Tessa, there's a chance it might actually make her cry.

"Sister?" the female says. "We know who Eric Dennings is, and you are not him."

"Doesn't make Kay *any* less my family." If it's possible, Trav's chest widens more as he continues to hold his protective stance. "Now, again…who the hell are you and what do you want?"

Grayson and I flank Trav on one side while E and Carter occupy the other. The couple in front of us is older, around my stepfather's age. The man is in what I recognize as a custom-tailored Armani suit under his unbuttoned wool coat, and on the woman, I can only see the stilettos and a genuine strand of pearls due to the buttons on her long peacoat being done up. There's a sinking feeling in my gut.

I have a hunch who they are, but having never met Liam Parker's parents, I can't be certain.

"Mr. and Mrs. Parker," E says, voice like steel, confirming my suspicions. "To what do we owe the *pleasure*?" He says the final word much the same as Trav did polite.

"So rude," Mrs. Parker chastises. "*Obviously* you weren't raised right."

"Make another dig against my father and I won't hesitate to call the police." E turns deadly serious.

The way the Parkers' eyes try to look over our shoulders, it's obvious they're waiting for an invitation inside, but we aren't having it. Mr. Parker lets out a dramatic sigh when he realizes this fact.

"We're here to talk about these *ridiculous* charges you *insist* on pressing against my son." How he can say that with a straight face, I'll never know. What I do know is I have the overwhelming urge to lay him out the same way I want to do to his spawn.

"Ridiculous?!" Trav bellows before I can.

E places a hand on Trav's shoulder, silently telling him to back down and let him handle the situation. We don't need any of us flying off the handle and making things more complicated.

"Mr. Parker." E waits for the patriarch of the Parker family to turn his attention to him before he continues. "I assure you there is *nothing* ridiculous about the assault and battery charges we brought against Liam. My sister had to have surgery to repair the cheekbone your son broke with his fist. That's not even taking into account the fact that he knocked her unconscious or the countless other bruises she incurred from his unwarranted attack."

"Unwarranted?" Mrs. Parker screeches. "Liam was only protecting himself."

"In what world would a guy who's over six feet tall and a football player to boot need to use his fists to 'protect'"—E uses air quotes around the word—"himself from a girl who doesn't even top five feet?" He pauses, waiting for a response. *"Please...*enlighten me. I would *really* like to know."

Color rises from Mr. Parker's neck up into his nostrils-flaring, jaw-clenching, ugly face while—I shit you not—Mrs. Parker clutches at her pearls like a 1950s housewife. It's clear they don't have an answer to E's argument, and a weighted, uncomfortable silence stretches on.

"You know..." Trav finally loosens his defensive posture. "It really is too bad the footage of what happened leaked onto social media." He looks at me over his shoulder, giving a *We can talk about it later* nod to my *What the fuck?* blink.

Trav runs a hand through his hair, shaking his head as if he *is* disappointed for the Parkers. "Good luck trying to peddle whatever bullshit your waste of sperm is trying to sell you."

As a group, we step back, E slamming the door in both their stunned faces.

"Explain. Now." I round on Trav.

He looks around, but no one seems to know what he was talking about.

"Shit." He scrubs both hands over his face when he realizes this. "I can't believe none of you have an alert set up for the UofJ411 Instagram. Or that you"—he smacks the back of his hand against my chest—"*still* haven't charged your phone."

He digs his own out of his pocket and scrolls until he comes to the appropriate spot. There, looping in a minute-long clip, is the moment when Liam Parker made the biggest mistake of his life.

#Chapter21

UOFJ411: How is @TightestEndParker85 still alive after this? #DeadManWalking #CasanovasGonnaGetYou

video of Liam stepping to Mason and Kay getting punched when she tries to intervene (only the overall noise of the party can be heard)

@Rock_n_read719: Holy shit! You really going to let that slide @CasaNova87 #DefendYourGirl #Kaysonova

@Shenanigator: Talk about taking the rivalry to a WHOLE new level #NotCool #KeepYourHandsToYourself #CasanovaWatch

@Sjenkins31: This is a declaration of war #DontMessWithTheFlock

Chapter22

A WEEK MAY HAVE PASSED since the drama that went down with Liam at the AK house, but campus seems to still be abuzz recounting the details, both true and exaggerated, of what happened.

The fact that Coach Knight and the guys were questioned about the footage now circulating the internet in their postgame interviews after the U of J defeated Wisconsin in the Big Ten Conference Championship in Indianapolis this past weekend is certainly keeping the story alive and well.

Even now, as I make my way from one lecture hall to another, my Hunter insulated knee-high boots making it easy to keep my footing as I keep my strides long, I can see the pointed glances and hands lifted to whisper behind.

Most of the bruising on my face has healed. There's only one small spot still tinged a deep purple, the rest fading to an ugly brown and mustard yellowish color. Thank god for that, and for Bette's professional makeup kit being stocked with heavy-duty concealer. I can't imagine how much worse the gossip would be without it.

On my left, I see a phone held up—not discretely, I might add—and aimed in my direction. I tug on the brim of my new black U of J fitted cap, the hat a match to the one my boyfriend always wears—a gift from, you guessed it, the man himself—letting the curls I left hanging loose swing forward, making sure anything the makeup couldn't hide is obscured as best I can.

After spending the last week recovering and generally hiding from all the things I don't want to but know I need to deal with, it's time for me to pull on my big-girl spankies and get shit done. That's why today I made sure to wear my white *Don't flatter yourself, I only look up to you because I'm short* tee underneath a fitted black and white flannel shirt.

Coach Kris still has me banned from The Barracks, declaring I need another week of taking it easy and to catch up on any schoolwork I may have fallen behind on when I had to avoid screen time those first few days with my concussion.

A group of co-eds loiter outside the doors to Jefferson Hall, and I curse my vertically challenged stature for making it harder to wade through the crush of bodies in my way. Normally I can handle the occasional jostle, but a rogue elbow or two could be damaging to my healing.

My spine stiffens when I see Adam's smarmy grin amongst the crowd. I honestly can't figure out his issue or what motivates him to be the douchebag he is, but he's always rubbed me the wrong way. A lot of it probably has to do with the sense of entitlement he wears around him like a cloak, but I just genuinely don't like him.

"Short Stack." Trav's voice washes over me from behind, and I grasp hold of it like it's a life preserver and I'm a drowning victim.

"QB1." I spin on my heel and wave. His typical playboy, lady-killer smile increases in intensity at the use of that particular nickname. There may be times when I'll call him T, but with Tessa having claiming rights of being the main T in my life, I had a hard time using that shorthand this week with both of them around.

An arm falls over my shoulders, and I'm pulled in for a side hug.

"McQueen." Adam's smirk turns slimier, his eyes crinkling in the corners in amusement.

"Hall." Trav, having never fully released me after his hug, tucks me in tighter against him when he feels me stiffen at Adam's greeting.

Adam looks Trav up and down. Though it should be impossible, his lips hitch higher, and now he looks like some demented preppy version of the Joker. "Shouldn't you be in a suit and tie?" He reaches up and wiggles his ear. "Maybe have a wire hooked in here?"

Trav angles his face around to see mine, his *What the fuck is he talking about?* written clear as day across his features. I hit him with a *Why are you asking me?* shrug.

"Oh…" Adam smacks a palm to his forehead, playing up the innocent act. "Was I wrong? Are you not playing bodyguard for the football queen?"

"Football queen?" I squeak, dread settling into my gut like a rock.

"One of your newer trending hashtags," Trav explains, keeping his voice pitched low in an attempt to shut out those being nosy around us.

My head falls forward. I should have known. Though it's different than it was in high school, social media still manages to affect my life in a way it shouldn't have any power to do. Every day I war with myself on what to do about it, and every day I fail to come to a decision.

Do I reactivate my accounts? If I do that, do I go full-on let the world know every detail about my life as a future WAG— what the wives and girlfriends of professional athletes are called—or will those who are curious be happy with whatever I decide to drip-feed? There can be perks to me getting involved and controlling the message.

Or do I keep avoiding it all? Pray that when the intrigue

about what happened with Liam lessens, things will die down? Hope that after the playoff game—and, if we win that, the subsequent national championship—is over, Mase and I lose our "media darlings" appeal in the offseason?

As tempting as it is to follow the latter plan, I can see the fault in it. Who's to say the cycle wouldn't start all over every time Mase has something happen in his career? In the upcoming months, he'll have the combine, the draft, and training camp. Mase will already have the stress of proving himself in his rookie season as well as us dealing with what will inevitably be a long-distance relationship. Is it fair for me to add the pressure of him worrying about us trending to all that?

Shit! I don't even want to think about him having to move god only knows how far away for up to eight months a year. That's another problem for future Kay.

"Ugh." I curl a hand over the brim of my hat, pulling it down in an effort to disappear.

A deep chuckle has me canting my head at my way-too-amused companion, and a section of recently-cut-by-Bette hair flops down and covers one of Trav's eyes as he tries to restrain his laughter. That grin I've witnessed drop a thousand pairs of panties comes out in full force when he catches my eye roll. My boyfriend may have been dubbed the campus Casanova, but his best friend should have been nicknamed Romeo. Trav's inability to turn *off* the flirting—though harmless—will have him sporting a constant bruise on his arm when Mase gets too caveman-y.

"Come on." Trav nudges me and steps to guide us around Adam and his cronies blocking the entrance. Not even the sight of a few phones pointed in our direction can take away from the kernel of happiness I feel at Adam being snubbed by one of his fraternity brothers. Though it wasn't anything overt, Trav completely ignored his bullshit. "Let's get you to class, little sis."

My smile grows big enough to hurt my still healing cheek, but I don't care; I can't help it. I heard all about Trav's big brother declaration during the showdown with the Parkers.

"I'm still wrapping my head around you calling me that," I admit.

Trav guides me over toward the wall out of the way of the other students trying to get to class. Both his hands come down on my shoulders, making sure he has my full attention. It's rare to see him without an underlying hint of playfulness, and this tells me what he's about to say is serious.

"You once told me I was important to Mason so that made me important to you." He tucks fingers underneath my chin. "Well, Short Stack...the sentiment works both ways."

Overcome with emotion, I throw myself at him, wrapping my arms around his middle in a hug, hard enough for him to let out an "*Oof.*"

"Love you, T," I say into his chest where my face is buried, still holding him tight.

His chin drops to rest on top of my head as he returns my embrace. "Love you too, Kay."

I hope he has a birthday in a month I already wear a ring for. I'm running out of fingers, and I get the impression Trav is going to be a member of my "family" who wouldn't be happy not being represented.

When we finally pull apart, he flicks the brim of my hat. "Now go be your nerdy self and get to class. I'll see you at the house tonight."

Due to NCAA regulations, the football team is only allowed to have fifteen practices in the weeks leading up to their bowl games. I plan on taking advantage of any extra time I can spend with Mase and the guys, but the reminder of tonight—or more the conversation I plan to have—dims some of the good humor I was feeling.

#THE GRAM

#Chapter23

UOFJ411: Long live the #FootballQueen #WelcomeBack #CasanovasGirl

picture of Kay walking on campus

@Simono9311: What's it been, a week? #TimelineUpdate #CasanovasGirl

@Smalltown_booklover: Aww...look. She has a hat that matches @CasaNova87 #Twinsies #CoupleGoals

UofJ411: Don't you two look cozy #BromancePrivileges #CasanovasGirl

picture of Trav with his arm around Kay

@Sparksandmoonlight: Is this some kind of love triangle? #DoesCasanovaKnowAboutThis

@Summerlynn83: I've always thought these too seemed a little too "close" #IfYouKnowWhatIMean

@TheQueenB: #SharingIsCaring

Chapter24

FINALS IS the only time the Alpha Kappa house doesn't have that air of...well, a frat house. During both the week leading up to and the week of finals, there aren't any parties held there. A number of our brothers are athletes, and it is crucial we manage to get passing grades to maintain eligibility.

With the demanding schedule that comes along with being a student athlete, keeping up with academic requirements can be a constant struggle.

The first time Coach Knight caught me sneaking out to get my pregame kiss from Kay, it was the realization that she was the reason he didn't have to hound my ass over my grades that kept me from running suicides until I puked.

It's why our group is currently spread out all around the den of the AK house. The room used to be my favorite at the frat, but since the night Kay was hurt, I haven't been able to bring myself to hang out in here without seeing her crumpled on the floor, blood forming a puddle around her head.

I have to actively shake my head to rid myself of that image creeping its way to the forefront of my mind. Precious seconds pass before I'm able to blink it away and focus on the actual scene in front of me.

Em and Grayson are back to quizzing each other with

flashcards now that she's returned from taking a phone call. Quinn's head is bent toward CK, close enough for her ponytail to brush him any time she lifts her face to ask him a question. Alex, Noah, and Kev are all pounding away on their laptops, and Bailey—though I'm not sure how I feel about it —is here, highlighter running over the pages of the textbook spread across her bent knees.

My girl is the only one missing. If she hadn't sent me a text earlier saying she had to take care of a few things before she came over, I'd be worried as hell. Though it would earn me both an eye roll and Kay calling me out for being an overprotective caveman, I wouldn't have hesitated to go to her dorm to check on her.

Her agreeing to let us move our study session to the AK house was a feat in and of itself. She already had a general dislike for anything fraternity life, but it still being unclear how Liam and his cronies gained entry during the party makes it exponentially more uncomfortable for her to be here. My gut may be trying to convince me otherwise, but the fact of the matter is, it was a frat party with hundreds of people crammed inside the mansion. It would be easy for someone to slip in without notice.

When Kay does show up, it's with a bang—literally. The swinging door from the hall slams into the wall with her entrance. Her strides are the longest I've ever seen her take, and I think if it were physically possible, she would have steam coming out of her ears. I throw an elbow back when Trav leans into my side to whisper a similar sentiment.

Kay flops down on the remaining open cushion beside me with a huff, her movements jerky as she pulls the strap of her book bag from her shoulder, aggressively tugging open the zipper, lifting her laptop free, and slamming it onto her lap.

When she stays silent instead of filling the now expectantly watching room in on what has her so worked up, I place my own MacBook on the low table and turn to face Kay, her body falling back against the couch's arm as I cage her in with my hands braced on either side of her.

Her torso twists my way, but she still refuses to look at me. "Hey." I tuck two fingers beneath her chin and push until her gray eyes rise to my greens. "Wanna talk about it?"

Her eyes shift down and to the left. "Talk about what?" She tries to brush me off, but I hear the strain in her voice.

"Oh, I don't know..." Trav props his chin on my shoulder like I'm a pirate and he's my parrot, stretching an arm out to circle a finger inches in front of Kay's nose. "Whatever it is that has you making...*that* face."

I can't see her because she's behind me, but I know it's Em who is the one to snort.

"Smooth, bro," Grayson coughs under his breath, joining in with Em's laughter.

"Whatever G." Trav finally remembers a little thing called personal space and backs up. "I'm just saying the look Short Stack is currently sporting is fiercer than Kev's when he's staring down a quarterback."

Kay blinks, the tempting lips I still haven't gotten a chance to kiss parting as she brings her attention to Trav. "You called him G." It's cute that she's surprised by this.

"You're my sis, he's your bro. That's what he goes by in this family, so why not?"

Trying to bring the conversation back around to what I need to know before I blow a gasket, I cup the side of Kay's face, running a thumb over the still healing cheekbone. She nuzzles into my hand as if seeking solace in my touch.

"My number has found its way into the hands of the few more...*persistent* reporters. I've been fielding calls from—and by fielding, I mean hanging up on—them for the last two hours."

"The fuck?" I rear back. A part of me can't blame the press and Instagram followers for their obsession with my girl; she's hot, charming—when she wants to be—and her and E's history makes for one hell of a compelling story. Combine all that with how attractive of a couple we make, and I get it. Doesn't mean I have to like it.

"Would it…" I trail off, the thought popping into my mind and blindsiding me.

Holy shit! Tell me you aren't actually considering this, Nova. The evil eye my inner coach is giving me has *nothing* on what Brantley's reaction would be.

"Would what, Mase?"

Kay's soft voice has me snapping back to the present. The instant way her stormy expression eases as she locks eyes with mine is the reason this thought of mine was born. *She* is the reason.

"Do you think they would lose interest faster if I announced that I'm not going to declare for the draft this year?"

The room freezes like someone pressed the pause button. All activity stops. *Fuck!*

"WHAT?!" Kay snaps, her earlier fury returning with a vengeance. *Shit!* This is more the response I expected from Brantley, not her.

My fingers flex around her skull. "I have another year of eligibility left. What if I play it out? I'm less of a story if I'm not a part of this year's draft class."

"That's a naive way to think." Ouch. In all the times she's sassed me, I don't think she has ever blatantly insulted me, but I feel like that's exactly what she just did. "You're too good of a football player for that to work." Her soft smile soothes more than the compliment. "Don't let *this* taint all the epic things coming your way. *You*"—she mirrors my hold, cupping my face—"deserve to live your dream *now*."

What if my dream has changed?

"Besides"—she waves a hand in the air—"their calls were more because the video with Liam still has traction." I know she worries about how I've been questioned about what went down, but why is she looking at Em when she says this? Why is she *apologizing* to Em?

My confusion only grows when Em brushes her off, adding, "This will all blow over and they'll get over it."

Who are they?

Kay doesn't seem convinced, the furrow between her brows deepening and her frown increasing.

Unable to see her upset over that fucknut who just won't go away, I scoop Kay into my arms and place her on my lap, pressing a hard kiss on her lips. It only takes a second for her to melt into me, the drama forgotten.

For now.

Chapter25

ALL THE ZEN I was able to find after coaching at The Barracks for the first time in almost a month disappears as I pull to a stop in front of the closed gates at Mason's family's estate. I haven't been back here since the night I accidentally slept over at the start of our relationship. I don't know why, but I feel intimidated being here now.

Could it be that you're finally going to have the lady balls to have that conversation with Mase and Trav about their split-personality ex, the one you've been putting off? I could do without the judgmental tone from my inner cheerleader.

With a deep breath, I roll down my window and type in the code Livi calls out to open the gates. She and her twin brother Olly have been bouncing with excitement in my back seat the whole drive. Since I knew I was coming here after coaching the Admirals practice, I offered to drive them, giving Grace Nova-Roberts—Mase's and their mom—a free afternoon instead of having to hang around The Barracks.

I follow the long curving driveway, taking note of the cars parked in it, and choose the spot next to Em's Lexus to park Pinky, my Jeep. Looks like G's basketball game is over and we're the last to arrive.

Tessa, who stuck around after the Marshals practice to join

us, has her eyes out on stalks as she takes in the massive gray stone mansion and large white columns. I can't say I blame her.

There's no one around as we step into the echoing foyer. "I bet they're in the game room," Livi says, walking down the hallway branching off to the right.

"Game room?" T asks, the whites of her eyes still visible as she does a full three-sixty.

"Does it really shock you that there's a game room in"— Olly spreads his arms out wide—"all this?"

From over her shoulder, T meets my gaze, and we share a *Holy shit!* head shake. First the theater room, which was pretty much a mini home movie theater, now a game room. What's next, a bowling alley? I swear this place could eat E's Baltimore home for a snack and still be hungry.

We come to a set of large mahogany doors, similar to the theater room's, cheers and shouts drifting out into the hall since one of them is propped open. I cross the threshold and come to an abrupt halt. The space is close to, if not the same size as E's home gym—and that's two thousand square feet of a gym rat's wet dream.

One wall has an eighty-inch flat-screen and a built-in entertainment center with every gaming console imaginable underneath. A large black leather sectional as well as four gaming chairs placed in front have me searching for CK in the room. I bet he's drooling over this setup. G is the only one he's allowed to see the video game he's designing, but I wouldn't be surprised if he lets Mase see it for a chance to play it here.

On the wall opposite gamer heaven is a black wooden bar with purple cushioned barstools. Another flat-screen, this one a modest fifty inches, hangs on the wall, and as I begin to walk again, I can see, in addition to the extensive liquor collection on display, there are both a wine and mini fridge.

There's also an old-school Mrs. Pac-Man machine, an air

hockey table, and even foosball. In one corner there's a dart-board with a custom Nova-Roberts scoreboard. I gotta give Brantley credit—the designer he chose to create the space did an excellent job not making anything feel crowded, each section of the room able to be utilized without anyone bumping into another.

I say hello, giving hugs and cheek kisses to any of my friends I pass until I come to a stop for a second time. I almost don't notice the sleekness of the black wooden pool table—a match to the bar—with smoke gray felt or the modern geometric glass ball lights above it. No, my focus is consumed by the one person who has seemed to master the fantasy-inducing bad boy lean—my boyfriend.

My eyes bounce as I try to take in every detail at once: the slash of his ever-present black backward hat across his fore-head, the sparkle of mischief in his seafoam green irises, the spot on his cheeks where those maddening dimples have popped out thanks to his devilish smirk.

My heart pounds and my breathing grows labored as my body goes molten at the dirty promises he's projecting.

As if my panties weren't already ruined from what was happening above the neck, what's happening below it would clinch the deal.

A black *Hawks Athletics* t-shirt strains around his biceps, the red and white writing only highlighting the breadth of the chest it's stretched across and the sinew of the forearms crossed under it.

His feet release from where they were hooked at the ankles, his stance widening as he reaches for the collar of my puffy coat to reel me into his body, my feet stepping between his in the space between his spread legs before his lips fall to cover mine.

Our height difference isn't as drastic as it normally is with him leaning, but I still press up onto my toes and wind my arms around his thick neck. I'm not sure if he meant for the kiss to be brief, but as soon as I feel the scratch of his stubble on my lips, I can't help but deepen our connection. When his hands shift to tangle themselves in my hair with a tug, angling my head better, his tongue stroking mine with a sigh, I know he approves.

It isn't until the catcalls start that we finally break apart. Nimble fingers tug down my zipper as Mase helps me out of my coat, spinning me to face out to the room, my back pressed to his front, my ass cradled against his groin.

"Nice shirt, Short Stack." Trav points to the stretchy long-sleeved *Bad to the Bow* tee I have on.

I clasp my hands in front of me, holding them near my heart, my knees bending dramatically. "So glad you approve, QB1. What *ever* would I have done if you didn't?"

"Brat." He flips me the bird and I blow him a kiss with a "You love me."

"*God.*" Tessa facepalms with an exaggerated flourish. "You two sound just like you do when you're with E."

The beaming smile that overtakes Trav's face speaks for itself. With one comment from Tessa, he has cemented his big brother status forever.

"How was it being back at work?" Mase buries his nose in my neck, placing kisses along the tattoo inked behind my ear.

"Amazing." I struggle to get the word out as he lets his teeth scrape against the tendon connecting my neck and shoulder. "Who won the game?"

G scoffs, and when I look over at him, he's miming being stabbed in the heart. "I see dating a football player has you doubting the skill of the stars of the school, Smalls."

Mase chuckles against my skin, his amusement at the accusation clear. True, I only had a passing interest in basket-ball until I became friends with G. Now that I have a personal connection to the game, I no longer only watch pieces of the March Madness tournament; now I'm a total basketball junkie. My lack of knowing the outcome of the game the U of

J played this afternoon doesn't have anything to do with football being my first love.

In a room full of football players, G's comment sets off endless ribbing and trash talk, which sets the tone for the rest of the evening.

G regales us with an animated retelling of how the Hawks beat the Michigan State Spartans by one with a three-pointer at the buzzer thanks to his truly.

CK wipes the floor—or more accurately, the pool felt—with anyone who challenges him to a game.

T and the twins debate with Em and Q about the chances of the Red and White Squads winning at nationals next month, occasionally pulling me in for what my thoughts are about the University of Kentucky Blue Squad's routine for the season.

I do my best to relax and enjoy the day off from studying before getting back to the grind tomorrow. It's not thoughts of my last final that have me actively trying to stay in the present. No, it's the conversation I know will happen after our friends call it a night.

T is the first to make her way over to where I've been wiggling my ass against Mase, not even attempting to hide my smile at the constant hard-on digging into my lower back as he leans around me trying to get my Mrs. Pac-Man to be eaten by the ghosts.

"I'm outie." T braces her hands on the side of the arcade machine, popping up onto her toes and leaning in to place a smacking kiss on my cheek.

"I take it you and Savvy watched *Clueless* last night?" I twist my face for my own, less enthusiastic cheek kiss. Along with their regular *Gossip Girl* binges, T and Savvy have an affinity for movies made in the 90s.

"It's a classic." She shrugs.

"How are you getting home?" I ask since I was her ride.

"King's outside the gate." She holds up her phone, waving

it side to side. "It's poker night." She does a little shimmy as she moonwalks out the door. Whenever there's the risk of the roads being icy in the winter, King hosts underground poker tournaments, and brilliant Tessa is his ringer. When she's finally twenty-one, the chick is gonna clean up at the casinos.

As the clock ticks closer to midnight, the rest of our friends start to say their goodbyes in groups. CK leaves with Em and Q, after confirming with G and me to meet in the library tomorrow for one last study session.

I already asked Trav to stay, so when the others who live at the AK house start saying their goodbyes, he remains seated on the couch.

I'm bent over laughing, watching Noah dance away from a scowling Mase after giving me a *Good game*-type butt smack. I roll my eyes; they really are overgrown children.

The twins have gone to bed, and by the time Mase pulls me to sit on his lap on the couch next to Trav, it's only the three of us left. I've put this off long enough—too long, really. No more stalling.

Based on the expectant way I see Trav watching me out of the corner of my eye, I get the feeling he suspects the reason I asked him to hang around. He may not know it, but I'm grateful he hasn't brought up the subject since I asked him about it when I was in the hospital.

Doesn't make this any easier…

Up and down, round and round, I make sweeping glides with my finger over the tribal ink on Mase's arm. Maybe if I focus on it, I'll be able to get this out.

"When…" I work to swallow around the nerves that have taken up residence in my throat all of a sudden. I clear it and try again. "When you both figured out the game Chrissy/Tina"—underneath me, Mase's entire body turns rigid—"was playing…who broke up with whom?"

"*Whhyyy?*" Mase drags out the question, but there's an edge to it.

"I need to know." I chance a glance through my lashes at Trav, and he's still as a statue. "It's important."

"Kayla…" Uh-oh. It's never good when Mase starts using my full name. "*She* doesn't deserve a second of your attention. She's irrelevant, insignificant, and inconsequential."

"Way to bust out a thesaurus on those adjectives, bruh," Trav teases.

"Fuck off, asshole." An arm tightens like a band around my middle with the curse, but I'm grateful for the joke. Mase is going to need the levity when I have to tell him how wrong he is.

Gurrlll, you let people toss you over their heads like most do a ball. Woman up—you're braver than this.

Heeding my inner cheerleader's advice, I take a deep fortifying breath and pray.

"The night of the rival rally, she showed up at my dorm."

"Who?" Mase asks, but it's not me who answers him; it's Trav.

"Tina," he says quietly.

"WHAT?!" Mase barks out, and I involuntarily flinch. Lips kiss the top of my head in an attempt to soothe me.

"She said she came to warn me."

"*Warn* you?" I nod when Mase repeats the word.

"I'd be careful. He doesn't always take no for an answer. I should know." Even now, my blood boils at her implication. Her lies are the type that sets victims of sexual assault back *years* in making progress toward getting justice.

"She tried to tell me you raped her"—I'm squeezed even tighter—"and when I wouldn't believe her absurd accusation, she tried to convince me Brantley paid her off to keep quiet."

Ragged breathing and the hum of the mini fridges are the only sounds in the room. When I can't take it any longer, I finally lift my head and spin to cup Mase's face between my hands.

"I *know* that isn't true either." Fire blazes in the green

depths of his eyes as I speak. "The *only* reason I asked about who broke things off is because I'm trying to figure out how much of a grudge she has against you." I look to my right at Trav. "*Both* of you."

"We did," Mase starts.

"Together," Trav finishes.

That doesn't surprise me. By confronting her and ending things together, it would be one more way to show the solidarity of their friendship.

"Fuck." A hand comes up to grip me by the nape, tugging me closer until I feel Mase's forehead resting on mine. My eyes close as I just breathe him in, the scent of his soap helping slow the erratic beat of my heart. "Do you have *any* idea how much it *terrifies* me that I feel like I painted this target on your back for all this crazy and there's *nothing* I can do to protect you?"

"Mase."

"It fucking *kills* me, baby."

This is not on him. Just as he worked to convince me what happened to me was Liam's fault and not mine, this is all Chrissy / Tina.

"Why come to you, though?" He tilts his head to the side in contemplation. "Brantley might not have paid her off, but she has to realize you would tell me, and there's *zero* chance he doesn't use his resources to try to scare her off."

"Liam paid her."

"The fuck?" Trav curses, Mase cutting him a look that says he shares the sentiment.

"She said even if I didn't believe her, it doesn't mean she couldn't get the press to, at least long enough to potentially convince teams you're a risk and should be considered undraftable." As much as I dread the rapidly approaching long distance of our relationship, I'll do everything in my power to protect his future.

"I told you I don't give a shit about the draft." Nails dig

into my skin as Mase tightens his grip on me. "Even if her bullshit keeps me out of it, that doesn't mean I can't get picked up by a team after I'm cleared."

"No." I'm shaking my head before he finishes his sentence. "That would cost you *millions*."

"Babe." Mase looks around the game room. "I'm not exactly hurting for money. *You* are what's important to me."

Fuck. My eyes grow hot, and I attempt to blink away the urge to cry but fail, Mase thumbing away the tear. "Dammit. You and your swoony words."

"They call me Casanova for a reason." One of his dimples pops out.

"You're an ass." I hate that moniker.

"You love me anyway."

"God help me, I do…Caveman."

He grows silent, a pensive look overtaking his handsome face. When he smooths a hand over his hat, my nerves flare up. "Maybe I really should consider putting the draft off until next year, let some of the heat die down."

I'm shaking my head before he can finish. I thought we put this ludicrous idea to bed weeks ago.

#Chapter26

THOUGHTS OF YESTERDAY plague my mind while I pack the bags I need for the almost week-long road trip to Texas for the Cotton Bowl. Typically when the team travels for away games, it's only for a weekend, but bowl games require us to be in the host city for all the pre-events and media requirements.

For as cool as it is to get to practice in the same stadium as the Dallas Outlaws, I can't banish my concerns for Kay. After dropping the Chrissy/Tina/Liam bombshell on Trav and me last night, she assured us she had the situation handled.

Who the fuck knows what she means by that? All I know is I'm not looking forward to being 1,600 miles away from her should something happen.

"Mason." The sound of my stepdad's voice has me pausing in zipping up my suitcase to look toward the open door of my bedroom. I haven't filled Brantley in on the things Kay told me, and based on the inscrutable expression on his face, I get the impression I'm going to be glad I haven't.

"Dad." I eye him with his hands shoved into the pockets of his pressed chinos a second longer before finishing my task with the zipper and setting the case off to the side. He may not be my father biologically, but he's been the only father figure I've known since the dad I share DNA with died when I was two. More often than not, I call him by the title he's more than earned.

He glances over his shoulder before stepping the rest of the way into my bedroom. I straighten at his approach, instantly feeling the full weight of the strain that has been on our relationship since the start of the season.

"Before you leave, there are a few things we need to discuss."

"Okay…" I fold my arms across my chest.

"I'm not sure this…" Brantley pauses as if searching for the correct word to use. When he finds it, I almost wish he hadn't. "*Girl* is the best thing for you."

My shoulders bunch, almost hitting my ears at the unexpected reference to Kay.

"Come again?" I choke down the rush of protectiveness I feel and remind myself this is my stepdad I'm talking to.

"I know you think you love her, bu—"

"It's not a thought. It's a certainty."

He sighs heavily, running a hand over his carefully styled hair. It doesn't matter that it's a Sunday and the rest of the family is in different variations of lounge clothes: a combination of sweats, faded t-shirts, loose Henleys, yoga pants, and, in Livi's case, taco-printed pajama bottoms. Not Brantley—nope, he's paired his chinos that have a crease sharp enough to break skin with a white polo shirt.

"Mason." He tries to patronize me.

On edge after last night, I warn, "I'd choose your next words carefully."

Not gonna lie, I'm a little perplexed. Sure, when I first started dating Kay, Brantley wasn't her biggest fan, though that had more to do with him blaming her—unwarrantedly—for Olly quitting football, but I thought we were past that. Olly is happier than I've ever seen him cheering for NJA, and with Kay as his coach, he has a good shot at getting a scholarship for it.

When things proved to be getting serious between Kay and me, Brantley tried to express concerns over a girlfriend pulling focus away from football. Mom shut that argument down real fast. If only Brantley knew Kay thinks the idea of me not following through with his plans for my career is laughable. I may have broached the subject with her a few times, but until I make an actual decision on what I want to do about the draft, I can't utter a word to Brantley.

Besides, with the exception of the game after I broke up with Kay—and yes I can admit I was a jumping-to-conclusions asshole—my stats in a single season have never been better. Hell, my girl knows the game in a way that means she can talk strategy with the guys and me on the rare instances she watches extra game film with us.

The worst was the time Brantley tried to insinuate Kay was a jersey chaser who only saw me as her future meal ticket. I laughed in his face over that one, though I was surprised he hadn't already run a background check on her and discovered her own personal athlete connection.

"I'm sorry, son." There's genuine emotion in Brantley's voice that helps soothe the beast inside my chest—marginally. "I'm just concerned she might have a negative impact on your career." *Fuck me, now he sounds like Kay.* "We've been working toward the NFL for most of your life." Always with the collective pronoun. "I don't want some girl and her drama to cost you everything we've worked for."

Whatever ease I was starting to feel vanishes at him referring to my girl, my Skittles, my *everything* as "some girl". I let it go for the moment and focus on the bigger issue at hand.

"It's not Kay's 'drama'." I use exaggerated air quotes. *I* am the one who has brought the drama, *not* Kay. It's the CasanovaWatch hashtag that led to the creation of the CasanovasMysteryGirl one. I don't care that Liam Parker is her ex. It was her connection to me that brought him back into her life.

"Liam Parker is her ex-boyfriend, is he not?" Brantley asks, picking up on my thoughts. I grind my back teeth together but reluctantly nod. He holds up his hands as if to say *I rest my case*, the lawyer in him shining through.

"*Liam*"—I spit out his name—"hadn't made contact with Kay in years. He didn't come slithering back into her life like the snake he is until he found out she and I were dating."

The reasons why Liam has taken on a personal vendetta against me and my girlfriend aren't important. He just needs to be gone. The motherfucker still needs to pay for hurting Kay too.

"There's video all over the internet of you looking ready to throw down with the guy." I barely restrain a very Em-like snort at him using the phrase *throw down*. "There's already speculation about if you're a hotheaded jock."

It's times like these I wonder if maybe I shouldn't have decided on using a family member as my agent. With Brantley's law background—specifically in contracts—it made sense for him to be the one to handle mine, but I'm starting to question that decision. There are days it feels like he forgets I'm more than a client to him.

"Does it not matter at all to you that that same video shows Kay getting hurt trying to protect *me*?"

Last night in bed, I did my best to drive home—

Yeah, sure, if you mean plowing your hips into Kay until she came twice was your method of "driving" your point home.

Shut up, I tell my inner coach. But, yeah…he's not wrong. *self five* Anyway…

I knew before I'd be able to get on the plane to Dallas, I needed to make sure, given last night's revelations, that Kay wouldn't make any other misguided attempts at protecting me that could put her in harm's way. Seeing her hospitalized like that is not an experience I would like to repeat—ever.

"That is correct," Brantley concedes, his face twisting in that *I have a plan* way it does when working on finding loopholes in the contracts he helps negotiate. "The media *is* loving that particular angle of the story…"

I hold my breath. Where is he going with this?

"Maybe if you played up your relationship on your Inst—"

"No!" I bark. Fuck, why would he go there? He's been hot and cold when it comes to Kay, and the frustrating thing is I can't figure out why. It also makes it impossible to keep up with what he wants. One second he doesn't want me with her then the next it's okay that we're dating if I can use her to my advantage. Not happening.

"I don't get it." I curl my hands over the brim of my hat, my head falling back from the added weight as I look at the ceiling like it has the answers.

"What don't you get?" I don't buy the veil of innocence he pulls over his features.

"First you don't want me to have a girlfriend, and then you do." He goes to answer, but I cut him off with a slash of my hand. To be honest, his opinion doesn't matter here, and I do have one critical point to make. "When, or better yet *if* Kay decides she wants to put parts of her life—*our* life on social media, it will be her call. I'm not going to use our relationship because you want to play up the whole 'media darling' thing."

Color works its way up Brantley's neck and onto his face. For all his merits, and there are a lot, his biggest fault is how poorly he takes not getting his way. Growing up with a silver spoon in his mouth followed by a career as a high-powered attorney, Brantley Roberts has grown used to the old adage: *What Brantley Roberts wants, Brantley Roberts gets.*

"You're young, on the cusp of starting a career doing what so few are able to achieve. Why tie yourself down now?"

And we're flip-flopping again. I'm going to give myself whiplash trying to keep up with his ever-changing opinions.

I despise this tactic. Yes, I've more than earned being called Casanova, but all that changed when a tiny blonde with rainbow highlights accused me of bringing her a coffee in an effort to have her blow me. From that moment, I knew I had to up my game if I wanted to prove to her I was playing for keeps.

"I love her," I state simply.

"I get it. *Really*, I do." There's another careful pass over his hair. "But you thought you were in love once before and look how that turned out." The reference to Chrissy/Tina has me close to snapping, my spine going ramrod straight in an effort to maintain my cool.

"*This* is what I don't get. A girlfriend is bad, a girlfriend is good—I need you to make up your mind here."

Brantley regroups, his shoulders rolling back, his stare calculating. "Why *this* girl? Why chose the one girl who is going to prevent you from achieving your full potential?"

That's it.

I've reached my limit.

I've tried to play it cool.

To play nice.

I tried to show my stepdad respect through his conflicting directives, but I can't listen to one more word coming out of his mouth.

Fuck him. He doesn't get to decide *who* I choose to share my life with, *especially* when what he really means by "achieving my full potential" is landing all the best endorsement deals and having the status of being one of the "faces" of whatever team I end up playing for.

There is zero chance of me telling him about what I've been considering or the threats made by one Christina Hale.

"That person"—I bare my teeth, doing my best to speak with them clenched tight enough to probably need the mouth guard I use when I play as protection—"you keep calling *some girl* is so much more than that. Kay isn't just my girlfriend, she's my *everything*."

The urge to fight, to defend, to protect courses through my body. *Fuck!* I need to get out of here before I do or say something I can't take back.

#Chapter27

UOFJ411: OH SHIT! OH SHIT! OH SHIT! #TooBadSoSad-ForYou #RideThatPine

clip of press conference where Coach Daniels confirms that Liam Parker will be suspended from playing for Penn State in their bowl game

@Christyheartsbooks: Karma's a bitch #DontMessWith-TheFlock

@Cmd427: I'm still waiting for @TightestEndParker85 to get the beatdown he deserves #BuyingMyTicket

@Cr8zysockbookblock: We're still waiting for this ^^ @CasaNova87 #DefendYourGirl

#Chapter28

EVERYONE THINKS the life of a professional athlete is *so* glamorous. The money, the cars, the houses, the velvet rope treatment, and endless perks all are supposed to add up to the life dreams are made of...but not everything is all sunshine and unicorns.

Don't get me wrong, E has it good—really good—and as his sister, I receive a lot of perks. My point is there's also the flip side. The time and dedication put in for workouts, during both the season and the offseason, maintaining a healthy diet, promotional commitments with the team, and any personal endorsements a player is fortunate enough to have.

All these things are part of the deal if one wants to play a sport professionally. In the grand scheme of things, they are small potatoes compared to, in my opinion, what is the biggest sacrifice—the time away from one's family for travel.

To be fair, the NFL probably has it the easiest compared to other sports, having only one game a week for the sixteen-game, seventeen-week regular season. The MLB plays one hundred and sixty-two games, and even though the NBA and NHL only play eighty-two, all three can have road trips that last for up to two weeks.

In the end, it all adds up to not always being around for

certain events or holidays. If we're lucky, Christmas will fall on a non-game day—like this year it's a Friday—so E won't have practice. Unfortunately, I am the reason I won't get to deck the halls on the Big Man in Red's day because I'll be in Texas cheering on my man playing in the Cotton Bowl.

Thankfully Coach Kris closes The Barracks for the weeks of Christmas and New Year's, and I was able to head directly to Baltimore after my final on Monday, allowing a few days with my family before flying south on Christmas Eve.

That said, squaring off with my brother in his kitchen as I'm currently doing is not my definition of a good time. Not even the fact that JT is here and I get to spend almost five full days with him is enough to brighten up my mood.

E stands on the other side of the island, arms crossed, nostrils flaring, jaw ticking as he glares at me across the quartz countertop. If I had to guess, I would say he's trying to come up with a way to strangle me from eight feet away.

"You can't be serious, Kay," he says in his hard-ass football voice.

"Of course I am, E." Twitch, twitch, twitch goes his cheek. "I'm not saying I like it—because I don't—but it's the plan."

I need to make my brother see reason, make him find the merit in my plan. Lord knows Mase is going to blow a gasket when I tell him.

That's why we won't be telling him until after the fact, my inner cheerleader singsongs in agreement.

"Liam needs to be held accountable for what he did to you." E point-stabs the counter with his finger. "He"—stab—"broke"—stab—"your *fucking*"—stab, stab—"cheekbone." He opens his palm, now slapping the counter with an echoing *smack*. "You had to have *surgery*." Slap, slap. "Fucking. Surgery, Kayla."

I sigh at the use of my full name, watching as he paces away from the island, doing his best to tug his hair out by the root.

"You think I don't know that?" I shout, holding back a wince at the twinge of pain I feel in the freshly healed bone. "You think I somehow forgot? Think the *concussion* he also gave me was enough to have me acting like a soap star with a case of amnesia?" Sarcasm bleeds out of me, coating each of my questions more thickly the longer I yell.

"That's not fucking funny."

I sigh again, my head tipping back, my shoulders falling as all the fight leaves me. "I know, E, but think about it…" I step around the island, slowly approaching him like one would a cornered animal. The description isn't too far off; all he needs is a giant ring through his nose to complete his impression of a raging bull. "You don't—and certainly *I* don't —want to be the news story." I lay the flat of my hand on his forearm, the muscle spasming with restraint under my touch. "This is the best thing I can come up with to help prevent that from happening."

This close, I can hear the grinding of his teeth. His dentist is going to give him one hell of a lecture on taking proper care of his enamel.

"Think of it as killing two birds with one stone—"

"I'd like to do some killing," E mutters, and I bite back a snort. He sounds like a teenager throwing a tantrum. It doesn't help that I hear JT whisper "Same" from the living room.

Bette strides into the kitchen, reaching up to pull a bottle of wine from the rack. "I hope you aren't expecting me to post your bail if you get arrested for homicide, E." She says more with one letter than most people can in full paragraphs.

"I wouldn't dream of it, dear." E shifts his body to face his wife, blinking with wide eyes, trying to portray the picture of innocence.

"Don't you *dear* me, Eric." She steps to him until their toes touch, her finger wagging in his face.

"Damn, bro." JT whistles through his teeth. "She Eric'd you. That ain't good."

"I know," E deadpans then nips at the tip of Bette's finger, causing her to squeak. "Don't worry, babe." He hooks an arm around her middle, pulling her flush against him. "I promise to behave."

"I highly doubt that." Bette levels him with a look that screams *I know how full of shit you are*.

I giggle behind my hand at the scene. Mase is always telling me he adores how I can give him shit in the same breath as telling him I love him. Well...I learned from the best.

"I promise." E holds up a two-finger salute.

Bette scoffs. "You weren't a scout, you ass." It takes her a few seconds to pull herself out of the daze caused by the kiss E lays on her, then she's turning to me, mom glare firmly in place. "You're going to have to explain your logic if you expect me to get on board with this."

That's what I do: I explain all the things I've been afraid to admit to. Fear of becoming *the* story for the press, having my life dissected and critiqued by strangers behind a keyboard and around me. Fear of Liam, and now Chrissy / Tina, digging in and hurting Mase's draft stock. Worry that if I can't handle the media—both social and otherwise—when I have Mase by my side, how am I going to do so when he is who knows how many hundreds, if not thousands, of miles away with the team that picks him up?

As I speak, my family gathers around, T and Pops moving in closer too as I purge everything from my system.

"Parts of the story are already out there," I say as I near the end. "By doing this, we can at least help control a portion of it."

No one speaks at first, and I appreciate them each taking a moment to digest what I said instead of offering their knee-jerk opinions.

"Kay"—Bette stretches her torso across the counter, linking her hand with mine—"are you *sure* you're okay with settling? *Really* sure this is what you want?"

"If you're asking if this is what I think Liam deserves for what he's done"—I shake my head, roughly brushing away the curls that fall forward when I do—"then, no. He'll barely feel the effects of the monetary loss."

Truthfully? I wish putting a person in stocks in the middle of the town square were still a legal punishment.

"Why the fu—"

Bette's raised hand cuts off E's curse.

"But if you're asking me if I can look at myself in the mirror every day and be able to smile at what I see"—I nod —"then, yes." I look past my sister-in-law's shoulder and meet my brother's steady gaze. "The only way for there to be a *chance* of Liam being held accountable for what he did is if we take things to trial. Yes, there's a lot of evidence and witnesses on our side, but I won't survive going through that media circus again."

I see the moment E concedes, a shadow falling over his features as he recalls the shit-show of the trial after Dad was killed.

"If we do it this way, we prevent the Parkers from spinning tales about how their *precious* boy is the real victim of a family raised by a convicted killer and drunk. Plus..." I inhale deeply, my chest puffing out with the action. I promised Mase I wouldn't put myself in danger trying to keep him safe. With this plan, I can honestly say I'm able to keep that promise. "Working in the clause about paying off Christina Hale while serving her with papers about bringing a slander suit against her if she decides to proceed with her lies takes away Liam's prized puppet."

While E made calls to Jordan Donovan and his lawyer to put our plan in motion, Bette and Pops cooked up a feast epic enough for his firehouse.

JT, T, and I are currently "sleeping" our food comas off on the couch while *Little Giants* plays on the television. T has her head resting on a pillow propped against her brother's leg, and my feet make themselves at home on JT's opposite thigh while I use a snoring Herkie as my pillow.

The movie cuts off as Becky is climbing the shelves in the supermarket to creep on Junior throwing rolls of toilet paper like footballs, the picture on the screen filling with the picture of Mase and me kissing after the Penn State game.

JT, proving once again why he earned the title of my ultimate bestie, stretches out his leg, using his toe to press the button on the remote to accept the video call.

"Hey boys," I say as the faces of my boyfriend and our friends come into focus.

"Hey, Skittles." Mase flashes his dimples, making me wish I could reach through the screen and bury a finger in their depths.

I shift against Herkie, who lifts his head and licks the entire right side of my face, while I wait the minute or so it takes for everyone to exchange greetings.

"What's up, guys?" I ask, nonchalant. I'm pretty sure I know the reason for the call, but I don't want to tip my hand if they haven't received the packages I have confirmed were delivered to the concierge at their hotel. Because Mase has no idea we're planning on flying out early—arriving on Christmas Eve and not late Christmas night—I wanted to make sure they got their presents now.

Each one of them are now proud owners of yet another Kayla Dennings-selected funny shirt, these in a football theme.

"I do have one question." Mase holds up a single finger in front of the camera.

"Yeah?" I twirl a lock of hair. "What's that, babe?"

The way he bites his lip tells me I'm not fooling him one bit.

"How'd you do it?"

"Do what?" I double down.

"Skittles," he warns. "Don't play stupid. You're too smart —it doesn't suit you."

It's not something that should make me swoon, but it does. It may be a stereotype, but not once has my hot jock made me feel bad for my nerdy girl tendencies. Quite the opposite, in fact. The only time he complains is when I don't let him distract me with *his* version of "studying".

"Did you know…" I sit up, folding my legs under me, facing the camera head-on. "Concierges at hotels are *very* helpful?"

"It would appear so." The twinkle in his seafoam green eyes promises retribution for being a smartass the next time he sees me. I can't wait until tomorrow.

"Well…" I clap my hands. "Don't leave me in suspense." I try to make eye contact with each of them. "Did you like your gifts?"

"Hell yeah, Smalls. Check it out." Kev rises to stand, showing me he has on his *LINEMAN. Because Impenetrable Wall isn't an official position* tee.

"Yay." I make exaggerated spirit fingers. "I'm so happy you like it."

"Fuck yeah!" Kev cheers before Alex shoves him out of the way to show off his own. His is a graphic tee with a playbook on it, the words *Oh! This was yours? Didn't look like you were using it* written beneath. I got both their shirts in tan, thinking it would contrast nicely with their dark brown skin. I should pat myself on the back for being right.

Noah pushes his way through them with a flourish in his *Laces out, Dan* tee. I may hate Instagram but figured if he liked the line from *Ace Ventura* enough to use it as part of his handle, he needed to have it on a shirt.

"Short Stack." Trav lifts the laptop, stealing it away from Mase and moving off on his own.

"Hey QB1." I have developed a soft spot for my boyfriend's best friend. The charming playboy was doing a good job of wiggling his way into my heart on his own, and the day he started referring to me as his sister, I was done for.

"*Please* tell me you didn't get this for B too?" He waves a hand under the *There are TWO KINDS of people in this world, and being a QUARTERBACK is better than both* lettering on his red t-shirt à la Vanna White.

"No. I got that one special for you," I assure him then lean in to whisper, "You know *you're* my favorite quarterback."

"What the hell?" B shouts from behind me. It should come as no surprise he showed up in time for dinner earlier. "Not cool, Little D. Not cool at all."

I wave him off while he complains to E about not raising me right and focus my attention back on Trav.

"Did Nana get hers?" Trav's Nana is one of the coolest people I've ever met. She gives off this Helen Mirren vibe with a royal air and a take-no-shit personality.

Trav nods. "I've already gotten a Snap from her in it, and she posted it on her Insta too."

It's pathetic that his grandmother is on social media and I'm too afraid to reactivate my account. I'm not the only one who thinks Nana is pretty much awesome sauce. Trav is constantly bitching about how she has more followers than him…and he has thousands.

Nana is another person who is a fan of all my shirts. I had a custom one made for her to wear when she takes on her role of super fan at Trav's games. It's black with red and white U of J lettering that reads: *Forget BINGO. This Nana yells TOUCHDOWN!* The O in down is a brown sequined football, and on the back is Trav's #7. I also replaced the McQueen nameplate with *Nana McQueen*.

"I'm so happy she liked it." I beam with pride.

"No." Trav shakes his head, his hair flopping down over his eye. "Love, Short Stack, *love*." He bats away the section of hair. "There was even a reference or two to you replacing me as her favorite." He tries to scowl, but a smile manages to break free.

"You can tell her the feeling is mutual."

Like I expected, a chorus of "What the hell!" greets my statement. JT goes as far as pulling my hair like we're back in kindergarten.

"As much as I love you, QB1"—I elbow JT back—"can I have my boyfriend back now?"

The image on the screen goes wonky as the computer is passed from one set of hands to another, until...finally my gorgeous man is front and center. Except...

My lips twist down in a frown. "You're not wearing your shirt." I pout for good measure.

"You *did* give me more than one." He arches a brow. "How was I supposed to choose?"

"Smooth," JT cough-says.

"*Anyway...*" I side-eye my best friend for his elementary behavior and focus back on Mase. "Call me later?"

"Wouldn't miss it." He practically smolders through the screen, his light green eyes darkening to the deep forest green I'm used to seeing when we're in bed—naked. Appropriate, I guess, given that I texted him earlier saying I had a gift I couldn't send with the others and he needed to be *alone* to get it.

Like at the beginning of the call, we all cycle through our goodbyes and Merry Christmases.

"Love you, Skittles," Mase says before hanging up.

"Love you too, Caveman."

I blow him a kiss. Later can't come fast enough, because Mase's *other* gift sure as hell won't land me on the Nice List.

Picking up the remote, I flip back to the correct input and restart the movie with a goofy smile on my face—at least until JT crushes my sugar-plums-dancing dreams.

"You do know he's going to flip when he finds out about your plan for dealing with Liam, right?"

#Chapter29

MY DAY STARTED LIKE THIS.

SKITTLES: I have an early Christmas gift for you.

ME: Don't you know it's not nice to tease me when I'm too far away to do anything about it?

SKITTLES: What? *shrug emoji* I'm not saying you have to wait to open it.

ME: Um, babe...did you forget I'm in Dallas? A little hard to open it from 1,600 miles away.

SKITTLES: *rolling my eyes*

ME: You know how I feel about making you roll your eyes *smiley face with teeth showing emoji*

SKITTLES: There are days I seriously question how effective your helmet is when you play. But whatevs, don't distract me—I haven't had my coffee yet.

ME: Wow *shocked face emoji* You must really love me.

SKITTLES: I do...clearly JT has dropped me one too many times while stunting.

ME: Smartass.

SKITTLES: You love me. But ANYWAY...I have something for you, but it's FOR YOUR EYES ONLY. I'll let you figure the logistics on how to make that happen. Now I'm going back to sleep. It's too early for this. Love you. Miss you.

Needless to say, the pounding I took at practice, the punishing workout in the weight room afterward, and all the media bullshit that comes with bowl games didn't seem so bad after that.

The issue I'm having now is finding a way to get alone to make it happen. For a normal person, this wouldn't be a problem. For me? Not so simple.

For one, being in Dallas with the team means I have a roommate. Second, my friends are ridiculously codependent. I swear I get less one-on-one time with my girl when the team is on the road than when we're home.

Dinner with the team is almost over, and I'm running out of time to come up with a solution if I'm going to make this happen before curfew and I'm forced to have Trav in the room with me. That's when the biggest pain in my ass himself plops down in the empty seat next to mine.

"You wanna tell me what has my little sis going all savage?" Trav holds his phone in front of my face, showing me his text thread with Kay.

SHORT STACK: If you ever want me to make chili or ANY food for you again, you will give Mase an hour to himself tonight.

SHORT STACK: That INCLUDES the other guys too.

SHORT STACK: *GIF of Stewie narrowing his eyes in the evil eye*

I snort, burying my face in my hand to hide my laughter. I shouldn't be surprised she has a handle on the situation. She's my pint-sized badass, that's for sure. God I love her.

I pick my head up, shooting my best friend a look that says *Do you really wanna know?* He catches the implication and scoffs in disgust.

"Nope. No way." He waves his hands in front of his face as if it can block the thoughts from forming. "I don't want to know anything about your kinky-ass sex life with my sister."

His chair screeches as it scrapes across the floor in his hasty retreat.

I can't wait to tell Kay about this.

After dinner, a good chunk of the team heads to the lounge the hotel set up as a gaming room for us to use. I put in some time with the guys, getting in on a game of Madden before excusing myself for my room.

There's a small part of me that still doesn't trust my teammates—we are a bunch of jock-holes most of the time—so I flip the metal hook that acts as a chain lock on the door.

Laptop in hand, I set it on the desk by the window. As I wait for it to power on, I pull my shirt over my head and drop it to the floor. Kay and I have never done the phone sex thing on any of my past road trips, thanks mostly in part to those aforementioned codependent friends. I'm not positive that's what *this* is, but I know she likes to look at my muscles and I am all about giving my girl what she likes.

If it does happen to lead to phone sex…

Kay is the first contact to pop up since we called her before we headed to dinner. I click on it and wait for the call to connect. When it does, there's no Kay in sight; only a pink animal print bedspread is there to greet me. I can hear her, though, and I can't help but chuckle.

"Come on, Herk, out."

There are sounds of a struggle, and I can only imagine it's her trying to physically move the dog who is practically the same size as she is.

"Look…I love you, boy, but your mama is not into the whole threesome thing, so you gots to go."

Woof! Woof!

"I don't want to hear it." I bite back a chuckle. She sounds like she's arguing with me and not the furball. "The whole head-tilt thing is not going to work on me."

The next noises are faint, and I can't quite make them out.

I wish the camera were facing them because I have a feeling it's a highly entertaining scene.

"Go find your Aunt T. I'm sure she has treats for you." Kay resorts to bribery, and it works based on the sound of nails scrambling across the hardwood floors.

"*Finally*," Kays says on a sigh, and I hear the door close and the lock engaging.

The display goes wonky as the computer is lifted from her bed and adjusted until my girl fills the screen.

And holy shit is she a vision.

In the time since our call earlier, Bette must have gotten to her hair. Once again, her long curly locks hang straight around her shoulders. I honestly couldn't tell you which way I like best on her; she's always hot to me. Upon closer inspection, it looks like, mixed in with the brighter blonde pieces, Kay was also given a refresh on the red and black streaks peeking out from the long layers. I love the U of J pride. It's hot as hell.

Her makeup is light, only mascara to darken her blonde lashes and a coat of shiny lip gloss. The way the red color highlights her plump lips has me sporting a semi. It's like I can *feel* them wrapped around my dick.

My semi turns into a full-fledged erection that's ready to bust out of my pants and climb through the screen to get to Kay as I take in the rest of her.

Fuck me!

She's wearing my Black Out jersey. You wouldn't think seeing her swimming in the dark, shapeless material would be hot, but in all the different ways I've managed to get my name on her, not once has it been with my jersey. Both my inner coach and inner caveman stand up and cheer at the sight. I want to ask her to turn around so I can see how amazing the NOVA #87 looks on her back, but I restrain myself…barely.

It's not an exaggeration when I say it's a good thing this is the alternate jersey for the team, because I don't think I'll ever be able to wear it again without thinking of how the giant red 87 on the front looks stretching across her tits as she tugs on the hem.

By the time my gaze makes the trek back up her body to meet her twinkling gray eyes, I know she knows exactly where my thoughts went.

"Like what you see, Caveman?" she taunts with a smirk that tells me she knows I do.

"Always, baby." I circle a finger in the air, gesturing to her hair. "I see you refreshed your school spirit."

"Do you like it?" She pushes her swoopy side bang out of her eye.

"Of course." It's my turn to smirk, adding a wink for good measure. "You know how I feel about your rainbow, Skittles."

A toothpaste-commercial-worthy smile takes over her beautiful face while a pretty blush stains her cheeks.

"Well don't be surprised if Bette does another refresh before the national championship. You know how she bitches about how quickly reds fade." She rolls her eyes.

"Before Bette starts buying extra stock of red dye, we need to win the Cotton Bowl first."

"Pfft." Kay waves off my comment. "The Irish were good this year, but they have *nothing* on the Hawks. Their quarterback can't read the blitz like Trav can, which means Kev will be *all* over him like white on rice. And with the one-two punch of you and Alex for the offense, their D isn't going to know who to focus on trying to cover first."

Man I love how into football she is. The guys always say it's hot when she "talks football". Her deep understanding and knowledge of the game and what it takes to play it at the highest level is a huge turn-on for me. The precum leaking onto my boxer briefs is proof of that.

Her unwavering confidence in my team and our abilities

is the biggest boost a guy can get, and I hate that I still have to wait *days* before I can kiss her for it.

"How's Texas?" Her question breaks me from my fantasy of bending her over the counter in the bathroom here.

"It's good. The team has been gelling at practice." Last year we made it to the championship but lost. Not this time. This is our year; I can feel it. "I miss you though."

Fuck! Do you hear yourself? You're lucky Kay insisted this was a private call, otherwise your boys would be demanding your balls. Oh how the mighty Casanova has fallen. *walks off the field*

The blinding, brighter-than-the-Christmas-tree-in-the-hotel's-lobby smile makes every sappy word I said and the scolding from my inner coach worth it.

There are days I feel like Kay doesn't understand the depths of my feelings for her. Or how I'm…

Nope. Best not to think it for fear I'll slip up and ruin the moment with a fight.

"Can I say *thank you* for your text to Trav? I thought he was gonna shit a brick with you threatening to cut him off from your cooking." I wrap an arm around my stomach as laughter overtakes me while remembering how pale his face was. Don't think I missed the way Kay checked me out in a blatant ogle…because I didn't. "It was the best part of my day."

"Was it, now?" Her eyes—still locked on my abdominals—grow heavy-lidded, her white teeth sinking into the red flesh of her bottom lip.

"Yeah." My voice grows husky as lust pumps through my system.

"Let's see if I can change that? *Hmmm?*" I about come in my pants like a teenager watching his first porno when she hums. "First…" Her left arm rises to reach behind her head, my ring winking at me from her finger as she gathers her hair over her shoulder. "I bet you're *dying* to see how this looks." She rises to stand, the laptop moving to the nightstand next to her bed. Keeping the grip on her hair, she turns, giving me her back to show the red NOVA and 87 that cover the entire length and width of her torso. "Is it everything you've ever dreamed of?" she taunts, glancing at me over her shoulder.

"*Babe,*" I groan. Now that she's standing, I can see my jersey is the *only* thing she's wearing. I have to clear my throat before I can speak again. "Where are your pants?"

Why the hell are you asking her about her pants? Why are you always trying to put clothes on her? Take. Them. Off. I swear I'm going to trade you.

"They didn't really go with your present."

"My present?" My brows rise until they hit the edge of my hat. "I'm pretty sure I don't play pantless."

Kay spins to face the camera again, her fingers lifting the hem of my jersey from where it fell past her knees. "You think me wearing your jersey is your present?"

Yes? I mean it *is* literally one of the things my dreams are made of.

"Oh, Mase." She giggles.

Her pupils dilate until her eyes are the color of deep charcoal as she scans every inch of my bare torso again. Without a word, her arms cross below her belly, grasping the bottom of the jersey and lifting it over her head in that sexy, effortless flourish that's the equivalent of the one-handed behind-the-neck shirt removal us men do. She holds my gaze with it pinched between her fingers before releasing it to float to the ground in a puddle of fabric.

I damn near swallow my tongue.

Holy fuck!

Her tits are plumped up and pressed together by red lace and contrasting black stitching, the curled-under ends of her hair outlining it all. Resting between them, calling to me like a bullseye to slide my dick against, is a black satin bow, punctuating her glorious chest as the gift it is meant to be.

It's one of those half-cup styles, the lace barely high

enough to cover the pink of her nipples—not that it matters, because I see the pebbled tips peeking through the material she's so turned on.

It's my turn to take a tour of her body with my eyes. Down the length of it they go, over the swells straining with each breath she takes, down the toned expanse of her belly and the ring with a jewel that has been switched to red to match decorating her navel. There's another few inches of smooth, creamy skin beneath the ring before I reach the top of the matching red lace panties.

The minuscule piece of fabric looks like it would tear at the slightest pressure and ties at the sides in a double set of matching black satin bows. I've never wished for something as hard as I currently wish I weren't over a thousand miles away. My hands itch with the need to pull on each of those ties and unwrap her.

The panties sit low enough that I can see most of the angel wings tattoo below her hipbone.

I palm myself through my joggers, grateful I'm not in jeans; otherwise I'd have one hell of a painful imprint on my dick.

"*Damn*, Kay." My groan echoes in my room and through her speakers.

"You like?" Her head tilts to the side and she twirls a lock of her hair around her finger, hip cocking out to the side.

"Fuck yeah." I increase the pressure of my palm on my dick. "I want to jump through the screen right now and show you how much."

"You haven't seen the best part yet."

There's more? My eyes widen until they are in danger of drying out. How the hell is her getup supposed to get *better*?

She tiptoes closer, angling the camera down to focus on her lower body. The closeup of the barely there triangle covering the V between her legs does not help the situation I have going on in my pants. Slowly she spins around again, filling the screen with one of my favorite parts of her body.

More precum leaks onto my boxers, the bottom half of her spankable ass exposed under the lace hem.

My dick officially breaches the barrier of my pants as the tease on the screen bends forward, placing her hands on the bed in front of her, arching her back and plumping her ass out in a perfect fuck-from-behind porn-style way.

God! If I were behind her right now, I'd grab her hips and be buried inside her to the hilt in a second flat.

Kay straightens before I can get the party started without her, red painted nails skimming across her back until they point to the keyhole cutout at the top of the panties. In the small circle, resting above the teasing hint of her crack peeking through, is a tiny rhinestone charm: 87.

"Holy shit."

By the time the camera is fixed to show Kay's entire body again, she's sporting the definition of a Cheshire grin.

"You've marked you better than I *ever* have," I admit.

"Oh, I don't know…" Her right hand plays with my birthstone band on her left ring finger. "You've come up with some pretty spectacular ways."

Hell yeah I have, and one day I'm going to slip a diamond so fucking big on that finger the people sitting in the nosebleed seats of whatever football stadium I'm playing in will be able to see it.

Her eyes scan my body again, stopping on where my hand is palming the head of my dick sticking out of my pants.

"I think you're a little overdressed." She gives a pointed look at my joggers.

And it's on like Donkey Kong.

I shuck my pants and boxer briefs in one swoop, my erection bouncing off my stomach in its excitement. My hand is on it the second I resettle in my chair, slouched down, knees spread, giving her an unobstructed view of what I'm doing.

She makes a hot-as-fuck *mmm* sound in the back of her throat as she watches.

"We're really doing this?" A hint of insecurity creeps into her voice.

"Only if you want to, baby," I reassure her.

Her lip is back between her teeth. "I've never done this before."

"Phone sex?"

"Yeah." Her fingers twist together in front of her belly, a clear indicator of how nervous she is.

"Neither have I." I inject a soothing tone into my voice.

Her eyes snap up to meet mine. "*Really?*" I don't take offense to the disbelief in her voice. It's a fair question—I *was* a total dog before I met her.

Still, I can't stop a puff of laughter from escaping. "Really, babe. There was never anyone serious before you. You don't call the jersey chasers for something like this, unless you want them to get the wrong idea." My cheeks heat at the admission.

It does its job, though, and her shoulders relax away from her ears. "Okay." She lets out a breath of relief. "How do we do this?"

Game on.

"As much as I'm loving this"—I wave a finger, indicating her boner-inducing lingerie—"I want to see you."

All of a sudden, her back is to me again as she looks around her bedroom. Before I can ask what she's doing, she rushes off, out of sight. A few seconds later, she's back with the chair from her bathroom's vanity. She positions it in front of her laptop, readjusting the camera once again, then mirrors my position.

Her hands go to her shoulders, fingers stroking across the bumps in her collarbone then traveling down to the top of the cups of her bra. Eyes locked on mine, her fingers dip, pulling the fabric down with them. Her breasts pop free, and with the bra left on, they are held up, on display as if to say *Yours for the taking.*

She takes a moment to tease the peaks of her nipples before running the flats of her palms down her toned stomach to the bows holding her panties together.

My eyes follow their path, my breath getting stuck in my throat as I watch her deftly untie the four bows. Since she's sitting, the material doesn't fall away on its own. Instead she twirls the black fabric around her pointer fingers before dropping them between her spread thighs and exposing the promised land to my gaze.

"God your pussy is beautiful." And it is. It's perfect. It's waxed bare, the lips plump enough to hide her clit behind them, and when they're spread, she's the prettiest shade of pink. I become damn near poetic when it comes to her naked body.

"Your mouth is so dirty." Her eyes are back on the hand stroking my cock.

"Isn't that the point of phone sex? The dirtier the better?"

"True."

"Touch yourself, babe."

"Tell me how." Our gazes meet again. The flush on her chest tells me she's no longer nervous and is as into this as I am.

"I get to direct the show?" A new surge of desire goes through me at the prospect.

"This is supposed to be one of your Christmas presents, so it only seems fair. Tell me how to touch myself." Her tongue licks across her top lip. "Like you would if you were with me right now."

God her words... For someone who, just a few moments ago, was unsure of how to do this, she's sure off to one hell of a start.

My voice pitches low and gravelly with want as I issue my instructions.

"First…I want you to *slowly* run your hands up your inner thighs." I swallow thickly as I watch her follow my commands. We've barely gotten started and I'm about ready to blow my load. I squeeze the head of my dick to hold myself in check. "Next, using both hands, gently open your pussy lips so I can see your clit. I want to see how swollen it is already."

Again, there's no hesitation in her actions. I think I could get used to this phone sex thing.

Her clit is swollen in a way that tells me it's not going to take much for her to get off either.

"God I wish I was there so I could take your pleasure button into my mouth."

"Pleasure button?" She lets out a broken laugh.

"What? Can't we have a little fun while we do this?"

"No it's fine. Just don't go calling my pussy my lady cave or anything."

"I love when you say pussy, baby." I give her a wink. "Now press on your…*pleasure button*"—I emphasize my new favorite term for her clit—"with two fingers of one hand while using the other to squeeze your tit the way I know you like."

She may be smiling from our joking, but she does what I say.

"I'm surprised you didn't call them my fun bags or something."

I let out a bark of laughter. This may be one of the most asinine phone sex sessions in the history of phone sex, but it is pure us. I wouldn't change a thing about it.

"They *are* fun," I tease. "Especially when you're on your knees in front of me, squeezing them around my dick while you lick the head of my cock."

"Don't you mean your love stick?"

"Please don't call Casanova my love stick. It's bigger than a measly stick anyway." Yes she nicknamed my dick after my own nickname around campus. What of it? She picked it, not me.

"Okay…love trunk. I'll call it LT for short." Her words break off on a moan.

"Whatever you say, Skittles. Now focus. I want you to imagine I'm there with you. Pull on your nipple and twist it slightly. Pretend I'm tugging it into my mouth, biting it between my teeth."

Another moan breaks out.

"Good girl." I encourage her as my hand skims over the head of my cock, spreading the precum down my shaft, lubricating my strokes. "Now move the fingers on your clit hard and fast." Stroke down to my balls. "Good girl." Up to the head. "Keep doing that until you come."

I can't see her pussy anymore as most of it is hidden behind her hand, but watching her fingers work between her legs is more than enough for me. I'll have a visual of what she looks like when she jills off to carry me through every away game in my future.

"That's it, baby. *Feel* how it swells and starts to pulse under the pressure of your fingers. I love when it does that. It's my first clue to how close you are to coming. I especially like when it does it when I'm buried balls deep inside you from behind, using it to control your pleasure as I fuck you hard and deep."

"Oh god, *Mase*."

Her hips wiggle in the chair as she loses focus on everything and starts to chase her pleasure.

The speed of my hand increases in sync with the tempo of the fingers between her legs.

Up.

Down.

My grip tightens, twisting as it travels back and forth along the length of my dick. I'm close.

"That's it, baby." I can tell she's at the tipping point and just needs a little push. "I'm gonna fuck you so hard when I see you you're going to be walking funny for a week."

"Mas—" My name is a broken plea as she comes, and I follow her over the edge, spraying my stomach with cum.

Our hands continue to work as we both bring ourselves down from our orgasmic highs. It may not be as good as actually being with her, but I can definitely get behind this whole phone sex thing when I have to travel for games.

It's a few minutes before we've come back to ourselves and Kay opens her eyes. She zeroes in on the mess I've made of myself.

"You got your love juice all over you." She smirks, and I laugh again.

"Only you can make me laugh and come at the same time. Where the hell do you come up with this shit?"

She gives me a shrug. "Would it help if I told you I'd lick it off you if I were there?"

"Holy hell, babe. You're gonna make me hard again."

Now she's the one winking.

"So did I do good with *all* your presents this year?"

"Fuck yeah you did." Her answering smile is my favorite thing in the world.

"I should probably get cleaned up and get back downstairs before someone comes looking for me." She sounds reluctant to do so.

"Me too. Our hour is pretty much up, and I don't need Trav bursting into the room just to be a dick."

"Text me later?"

"You know it. Love you, baby."

She blows me a kiss. "Love you too, Mase."

I close my laptop and head to the bathroom for a towel to clean myself up, smiling the entire time.

Merry fucking Christmas to me.

#Chapter30

EARLY WAKE-UP CALLS to travel are their own special form of torture. Mornings suck in general, but the whole hurry up and wait that comes with dealing with flying only tends to add to my not-so-bright-eyed-and-bushy-tailed demeanor when the clock reads single digits in the hour column.

If anyone has any doubts about how I'm feeling this morning, all they have to do is read my *Just because I'm awake DOESN'T mean I'm ready to do things* slouchy off-the-shoulder long-sleeved shirt.

"You do realize we're on our way to see *your* boyfriend, right?" JT bumps his hip into my side, our carry-on suitcases rolling behind us. Guess my face is broadcasting my feelings as much as my shirt.

"Your point?" My voice is gruff thanks to it being stupid o'clock. It's like my body doesn't care that I already downed a full cup of coffee before leaving E's. Neither it nor my brain feels like it will be satisfied unless I have an IV drip of the caffeinated brew.

"You could at least *pretend* you're excited." He chuckles at my side-eye as we step onto one of the moving sidewalks inside BWI. It's Christmas Eve, and the airport is packed with other early holiday travelers.

"I *am* excited." My jaw unhinges with another yawn. "Mase is gonna flip." He thinks we aren't flying in until late tomorrow night because that was the original plan, but with E traveling for his own away game, he suggested Bette change our tickets to today in case there were any weather delays.

We sidestep our way around a man on his phone, continuing through the terminal toward our gate. "Besides…you've traveled with me enough for competitions to know I hate this crap something awful."

"Truth." It's my turn to hip-check him at his devout-testify hand wave. "It is lucky you were such a damn good cheerleader, otherwise we would have left your ass behind at The Barracks."

I scoff. "Jerk." I get him with an unsuspecting elbow back into his gut. "And what do you mean I *was* a damn good cheerleader? I still kick ass."

"Love you, brat," he says instead of answering.

I scrunch my nose and pucker my lips, telling him without words how I feel about him in the moment before reluctantly agreeing, "Love you too." I pause as JT helps us weave through other travelers. "But I think Trav might be replacing you as my favorite surrogate brother."

He guffaws and hits me with an eye roll. "*Please.*"

"What?" I shrug. "I'm just saying he's a lot nicer to me…"

"You guys are still in the honeymoon stage of your friendship. Once that wears off, he'll start treating you like the rest of us." The rest of us being him, G, CK, B, and, of course, E.

We make it to our departing gate and look around for a cluster of free seats to accommodate our traveling party.

"The honeymoon stage is not a friendship thing." It's my turn to roll my eyes. "It's a *dating* thing."

"Bullshit." JT turns sideways in his seat to face me, laying his arm over the back of mine. "Right now you and the quarterback are in that"—he clears his throat, adding a girlish lilt to his voice—"*you're my new best friend, I love you so much, how have we not been friends before this* stage."

I glower at him with narrowed eyes. And Mase says *I'm* the smartass. He would never survive hanging with my bestie for an extended period of time.

"Soon enough, that new-friend shine will fade and Trav will recognize you for the real pain in the ass you are." JT boops my nose.

I bat his hand away. "You're an ass."

"I know." He pops a shoulder, unaffected. "But as previously stated, you love me anyway."

Currently, not so much. I kind of want to hit him right now.

"You're wrong, though. Trav and I have never been the gushy-over-our-new-friendship type. The closest he's come to declaring his undying love for me is when I feed him."

"They say the way to a man's heart *is* through his stomach." JT leans back and circles a hand over his, nodding.

T and Savvy are laughing from their seats across the aisle, clearly entertained by our antics.

"Careful, Jim," T warns her brother. "It sounds like you're at risk of losing your spot at the top of PF's list."

Bette, having had to check her bag to bring the scissors and clippers needed to style our guys' hair, returns at that moment. My gaze homes in on the large coffee carrier in her hands.

"What'd he do now?" She gestures at JT with the carrier but directs the question to T.

"Nothing," JT answers, accepting the Dunkin' cup Bette holds out to him. "I was just trying to get PF to smile."

Bette belly-laughs as she passes out the rest of the coffees.

"You know it's hazardous to your health to mess with Kay this early." I catch the smirk Bette tries to hide behind her cup.

I tuck my feet beneath me and cradle the paper cup

between my hands, inhaling deeply while I have a private moment with my salvation. This white chocolate latte is the only best friend I need.

"*Really* feeling the love people," I grumble.

"Oh hush." JT tucks a finger under my cup and tips it toward my mouth. "Drink your coffee."

Bette, being the most organized person on the planet—I swear it was the reason why being a long-distance newlywed was easy for her—arranged everything about the trip for not only us with her, but everyone joining us.

Somehow, someway, she was able to work out flight arrangements that had the five of us flying in from Baltimore, G and D from New York, and CK from Kansas landing in at Dallas/Fort Worth within an hour of each other.

Em and Q are also arriving in Dallas today but will be tied up with their commitments with the Red Squad, so we won't see them until later this evening.

After collecting Bette's bag from baggage claim and meeting up with the rest of our party, we walk outside, all of us sighing at the comforting heat that greets us. Sixty degrees may not seem all that warm, but when you live in the northeast and you're used to your winters typically being in the thirties, if not colder, this is t-shirt weather.

Bette leads the way like she's Mama Duck, and we follow like her faithful ducklings until she comes to a stop at a man holding a white dry erase board with *Dennings* scrawled across it in messy black marker.

Being the smallest of the bunch, T, Savvy, and I tuck ourselves in the back row of the Yukon XL Denali. When we hear Bette confirming with the driver that he will be dropping our bags off with the front desk at our hotel, we share a laugh at the military-esque precision Bette used in her approach for planning our travels.

Not only was she able to secure a four-bedroom suite in the same hotel the U of J is staying at, she also called in one of her own personal connections to arrange a private tour of AT&T Stadium.

Miles Dennings—running back for the Outlaws and a player on my fantasy team, the Dennings Family Reunion— had grown close with E during their multiple Pro Bowl appearances together, but it was how easily Bette and his wife Denise hit it off that led to the friendship between the two Dennings families.

As was the case any time I attended games for E, Bette and I would hang back, doing our own laid-back thing out of the spotlight of all the hoopla. When Denise—a *Sports Illustrated* swimsuit issue cover model—overheard our plans to spend the hours before the Pro Bowl getting manis and pedis instead of attending the fancy party the NFL put on, she jumped at the chance to join. And the rest is, how you say, history.

With all the press and media coverage surrounding the Cotton Bowl—the bowl game not the stadium, since the game is no longer played in its namesake—we wouldn't normally risk being near the epicenter, but today is one of the rare days when the U of J's practice is closed to both the press and the public.

I do feel a mild amount of trepidation, but the tour will be private and an awesome experience, especially for those who have never done anything like it before. I'm not planning on surprising Mase until tonight back at the hotel, so it should give me the opportunity to see him—even if it will only be from a distance.

We make the drive to the stadium in less than thirty minutes, and by the time we pass through security and pull up to the players' entrance, Miles is outside waiting for us. T and Savvy sigh at the sight of him leaning against the side of the stadium, and I laugh at the dreamy sound.

Miles is a good-looking man: a few inches shorter than E with a camera-ready smile that stands out against his dark skin and a close-cut fade I'm sure Bette will be decorating sometime before we leave Dallas. He's dressed in tapered dark wash jeans, gray suede loafers, a white collared shirt, and a dove gray lightweight sweater, both pushed up to the elbows and exposing his tattooed forearms, and he has matching diamond studs in his ears. I'm sure his supermodel wife is to thank for his impeccable fashion sense.

Miles folds Bette into a hug and does the same with T, Savvy, and me as we make our way out of the vehicle. I hear another round of those sighs.

"Whoa, Little D," Miles says, having also taken to calling me the same shorthand for Little Dennings that B does, as he flicks a section of my hair over my shoulder. "I don't think I've ever seen you with your hair straight."

"You're a guy—why would you ever notice a thing like that?" I tease.

"Um…" Miles hooks a thumb back at himself. "My wife's a model. I've been conditioned to notice these things." He swipes a keycard over a sensor and holds the door for us to enter the stadium.

"Glad to see DeeDee has you so well trained." Bette loops an arm through Miles', and the two of them take the lead through the tunnels.

"You know…you're the only one she lets call her that." His confession has Bette's head falling forward with laughter.

"Not even you?" she asks.

Miles shakes his head. "I tried." He extends one finger. "*Once.*"

This time we all join in on the laughter.

We continue down the long corridor, taking turns through

the maze-like system until Miles comes to a set of blue doors that lead to the locker room the Dallas Outlaw Cheerleaders use. The room is huge and high class. There's high-pile blue carpeting under foot, and the cubbies that make up each cheerleader's locker space are made of high-gloss white wood with a mirrored back and a row of vanity lighting. There's a locked drawer under each extended seat area, and above each locker is a three-foot-high portrait of each individual cheerleader in their uniform.

I may not be a Dallas fan, but I've always thought, hands down, their cheerleaders have the best uniform in the league. I may be partial to it since the shorts for my old Admirals one are super similar.

Miles also takes us by the locker room for the Outlaws, and Bette and I even take a picture inside his locker to send to E.

We spend the next hour or so seeing all the highlights the massive stadium has to offer: the pro shop, the press box, the offices, the VIP lounges, and the room where they do their official postgame interviews. A few times we get a glimpse of the field, and I grin each time I spot number eighty-seven in the mix.

T and Savvy joined trouble-making forces with D, and the three of them are currently walking down the concourse of the executive suite level like they are in *The Wizard of Oz*.

"It's shit like this"—G stretches the arm that is around my shoulders, his forearm brushing my cheek as he points at his brother—"that I think is the real reason why Dad and Mama didn't want to fly in with us today."

I bury my face in his side to smother my giggle.

Miles finally comes to a stop at one of the suites, the plaque next to the door declaring it the owner's box. Why are we here? I've been in the box for the Crabs' owner before with Bette, but there's no way this would be included on a public tour.

"Miles?" Bette asks, the furrow between her brows telling me she's thinking along the same lines as me.

"Um…" The man in question trails off, rubbing at the back of his neck.

"Spit it out already, Dennings." Bette pulls out her mom voice.

Miles clears his throat, looking a little green beneath his dark brown skin. "When I was arranging everything for today, Bossman"—he uses the nickname most of the league uses when referring to the Dallas team owner—"found out who I was doing it for."

"Oh-kay…" Bette makes a rolling motion with her hand, all of us lost as to why *Bossman* would care.

"Let's not kid ourselves." Miles opens the door, and we step inside the most luxurious suite I've been in—ever. It's almost a shame I'm too distracted by this bizarre conversation to appreciate it. "We all know he may own the Outlaws, but we also know he has way more control in the league than your typical owner. He's well aware of who you are…but more importantly, who your brother and boyfriend are."

Miles has known our family long enough that he knows of my…aversion to being in the spotlight. Yes, since being with Mason, I have started to metaphorically dip my toe in the social media waters again. What Miles just admitted about his boss? That's next level.

Personally, I'm not sure how I feel about this revelation, and I need a moment to compose myself before I overreact. As everyone explores the multiple *rooms* of this over-the-top suite, I cross the length of it and open one of the sliding glass doors that lead to the seats overlooking the fifty-yard line. Choosing the row closest to the field, I settle into the plush leather chair and scan the players scattered below, searching for my boyfriend.

The anxiety bubbling inside me calms the instant I spot Mase lined up with the offense. The things that man does for football pants. The snap of the ball drags my eyes off Mase's tight end *hehe* and onto Trav, watching the play develop as he drops back into the pocket, searching out his eligible receivers then launching a sweet spiral to where my man is waiting for the pass, catching it for a forty-yard completion.

The team does look good; I can see what Mase meant by them gelling. I watch a handful of plays before I feel Miles' presence.

"I don't get it." I keep my eyes trained on the field while he tentatively slips into the empty seat next to me. "Outside of all-star cheerleading, I'm a nobody. Why the hell would he care?"

Silence stretches between us, and for the first I can remember, it's an awkward one.

"I think…" When Miles doesn't continue after letting his words trail off, I dip my chin and meet his contemplative gaze. "I think he wants to play up the whole 'football royalty'"—he goes as far as to use air quotes—"angle you two have going on."

I growl. *Thanks a lot, UofJ411.* "How? It's just a stupid hashtag a college gossip account started using."

"True, but it's a hashtag that has trended to national reach thanks to the U of J clinching the title of Big Ten champs and it being tagged in a video of two top draft picks for this year looking like they are about to throw down."

Fucking Liam Parker. I have to remember to check with E to see if Liam and his parents signed the papers.

"Look." Miles leans forward, his forearms resting against the ledge wall in front of us as he glances back at me. "All I'm saying is it wouldn't surprise me if you get approached by someone from the front office asking about changing your seats for the game on Saturday."

Fuck!

I focus my attention back to the field. I see they've already swapped out the Outlaws' end zones, the turf on the right representing the U of J and the left Notre Dame. The Texas star usually sitting in the middle of the fifty is also gone, in its place the Cotton Bowl logo.

It amazes me how quickly the grounds crew can make these changes. By the time the Outlaws play here for *Monday Night Football*, you'll never know anything was different less than forty-eight hours prior.

Grace, Mase's mom, invited us to join them in the suite they purchased for their family and Nana McQueen, but I opted to get seats in the stands since Mase likes to look for me during a game. Plus, if the television cameramen pan to show players' families, the suites are the first place they will go to.

Personally, I like being closer to the action. The smell of the turf, the clash of the pads, the call of the plays—that's what the game is all about, not bullshit hashtags.

Chapter 31

GRABBING a paper cup of Gatorade from the hydration table, I rub a hand over my sweat-soaked hair as I down it, counting the seconds until the end of practice. Tomorrow is a no-pads practice for the team, and Coach Knight is making sure to put us through the ringer today. The man is a beast, but he's one of the greatest coaches I've ever had the privilege to play for. He is the reason the U of J has one of the top collegiate football programs in the country.

In my tenure as a Hawk, we've made it to the top-tier bowl games all three years and the national championship last year. With each shrill of Coach Knight's whistle and shouted "Again" for yet another drill or repeat play, it's almost like a physical push toward winning it all.

After all the hoopla that comes with this type of bowl game the last few days, it's a little eerie here without the press today. The way AT&T Stadium was built, it's like the seats hover over the field. It makes for one trippy optical illusion when running plays while the stands are empty.

Another thing different about today is we haven't seen the usual tour groups milling around the stadium, only the staff getting things prepared for the game on Saturday.

Some of my teammates were saying they saw people in

the Outlaws owner's suite, but Trav and I were busy working on perfecting a trick play Coach Knight made. When I'm on the gridiron, football is my only focal point.

It's during these moments of downtime, when I pause to take a breath and hydrate, that my thoughts are able to drift.

A playful screech rips through the air, cutting through the clash of pads and grunts happening on the field. Looking over the rim of my cup, I lift my gaze in the direction of the owner's box, and sure enough, there are people in it. I dig my knuckles into my eyes, rubbing across my closed lids, convinced I'm seeing things.

"Fuck I miss Kay." The words tumble out as I continue to stare at the departing group. I must miss her more than I originally thought because I would swear the blonde hanging upside down over a big guy's shoulder could be her.

"I know, bruh." Trav claps a hand on my shoulder pads. "Only a couple more days then you can kiss your girlfriend."

My mouth turns down in a frown. Kay and our friends are flying in tomorrow, but it'll be after curfew by the time they arrive at the hotel. I may have to see if I can persuade Trav to cover for me if Coach does a surprise bed check so I can sneak out to see her, even if it's only for a minute.

My need to see her isn't about sex either. Yes, I still get to talk to her throughout the day when I'm on the road, whether by phone, text, or video chat, but it's not the same as being able to touch her, hold her hand, or kiss her whenever the mood strikes. Sure, that may make me sound like a pussy, a whipped sap, but I don't give a shit. I'm fucking man enough to admit the woman owns my balls as much as my heart.

A whistle blows then Coach Knight calls for the team to bring it in, and we huddle around him, ready to hear whatever closing speech he has for the day. He may kick our asses in the weight room in the morning and out on the field during these practices, but what has earned him the respect of his players is how he isn't afraid to sing our praises for a job well done.

By the time he's finished, ten minutes have passed, and the previously exhausted group of athletes is amped up and ready to do battle like we haven't just had our asses worked into the ground for hours.

Cleats clack as the team shuffles toward the entrance of the tunnel that leads from the field to the locker rooms. Trav and I wait for the others at midfield before making our way as well.

"Wonder what's going on," Noah comments as a bunch of our teammates congregate in a group at the mouth of the entrance.

"There were rumors that Miles Dennings was spotted earlier—maybe it's him," Kevin muses.

"Doesn't Kay have him on her fantasy team?" Alex asks, his helmet bouncing off his leg as he swings it around.

"Yup." I nod. "She's stacked her team with all the Dennings players in the league."

"You mean E, too?"

I nod again. "And Tyron and JJ." When I mention the other running back and wide receiver on Kay's roster, Alex lets out a long, slow, impressed whistle.

A handful of footballs are still scattered around the field, so we scoop them up in an effort to help collect them for the support staff.

"Fuck I'm hungry." Trav rubs a hand over his belly. "I feel like I could eat the ass end of a horse right now."

I roll my eyes and can't help but smile to myself about reacting the same way Kay probably would.

"Always thinking with your stomach, bro." I shove Trav hard enough for him to shuffle to the side a few steps. He retaliates by shoving my helmet into my gut.

"It gets me in less trouble than when I think with my dick." He waggles his eyebrows at me.

"That's not what you were saying last night, McQueen." Kev references the Texas beauty queen Trav picked up in the hotel bar when he gave me the room for my call with Kay last night. Thank Christ for it too because that was the hottest fucking phone call of my life. Even dog-ass tired from practice, I feel my dick twitch behind my cup as I think about it again.

"Mase!" A feminine voice that sounds surprisingly like my girlfriend cries out.

Damn I'm starting to really lose it. First I think I see her, and now I'm hearing things. Tomorrow night can't get here fast enough.

But when I turn in the direction the voice came from, I swear it really is her running toward me. Reacting on instinct, I catch the blonde jumping into my arms. When I realize what I've done, I release my grasp and hold my arms out to the side, not wanting to encourage this crazy person further. Then lips crash onto mine and I'm hit with the familiar scent of vanilla and peppermint. The realization that this *is* Kay slams into me at once, and automatically I bring my hands back to cradle her ass, my helmet falling to the ground as I squeeze her to me tighter.

My tongue strokes inside her mouth, the unsurprising sweet taste of coffee lingering on her tongue. She hums in approval, the sound and vibration of it going straight to my dick as her legs squeeze tight against my sides. The world fades away as I get lost in the kiss, and the only thing on my mind is what's the fastest way I can have her naked and under me. Hell, I'll take her up against a wall if it'll have me inside her sooner.

"Little D," a deep voice says around a hearty chuckle. "I don't think you dry-humping your boyfriend is the type of touchdown your brother wants to hear about."

The interruption of our reunion causes Kay to lift her lips from mine, and she twists in my arms to look at the person who spoke. Peeking through the spot over her shoulder, I see that, sure enough, it *is* Miles Dennings.

"Really?" The eyebrow closest to me rises with Kay's sarcastic question. "I've actually heard he's *quite* the fan of…*those* types of touchdowns."

Bette, who's standing with her arm looped around Miles' waist, blushes crimson. Oh there's definitely a story there.

As she unwinds her limbs from around me, I help Kay lower herself to the ground, cursing the padding of my uniform for creating a barrier against feeling the full slide of her body against mine.

"You're sweaty." Her nose gets the cutest crinkle at the top of it.

"I thought you weren't flying in until tomorrow night?" I ask.

Both of us seem to fall into stating the obvious, but in my defense, it's the only thing my brain can think of since most of my blood has redirected itself to my dick.

Her kiss-swollen lips twist to the side as she makes spirit fingers with her hands. "Surprise?" It comes out more question than statement, as if she's not sure if I'll be happy she's here early. Yeah fucking right.

"The *best* fucking kind." Her answering smile is brighter than all the lights around the stadium, her gray eyes dancing with happiness as she holds my gaze.

Our private moment is broken yet again as the guys rush her and pass her between them for a round of bear hugs, the nose crinkle back in full force. "You guys stink."

"Wrong." Alex pulls her into a headlock. "That's the smell of awesome, Smalls."

Kay's eye roll says otherwise.

Rescuing my girl from our friends, I loop an arm around her body and tuck her close to my side, pretending she didn't complain about me smelling, and start to guide us in the direction of the locker room. "I can't believe you're here."

Her head tilts back on my bicep to meet my eyes, the scent of peppermint wafting up as her hair fans out along my muscle. "It *may* have always been the plan to try to come today."

"Why didn't you tell me?"

"With so many pieces to coordinate, I wasn't sure if it was a done deal. I didn't want to get your hopes up only to have to be like *just kidding*." She dips her chin, dropping her gaze to the floor. "I know in a few months we'll have to figure out how to manage living in different states—"

My gut clenches at the mention of the not-so-distant future.

"—and all I knew was, if I could do something about it, I didn't want to spend our first Christmas that way."

My feet stop moving as I stare down at her in shock, the urge to *really* talk to her, to explain these aren't mere thoughts I've been kicking around getting stronger. Not wanting to fight and ruin this unexpected surprise, I go with, "E was okay with you not spending Christmas with him?"

"Yeah. The Crabs are away this weekend anyway, and he was the one who insisted on buying everyone plane tickets. He even purchased tickets and got a separate suite for the Graysons to join us tomorrow." Now it makes sense why Grant and his brother were able to be here.

"So…" I jerk my chin as our friends pass us. "You know Miles Dennings, huh?" I keep my question casual, not giving her any ammunition to use for teasing me about being a fanboy. She only shrugs.

"I love that you're so blasé about my pro connections." A furrow forms between her blonde brows. "You make me feel normal." There's a sad underlying tension to the statement.

This time when I stop walking, I guide us to the side until her back is flush against the wall, trapping her between it and my body. With a finger curled under her chin, I tip it up until I have the full focus of her stormy gaze. "Baby," I coo when she looks away. "You aren't normal." Her tiny body stiffens. "You"—I pinch her chin for her attention—"are fucking *spectacular*." The softest gasp falls from her lips. "Don't you *ever* forget it."

She sags against me, and I have her off her feet, into my arms, and pinned to the wall before my next breath. There are times our foot-and-a-half height difference can be annoying, but never when we are like this. This is effortless.

Spreading my feet apart, I angle my hips to take the bulk of her weight, freeing my hands to touch. I thread the fingers of one into her colorful hair, running them from the base of her skull down to the ends curling around the undersides of her boobs. It looks different when she wears it straight, but I love it all the same.

Kay's head lolls against the wall, basking in my ministrations. She's always been transparent about how my touch affects her. I love how responsive she is, both in and out of bed.

It's a damn good thing the press weren't allowed in today because these are the type of shots they've been jonesing for since they started running with the football royalty angle freaking Instagram started.

"NOVA!" Coach Knight bellows. "Get your ass in here and shower so the trainers can work on—" His words cut off when he catches sight of Kay in my arms. Guess he left the field before she arrived. I make a mental note that he doesn't look unhappy to see her with me. *Interesting.* Looks like my hard-ass coach *does* have a soft spot for my girl. "Miss Dennings."

"Coach." Kay taps my shoulder to put her down, a request I pointedly ignore. Her eyes narrow to slits, and I know I'm going to lose this battle. "You know how I feel about you skipping sessions with the trainers."

When I shift my attention back to Coach, he is very obviously fighting back a smile at my pint-sized tyrant. "I knew there was a reason I liked this girl."

That has Kay beaming ear to ear, every one of her white teeth on display. "Go." She jerks her chin toward the locker room doors. "You really do stink." She pinches the tip of her nose with a smirk.

"You didn't seem to mind a minute ago."

"That's because I love you." She arches a brow in question. "Can you say the same about your trainers?"

"Always the smartass."

"Blame Bette."

There's an offended scoff from somewhere nearby followed by a bark of laughter.

"Bullshit," JT shouts. "You were *always* like this. The force only got *stronger* when Bette moved in."

Kay leans around me to scowl at her best friend, but neither she nor Bette deny the claim. Having learned the details about her mother, I have a better understanding about their closeness. It didn't matter that Kay was already sixteen at the time; Bette truly is her surrogate mother.

"Go do what you gotta do." Kay pushes up onto her toes to press a kiss to the underside of my jaw then moves to step around me. "I have enough people with me to keep me entertained until I can see you later."

Before she can get far, I hook an arm around her middle and pull her in for a deeper, proper kiss, not giving one fuck about our audience. When I finally let her go, I'm satisfied to see she looks slightly dazed.

"Love you, Skit."

"I know, Caveman."

"Did you just Han Solo me?" I chuckle.

"Blame JT—he's the one who mentioned the force."

"Thanks, Cheer Boy," I toss out, not taking my eyes off my girl.

"You're welcome," he returns, as much a smartass as his best friend.

With one last wink from me and a blown kiss from Kay, I allow myself to be ushered into the locker room, already counting the seconds until I can excuse myself from the team and get back to her.

#THE GRAM

#Chapter32

UOFJ411: Merry Christmas to @CasaNova87 #Christmas-CameEarly #Kaysonova

picture of Kay and the group checking in at the hotel

@Suntan_malone: *heart eyes emoji* The queen loves her king #SomeoneWasAGoodBoyThisYear #CasanovaWatch #FootballRoyalty

@The_book_queen: Anyone else wanna know what room she's going to sleep in? #CuddleBuddy #Kaysonova

Chapter 33

MUCH TO MY ANNOYANCE, it's *hours* before I get to see Kay again. I know I shouldn't complain—she wasn't even supposed to be here until tomorrow—but fuck it, I want to be with her.

Still, I behaved and went to my session with the trainers, had lunch with the team, and watched game film. Basically, I was a model football player.

There's press milling around when the team bus pulls up to the hotel, but that's typical of how our time here has gone, and I'm sure it's the same over at the hotel Notre Dame is staying in. The potential of getting an exclusive interview or comment from a future draft pick increases if you can catch them during downtime when one's guard is lowered.

Except as my feet hit the asphalt, the slew of questions directed toward me—particularly my thoughts on how I feel about having my girlfriend in Texas to cheer me on—have increased tenfold. How do they know she's here?

"Bruh." Trav discreetly holds his phone out for me as we do our best to push through the small cluster of flashing cameras and recorders held out in our direction. I grind my teeth when I see the post from UofJ411. I wonder if I can report their account and get them shut down.

Whatever. I'm going to put all the needs-to-get-a-new-hobby people from my mind. The team has the rest of the night free until curfew, and I'm going to spend every one of those hours with my girl.

With a quick detour to drop our bags in our respective rooms, the five of us pile back into the elevator, this time taking it up to the nineteenth floor where Kay and our friends are staying.

CK is the one to answer my knock, bumping knuckles with each of us as we enter. Every now and then, he still holds himself separate from us—Kay explained some of his history with jocks—but the guys and I have worn him down over the course of the semester.

The suite is luxurious and more than big enough for everyone to hang out in comfortably without any prying eyes. The living room is a large square with a gas fireplace against one wall and a full-sized kitchen directly behind it, and I can even see a small office workspace tucked into the alcove off to the right side by two of the four bedrooms.

"D, stop. That's cheating," Kay yells, but her words are choppy because she's laughing. "Sto—stop." A deeper chuckle joins in with her tinkling laughter. "Oh my *god*. Stop, D." It sounds like she's struggling to breathe. "Ahhh! G…*save* me from your brother."

"No way, Smalls." Grayson smiles, focusing all his attention on the video game he's playing and completely ignoring the fact that Kay is all but squirming around on the couch next to him.

Kay also has a game controller in her hands, but her head is hanging upside down off the couch as she does her best to avoid Dante's attempts at tickling.

"Not"—a laugh—"my"—a giggle—"fault"—a gasp for air —"you don't like"—a screech—"losing to a girl."

I come to a stop at the back of the couch as Kay lets out

another ear-splitting screech. "You alright there, Skittles?" I ask, looking down at the scene.

"*Eeep.*" She lifts her head from its tipped-down position, her cheeks pink from exertion and probably from the blood rushing to it. I get a flash of worry over if that's okay for her cheekbone, but it's been four weeks, so I try to relax. "Mase." She lets out a sigh of relief. "Can you please go all caveman and save me from the *annoying* Grayson?"

I wrap my hands around her flailing ankles and lift her from the couch, easily maneuvering her right side up and down to her feet.

"Wanna explain what I just witnessed?" I hug her to me and drop a kiss to the top of her head.

"She was kicking D's ass, and the sore loser was trying to distract her," Em explains as she walks into the room, dropping into Kay's old spot and picking her controller up off the ground, taking her place in the current game of NBA2K being played.

"Start figuring out what you want..." Bette pauses with the ends of Quinn's hair pinched between her fingers and gestures to us with her silver scissors. Based on the multitude of colors I see in the strands gathered on the white sheet under Quinn's chair, she was not the first cut of the night.

"There's hella food in the kitchen if you're hungry, too," Tessa offers, carrying in a loaded plate and perching on an armrest close to Grayson. Without missing a beat, he filches food from the plate, much the same way he does to Kay at lunch all the time. However, unlike Kay, Tessa shifts her hand closer, making it easier for them to share.

"For reals." Savvy isn't far behind with her own feast. "I think Bette ordered every single thing on the room service menu."

We make our way around, saying hi and filling plates of food before we find our own seats around the suite. Making the most of every second, I pull Kay onto my lap, letting her hold my plate so I can hold her.

The game controllers change hands a few times as people lose and a new game starts while we catch up on everything and nothing.

Bette is putting the final touches on the football surrounding the large 91 shaved into the hair on the back of Kev's head when there's a knock on the door. Alex, being the closest, offers to answer it, and promptly loses his shit…well, more like goes still as a statue.

"Are you sure this is the correct room, babe?" a feminine voice asks.

"Yeah." I recognize Miles Dennings' voice from earlier today. "I think he's just starstruck."

Kay giggles, hand flying to her face as she snorts water through her nose.

"Not for me." Miles chuckles. "For you, babe." There's the smack of a kiss. "I swear you forget how fucking hot you are."

"DeeDee," Bette cries, rushing to the door and pushing a still stunned Alex out of the way.

Can't say I blame him for standing there gaping like a fish as Denise Regan, now Denise Regan-Dennings, steps into the suite. The American-born Brazilian looks a lot like her Victoria's Secret co-worker Alessandra Ambrosio. With her chocolate brown hair and matching eyes, her natural golden skin seems to glow. She is even more stunning in person than on the magazine covers she graces.

"Betty Boop," Denise returns in the same manner, the two women bouncing as they hug.

Miles, doing what any man in a long-term relationship with a woman does, steps around them, not interrupting their reunion.

Pfft. Listen to you talking like you're this expert *on long-term relationships. It's been four months and you broke up once.*

I mentally flip off my inner coach.

"Damn, Bette." Miles circles Kev, checking out the nearly complete shaved artwork. "I didn't think it was possible, but you're even better than the last time I saw your work."

"Thanks." Arm in arm, the ladies stroll over to join Miles, and Bette makes the formal introductions. "Alex." Bette snaps her fingers in his direction. "You wanna snap out of your stupor and rejoin the land of the living?"

He shakes his head as if to clear it while the rest of us don't even bother to restrain our laughter.

"Where's our girl?" Denise looks around the room.

"Hey DeeDee." Kay extends an arm up to wave, remaining snuggled in my lap. I love that she's stayed within touching distance the entire time I've been in the suite.

"Why does she get to call you DeeDee?" Miles complains around a mouthful of food.

"Letter nicknames are her thing." Denise shrugs without a care, moving closer to Kay and lifting one of her feet in the air. "You're wearing the boots I sent you."

I drop my gaze to Kay's leg, following the long toned line of it to where her stretchy black leggings disappear inside a pair of simple black leather mid-calf cowboy boots.

"I figured when in Texas…" Kay says with a wink. I lean in close, whispering to her how much I do like it when she rides me reverse cowgirl, nipping at the back of her shoulder when I feel her shiver at my dirty words.

"But I'm your *husband*," Miles complains again. "You withheld sex for three days when I tried calling you D—" He cuts himself off when Denise arches a brow. "That," he finishes with instead.

Like there's this weird psychic connection that only comes from having two Xs in your chromosomes, every female in the room manages to lock eyes then promptly fall into a fit of giggles. With all that's happened this last month—the drama leading up to the rivalry game, Chrissy/Tina showing up, everything after the game with Liam, the hospital, Kay's recovery, all the legal stuff, and finals—it's been a while since I've gotten to see Kay this light and carefree.

Denise struts over to her husband much the same way she does down a runway, the entire room falling silent as we watch the lithe way she glides her hands up the plane of his chest and loops her arms around his neck. Miles automatically shifts, his legs spreading for his wife to step in closer. The moment is almost too intimate to watch, but they are simply captivating.

With Miles on one of the barstools at the kitchen island and Denise's model height, they are eye to eye. I expect them to either make out or start whispering sweet nothings to each other any second. Knowing Kay and how she is with me and how her sister-in-law is with her brother, I should have expected what happens instead.

"You'll live." Denise places a smacking kiss to the tip of Miles' nose, leaving behind the shine of sparkly lip gloss.

"See how mean she is to me when she's around you, Little D?" When Miles pouts in her direction, Kay buries her face in the crook of my neck, her warm breath teasing across my skin, and now I'm the one with the shiver sliding down my spine as my dick hardens under the curve of her delectable ass.

"I hate that you and Ben call her that," Denise complains. "It sounds like you're calling her Little Dick."

That sets off a whole new round of ribbing, and the rest of the hours before the team's curfew are spent with both an ache in my stomach from laughing and one in my dick from being near Kay and not *in* her.

At some point, Miles video-calls E, claiming he was being "ganged up on" by the wives. Bette, not offended in the least, continues to rotate each of us in and out of her chair, cutting and styling hair while seamlessly carrying on conversation. I mention something of the sort to Kay, but she only points out it's what Bette does all day long at her salon.

When it's finally time for me to leave, Kay offers to head down with us, stretching out our time together for as long as possible. There's a round of goodbyes and a collection of kisses on the cheek before my guys all disappear into their rooms, giving me a few minutes to say good night to my girl in private before bed checks.

For hours, I've been teased and tempted by the swells of her breasts peeking out any time her shirt shifted to fall farther down her arm, by the curve of her ass brushing along my dick any time she wiggled to reposition her seat. As soon as the door clicks shut behind Trav, I have Kay in my arms and pressed against it.

"We probably shouldn't do this out here." Kay traces a finger along the freshly cut hairs sticking out beneath the brim of my backward hat at the base of my skull. I love when she does that. "What if someone comes by and takes a picture?"

"Fuck 'em." I steal a quick kiss before pulling back. "Besides...if I don't pick you up, I get a crick in my neck."

"Don't pick on me for being vertically challenged." The way she squeezes her thighs against me to kick her heels back into my ass has me groaning with a fresh wave of need to be inside her. "I don't make fun of you for being stupidly tall."

A laugh rumbles out of me. This chick loves putting me in my place.

"I'm not. I adore how pint-sized you are." I kiss the tip of her nose.

"I prefer the term 'fun-sized', thank you very much," she says with a pout.

"Oh, you *are* fun-sized." I waggle my eyebrows as I grind my hips against hers.

It's her turn to let out a moan, and I'm instantly rock hard, tempted to say *Fuck it* and turn the playful move into a serious one.

"Don't start something we can't finish right now," she warns, her head thunking against the wall.

I know she's right, but it doesn't prevent me from taking her mouth with mine, claiming it until the alarm I set on my phone goes off, alerting me to the fact that I have one minute until curfew. We're both breathing heavily, our chests bumping into each other with each inhalation.

"You're happy I came a day early?" she asks when I rest my forehead against hers.

"Very. Not sure how much I'll actually be able to see you tomorrow with all the pregame shit we have going on, though."

"I told you, I get it. Don't worry about me, babe."

The second alarm sounds, announcing curfew. Kay places one last kiss to my lips before unhooking her legs from around me.

"Love you, Caveman," she calls out as she skips down the hall toward the elevators.

"Love you too, baby," I return.

She blows me a kiss as she disappears behind the closing doors. What do I have to do to make her understand I'll *always* worry about her?

Chapter34

TESSA'S ARM flops across my face as she stretches, still half-asleep. I'm no stranger to sharing a bed with the younger Taylor—years of travel for cheer competitions will do that—but I don't think one can ever get used to sleeping with a person who is essentially an octopus in their sleep. How Savvy survives this a few times a week, I'll never know. I should have taken the couch like I planned to instead of letting her convince me to take the bed.

JT is a much better bedmate than his sister; at least with him I don't have to worry about waking up with bruises. Truth be told, he was concerned about what Tessa might do to my cheek in our sleep, but I convinced him that was too much of an overreaction. The bone is pretty much healed, I'll be cleared for stunting and tumbling sometime next week, and there's no way she would hit me with enough force to re-break it.

The door to the bedroom opens without a knock, and the other Taylor plops down on the mattress. "Told you she'd try to beat you up, PF." He peels this one's arm from where it's covering my eyes and scoots in between us.

"Yes, please do come in," I say sarcastically. "So *nice* of you to join us this fine morning." I roll to my side, trying to bury myself deeper into my pillow.

"Calm your tits, sis." JT steals my pillow out from under me. "It's after ten."

Before I can actually murder JT with my eyes my death glare is so strong, G walks in carrying coffee, stretching out along my free side and offering the mug to me. "Rookie mistake, Taylor." G leans back against the padded headboard. "You know better than to engage her without caffeine in the morning."

Sitting up, I run a hand through my once-again curly hair, pushing the riot of bedhead from my face, and accept the java goodness. "You're my favorite of all my brothers," I tell G, blowing across the rim of the mug and taking a small sip. *Perfection.*

"You're mean in the morning," JT grumbles.

"No." I shake my head, looking at him out of the corner of my eye. "I'm undercaffeinated."

"You know her attitude is on a sliding scale with her caffeine intake," CK adds, leaning in the open doorway, his shoulder propped on the jamb, his own mug of coffee cradled between his hands.

"Everybody's got jokes." I take note that they are all still in their pajamas. At least I can loaf it up if I have to be awake.

"Food's here," a rumpled-looking Savvy announces. "I swear your sister-in-law doesn't know how to *not* order every available item."

We all laugh, knowing how accurate the statement is. To be fair, she's used to feeding E and B on the reg, along with any teammates who happen to swing by. In case you didn't know…football players eat *a lot*.

Needing the others to move so I can get out of bed, I wiggle a knuckle between two of G's ribs, causing him to let out a girlish squeal.

"A sound like that should *not* come out of a man your size." T snickers, sliding on her butt to the foot of the bed. She's not wrong; I think the high-pitched sound he made was meant more for Herkie's ears than ours.

"And to think"—G scowls down at me, the look losing its effectiveness when his face breaks into a smile after a few seconds, never one to be able to hold on to his mad long—"I made your coffee this morning."

"Love you, G." I blow him a kiss.

The others shuffle out of the room to eat while I pull on a pair of tube socks—these white with red stripes around the top—adjusting the elastic to rest a few inches above my knee. Sure, I could have pulled on a pair of leggings to keep warm, but the Soffe shorts I wore to bed are too comfy.

I make a pit stop in the bathroom to pee and brush my teeth before adjusting the twisted band of my sports bra. When I make it to the kitchen, I'm not surprised to see the twins are here. Olly and Livi have chosen to spend most of their time since arriving in Dallas with us instead of their parents.

"Hey Coach." They greet me in their typical in-unison fashion.

"Hey guys." I reach out a fist for them to bump.

My stomach rumbles audibly at the sight of the feast spread before me. There are silver chafing dishes filled with French toast, pancakes, scrambled eggs, bacon, sausage, and sliced steak. Glass bowls filled with freshly cut fruit and carafes of multiple juices take up the remaining table space.

After perusing the options, I load a plate with some of the French toast and smother it in butter and syrup before rounding out the dish with a handful of strawberries and a few slices of bacon.

"Do you know what your parents' plans are for later?" I ask the twins around a mouthful of crispy pork fat.

I'm hesitant to bring it up—the twins are a little salty over the fact that they weren't allowed to get tickets with us in the stands, their parents insisting they join them in their box like they do at the home games—but I figure if I can coordinate our trips to and from the stadium, it might appease them some.

"Yeah. Dad said we need to leave here by two-thirty so we have a solid hour to get there and settled into the suite." Olly's tone does nothing to hide his unhappiness.

I was tempted to purchase them tickets in our section anyway but refrained. There's already a weird tension between Brantley and me; I don't need to do anything to add to it.

"Solid plan." I search around, trying to catch Bette's eye, and when I do, I get the nod I was looking for. "We'll head over when you do. We can hang around the main concourse and stuff until pregame starts."

"You know"—Bette braces her elbows on the counter, leaning in so we can hear her better now that we've moved to the couches—"after seeing the suites yesterday, I'm almost disappointed we didn't get a box ourselves."

I've mentioned before how much I love my sister-in-law, right? Her maternal instincts are top notch, like Lombardi Trophy-worthy; she can so easily read any situation. Whenever she and E finally decide to give me the nieces and nephews I've been begging for, they really will have the most amazing mom in existence.

"Is that—" Livi breaks off in the middle of her question.

Out of the corner of my eye, I see Olly shaking his head at his twin, and I shift to fully face him. "Olly?" I ask. When he stays silent, I turn back to Livi. "Livi?"

The two of them are fidgeting, and that is so unlike them. I have no idea what brought on this wave of nervousness. Something is definitely up.

Livi looks to her brother, waiting for his nod before she's

willing to continue. She blows out a heavy breath then begins to speak. "So…" Pause. "This morning…" Another pause. This time I have to curl my hands into fists to resist the urge to shake her and tell her to spit it out. "These two guys in suits came to our suite."

The Roberts and McQueens are sharing the penthouse on the top floor of the hotel. If we thought our suite was nice, it's practically a cardboard box compared to the one Brantley rented for their stay. For all its luxury, the thing I'm most jealous of is the ten-foot-high, fully decorated Christmas tree it features.

"Oh-kay," I drag out, still not understanding.

When Livi's eyes swing back to Olly, he takes over the story. "They were from the Outlaws' front office." The pieces I'm missing start to come together, and I'm not sure I like the picture they're forming. Miles' words from two days ago echo in the back of my mind. "They came to extend an invitation to watch the game from the owner's box."

Holy shit.

Never in a million years did I think they would take this approach. When we had Miles relay our "thanks but no thanks" response, we thought that was the end of it. It *should* have been the end of it. Hell, it should never have been an *it*.

I take a deep breath, letting my shoulders roll back with my tension. "Let me guess…" I shift forward to place my now empty plate on the coffee table. "They made sure the invitation included me as well?"

"Bette too," Olly adds.

A frown tugs at the edges of Bette's lips when I spin to look back at her. I'm sure my expression mirrors her own. None of this makes sense. Bette I understand—sorta; she's a WAG, E is a top player, and his contract is coming up soon. Maybe Dallas is hoping to put a bug in her ear, feel her out on what E has been thinking. But me? *Why* me?

Yes, Mase is a damn good football player.

Yes, Mase is fuck-hot.

And yes, I can admit we are an adorable couple. But the interest in us, as…well, an *us* is ridiculous.

Plus, Mase is going to be a draft prospect. He and *I* have zero say in what team he plays for. What purpose does my presence really serve?

I'm supremely glad Mase is busy with the team. I chose not to mention anything to him about Miles' suspicions; no need to have him go all caveman over us being used for another's gain. He's been extra sensitive lately.

Plus…

It. Makes. No. Sense.

At least there are only a few more months left before the draft. Then we move on to *other* challenges.

"How'd you know?" Livi curls her legs under her.

"It doesn't matter." I brush off the question. "What did your parents say?"

"Dad was quick to accept."

Of course he was. I'm sure Brantley sees rubbing elbows with one of the most powerful people in the NFL as a major coup for Mase's future career. I can't fault him for it.

That being said…

"But Nana was quick to inform them that you *always* watch the games where Mase can see you and as nice as their offer was, it was doubtful you would be joining us," Livi tacks on quickly.

Have I mentioned Nana McQueen is one of my favorite people in the world?

"I love that woman," I say offhandedly.

"She's the best," the twins answer—in unison.

With them not having any living grandparents, Trav's Nana proudly fills the role for all the Nova and Nova-Roberts children, a situation very similar to the one between the Dennings and Taylor clans.

There's rhythmic knocking on the door to the suite, causing the room to fall silent. Based on the questioning looks everyone shoots each other, no one has a clue who it might be.

D, the closest to the door, is the one to answer. Unfortunately, I can't make out who it is, his over-six-and-a-half-feet bulk serving as a door of its own.

"Hey, man," he greets our visitor. "Don't you have a game to get ready for?"

"Gotta get my good-luck kiss first," a familiar voice says before D steps to the side, revealing my boyfriend.

"Mase?" I rise from the couch, automatically walking in his direction even if I'm still confused on how he's here.

"Skittles," he drawls.

"What are you doing here? Doesn't the bus leave for the stadium soon?"

"Yup." Out come those dimples. "I have less than five minutes to get my ass on it before Coach Knight rips me a new one for being late." He wraps his arms around my waist as soon as I'm in reach.

I smooth my hands up the hard expanse of his muscular chest, hooking them behind his neck. "Sounds risky."

Not giving a damn about the audience around us—which is typical behavior for him—he pulls me closer, eliminating the space separating our bodies.

"I figured I'd come to you for my kiss since you can't come to me."

I swear some of the things this man says to me are straight out of one of those romance books T loves to read.

"Now come on." He puckers his lips and taps them. "Lay it on me so I can get on the bus before it leaves without me."

Another tug on my hips and I'm placing my sock-covered feet on top of his sneaker-clad ones, pushing onto tiptoes, and giving him what he wants. When I trace the seam of his lips with my tongue, I'm suddenly airborne, Mase striding out of the suite and pressing me against the wall in the hallway within seconds.

"Um…why are we in the hallway?" I ask when we finally come up for air.

He smirks, flashing me his dimples again. "I always pin you to the wall before a game."

"Okay." My head bobs. "The hallway?" I ask again, seeking clarification on our relocation.

"Figured you'd rather I didn't maul you in front of your family."

A giggle bubbles out of me and I roll my eyes at his ridiculousness, causing him to nip at the tip of my nose when I do.

"Some of *your* family was in there too." I use my chin to gesture to the door next to us. "The twins are inside," I explain when he arches a questioning brow.

"They are?"

"Wow." Another laugh escapes me. "You really didn't see them? Livi was sitting next to me on the couch."

"Nope." He shakes his head. "You're like end zone for me —I focus on you like I do when I'm running for a touchdown."

"I adore when you use football metaphors to describe our relationship." I'm only partially sarcastic, knowing I'm guilty of doing the same. I blame our corniness on my affinity for punny t-shirts. "Okay, hotshot." I tap his shoulder, my hand squeezing the ball of muscle under his U of J football hoodie. "Time for you to catch a bus."

He grinds his hips against me instead of releasing me, and the hardness behind his zipper presses against my hot center, the friction causing me to bite back a moan. My red Soffe shorts don't provide much of a barrier against the feel of denim and an erection.

He steals another kiss before finally lowering me to the ground. I watch him as he steps onto the elevator.

"Make sure you send me a pic of your shirt before the game," he calls out before the doors finish sliding shut.

Picking out my Nova-boasting shirt for today is going to be fun.

Chapter35

GAME DAY.

The Cotton Bowl.

The final game between us and the national championship.

Game on, baby.

As the higher seed, the Hawks are considered the home team today. The Fighting Irish are going down.

This entire day—hell, the entire week—has been a whirlwind of activity. Most people would be drained by the grueling schedule of workouts, practices, and media requirements, but D1 athletes are not most people, and athletes who play for the U of J could even be said to be a cut above the rest. The school is known for having some of the highest number of students turn pro in basketball and football compared to any other major university in the country. We've made this week our bitch.

Getting to play in a pro stadium today is a preview of what my future will be like. It's not ego talking; it's fact. All the experts discuss where they think I'll fall in the draft, and not one has me placed lower than the top five. Yeah, I'm the man.

The biggest downfall of not playing at home is that Kay

isn't able to come down to give me my pregame kiss. Honestly, I'm sure she could have swung it, but with all the extra press around, it's probably a good thing she didn't.

Not wanting to give up my good luck kiss completely, I risked the wrath of Coach Knight—and in case you were wondering, yes he did rip me a new asshole when I got on the bus four minutes late—to claim my kiss before I left the hotel. I gave it to her extra good to make sure it carried me through the five-plus hours until kickoff.

God, I'm so happy I did too. My baby looked so damn cute in her pajamas: one of my football shirts that's pretty much a nightgown and thus hits below her knees if she doesn't tie it at her hip, a pair of those tiny shorts that always manage to have me hard faster than it takes the center to snap the ball, and classic white tube socks with matching red stripes.

Her natural riot of curls was back, looking all bedhead messy, provoking thoughts of what it looks like after sex. *Shit!* There I go chubbing up again.

Fuck, Nova, get that shit under control. Think of the smell of Trav's gym socks, us losing today, anything to get your erection under control. The locker room is the last place you should be getting a boner.

The scolding from my inner coach works until I start to think of how she tasted, all minty toothpaste and sugary sweet from her coffee…

God I wanted to eat *her* for breakfast.

I'm fucking kicking Trav's ass out of the room tonight to spend it buried between my girl's legs…hopefully in celebration.

"Stop thinking dirty thoughts about my little sis." Trav plops down beside me.

"How'd you know?" I try and fail to wipe the smile from my face.

"You always make this dumbass smirk when you do." He circles a finger in front of my face.

"Can't help it, bro. She's very…inspiring." He mimes gagging. "You never had a problem with hearing about my sex life before," I say, reaching inside my locker for my phone.

"None of your girls have lasted long enough to feel like family to me before. How would you feel hearing about Livi's?" He gives me a knowing look, and I fight back my own gag.

As a junior in high school, I'm surprised the subject of boys hasn't already come up. If I had my way, though, she wouldn't date until she was thirty.

"Point taken."

My phone buzzes in my hand, and I look down to see a picture message from Kay. The shirt she chose for the game is one of the ones I gave her: a white long-sleeved scoop neck with football elbow patches and black and red lettering reading *My boyfriend SCORES more than yours*. Bracketing the word "My" are two hearts, and the O in scores is a football. The lettering is black, and the hearts and football are red. And, of course, NOVA #87 is on the back.

It's one of my favorites that I've given her, a little bit of sap with a double entendre mixed in for good measure.

I can tell Bette must have done her makeup. Her gray eyes are more prominent thanks to the winged liner, and her lips, which are blowing me a kiss in the image, are a deep blood red. *Fuck I love when she wears red lip stain.* Again, I have to will away the blood rushing to my dick.

The hand not holding her phone is threaded through the hair on top of her head, pushing her bangs and curls away from her face. Flanking my flirting girl in the customary mirror selfie are her two best friends, Grayson winking and JT holding up his hands in the shape of a heart.

Quickly I type back a response.

• • •

ME: Sorry boys—the blonde in the middle is much more my type than the two of you.

I tilt the screen so Trav can see the shenanigans our friends are up to, causing him to laugh.

SKITTLES: JT said you broke his heart.

ME: I'm sure he'll survive.

SKITTLES: I know. Plus, he can't have you. You're mine.

I love when she gets all possessive.

SKITTLES: Headed to the stadium now. I'll see you after the game. I'll be the hot blonde cheering you on from the stands. Go kick some Fighting Irish ass, babe.

ME: *GIF of Tom Cruise in *Top Gun* saying, "Yes ma'am"*

SKITTLES: *rolls eyes* Love you.

ME: Ditto, baby.

. . .

Locking the screen, I toss my phone back inside my locker. Time to suit up. We have a football game to win.

Chapter36

THERE'S a beautiful chaos that only happens during playoff games. It doesn't matter if it's high school, college, or the pros; I've discovered the vibe is the same.

The main concourse into AT&T Stadium is packed with fans as we slowly meander our way around. It looks like there are as many sporting the black and red of the U of J as those in the Fighting Irish's blue and gold.

As promised, we spend as much time with the twins as possible. We take multiple—and highly inappropriate—pictures with the twenty-foot inflatables of each team's mascots set up in one of the fan game break areas.

As expected, Brantley pulled me aside when we first arrived in an effort to convince us—me—to reconsider watching the game with them in the owner's box. As politely but firmly as I could, I declined.

Originally we had all planned to watch the Orange Bowl —the other bowl game selected for the playoffs—later. In an effort to smooth what I could tell were Brantley's ruffled feathers, I promised our crew would attend the aftergame party they had planned in their suite back at the hotel instead.

Nana and I take pictures in our custom shirts, and I even

go as far as to let her post one of them on her Instagram. For something that would typically give me hives just thinking about it, I'm actually excited to see how Trav will react when he sees the hashtag she used.

When we do finally go to our seats, it doesn't shock me in the least that Bette was able to score us tickets in the front row behind the U of J's team bench near the fifty-yard line. We missed both marching bands performing, and each are gathered by the inflatable renderings of their respective school's football helmets. We're too far away to make out their faces, but Em and Q are lined up with the Red and White Squads, creating the pathway the Hawks will run out through.

The combo hype video for the Cotton Bowl starts to play on the massive one-hundred-and-sixty-foot jumbotron, and as the seconds tick off the clock, the crowd of eighty thousand roars and pyrotechnics explode in a burst of golden sparks as each team takes its turn running out onto the field.

We remain standing for the national anthem and as the team captains meet at the fifty for the coin toss.

Mase looks fine as ever in his black football pants and red jersey, helmet hanging loosely from two fingers when he steps behind the bench to blow me my kiss. T squeals in excitement when she notices him taking part in our family's competition tradition, thrusting both her arms up and waving her Y-shaped hang-loose hands in the air.

I want to say the game is exciting—I mean it's football; it's *always* exciting—but the Hawks own the game from the second the Fighting Irish kick off, the final score 30-3 in favor of the Hawks.

Despite it being a completely one-sided game, my family and I still manage to scream ourselves hoarse.

We hip-check, shimmy, and raise the roof, and I think I saw D doing the shopping cart as we happy-dance in our seats while the team celebrates down on the field.

The Hawks are officially going to the national championship.

I'm so proud and excited for them.

Wrapping my hands around the railing in front of me, I search the massive cluster of bouncing football players for my boyfriend. I'll have to wait until we're back at the hotel to properly congratulate him, but I can at least blow him a kiss of my own.

My breathing hitches when those light green eyes find me over the crowd. How Mase manages to look sexier now, when he's a sweaty mess, I'll never know. His dark brown hair sticks up in places and is flattened in others from his helmet, his eye black is smeared down his cheeks, and even though the field is turf, his jersey still has stains on it.

Without warning, he starts to run, jumping up onto the stands and hauling himself high enough that we're face to face. He puckers his lips for a kiss, and I don't hesitate in fulfilling his request. Taking his face between my hands, I pay no mind to the sweat clinging to it as I thread my fingers through his short hair and lay a tongue-dueling kiss on him. It isn't until I feel his muscles start to shake from holding his position that I break away and he drops back down to the ground.

"Good game, baby." I brace my forearms on the railing and lean forward to be heard over all the noise.

"I'll be collecting my trophy later." He issues the dirty promise with one of his signature winks and jogs off to rejoin his teammates.

"*Some*one is going to be trending tonight," JT singsongs, looping an arm around my neck and tucking me into his side as we start to make the slow trek out of the stadium. It feels a lot like how I imagine salmon do trying to swim upstream.

"Eh." I do my best to shrug under the weight of his arm. "I figure if I'm trying to learn to not be afraid of it, I should throw them a bone every once in a while."

"Do you hear that?" G turns to walk backward, cupping a hand around an ear. "That's the sound of keyboards clacking as the UofJ411 rushes to be the first to share the newest Kaysonova football royalty pic."

#THE GRAM

#Chapter37

UOFJ411: Were we right about what's been going on between her and @QB1McQueen7 because peep that hashtag #MissingPuzzlePieces #CasanovaWatch

REPOSTED—picture of Nana McQueen and Kay at the Cotton Bowl—TheNanaMcQueen: Rocking my new Christmas gift today thanks to this girl right here #NewFavoriteGrandchild #GoHawks

@The-mumma-life: Is there like an application I can fill out to apply? #AskingForAFriend

@UnCheckedOther: Don't hoard the football players #ShareTheWealth #CasanovasGirl

UofJ411: WE'RE GOING TO THE NATIONAL CHAMPIONSHIP!! #HawksWin #WeAreNumber1

picture of the final scoreboard from the Cotton Bowl

UofJ411: No surprise this is how @CasaNova87 chose to celebrate #Kaysonova #FootballRoyalty #TheKingsFavoriteTrophy

picture of Mason jumping into the stands to kiss Kay

@Work2play: I wanna be kissed like that #PleasePlease #Kaysonova #FootballRoyalty

@_Bsdmbutch: That kiss though #TheyCouldTeachAMasterClass #Kaysonova

@_The_art_of_reading_: This belongs on a postage stamp #KingAndQueen

UofJ411: Now THAT'S a sandwich I wanna be a part of #IllBeYourFilling #MissingPuzzlePieces #CasanovaWatch #Kaysonova

candid shot of Kay laughing between Mason and Trav

@68blackburnc: The three of them SURE DO spend a lot of time together #PuttingThePiecesTogether

@TheQueenB: Throuples are a thing #JustSaying

#Chapter38

ON OUR WAY back to the hotel, Mase texted that he and the guys were going to stop at their rooms to change out of their suits before swinging by my family's suite on the way up to his. This was the perfect plan for me as it allowed for downtime and gave Em and Q time to join us too.

I debated changing, not at all sure what type of party we would be walking into, but when Mase showed up wearing the *I got this shirt from someone who thinks I'm pretty AMAZING* shirt I gave him for Christmas, I knew there would be no update to my wardrobe.

A wave of doubt hits me when we step inside the already lavish penthouse suite, entering a party that seems more fitting for a cocktail hour at a wedding than a low-key football game celebration.

I lose count of the number of buffet tables draped in fine white linens set up around the room; the amount of food on display couldn't possibly be consumed in one evening.

Two bartenders dressed in white Oxford shirts and black vests man the large oak bar that is a feature of the suite, and as we make our way around, saying hello to people I mostly don't recognize, I think I see a carving station set up in one of the corners.

Not long after we've arrived, Brantley commandeers Mase, pulling him into a conversation with another group of men whose identities are completely unknown to me. I opt to remain in the wingback chair we were sharing prior to his stepdad's interruption.

The only saving grace—okay, not *only* because the food is bomb—is that all the televisions scattered throughout the suite are tuned to the Orange Bowl. The winner of this game will be playing the Hawks in the national championship in two and a half weeks.

Unlike our game earlier, the battle between Alabama and Oklahoma is much closer.

"This brisket may be the tits," Trav mumbles around said brisket in his mouth as he squeezes his butt onto the armrest of my chair, "but I much prefer a post-game brew in the bar."

"Truth," Noah and Alex agree.

Periodically, I glance over to check on Mase, and any time I do, he's already looking my way. The tension at his jaw tells me how much he's not enjoying himself, and I hate that for him. This should be his night, not Brantley's and whatever agenda he's pushing.

The one bright side to attending this shindig is the twins seem to be the happiest I've seen them these last few days, with T and Savvy rounding out their happy foursome. Grace even commented about the change in her younger children when she and Nana joined our crew, taking a break from the festivities in the other room.

"Wanna get out of here?" Mase leans down to whisper in my ear when he returns. Everything from his hot breath to the soft brush of his lips as he does has all my girl parts shaking their nonexistent spirit fingers.

"More than anything."

My hand is clasped in his and I have to double-time it to keep up with his long-legged strides as he serpentines through the partygoers, doing his best not to get stopped by the numerous people still vying for his attention.

By the time we make it out the door and into the elevator, I'm breathless. "Where are we going?" I ask, sucking in air.

Mase moves, the cool wall of the elevator jolting me as he cages me against it. In my peripheral, his forearms ripple as his hands spread out on either side of my head. He's so manly it's overwhelming at times.

"My room." He nips at the tendon running down the side of my neck. Whatever breath I was able to find hitches at the bite left from his teeth.

"Wh-what about Trav?"

The elevator dings, announcing our arrival on his floor, the doors sliding open before he can answer. Instead, my hand disappears in his and once again I'm being tugged, my feet tripping over themselves to keep up.

I couldn't tell you if any of Mase's teammates are around; the entire hallway is a blur then I'm inside the room Mase shares with Trav, lifted off my feet and pressed against the now closed door with my shirt off before I have any time to process what's happening.

"I told him to sleep in your suite tonight." The words rumble through my bloodstream as Mase speaks against my skin. Like he did with my shirt, he David-Copperfields my bra, making it disappear in a blink.

"He agreed to that?" I wonder if he knows he has to sleep on the couch.

Mase trails a path of kisses down the length of my neck and I moan, my head thunking against the door as it falls back, granting him better access.

"I didn't give him a fucking choice." His mouth finds the soft spot where my neck meets my shoulder, sucking, and I see stars. "I can't remember the last time I had you all to myself." Kiss. Bite. Suck. "I'm rectifying that *right* now."

I moan again, and shit, I totally hear my inner cheerleader

telling me I'm starting to sound like a porn star. It's not my fault. He never shaves when he travels for away games, and his stubble is even longer than usual; the way it scratches across the sensitive skin of my heaving breasts then over my budded nipples only heightens my awareness of it.

"Ar—" My voice breaks on—you guessed it—another moan when he places his hot mouth over my nipple and… sucks. "Aren't you hungry?"

Brantley had him tied up at the party, playing the role of his future agent, so Mase never got to enjoy any of the food Grace selected.

"Starving," he growls, pulling me from the door and tossing me down onto one of the queen-sized mattresses in the room. My body bounces twice from the force before coming to a stop when he climbs on top of me.

"So then—" Again my words are cut off, this time from his stubble traveling down the length of my stomach, pleasure shooting a direct line to my clit. His tongue smooths away the abrasion of his prickly hair, swirling around my navel before his teeth latch onto the jeweled ring pierced through it with a tug.

Dexterous fingers pop the button on my jeans, the hiss from the zipper ringing out seeming obscenely loud to my ears. A whoosh of cold air hits the overheated skin of my thighs as the denim is jerked down my legs. The curse Mase mutters when my pants get stuck on the cowboy boots I wore again—because, Texas—has me giggling.

All humor fades with a shocked gasp as he slaps my pussy over the red lacy thong covering it. I don't know if it's the unexpected move or the pure unadulterated lust radiating off of him, but I'm this close to coming on the spot.

The thud of the boots' heavy heels hitting the carpet as he tosses them over his shoulder is an audible representation of his determination not to be deterred.

Then all bets are off.

The soaked material of my panties tears easily under his fingers, and if I had any doubt about what he wanted to eat, it's gone now. Me—*I'm* the meal.

Mase pushes his way between my legs, throwing them over his shoulders, latching his mouth onto my clit without preamble. He feasts like he's starving and I'm the buffet, the bite of teeth soothed by the swirling of his skilled tongue, only to repeat all over again.

My orgasm crashes over me like a tidal wave.

My heart pounds furiously, battling it out with my lungs as to who will be the victor in escaping my ribcage first. Before I get the chance to catch my breath, he shoves two fingers deep inside me, my walls squeezing them as he sucks my clit all the way into his mouth.

"Oh…god…*Mase*." I knock his hat away, my fingers ripping at his expresso-colored locks. If he keeps this up too much longer, he might not have any hair left for me to grab hold of.

All the stars in Texas explode behind my eyelids when his fingers scissor and a second orgasm slams into me.

I wiggle, trying to get away, the sensations too much, too intense, but Mase's strong arms are curled around my legs, anchoring my hips to the bed as he continues his onslaught on my pussy. It isn't until a third orgasm and the last bit of strength in my vocal chords are wrenched from me that he finally drops my legs from his shoulders.

I'm weak, limp, full-on noodle-limbed—*when the hell did he remove his shirt?*—as his calloused hands slip under my knees and he readjusts my legs around his hips. In a single breath, he drives the full length of his cock inside me with one thrust.

My mouth falls open on a silent cry at the sudden fullness. It's rare for Mase to fit the entirety of his cock inside me—his overwhelming size extending to *all* of him—in one go.

"God, babe." Hot breath hits my neck when he groans, the

soft strands of his hair tickling my ear. "You're a fucking *puddle*."

That explains his easy entry.

The ability to speak left me two climaxes ago. The only things I'm capable of as he pumps himself in and out of my body are incoherent *mmms* and choked breaths.

There is nothing sweet about our lovemaking tonight. It is pure animalistic fucking, the adrenaline from the win fueling each drive of his hips.

Just when I think it isn't possible for me to come any more for fear of drying out, the first stirrings of a fourth—impossible—orgasm begin.

"That's it, baby," he coos. "Give it to me. Come on my cock the way you did for my mouth and fingers."

Mase's dirty words give me the final push over the edge. I feel him spill inside me as I crest the highest peak, an arm snaking under my back to squeeze me to him tighter.

His thrusts turn lazy as we ride out the last few moments of pleasure.

Always cognizant of our vast size difference, he rolls to his side, taking me with him, tucking me into the hollow space above his armpit and pressing a soft kiss to the top of my head.

"Fuck I love you, baby."

Mase's awestruck confession is the last thing I'm conscious of before I fall asleep.

Chapter39

AFTER SPENDING an entire uninterrupted night together after the Cotton Bowl—fucking, pigging out on room service, making love, and binge-watching a season of *Ballers* on HBO —Kay and I reluctantly rejoined society.

So many things seemed to happen at once after that and we entered the new year in a blur of activity.

First, the picture of my celebratory kiss with Kay did go viral. Thankfully she wasn't upset, almost as if she expected and came to terms with it before it even happened. I'd complain, but if she's not bothered by it, I can't find it in me to fake that I am. I've set that gorgeousness as the home screen on my phone.

There has been one added bonus I didn't expect: it seems the more attention we get for our—and please don't have my balls for saying this—love story, the less concerned people seem to be about the details of what went down with Liam Parker. I'm sure that will change when he goes on trial for the assault and battery charges brought against him, but I'll take the reprieve for now.

Colleges and universities are on winter break for academics, but the same cannot be said for sports. While Kay and her family—Bette, Tessa, and Savvy—flew to New England to see E and the Crabs play and CK headed home to Kansas, Grayson, the football team, and the cheerleaders flew back to Jersey, and JT and Dante returned to Kentucky.

Dr. Nikols officially cleared Kay to resume her normal activity, and she has spent every day since practices resumed working at The Barracks, whether coaching or running stunting clinics.

Still having to adhere to the NCAA's restricted practice schedule and with no commitment of having to attend classes, my newfound freedom should be seen as a good thing. Sure, it's allowed me to spend more time with Kay, but it also makes it so I don't have a ready excuse for when Brantley summons me to the house.

I bring my wingman with me, but Trav ditches me to find the twins the second we step through the front door, leaving me to make my way to Brantley's home office by myself.

With two quick raps on the door, I enter to find my stepdad sitting behind his desk. Brantley's office is everything you would expect from a man who is the king of his castle. It's large, with a massive oak desk the main feature in the room. There's a working fireplace, wood burning and crackling as a fire burns in the hearth to help combat the chill of the winter. The wall behind the desk is floor-to-ceiling glass overlooking the manicured back yard, with the other prominent wall made entirely of matching oak bookcases filled with leatherbound law books and priceless first editions.

Two studded, tufted, camel-colored leather wingback chairs sit at forty-five-degree angles in front of the desk, and I make my way to one of them to take a seat.

"Mason," my stepdad says, stepping out from behind the desk and taking the open seat beside me. "Son."

Both the move to change his position and his word choice have me instantly on alert, confirming what I already expected—I'm not going to like what he has to say.

"I thought it was important we spoke before the team flies out to Santa Clara."

I nod, thinking it's safer than opening my mouth to speak, unsure what might come out. I'm also trying not to think about how, in three days, I have to yet again leave Kay for another week when the team travels to play in the national championship. It doesn't help that since school is on break and NJA is back to practicing, she's been spending more time in Blackwell than on campus and Liam Parker is *also* from Blackwell. I hate that I feel like I'm leaving her unprotected, even if it's highly illogical.

"I understand your reluctance to talk about your connection to the Dennings girl—"

Can we pause for a moment so I can say how much it makes my fucking blood boil that he *still* undermines my relationship with my girlfriend?

"—but this complete radio silence thing you're doing whenever you're asked about her isn't helping people forget about it."

"Brantley…" I suck in a breath, checking my temper. "I thought I made myself *perfectly* clear—time and time again, I might add—on where I stand on this subject." Another deep inhalation for good measure. "Kayla is a *hard* limit for me." The use of her full name is another indicator of how close to the edge I am.

"I know," Brantley concedes. "I get it."

But do you? Because I'm pretty sure the only time you talk favorably of her is when you want to use her to some unexplained advantage.

"The thing is"—he shifts forward, resting his elbows on his knees—"what you aren't seeing is that by refusing to talk about her *but* kissing her in a way that trends all over social media, it only makes the press think there's a bigger story they aren't seeing."

I nod again, because he isn't *completely* wrong.

"If you give them even the smallest nugget of information, it might help take some of the intrigue out of things."

My instincts scream at me to reject the idea outright, to hold firm on the stance we've taken. If this were months ago, that's exactly what I would do, but somehow I manage to curb those thoughts enough to actually consider what Brantley is suggesting. I've seen how Kay has been changing. It's not only the kiss pictures she hasn't freaked over. Maybe his idea does have merit.

"I need you to keep this in mind while you're in California. This isn't just the end of the football season for you—this is also the start of your career. How you handle yourself with the press will show teams you aren't only an asset on the field, but off it as well."

I work my jaw side to side as I mull it over.

"Teams won't be the only ones keeping an eye on you. This is your first opportunity to prove to sponsors and companies how marketable you are. If you impress them enough, we may be able to score a top-notch endorsement deal."

And we're back to the money thing. It's always about the money with him. Doesn't he have enough? How many more zeroes does he need in his bank account?

"I'll talk to Kay about it." It's not that I need to ask permission, but I need to show him that she and I are a team. Brantley has a habit of forgetting this very important fact.

Originally, the plan was to meet up with Kay after she was done coaching the double practices at The Barracks, but after my…talk with Brantley, I need eyes on her now, not in a few hours.

It's why I offered to drive the twins to their Admirals practice, opting to spend Trav's and my last free weekend at

The Barracks. Olly and Livi direct us to the stairs that will take us to the family viewing area on the second floor while they rush off to the locker rooms in the state-of-the-art all-star gym to change.

I'm surprised to see a familiar blonde in the row closest to the ledge overlooking the main gym area, her arms folded on the edge. Trav nudges me when he notices her as well.

"Hey." I greet Savvy King as I take the open seat to her left.

Tilting her head but never lifting her chin from where it rests on top of her folded arms, she casts a glance in my direction and looks past me to Trav before returning her focus to where the Marshals practice is coming to an end. "Yo."

She's nowhere near as quiet as her brother, but I've noticed the younger King doesn't rush to fill the silence with useless words like most girls her age—aka my sister—tend to do.

Kay and the other coaches call an end to the practice, and the two dozen or so girls on the blue mat disperse. Kay makes her way to a cluster of duffle bags on the blue camouflage pathway surrounding the spring flooring, pulls out what looks like an instant ice pack from one, and sends it sailing through the air at Tessa. We're too far away to make out what's being said, but the wild arm movements from both of them tell me it's not the calmest of conversations.

"What's with the sibling rivalry?" I point to where Kay is now reaching up to hold the cold pack to one of Tessa's shoulders.

"Tess took a nasty hit from one of her flyers falling on her when they were tweaking the pyramid sequence earlier. Kay wanted her to step out to see the trainer, but all T did was point to Kay's shirt and get in place to go again."

My lips twitch and I swipe open my phone to see the pic Kay sent earlier of her in a black racerback tank. In the same graffiti-style writing I've noticed NJA uses on a lot of their clothing are the words *Sweat dries. Blood clots. Bones heal.* She said it was a nod to her own recently healed injury, but the part that was the pure Kay sass I've come to know and love is the words scrawled in silver glitter underneath: *Suck it up, Princess.*

It doesn't surprise me that the tiny Taylor found a way to use her sister's wardrobe against her. I'll have to keep that in mind for myself.

"Do you cheer for one of the other teams?" I ask Savvy, figuring that's why she's here and hanging around until her best friend gets done with her practice.

"No." How she's able to make me feel like I should have known the answer to my question before asking it I'll never know. *Women.*

"Bitchy!" The three of us look up when Tessa calls out for her bestie, but she's looking down at her phone while she walks our way. "I'm gonna need to crash for a few before ton—" Tessa stops walking, her words halting with her steps as her head tilts to the side upon spotting Trav and me. "Mase?"

"Hey, Tiny Taylor."

Her lips twitch at the nickname I've started using for her. "What brings you boys to our home away from home?" Tessa circles her arms wide to encompass the gym.

"I'd imagine the same reason I'm here," Savvy says dryly.

"You wanna bang Short Stack too?" Trav perks up like an overeager puppy. "Hot!"

I cuff him in the back of the head. There are days I question my sanity based on my choice of best friend.

"Sorry to ruin your girl-on-girl fantasy, Mr. Quarterback." Savvy stretches an arm in front of me to pat Trav on the hand. "They may call Kay 'Little D', but she's not the type of D I go for."

Tessa snorts and falls into a seat with a plop. "Savvy comes to practice any time she stays over."

"I'm like the freaking NJA mascot," Savvy mutters under her breath.

The last thing I would have ever expected is to be entertained by hanging out with a couple of high school juniors, but these two are not your typical breed.

The next few hours fly by while we watch the Admirals. It's impossible for me to take my eyes off Kay as she puts her athletes through the paces, her voice strong enough to carry up to us as she calls out the count for the pyramid sequence they're practicing. I can't get over what a commanding presence she is when she's coaching. When I was with her while she helped JT and his partner Rei put together their partner stunt routine for the collegiate nationals, I was impressed, but being here? In her house, it's like it's magnified. It makes my dick hard.

Or could it be the way her ass looks in those leggings?

Gotta say, the inner coach might be onto something with that one, because even from this bird's-eye view I have going on, it looks spankable.

"Come on." Tessa stands as the members of the Admirals start to scatter. Savvy loops her arm through Tessa's while Trav and I pull up the rear.

Down the stairs and around a corner, we follow as Tessa scans a keycard and walks through the blue door leading into the gym. I didn't think we were allowed on the gym floor, but I guess it doesn't matter if we're with one of the cheerleaders.

From down here, it's like a whole different experience. The hundreds of banners hanging from the ceiling for each national and world title teams from NJA have won make more of an impression when you're standing under them instead of seeing them closer to eye level.

"Mase?" Kay's sweet voice has my attention snapping around to her, my neck cracking as I shift it from the ninety-degree angle I held it in to inspect the organization's achievements.

"Hey, baby." I stalk her way, my steps stuttering as the floor goes from a solid surface to the spring-loaded competition mat.

"What are you doing he—"

I pinch her chin and tilt her face to mine for a long, slow kiss. "I missed you," I murmur against her mouth.

When she lets out a breathy "Oh-kay," I know coming here instead of waiting was definitely the right thing to do.

#THE GRAM

#Chapter40

CASANOVA87: How the hell do @NJA_Admirals make this look so easy? #IllStickToFootball #CheerFail

> ***video of Mason trying to lift Kay over his head in a full extension and dropping her (on her feet) with Kay laughing the whole time***

> **@QB1McQueen7:** Your shoulder game is weak, bruh. You better up those weights if you can't handle holding Short Stack over your head. #AshamedToCallYouMyBestFriend

CasaNova87: I swear @QB1McQueen7 you are the biggest shit-talker I know. But the proof is in the pudding…you failed too. #StopTalkingSmack

> ***video of Trav trying to do the same with Kay with the same failed result***

> **@QB1McQueen7:** Whatever! Talk to the *hand emoji* #IMeantToDoThat

CheerGodJT: You're BOTH idiots @CasaNova87 and @QB1McQueen7. Peep the t-shirt and take note of how the professionals do it, because if you break my bestie, we're gonna have words. #GetYourPenAndPaperReady #ThisIs-HowYouTellTheMenFromTheBoys

*slideshow of a picture of JT in an *If cheerleading is so easy…why can't you pick up girls?* shirt and a video of JT and Kay stunting during a practice*

@TheGreatestGrayson37: Shit that's some major shade you're throwing #DoYouNeedACoat

@QB1McQueen7: We are TOTALLY having a beer next time you're home #MyKindOfPeople

@CasaNova87: I have ZERO doubt why YOU are my girl-friend's best friend #SurroundedBySmartasses

Chapter 41

THE FIRST FEW weeks back at NJA after the holiday break usually go one of two ways. Either it takes a few days for the teams to find their groove again, or it's full steam ahead.

Luckily for us, the latter is the case this year. The NCA Nationals are just under two months away, and we've jumped right into tweaking our stunting, pyramid sequences, and tumbling passes to increase the difficulty level as much as possible while being able to hit zero (no drops or falls).

Things have been much easier since I was cleared by Dr. Nikols to resume regular activity. It's not that I need to be able to demonstrate my ideas firsthand, but Coach Kris likes to call me her "secret weapon" because of my ability to jump right into a stunt group if needed. We've found it helps our athletes master things a lot quicker when I do, and until I'm too old to do so, you bet your basket toss I'm going to do my best to help keep NJA on top. Plus, keeping up my stunting and tumbling skills is an easy way for me to keep my ass in shape, both figuratively and literally.

My Admirals are spread out warming up as I confer with Coach Tim, the other full-timer besides Coach Kris. With a quick glance toward the latter's office, I can see she's still talking with Pops and T about tomorrow. Guess we should get practice started without her.

"You're jumping in tonight, right?" Tim asks. He aged out of NJA two years before JT and me and now attends BTU, one of the other Division 1 universities in the state. They are more known for their hockey than their football. He was always one of my favorite teammates, and getting to coach with him is like a dream.

"Yup." I bend lower into a split, finishing off my own stretches.

After filling the team in on what the plan is, Tim pulls the flyer out to stand with him at the edge of the mat and I take her place. Excitement sparkles in Livi's dark eyes when I line up beside her and we wait for Tim to count us off.

"One, three, five, and seven." Tim's sure voice counts as we work through the stunt.

It's during one of the transitions down into a handstand hold that I can feel a hand out of place, and when I spin around before the final trick, the spacing under me is a hair off. It's so slight it's no wonder we couldn't spot it when we reviewed our practice tapes.

I explain what needs tweaking and switch places with my flyer. They nail it on their first try, and I can't hold in my excited whoop when they do. These kids want their Worlds title back, and nothing is going to stand in their way.

I'm as much of a sweaty mess as the team, and I wish I had enough time to shower before having to catch the red-eye to California. The commotion happening at the gym's entrance confirms it is time to leave when I look over and see E, Bette, and B have arrived. Sadly the Crabs were knocked out in the second round of the playoffs this past weekend, but the plus side is now my family is free to attend the national championship with me.

"I still can't believe Eric Dennings is your *brother*," Livi says with awe.

"Holy shit!" Olly curses, and I'm sure if Grace were nearby, she'd chastise him for his language. "Is that Ben Turner with him?"

I didn't think it was possible, but the two of them might be more adorable in their fanning out than their older brother.

"You wanna meet 'em?" I offer, only to get twin—pun intended—slack jaws in response. I roll my eyes, take both of their hands in mine, and pull them with me to my family.

Pops steps out of Coach Kris's office, and I leave the twins to bask in the moment and head his way. "You sure you're okay going in my place?" he asks after hugging me tight.

JT isn't the only Taylor sibling to be highly sought after for college teams. T may only be a junior, but already the top all-girl college cheerleading teams have been showing interest, including the U of J's White Squad, the University of Indiana, the University of Louisville, and the team playing our Hawks in the national championship, the University of Alabama.

Since we were already planning on attending the game, we made arrangements for Tessa to meet with the head coach for the Tide while we're there. The firehouse is currently short-staffed, meaning Pops has to work a shift, so I offered to serve as T's guardian for the meeting.

"Hell yeah," I assure him. I may not have accepted any of the offers I received, but I did go through the whole dog and pony show of the recruitment process with JT and know what to expect. Plus, I do have a little bit of an ulterior motive.

"Yo, Squirt," E bellows, causing Pops and me to look his way. "You ready to get this show on the road?"

"Yeah…" B tries to hide a laugh behind his hand as he drapes an arm over E's shoulder, leaning into him. "The sooner we leave, the sooner you get to see your lover boy."

I swear he and E must have bought a thesaurus so they could come up with every variation of Mase's Casanova moniker. Lover boy is one of the tamer ones, which is a good thing seeing as we are around so many people at the moment.

"You do realize it doesn't matter when we leave here because the plane isn't going to depart any earlier than its scheduled time, right?" T sasses, and Pops coughs in an effort to cover up his snort.

I want to give her props for her sarcasm, but after being separated from Mase for a week, I'm missing him more than I'd like to admit.

A weight I've grown familiar with settles in my chest thinking of all the time I'll be spending away from him next year.

I shake it off, something I've gotten good at doing, especially before I video-chat with Mase. When he sees me sad, he starts back up with his craziness about putting off entering the draft.

I'll learn to get used to the distance. I don't need him feeling, I don't know...guilty? Not sure if that's the right word or not, but I'm doing everything in my power to not give in to old insecurities. I also refuse to let him give in to them.

#Chapter42

UOFJ411: So many rumors floating around about if our #Kaysonova is really a #KaysonovaQueen but look at all this proof we found that @CasaNova87 and @QB1McQueen7 have shared in the past

slideshow of pictures—hugging, kissing, cheek kissing, heart hands—of Mason with Chrissy/Tina and Trav with Chrissy/Tina

@Acolon1729: I KNEW @QB1McQueen always seemed a little TOO FRIENDLY with her #ISeeYou

#Chapter43

ANOTHER BOWL GAME.

Another week away thanks to travel and promotional requirements that come with it.

Opposite coasts.

A three-hour time difference.

None of this helps when I'm already missing my girl something fierce.

At least the weather in Santa Clara is a nice balmy seventy degrees unlike the snow Kay was bitching about them having back home the other day.

Tomorrow we play Alabama for the title of national champions.

For the four days leading up to the game, the SAP Center is transformed to give the residents of the Bay Area, as well as all the fans traveling for the game, what they call a championship campus experience.

It all culminates in the ultimate fan event—Media Day. The free event provides fans the unique opportunity to watch and listen as members of the major national media outlets conduct their interviews with coaches and student athletes from both the U of J and the University of Alabama.

In the past, I've never really had an opinion on Media Day.

In fact, if asked, I probably would have said I quite enjoy it.

Trav and I have been known to do our interviews at these types of things together, and the press has always eaten up our story like potheads with the munchies. Childhood best friends turned teammates, offensive powerhouses with *GQ*-model good looks, future pro ballers—all of it is a reporter's wet dream.

I think the reason Brantley has been having such a hard time adjusting to the new "no comment" stance I've taken with the press is because I've never shied away from their inquiries in the past. Trav and I used to play up our story as much as we could.

What he's failing to comprehend is it isn't just about me anymore. If Kay didn't have the history she did with the press, things might be different, but for all their "media darling" stories and questions thrown out now, it doesn't change the fact that Kay has lived through the ugly side of being in the public eye.

Side by side, Trav and I make our way through the SAP Center decked out in the new custom sweatsuits Nike has provided both teams for the event. It sure beats the monkey suits we have to wear after a game, that's for sure. Over my heart is the Nike swoosh and the championship year, with the U of J Hawk logo and my number on the opposite side of my chest.

There are half a dozen smaller press conference setups spread throughout the space for the athletes who will be interviewed and one large stage with the CFP's black and gold backdrop for the coaches.

We're stopped by fans for selfies and autographs, and I do my best to enjoy the moment and not worry about how quickly these pictures will find their way onto UofJ411's page.

When it's our scheduled time, we walk to the platform underneath the electronic sign boasting both our names and sit behind the table sporting dual microphones.

Things start off fine. The first ten minutes are spent talking about the team and how we feel being the underdogs in tomorrow's game. We even have a reporter or two chuckling at our cocky answers.

Then things take a turn.

"Mason." I look at the journalist who called my name and give him a nod. "Will Kayla be at the game?"

Under the fabric-draped table, where others can't see, Trav knocks his knee into mine as a reminder to *Be cool.* As frustrated as I was with my conversation with my stepdad before I left Jersey, I took what he said to heart. Kay even shocked the shit out of me by agreeing. It's how the epic cheerleading failure happened—showing a little bit of our private life to the public without them getting to know too much.

"She'll be in the stands rooting for the Hawks to take down the Tide," I answer, keeping the team at the forefront, not my personal connection.

"How do you think she'll handle you playing for a different team than her brother next year?" a different reporter asks.

It takes everything in me not to rub the tension headache forming between my eyes. I haven't officially declared my intention to enter the draft yet, but everyone is acting like it's a done deal.

It also bugs the shit out of me how they phrase their questions any time the draft does come up. It's like they're looking for drama to stir up. Depending on the team I get drafted to, there's a distinct possibility that E and I don't play each other in the regular season.

"It should be interesting," I say diplomatically.

"Nah"—Trav props his elbow on the tabletop, resting his chin in his upturned hand—"Kay will tell E he has Bette to cheer him on so Mase can have her all to himself." One of his large hands claps me on the shoulder, and he really hams it up by giving me a wink. "The real test will be when *I'm* playing."

I scratch at the back of my neck, subtly giving him the finger. I get another wink in response. He's such a jackass.

"So the rumors are true?" The question has both of us turning from our private moment and looking out over the crowd of microphones and cameras that have seemed to double in number. "Kayla Dennings is dating both of you?"

This fucker posing as a reporter will be responsible for launching a thousand memes thanks to the *Did this moron really just ask us that?* faces Trav and I make.

"The fu—" Trav manages to catch himself, cutting off the curse before it's completed. Dropping f-bombs in front of the press is a sure-fire way to have Coach Knight thoroughly ream us out. "I'm sorry, I thought they only let *legitimate* journalists into Media Day, not storytelling paparazzi." He flattens a hand over his heart, doing his best to look contrite. "My mistake."

A buzz of discomfort rolls through the crowd gathered in front of our table. Trav's charming persona isn't just something he's known for with the ladies; it extends to his reputation with the press. Unlike me, he's never been known to lose his cool. Him being the one to put this gossipmonger in his place? Yeah, that speaks louder than words.

Trav chuckles, but there's not an ounce of humor in it. "And you wonder why my boy here"—another clap on my shoulder—"refuses to talk about his girl when you ask." He shakes his head like a parent disappointed in his child.

I wisely keep my mouth shut. I was seconds away from epically losing my shit this morning when those old pictures from the time when Chrissy/Tina played us started circulating on UofJ411. If Trav hadn't dragged me to the weight room inside the hotel as soon as they did, who knows if I would still be eligible to play tomorrow.

"I will say this once and *only* once." Trav holds up a single finger for emphasis. "Honestly, I can't believe I even have to address this bull to begin with." This he says more to me, but since he didn't cover the mic, it carries.

He's doing his best to project a devil-may-care attitude, but the vein pulsing at his temple tells me he's as close to losing it as I am.

"Kayla Dennings is Mason Nova's girlfriend—*only* Mason Nova's girlfriend." Trav hooks an arm around my shoulders, pulling me into an almost chokehold. "Mase here is my best friend, my brother from another mother, my comrade in arms on and off the field. Automatically, that makes any person important to one important to the other. If you're going to insist on trying to turn this into something it's not, we're done here."

A hushed, stunned silence follows Trav's decree, the echo of his chair scraping on the stage as he stands abruptly punctuating his words. Off to the side of the stage, I see the other guys coming closer in case we need backup. Even Coach Knight has paused in his own interview, giving us his attention.

"Does it make you nervous at all dating someone who comes from such a pedigreed football linage?"

I would say a classification like that is a bit of a stretch. Yes E is a top player in the NFL, but he's the only person in their family who has played professionally. It's not like the Dennings are the Mannings, but whatever's going to get the link clicks, right?

"Puh-lease." I mime brushing dirt off my shoulder. "This is *me* we're talking about." I haven't pulled out the cocky Casanova persona in a while; now seems appropriate.

"But you play the same position as Eric."

"Was there supposed to be a question in there somewhere?" That came out with a little more bite than it should have, but I'm approaching my limit here.

Trav barks out a laugh, going as far as wrapping an arm

over his stomach and smacking the table.

"Bro?" I ask.

When he finally composes himself, he wipes away a tear from under one of his eyes. "Sorry. I just find it hysterical they think E is the tough critic in the family."

Now I'm joining in his laughter, the two of us acting like we aren't in a formal press setup. "Gotta hand it to my boy here." I nudge Trav with my elbow. "There's no tougher Monday morning quarterback than Kay." I cup my hands around my mouth, angling toward the coaches' podium. "Sorry, not sorry, Coach." Coach Knight only touches the brim of his ball cap and tips his head at us.

"Hashtag fact." Trav makes dual peace signs and double taps them together.

"Tell me you didn't seriously hashtag in real life." If ever there was a time to channel Kay and roll my eyes, now is it.

"What?" Trav lifts his hands in the air, shrugging as if to say *What are you going to do?* "Sometimes you gotta talk in hashtags to get your point across."

"Why are we friends?"

"Like you could function without me," Trav retorts as we continue to bicker like we're not in front of over a dozen members of the press core.

I can't wait to see what Kay is going to say to you when she sees this online later.

The comment from my inner coach has me sobering instantly, and I clear my throat before refocusing my attention where it belongs to wrap this up.

"Anyway…" I clap my hands together. "Our time is up, but we'll see you all"—I snap and make finger guns at the reporters—"after the Hawks win tomorrow night." I let out a hawk cry, and the rebel yell echoes throughout the arena as all my teammates and our supporters return it.

If things play out the way I expect they will, the football game won't be the only thing they're reporting on.

#Chapter44

THE CFP NATIONAL CHAMPIONSHIP.

The big show.

The Super Bowl of Division 1 college football.

The battle for a trophy.

Playing for a ring.

The pomp.

The circumstance.

Every college player dreams of making it here. For some, it's the closest they'll get to feeling like they're playing in the NFL.

Then there's me.

I'm grumpier than a T-Rex with a back itch. Those short-armed motherfuckers never had a chance.

Why am I what Kay would call a grumpus right now? Well let me tell you. It's *because* I couldn't see her for my pregame kiss.

I *need* my pregame kiss. It's sacred.

Now I know you're saying to yourself, "Why wouldn't you get your pregame kiss, Mason? You were able to get it before the Cotton Bowl—wouldn't today be the same thing?"

And me, I would say to you, "Why yes, you would think so."

But no.

Nothing went like I planned this morning.

I blame the damn time difference. The game might be an eight o'clock start for those watching at home, but that means kickoff is at five here on the west coast.

First, Kay wasn't answering any of my texts.

So I went up to the suite she is sharing with her family, only to find out she wasn't there. The only thing to come out of that small field trip was solving the mystery of the unanswered texts—Kay accidentally left her phone behind.

I was already on the team bus heading to Levi's Stadium when I finally heard back from her. Outside of telling me she was out with Tessa, she wouldn't give me any other details, and my mood only darkened from there.

SKITTLES: Will you relax?

ME: Fat chance.

SKITTLES: *rolling my eyes* I promise it will be okay.

ME: Not likely.

SKITTLES: Wow. *wide-eyed emoji* You MUST be upset if you aren't going to make an innuendo out of my eye rolling.

She's got that right. When she still can't get the reaction or response out of me that she wants, she starts bombarding the guys' phones instead. I've lost count of the number of times

Trav nudged me with his elbow to show me his phone or Noah draped over the back of the seat to do the same. Luckily Alex and Kev took a calmer approach and only turned around so I could see theirs.

Not even a barrage of funny texts, pictures, and GIFs can make me okay with missing my pregame kiss.

I position my headphones over my ears, "Amen" by Halestorm blaring through them in my attempt to get into the zone as we step off the bus and make the trek to the locker room.

I've pulled on my pants, leaving them and my cleats untied as I lean back against my locker, when my phone vibrates with another text.

SKITTLES: What about this? Do they cheer you up at all?

Dammit! She had to go and make me crack the barest of smiles. Winking at me from the screen of my phone is Kay in today's gameday shirt—one of the ones I got her. The weather is warm enough she can get away with wearing the gauzy cropped-style shirt. The tee itself may be a looser style, but it clings to her curves and there's the slimmest sliver of skin visible between the shirt and the high-waisted band of her leggings.

The shirt itself is red, and in black reads *I like the game BUT I love the player*. There's also the outline of a football with *MASON* and *87* stamped in the middle of it.

I run my thumb over the image, her beautiful face fully on display thanks to the thick side braid ponytail thing she must have had Bette do. My favorite part is with her hair gathered together, it won't block the large NOVA #87 on the back of the shirt. I'm sure that comes as no shock to you.

Another message alert pings, and I swipe to see she also

sent me a picture of her shoes. She's rocking her red Chucks, but this time she's switched out the plain laces for ones with mini 87s printed on them.

SKITTLES: I love you. Just think about the victory kiss I'm going to lay on you after the game.

SKITTLES: *GIF of fireworks exploding*

ME: Yeah...I'm going to need much MORE than a kiss to make up for this insult.

SKITTLES: Fine. *sighs* I'll hump your brains out too.

ME: Oh you'll be sighing later for sure. And moaning, and screaming, and...

SKITTLES: Stop trying to sext me from the locker room. Listen to Zac Efron

SKITTLES: *High School Musical GIF with "Get your head in the game"*

SKITTLES: I know it's basketball, I don't wanna hear it.

She's insane, but my bad mood is officially gone.

. . .

ME: Love you too, baby.

I power down my phone and lock it away in the small safe at the top of the locker. Time to shake off the last of my nerves from not getting my kiss and follow Kay's—or I guess, Zac Efron's—advice and get my head in the game.

If last year taught us anything, it's that Alabama is one hell of an opponent. History will *not* be repeating itself.

I rip out a hawk cry, and every single person returns it.

Fuck the Tide. The is the year of the hawk.

#Chapter45

A SMALL KERNEL of guilt forms in my stomach as the guys continue to blow up my phone with texts about Mase pouting like a four-year-old because he couldn't get his pregame kiss. I'm hoping what I have planned will more than make up for the stress I've caused. Damn athletes are such superstitious fools.

My thumbnail—painted red, of course—spins the peridot band around my ring finger as I do my best to settle my nerves. What I'm about to do goes far beyond satisfying a superstition, and I'm not sure how much longer I can listen to T wax poetic about how this is my grand gesture. I brush it off any time she says that. The only person I'm doing this for is Mason, no one else.

He thinks I can't tell, but I see the way he tries to shield me when we talk, as if him censoring himself is what I need to be able to handle our upcoming reality. Or who knows, maybe he doesn't want me to think badly of Brantley.

It doesn't matter. What does is that it's time for me to stop hiding, time to step up and control *my* narrative.

Watching the footage from Mase and Trav's interview during yesterday's Media Day confirmed something for me. There will always be rumors, always be someone looking for an angle to sell a story, but it wasn't until I listened to how Trav defended both Mase and me that it hit home that I'm not alone in this battle. Also, holy shit you can*not* tell my family I said that. They'd be pissed.

I have no issue embracing who I am at The Barracks. No, PF Dennings knows she's a badass and isn't ashamed to admit she's the best damn flyer there is. It's time for me to take that attitude and apply it to the Kayla Dennings side of my life.

Better late than never.

Yes my older brother plays in the NFL and I'm so fucking proud of it. While people think this is the most important thing about him, to me it's how he altered his life to raise me when Dad died.

Yes I've experienced heartbreak—who hasn't? My loved ones refused to let my bullies win. They protected me, did their best to help create a life I was comfortable with in the wake of everything. What I didn't realize until I lost Mase all those months ago was that *I* was still letting them win.

I almost let the fear of history repeating itself keep me from experiencing the type of one-of-a-kind love my brother shares with his wife.

Mase was too stubborn to let me push him away. He wanted me, knew I wanted him too, and refused to let me deny it. Thank god for it. I love him in a way I didn't think was possible. He fought for me, for us.

So this? Me walking through the tunnel that will take T and me to the field inside Levi's Stadium? This is me taking a page from my boyfriend's playbook and showing him he's not the only one who's playing for keeps.

"Can you stop bouncing?" I put a hand on T's arm, trying to still her. She's been Miss Ants In The Pants since this morning.

"I'm sorry." She continues to push up and down on her toes. "I'm just so *excited*." That might be too tame of a word to describe her current state. She's more like Tigger after downing one of Lyle's triple espressos at Espresso Patronum.

"You don't even feel a little bit guilty, do you?" For as much as this is supposed to be my grand gesture, T is the architect of the plan.

"What should I feel guilty about?" She lays both her hands over her heart and innocently bats her baby blues at me.

"Oh, I don't know." My sarcasm ricochets off the walls back to me. "Maybe because you accepted these field passes from the Bama coach to meet with the team knowing full well you're going to end up going to the U of J."

I gotta give Coach Price props, too. Inviting Tessa to meet the members of the Crimson Tide's all-girl cheerleading squad during a game setting—such a high-profile game at that—is an experience she wouldn't get on other recruiting trips.

"How do you know I'll pick the U of J?" T challenges.

I roll my eyes as if to say *Puh-lease*. "For as close as your brother and I am, you and Savvy are a whole other level."

If I didn't know how much of a good girl T is at heart, I'd probably be afraid of the devilish, it-spells-trouble smile blooming on her pretty face. She's much too proud of herself. She can't deny it's true though.

"Have you figured out how you're going to get to Mase to kiss him?" she says, changing the subject, not wanting to admit I'm right.

I shake my head. I only have a small window to work with, and I already feel like I'm running out of time.

For those of you who've never been to a football game, the first time a team takes the field isn't when they are announced with all the fanfare that comes with hyping them up. No, before all that, both teams take to the gridiron to warm up.

Do you see what my plan is?

Mase will be on the field…

I'll be on the field…

I worry the thick lanyard around my neck, pushing away all the concerns about figuring out the *getting to Mase to kiss him* logistics, and inhale a deep breath, soaking up the grandeur in front of us as T and I step out of the tunnel onto the turf. No matter how many times I've experienced it, field access will *never* get old.

The stands are still more than half empty but will continue to fill the closer we get to kickoff.

Linking her arm with mine, T guides us toward where both Alabama cheer squads work through their own warmups. Knowing she won't walk me into anybody, I let my gaze track across the football field, searching out my man amongst the sea of white jerseys. Mase's back is to me when I finally spot the large red 87, and I take a second to admire the way his butt looks in his tight red football pants.

He really is the sexiest tight end—all the puns intended *spirit fingers*—in all of college football.

My giggle has T turning around to face me, and when she follows my line of sight, I can tell by the shake of her head she knows exactly where my, and my inner cheerleader's, thoughts have gone.

There are more than a few questioning looks sent our way as we walk along the sideline for the Crimson Tide. Maybe we should have changed into our U of J gear *after* our meeting.

"Why do I feel like we're going to be drawn and quartered for wearing enemy colors?" T says out the side of her mouth.

There's no way to stop the laugh that escapes me. "It's scary how easily you Taylors read my mind."

Having only ever cheered for a club team, this is the first time I've gotten to experience gameday preparation up close. Poms are ruffled, megaphones are stood up, and signs are stacked and laid out in order for easy access to guide the crowd in cheers for their team.

"You ladies are going to have people questioning my loyalty to the Tide coming here like that." Coach Price points to my Nova shirt and T's own *More extra than the point after a touchdown. GO HAWKS!*

"Not gonna lie"—I shake the hand held out to me—"Tessa and I are a little concerned about making it out of here alive."

"You'll be fine. I doubt anyone would want to do anything to piss off your guy." Coach Price points to Mason's name on my shirt, and I grin as he takes us around and introduces us to his cheerleaders.

It doesn't take long for them to put together who both T and I are—for cheer connections, not football—and to call over some of the co-ed squad. There's been so much focus on the whole Casanova's mystery girl side of things, I kind of forgot most of this started by my identity being leaked from a cheerleading video. It seems the viral video of JT and me messing around with stunts in a hotel's banquet hall was quite memorable.

The curiosity only grows once they realize Tessa is JT Taylor's younger sister. A blush overtakes T's creamy complexion, and for as much as I want to go into full-on older sister bragging mode, I choose to stay quiet as to not add to her embarrassment.

With T fully entrenched with the Bama cheerleaders, I step to the side to see if I can use this as my opportunity to put my own part of the plan into action.

In a stroke of luck, Em and Q are actually the first to notice me, both their jaws hanging open in shock when they do. Q's eyes dart around like *How the hell are you down here?* as one of Em's perfectly sculpted eyebrows rises in a *You do know you're on the wrong side, right?* I hook a thumb to where T is surrounded by Bama cheerleaders then point to our football team, hoping she picks up on what I need her to do.

As any good best friend would do, Em does, and I hold my breath as I watch her jog over to where Mase and Trav are huddled by their team bench. I'm too far away to read her lips, but she pokes Mase in the shoulder pad then points to me.

From across the field, I can make out the confusion written on both their faces, until they follow the line of Em's arm. The moment Mase spots me, his entire expression shifts, a wolfish smile replacing the scowl that was on his lips. Without hesitation or regard for Coach Knight shouting at him, Mase darts across the turf to the enemy's sideline.

I let out a startled squeak as I'm lifted into his arms and spun in a full circle. When he finally sets me down, my foot brushes the helmet he must have dropped to the ground to pick me up. I step on it, but even with it to stand on, there's still a few inches of height difference between us. I wrap my arms around his neck, resting my forearms along the space left between it and his pads. "Hey."

"Hey?" Mase's arms loop around my middle, pulling until my body is flush against his. "That's all you have to say for yourself?"

Ooo, some*one's still in a mood,* my inner cheerleader singsongs.

"What?" I run a thumb over the 87 Bette shaved in the side of his head last night. "You said you *needed* your pregame kiss."

He growls, legit *growls* at me and squeezes me tighter. "Do you have *any* idea how pissed I was thinking I wasn't getting it?"

"Well if the guys' texts were any indication…" I let my words trail off as I giggle. If the narrowing of his eyes is anything to go by, I'm the only one finding humor in the situation.

"Give me my damn good luck kiss, woman," he demands.

Pushing up onto my toes, I stretch up to close the last of the inches the helmet couldn't give me and seal my mouth over his.

All other thoughts cease to exist. I don't think about the thousands of people who can see us, or how many of them might be taking pictures of this, or how this is why we are "media darlings".

All my focus is on how Mase's large hands spread out on my body, covering most of my torso with one braced on my back, the other flexing along my side. The stroke of his tongue dueling with mine, the salty taste of sweat already beading on his skin…

I clutch him, my fingers kneading the muscles at the nape of his neck, wishing to be closer.

"You do know E is in the stands, right?" T's shout is like a Gatorade bath to the senses.

We end the kiss, but Mase doesn't pull away from me fully, instead resting his forehead against mine, a feat made easier by my standing on the helmet. The hard plastic of his chest protector pushes into me with each heavy breath working its way into his lungs. Peeking out between the fringe of his inky lashes, his typically light green eyes are the color of pine, and I bet if he wasn't wearing a cup, I'd be able to feel how much he is affected by our pregame ritual.

"Guess it's a good thing he's on the other side of the stadium, huh?" he asks T, but his eyes never leave mine.

"Um…" The uneasiness in T's voice has us both looking her way. Her arm is stretched out toward something to my left, Mase's right. As we swivel around to see what she's pointing out, there we are, on the jumbotron. The image of me cradled in Mase's arms is a few stories tall.

I bury my face into Mase's chest. "Shit."

"Guess we'll be trending two times today," Mase says with an air of pride.

"Two times?" I furrow my brow. Was UofJ411 already at it and T forgot to tell me?

"Yeah." Mase kisses my nose, and I almost lose my footing from swooning so hard. It's such a gentle gesture when he's all dressed for battle. "Don't pretend today's celebration kiss won't go viral like the others."

"That confident you guys will win?" I can't help but tease.

"Now that I got my kiss"—he goes in for one more drugging kiss on my lips—"you bet your sweet ass we will." He reaches down and gives said ass a squeeze.

"*Mason.*" I squeal, giving him a backhand to the chest.

"Sorry." He sounds anything but. "I couldn't resist."

"*Oooooo.*" T's voice cuts in again. "E is going to kill you," she singsongs, bouncing a finger at the jumbotron again.

"Totally worth it." Mase's grin is pure cocky Casanova. "Gotta go, babe. I'll see you back here after the game."

"Only if you win," I taunt, stepping down from my perch.

Bending over, he scoops his helmet from the ground. "You're gonna pay for that later," he whispers in my ear before straightening all the way, the dark promise making me wish it were later now.

He's halfway across the field before my wits return enough for me to call out, "Promises, promises."

His wink tells me he plans on delivering.

Oh man. What did I just get myself into?

#THE GRAM

Chapter 46

UOFJ411: Not even a road game can keep our king from getting his pregame good luck kiss from his queen #Kaysonova #FootballRoyalty #CoupleGoals

    picture of Kay standing on Mason's helmet as they kiss

    @Annielaurel: They are like a human kiss cam #KissCam #Kaysonova

UofJ411: I don't think @CasaNova87 is bothered by this at all #CoachIsGonnaBenchYou #Kaysonova

    TikTok of Mason and Kay kissing followed by Coach Knight hitting Mason upside the head with his laminated play sheets

    @AshWonderWoman: Oooo…someone is in trouble #NotHowYouWarmUp #CasanovaWatch

UofJ411: It's a good thing you're such a big guy @CasaNova87 because @EricDennings87 does NOT look impressed #IAmEntertained *picture of E, B, Bette, and CK in the stands, E and B with their arms crossed, Bette giving two thumbs-up, and CK shaking his head*

@Beccalynn1010: Oh to be a fly on that wall #OverprotectiveBrother

#Chapter47

THE ATTENTION from wearing U of J gear in Alabama territory was like the warm-up compared to the eyes I feel locked on me after the whole jumbotron incident. Not wanting to risk being swarmed, T and I beat feet back to our seats with our family.

Thanks to the six inches she has on me, I practically have to skip to keep up, and by the time we collapse into the empty chairs saved for us, I'm out of breath.

"Eighty-seven feeling alright?" B throws an arm around my shoulders with a knowing smirk.

"Yeah. Why wouldn't he be?"

CK stretches an arm between the chairs, waving a hot pretzel in my face. I look over my shoulder, giving him a wink of thanks.

"Just checking." B shrugs, staring off at the football field with a blank expression on his face. "Your tongue spent a lot of time inspecting his tonsils, so I wasn't sure."

I blink, freezing with my jaw open, pretzel halfway to my mouth. When B tips his chin and catches sight of my expression, he falls over, guffawing.

"You're an asshole."

The jerk has the audacity to try to steal a bite of my snack.

"Don't pick on my girl." Bette leans across the seats to cuff B on the back of the head. "Mark my words, Benjamin"—she wags a finger in his face—"one day you're gonna meet a chick who's gonna knock you on your ass, and payback is going to be a bitch."

"Yeah, a tiny one," B chokes out around a laugh, dodging the second head smack from Bette.

I love this woman so much. I know I've said it before, but I don't think I'll ever be able to say it enough. I would love her forever just for loving my brother the way she does, but everything she's done for me in the six years she's been in our lives has earned her a permanent spot up on a pedestal in my mind.

"Well this is a change," CK says, passing his phone to me.

"What is?" I respond, keeping my eyes on him and not the screen.

He points down. "You guys usually wait until the *end* of the game to go viral."

Finally looking down, I see a snapshot of our kiss. Our size difference has never been more obvious. With Mase in his full football gear and me standing on the helmet, I almost look like a child compared to his massive bulk.

There's nothing childish about the kiss they captured, though. My front is pressed so tightly against his there's not even a sliver of light peeking through. My hands are clutching his hair, and the fingers of one of his hands are splayed out, creeping down to cup my ass.

The shot was taken on a forty-five-degree angle instead of directly from the side, and combining this with the side-braided ponytail Bette did my hair in, the NOVA and #87 on my back are plain for the world to read.

Oh, he's going to be so happy about that.

"That's hot, but these are my fave." T jumps into the conversation, scrolling through the other posts shared by UofJ411.

"This is ridiculous." I shake my head but can't help but laugh as the TikTok video of Coach Knight scolding Mase replays.

"Fucking right it is," E grumbles. The tension in his jaw is the first sign of something darker, almost dangerous brewing under the surface. Nothing can flip E's switch faster than thinking something could hurt me, or use me.

Which reminds me…

I need to make a conscious effort to keep E away from Brantley. I do not foresee the two of them in a room together going over well.

I still can't believe E went along with my plan for Liam. He was so hell-bent on revenge I had legitimate doubts he would be on board.

Are you ever going to tell Mase about what you did?

Well shit. That is *not* the type of reminder I need from my conscience. I am putting *that* conversation off as long as I can get away with it.

Bette must sense the same thing in E that I do, because she smooths a hand along his jaw and pinches his cheek. "You two really do share some epic kisses." She jerks a chin down. "It's like something out of a movie." She's all dreamy-like, really gushing over the picture.

I know what she's doing. If the way she wiggles her eyebrows at me is any indication, *she* knows I know what she's doing. E is the only one not onto his wife's plan. That's probably for the best, because if he were, he might not take the distraction bait.

"I'll show you a kiss good enough for the movies, woman." E hauls Bette out of her seat and into his lap, dipping her back and laying one on her.

The rest of us, along with probably our entire section, cheer and catcall. B snaps pictures like the paparazzi. By the time my brother releases his wife, her face is flushed and she's looking a little dazed. E leans back in his seat, a satisfied smug expression on his face.

"Try to tell me *that* won't go viral." He snatches B's phone from him and posts a few of the pictures to his Instagram.

The marching bands for both schools each take their turn doing their thing for the pregame entertainment, T dancing in her seat and pulling B in to join her. CK rests his head between my shoulder blades, his body shaking with restrained laughter when B starts to vogue. I slyly record these fools and send the video to G, who couldn't travel with us this time because the Hawks basketball team has a game of their own tomorrow.

Both Alabama and U of J use AC/DC's "Thunderstruck" as their entrance songs when they play in their home stadiums, so when it blares from the sound system, a familiar rush comes over the entire crowd. Seventy-five thousand fans scream and cheer as a sea of red and white take the field. Not much of a color variance between the schools.

A pop star sings the national anthem with a fighter jet flyover as the big finish.

There's an undercurrent of anticipation as Mase and the other captains head out to the fifty for the coin toss. This game isn't just a national championship; it's a rematch, a game of redemption for the Hawks.

With his hands hooked into the collar of his jersey and pads, Mase stalks behind the team bench for our other game-time ritual. Kissy sounds fill my ears, and I see E and B each blowing exaggerated kisses down to my boyfriend.

E goes stock-still when Mase holds his hand up in our family's hang-loose gesture. With wide eyes and a hung jaw, he swivels to face me. "That's our thing."

I bite the inside of my cheek to hold back a laugh and nod. Why does he sound betrayed?

"He knows what it means?"

I shake my head. "He's never asked." Mase knows the

basics—it's why he's been doing it since he surprised me at one of our cheer competitions—but he doesn't know that the gesture stems from E.

"Hmm," E hums. "No wonder you're willing to freeze your butt off in the stands to cheer him on when he plays."

Aww. I think someone is feeling a bit salty.

"Leave your sister alone," Bette chastises. I'm surprised she didn't say anything when she saw Mase do it during the Cotton Bowl. E tugs her close and kisses her temple. Joining Bette in the WAGs box is why I typically don't watch his games from the stands once the mercury on the thermometer no longer reaches north of fifty degrees.

Me sitting my butt in the stands in more layers than I can count and letting myself get pelted by rain was one of my brother's first clues to how deep my feelings are for Mase.

But like my inner cheerleader said...he's salty about it. Doesn't stop me from reminding him how today it's a balmy seventy degrees here in Santa Clara. Sure as hell beats the four inches of snow we left behind in Jersey.

"*Eep!* I'm so excited." T's ants are back in her pants as she wiggles around in her seat clapping.

"Me too," CK agrees, causing all of us to look at him in surprise. "What?" He shrugs, blushing at all the attention. "Is it wrong that I'm looking to forward to seeing E have to root for the Hawks?"

T snorts, reaching out a fist for CK to bump. "Oh yeah, I bet it breaks his little Nittany Lion heart."

E scoffs. "Who says I'm not cheering for the Tide?"

"*Right...*" CK drags the word out into long multiple syllables.

"You would never," T confirms. "You value your eyebrows too much."

When T and I fall over each other in laughter, B perks up, sniffing out the potentially embarrassing story about his friend like Scooby-Doo looking for Scooby Snacks. We promptly fill him in on the time E and JT had an unfortunate encounter with a buzzer growing up.

With the shrill of the referee's whistle, the first half starts and the battle of the offenses begins, each team trading touchdowns.

"I know everyone has been talking about Mase declaring for the draft, but has Trav made any noise about it?" B asks after the man in question throws a bomb of a spiral to Alex for another Hawks touchdown.

I breathe through the anxiety that comes on any time someone brings up the draft and the reminder that this routine we've settled into, this life we are creating is going to look completely different in a few short months.

"Noah is the only one who has said anything." Our resident jokester is a senior, and with his golden toe, he's a shoe-in to get drafted.

Trav is the wildcard. He redshirted as a freshman, and based on things he's said, I get the impression he wants to play out one, if not both, of his eligibility years.

Thankfully, a wide receiver for the Crimson Tide breaks a tackle and runs the ball into the end zone, bringing our attention back to the once-again tied game.

Whichever defense is the first to make a stand will end up the victor.

I fucking love football.

Chapter 48

BACK IN THE locker room for halftime, Kev throws his helmet, causing it to bounce off the back of his locker and roll onto the floor. The room is silent as we watch him stalk his way around it, his frustration clear every time his feet pound into the ground.

No one says a word, each of us keeping our distance while Kev works through his shit. I get it. The defense isn't playing bad per se, but they also haven't been playing up to the standard they set for themselves this season.

"Listen up, Hawks." Coach Knight walks into the center of the room, his bellow drawing the attention of each of his athletes immediately.

Slowly and with great purpose, he rakes his gaze over each and every one of his players, not stopping until he comes to Trav standing beside me. We wait, Trav's shoulder pads clacking against mine as he sucks in a breath in preparation for Coach Knight's speech, but it never comes. All Trav gets is a small nod, and his relief is palpable at the silent *Just keep doing what you've been doing.*

Coach Knight scans the huddle again. "Sanders," he says, locking eyes with Kev. "You and the D need to shake off the first half." Kev nods. "It's a tie game. We get back out there starting fresh." Another nod. "Bama starts with the ball, so come out hitting hard. Show them the Tide doesn't stand a chance against a flock of Hawks."

A wall of sound hits Coach as every person in the room releases a hawk cry.

"Show them who we are." Coach thumps a fist to his chest. "They may think they want it. But"—*thump*—"we"—*thump*—"want"—*thump*—"It. More." *Thump. Thump.* "They"—he thrusts an arm at the doors to the locker room—"*robbed* us of the win last year." He swings his arm around and aggressively points to the ground. "*History*. Will. *Not* be repeating itself this year."

This time, he's the first to let the hawk cry rip.

Adrenaline surges, energy pumping through the team, rolling off us in waves as we rush down the tunnel and back onto the field for the second half, ready to dominate.

We surround Kev, smacking the hawk on his helmet, pumping him up to get to work. Trav, Alex, Noah, and I stand shoulder to shoulder, arms crossed as a unit, and get ready to enjoy the show.

Whatever was missing in the first half has sparked to life and radiates off the defense as they get into position with the Alabama O-line.

First down is a two-yard gain.

The second only gets another three.

On third and five, Kev intercepts a pass meant for one of Bama's wide receivers, stiff-arms a lineman out of the way, breaks a block, and with no one else there to defend, runs it in for a touchdown. Pick six baby!

With the Hawks scoring, the Tide gets another attempt at offense, but Kev and the D hold them to a three and out, making them punt.

The momentum officially becomes ours.

Time for us to do our thing and see if we can extend our lead by hopefully another seven points.

We work our way down to the Bama twenty.

Trav pump-fakes. I tuck the ball tight to my side when he hands it off to me, find a hole, and don't stop running until I cross the white paint of the end zone.

Time ticks down, and with a beautifully launched spiral from the Alabama quarterback, they cut our lead back down to seven.

Halfway into the fourth quarter, Coach Knight takes a risk on fourth down, calling for Noah to attempt a fifty-four-yard field goal. It's only a risk in the sense that if he misses, the Tide will start with great field position—but this is Noah we're talking about. The pigskin sails through the uprights, once again making it a two-score game.

With a quarterback sneak from Alabama, we're only up by three.

An onside kick and seven plays culminating in a touchdown later, Alabama has the lead for the first time this half.

Time only seems to speed up the closer we get to the two-minute warning.

We huddle and clap to break.

Trav calls the play.

I line up on the outside.

Alex lines up in the slot.

The center hikes the ball.

I take off like a bat out of hell.

The O-line holds firm, giving Trav enough time to settle into the pocket, launching a bomb into my waiting arms.

Touchdown.

Timeouts are called to stop the clock from ticking down.

Sweat trickles down the back of my neck under my jersey, but I pay it no mind, keeping my hands hooked into the collar, my fingers digging into my shoulder pads as Alabama fights for yardage until it's fourth and inches. They need to go for it, still too far away to attempt a field goal.

Hut-hut.

The ball is snapped, and it spins in the quarterback's fingertips as he looks for an eligible receiver, the lack of time forcing him into a passing play.

The roar from the crowd is deafening as we collectively hold our breath to see what will happen. It all comes down to these last few seconds.

Bam!

Kev drills the quarterback into the turf, his sack securing the win for the Hawks.

The benches clear, the coaches and players meeting midfield and shaking hands for the cameras.

Dumping my helmet on our bench, I round it to where my girl is jumping up and down, losing her mind cheering for our win.

"SKITTLES!" I shout up to her.

She stops jumping when she hears my voice, grabbing the rail in front of her, bending down so I can hear her better. "Congratulations, Caveman." Her smile shines brighter than the golden championship trophy.

"Get your fine ass down here."

She gives me a look like I've lost my mind. "Are you crazy?"

"Nope." I hold my arms up, making *come here* motions with my hands. "Climb over, I'll catch you."

It's barely a drop at all, and she looks to her brother and Bette. With their green light, she lifts a leg and climbs over the side, hanging into a crouch and dropping into my waiting arms.

"Hey, babe." I lower her to the ground.

"You're nuts. You know that, right?" Kay's arms wrap around my neck, not caring that my jersey is soaked with sweat.

"You love me though." I bend to take my victory kiss. I keep it shorter than I would like, knowing there are post-game interviews I'm required to give. At least this way I get to have her with me.

Hoisting her up by the hips, I settle her ass to sit on my shoulder.

"What the *hell* are you *doing*?" She squeals as I adjust her to wrap my arm over the top of her thighs, anchoring her against me nice and tight.

"Taking my trophy."

"They haven't presented it yet, you goof."

"When are you going to learn?" I turn my head to nip at her thigh. "You're my trophy." I find the guys huddled together and drop Kay in the middle.

"Short Stack."

"Smalls."

"Your Highness." Noah punctuates his greeting with a bow, earning him a shoulder shove from Kay before she's passed around for another round of sweaty hugs.

"I'm so happy for you guys." She beams, all her focus on us and not the melee happening around us.

She's still bouncing on the balls of her feet when I tuck her back under my arm, her fingers automatically coming up to trace the lines of my tattoo. She starts recounting all her favorite highlights of the game, and it's adorable how amped up she gets from watching us play.

I don't want to hear it, I warn my inner coach, cutting off what I know would be his response to calling Kay adorable. I don't care. She is, and she couldn't possibly be more perfect for me.

Red, black, white, and silver rectangular squares of confetti dance and swirl in the air, pieces of it getting stuck on us as they land. Camera flashes pop all around us, but we stay in our small circle.

My eyes cross at the silver sparkle on my nose, and Kay

reaches up to pluck it away as the first on-field reporter finds his way into the fold. I relax the hold of my arm, but Kay makes no attempt to back away.

Her smile stays firmly in place as she listens to Stan, the reporter, do his thing. I'm not sure she's aware she's doing it, but I feel her tense any time the draft is mentioned. With all the other drama in our lives, she's never really allowed us to discuss our future. Any time I've brought up delaying entering the draft, she's either blown it off or told me I'm being ridiculous.

Deep down, I know being drafted to a city far away wouldn't end our relationship. Kay is my future, and I'm hers. That doesn't mean I haven't thought about what that future should look like in the upcoming years.

I have.

Long and hard.

"So, Mason." Stan twists to give me his full attention now that he's done with Noah. "All year you've been projected to be a top-five pick if you were to declare for the draft. Anything you'd like to say now that the season is officially over?"

I look down at Kay. She's still smiling, but I see the strain behind her gray eyes, and her pulse beats erratically beneath my fingers on her nape.

"I've actually been thinking about the draft a lot this season, Stan."

Kay's nails pinch hard through my jersey as she clutches at me, nervous energy radiating from her. I lock eyes with her while I speak to Stan.

"I've decided I'm *not* going to declare this year."

"*What?*" Her voice is a shocked gasp as she turns to stone under my arm.

"I've decided to play out my eligibility with the Hawks."

I'm vaguely aware that the guys are reacting to the news

as well, but I ignore them and the barrage of questions coming from Stan. Every bit of my consciousness is on the silent girl at my side, storm clouds rolling inside the glare she sends my way.

"Skittles?" I smooth a thumb along the hard jut of her jaw.

"What the—" She cuts off the curse, aware of the camera trained on us. "What the *what*?"

I chuckle. I told you she was adorable.

"Yeah, babe?" I cup her cheek.

"You *can't* be serious." It's a statement, not a question. To her, Brantley, and hell, most of America, me declaring for the draft was a forgone conclusion. If you had asked me prior to September, I would have agreed. Then I saw Grayson spinning her around inside The Nest and the trajectory of my future changed.

"As a heart attack, baby."

Kay's eyes flare, a full ring of white showing around her irises, incredulity bleeding off her as she knocks the heel of her hand to my forehead. "Are you concussed? Is that it? Did you take a hard hit to the head with one of your tackles? This is *nuts*."

There's that sass I love so much. It doesn't bother me in the least that it's being broadcasted to the millions across America watching us on TV.

"Why?" I ask, and she growls when I deepen my dimples.

She blinks. And blinks again. And again. "It's the NFL."

"So?" I shrug.

"*So?*" Oh that's not a good octave. "Mason, it's the National Football League."

Ooo, full-named. Careful…someone is getting feisty.

"I'm well aware of what the acronym stands for, babe." I reach for her as she steps out of my hold.

"But it's your *dream*." Her voice softens, almost sounding like she's heartbroken as she says it. *God.* The way she wants this for me as badly as I have my entire life is why I'm ass over cleats in love with her.

"And it will still be my dream next year." I cup her nape again and bring her back to me. "You're now a part of that dream." I tighten my grip at the shine overtaking her gaze. She looks at me like I've hung the moon. A guy could get addicted to that. "It's a win-win for me. I get to try for a repeat"—I hold my helmet out and the guys bump it with theirs—"*and* get to spend more time with you before moving to god knows where and being apart until you graduate."

I wait, prepared for her to issue another argument, but it never comes. Instead, her hands come up, clutching my jersey tight in her grasp, the move catching me so off guard she manages to tug me down to her, sealing her mouth over mine. Our lips, teeth, and tongues clash in the most fervid kiss we've *ever* shared.

Who knows how long it takes for me to remember our audience and the interview I'm supposed to be in the middle of. When I do, I pull back, whispering, "Later," against her lips.

It take a moment for Kay to do the same, and when she blinks herself out of her daze, she buries her face into my sweaty, game-played armpit in mortification.

My dick is pressing against my jockstrap in painful fashion, but at least it's preventing me from embarrassing myself on national television. I have to clear the passion from my throat before I can continue.

"So yeah…" I bring my attention back to Stan. "That's the plan." After saying our goodbyes and thanks to the reporter, I scoop my girl into my arms and get ready for the trophy presentation.

The trophy.

The reporters.

The flashing cameras.

The cheering fans.

None of it matters the way the blonde with the rainbow-colored highlights who's wearing my name on her body and filming us on her iPhone does.

If they didn't know already, now the world knows it too. I dare them to try to come between us.

#Chapter49

AFTER MASE PROFESSING his love for me over football, on national *freaking* television, I have been walking around in sort of a daze. I couldn't begin to tell you how I ended up back at our hotel's bar, in a back booth sandwiched between my brother and B.

There's food, drinks, and multiple conversations going on, but I'm stuck in this kind of hazy blur trying to figure out if this is real life.

This man…this handsome, talented, future hall-of-fame-worthy football player would risk the millions of dollars guaranteed for a top-five draft pick to be with me. *Me*. Kayla Dennings, the girl who wasn't good enough for her mom to stick around for, is being valued above a lifelong dream. I can't quite wrap my brain around it.

Every flat-screen hanging around the posh bar is tuned to the postgame coverage, the highlights and interviews playing on an infinite loop.

The sound of Mase's deep voice telling me—and the millions of viewers watching—that I'm his new dream replays again, and T lets out a dreamy sigh—again. I fold my arms over the tabletop, burying my face inside them and wishing I could apparate to my room like Harry Potter when I feel the heat of everyone's gaze on me.

"He's like a real-life book boyfriend," T comments. Chick loves her romance novels.

"Who knew my brother had it in him to be so swoony." I hear Livi agree, the twins having met up with us once they made it back to the hotel.

"I don't know…" All my girly bits stand up and shake their pom-poms at the sound of Mase's deep voice in person. "I thought I already had a pretty good track record." He presses a kiss to the back of my lowered head and strokes a finger along his birthstone band I wear.

"That was when you were trying to win her back," Livi counters.

"Yeah." I don't have to see T to know her arms are folded across her chest as she leans to the side with a *Who are you to say?* attitude. "It's totally different when the things you do are to redeem yourself for being a *moron*."

Em snorts and Q giggles, the air shifting with what I can only assume are arms being stretched out for knuckle bumps of appreciation.

"*Dayumn*," Trav whistles. "Burned by the little sisters." He tells the girls to scoot to make room.

With my head still resting on my arms, I turn my face so it's no longer buried and look toward my boyfriend.

Holy hotness, Batman.

There are many, *many* looks of Mase's that I love—his ever-present backward ball cap, him in full football gear, and of course, naked—but this right here? Yup, it's pushing its way to the top of my list.

Putting Christian Grey to shame, Mase wears what can only be a custom-made three-piece suit. Yes, you heard that right, *three-piece*, vest and all. The fabric looks as soft as million-thread count sheets, hugging his broad shoulders and molding to the muscles of his arms such that, even when relaxed, you can tell how big they are. The button on the jacket is undone, displaying how the vest accentuates the tapering of the V-line of his waist.

His crisp white button-up contrasts with his olive complexion, making his unshaven jaw fashionable. The scruff may be longer than usual, but it's still short enough not to hide his panty-melting smile or brain-cell-killing dimples. Shit, between them and his declaration, I practically turned into a puddle on whatever yard line I was standing on earlier.

There's a green small-weave plaid in his tie that brings out the brightness of his seafoam green eyes, highlighting all the different colored flecks swimming in my favorite irises.

To sum it up, he's sex on stupidly tall legs.

I need the fuzziness in my brain to clear so I can properly calculate how long we have to stay here before I can drag him off by that tie of his. Everything about him calls to me, and the insides of my thighs burn remembering how his scruff felt between them the last time it was this long.

I swallow thickly as I watch him take me in with similar intensity.

"Shit! I feel like I need a cigarette just looking at you two." B rises from the booth so Mase can take his place.

"Not something a brother should have to see," E complains.

"Hear, hear." Trav thumps his fist onto the tabletop twice.

I jackknife in my seat, whipping my head around to face my brother so fast my ponytail swings around and hits me in the face. "Are you flipping kidding me with this?" I thrust an accusatory finger in E's face then wiggle it between him and Bette. "When you two first got together, you couldn't be more than five feet from her at *all times*. If you were in the same room, you were *always* touching." I hold my hand out, palm facing up, waving my arm up and down. "Nothing's changed." E has his arm hooked over Bette's leg that's closest to him, his hand cupping her knee, drawing figure eights with his thumb over the denim-clad joint. Bette chuckles at his side, and E wisely chooses to keep quiet, knowing I'm right.

Honestly, I love how even six years into their relationship, they feel the need to always be touching, but I'm not going to let him get away with being a hypocrite. It goes against my nature.

Noah, Kev, and Alex find their way over to us, and although we've chosen one of the large rounded corner booths, they need to drag over chairs from nearby tables to fit.

We're a mishmash of chaos. There are shouts, jokes, and FaceTime calls to wake G up and to rub it in to JT that he's missing out. Any food that was left is consumed in seconds, and we place an order for another round with the waitress.

"If you don't stop looking at me like that, I'm going to drag you out of here right fucking now, Skittles," Mase whispers hotly into my ear, dragging his teeth along the outer edge.

A bolt of heat zips down my spine, and I shiver. "Like what?"

"Like you want to rip my suit off, buttons flying, so you can fuck me...hard." He punctuates the last word by biting down on my earlobe.

Holy hell. I really need to start wearing underwear with leggings around him.

I need to swallow, twice, to clear the saliva pooling in my mouth and be able speak. "Who says I *don't* want that?"

"*Fuuuck*, babe. You ha—"

The rest of his sentence is cut off by Brantley storming up to our table. "Mason. A word." It's not a request; it's a command.

Slowly, without a care in the world, Mase shifts to face his stepfather, an arm dropping behind my back and hooking over my hip protectively.

From beneath my lashes, I surreptitiously glance in the

direction of my brother to find his back ramrod straight, eyes locked onto Mase's stepdad. This could get ugly fast.

"Now's not the time." Mase's voice is hard, harder than I've ever heard it before.

"It certainly is if we're going to fix this," Brantley retorts.

The tension around the table crackles violently.

"Nothing's broken." The grip of his fingers on my hip turns bruising.

"The hell there isn't." Brantley crosses his arms over his chest. "This is your *career* we're talking about."

Mase lets out a frustrated growl, his hand running through his carefully styled hair. "You know what?" He rises from the booth, grabbing my hand and pulling me along with him. "We'll see you guys in the morning," he says to our friends and family, ignoring his stepdad completely.

"Mason," Brantley shouts, but Mase never slows his long strides. His steps are angry, and I have to jog to keep up or risk of being pulled behind him like *Just Married* decorations on a limo.

The way he punches the button for the elevator like it personally offends him makes me think he's imagining it's Brantley's face. This side of him, the barely restrained protective caveman is what has me scared of how he'll react when he finds out he's not the only one who made a life-changing decision.

Knowing this is why I can't yell at him for deciding what he did without talking to me about it.

There's a ping announcing the elevator's arrival, and he stalks inside as soon as the doors slide open. Another pair of people attempt to get on with us but wisely step back when they catch the look of danger dancing in Mase's hooded eyes.

He doesn't wait for the door to fully close before he's boxing me in against the wall. His palms flatten on either side of my head, his knuckles blanching as he flexes his fingers, trying to rid himself of the anger coursing through his body.

His hard chest brushes mine with every nostril-flaring breath.

My eyes fall shut in anticipation of a kiss that never comes. Instead, I jump when the prickly hair of his scruff drags down the length of my neck, my head tilting to the side to grant him better access.

The vibrations underneath my fingertips should scare me, but at my core I know I have nothing to fear when it comes to Mason.

Doesn't change the fact that I'm in trouble.

#Chapter50

THE ADRENALINE FROM THE GAME.

The high of the win.

The relief from finally admitting and solidifying my plans about delaying entering the draft.

The way Kay eye-fucked the shit out of me when she saw me in my Tom Ford suit.

Brantley trying to forcibly voice his displeasure about *my* decision for *my* future.

All of these things are like ingredients in a recipe, but instead of a delicious dish, I feel more like a 2-liter bottle of soda getting Mentos shoved into it.

All I want to do is bury myself inside my girlfriend and forget anything else except the way she feels wrapped around me until morning, except I'm feeling so fucking volatile I'm afraid I'll break her.

Ding!

The elevator arrives on my floor and I spin on my heel as the doors open with a whoosh, dragging Kay out of the steel box like the caveman she jokingly calls me. As I hear her footsteps rushing to keep up, I take heart in the fact that at least I'm taking her by the hand and not the hair.

The keycard gives me issues, the force of me shoving it

into the slot causing the plastic to bend during the first two attempts at unlocking the door. When the green light finally blinks, I throw the door open and haul Kay inside.

The door slams shut, the sound echoing my ferocity. The only illumination in the room comes from the bathroom light bleeding out around the open door. The light is limited, but what I can see shocks the shit out of me.

Instead of wide-eyed apprehension, heat is the only thing burning in Kay's stormy gaze. She wants me; that much is plain to see. If I go to her now, there's no way her under-five-foot frame will be able to absorb the pressure brewing inside me.

I roll my shoulders back, shrugging out of my jacket and dropping it to the floor like it's a towel after a shower and not a piece from a five-thousand-dollar ensemble.

My hands come up, working to loosen the knot of my tie but not completely undoing it. Next up, I start to work the buttons on my vest open, Kay's eyes tracking each one as it slips from its buttonhole.

As the vest flutters to the ground in a whisper of silk, she snaps out of her trance, her chin tilting up the slightest inch before she does the same with her red shirt, pinching the material between two fingers, holding it out, eyes daring me as she lets go. She's beyond aroused, the rapid rise and fall of her chest as well as the pink blush covering it telling me as much. The black lace demi bra cupping her breasts has me wanting to tear into it where her nipples poke through the spaces in the flower detailing.

She toes off her red Chucks, only breaking eye contact when she bends with a flat back to peel her leggings down her toned legs. There's nothing overtly sexual about her movements, but the fluidity of them makes it seem like the hottest strip show.

Fuck!

I'd forgotten that she prefers to go commando when she

wears leggings, and I bite down on my cheek hard enough to draw blood when I see the evidence of her arousal glistening on the bare lips of her pussy.

Her arms bend, elbows sticking out to the sides as she reaches behind her to undo her bra, giving it the same treatment as her shirt. I'm so mesmerized by the sight that my fingers stop halfway through undoing the buttons on my Oxford shirt.

Fuck me if I couldn't come on the spot just from looking at her. Nothing, I mean *nothing* is hotter than Kay naked.

Precum leaks onto my boxer briefs with each soft padded step she takes in my direction.

My body locks up for an entirely different reason as she drops to her knees and reaches for my belt. I don't move a muscle as she deftly works the leather through the silver buckle and carefully drags the zipper down over my straining erection, her small hands lifting my cock and my balls over the elastic band of my underwear. My dick is nothing to sneeze at—I'm six foot five and proportionate *all* over—but in her tiny hands, it looks like a fucking beast.

I reach out to brush a rogue curl from her beautiful face, and without warning, she deep-throats the shit out of my cock, her lips kissing the skin at the base as she swallows around my length.

"*Fuck Kay,*" I hiss, doing my best not to explode on the spot.

When she moans, the only sound she's able to make with a mouth full of my dick, the possibility of embarrassing myself increases tenfold with the way it makes her vibrate around me.

My fingers dig into her hair, fucking up the braided whatever she has going on, holding on for dear life at the eroticism of my naked girlfriend bobbing on my dick like it's her job while I remain mostly clothed. My head thunks against the door at how the tables have turned. Here I was worried I would devour her when in reality it's my little pixie who gets to claim the honor.

The tell-tale tingle forms at the base of my spine, and I tug on her hair harshly until she releases me with an audible pop. I plan on coming multiple times tonight, but I'll be damned if the first time I do it's down her throat.

"I *need* to fuck you." My voice sounds like I swallowed gravel.

She arches one of her sculpted brows. "Isn't that what you were just doing?" She's the one down on her knees, but fuck me if she doesn't own me.

"Go to the dresser," I instruct.

One of the first things I noticed when we checked into our room was the giant rectangular mirror hanging on the wall above the long dresser. Since the time I took Kay in the bathroom in our hotel in Kentucky, I have been trying to find any way I can to fuck her bent over in front of something reflective. It allows me to get the visual stimulation of fucking her from behind while simultaneously watching her face contort in the pleasure I make her feel. Best of both worlds.

I slide my shoes off, kicking my pants and boxer briefs away as I stalk to the lamp in the opposite corner of the room. I'm going to need more light if I'm going to fully appreciate this. I finally finish removing my shirt, but when I reach for my tie, an idea hits me and I leave the knot intact as I slip it over my head.

With my left arm, because I know what the sight of my tribal ink does to her, I reach for Kay, capturing both her wrists easily, and place the loop of the tie around them, pulling the skinny end until it's tight. It's barely a restraint—all she has to do is separate her wrists and she'll be free—but it doesn't stop her pupils from being fully blown out with lust. Personally, my favorite is how the bound position has the added bonus of thrusting her tits out.

My turn to get on my knees.

The plush carpet is relief on my joints, but it could be rock-hard concrete for all I care.

I cup a breast in each of my hands, kneading the flesh and sucking a nipple into my mouth before giving the other equal treatment. I bite and suck all over the creamy globes, a trail of light pink beard burn evidence of the path I take down Kay's tempting body.

I follow the spatter of beauty marks over her toned stomach like a treasure map to her dripping pussy, the musky scent of her arousal filling my senses.

Fuck I *love* how turned on she gets from giving me plea-sure, the bud of her clit trying to peek through the plump lips of her pussy. My hands follow the line of her curves, into the dip of her narrow waist and along the flare of her hips then sliding around to cup her ass, anchoring her in my hold as I pull her toward my mouth and seal it over her cunt.

"*Mase.*" The broken plea of my name is everything.

I have no patience to tease. I need her to come all over my face, and I need her to do it right fucking now. My tongue spears her entrance, lapping up the honey dripping from it, rolling it up to her clit, and pulsing until she explodes.

Kay screams her release, my mouth never leaving her body until she comes down. Resting back on my heels, I wipe the excess from my face and rise to my feet, spinning her around to face the mirror.

"Hold on tight to the dresser," I command after freeing the tie from her wrists.

Like a good girl, she bends over, arching in that perfect way she knows drives me out of my goddamn mind. Her elbows anchor her, and her forearms stretch long until her fingers curl over the edge of the dresser. In the reflection of the mirror, she meets my gaze, another dare swimming in their depths.

Fuck me she's a wet dream.

I crowd her until the fronts of my thighs hit the backs of

hers, lifting her leg until her knee is also resting on the dresser top, fucking grateful for the ridiculous flexibility all her years of cheerleading afford me. Gripping myself at the base, I run the head of my dick through her wetness, her head falling forward as I slide along her slit and tease her swollen clit with the tip.

Wanting her eyes on mine as I fill her, I wrap her ponytail around my hand and tug until her head rises and those pools of charcoal stare back at me.

I breathe, taking it all in.

Bracing my elbow next to one of hers, I lean over so my body blankets hers. "Watch, baby," I murmur against the shell of her ear. "Watch me take you." A tremor racks her body as I drag my cheek down the column of her throat.

Bending my knees, I line myself up with her entrance and push inside her...slowly, looking down to do my own watching as, inch by inch, my dick disappears inside her body. The second I'm buried to the hilt, the last of my restraint vanishes. I draw my hips back and snap them forward with a ringing clap of skin on skin.

Back.

Forth.

In.

Out.

Pump after pump.

A moan for a moan.

I may hold the dominant position over her, but my sassy girl isn't one for lying there and taking it. Her ass pushes against me with every thrust of my hips, and she rises onto her toes then drops down with a little wiggle.

I have a white-knuckled grip on the leg I have raised, the haze of lust too much to allow me to think about the possible bruises it could cause.

"Oh god. *Mase*."

There's this sound Kay makes in the back of her throat

every time I enter her. I can't describe it, but it's somewhere between a gasp and a moan. It's the hottest fucking thing I've ever heard.

"I'm going to come," she cries.

"Don't fight it, baby." I increase the tempo of my thrusts. "Come all over my cock. Soak my balls."

"God." Gasp. "You're such a perv. *Mmm*."

A gush of wetness hits me as she does as she's asked, her pussy milking my dick, pulling my own release from my balls. I continue moving until it feels like there's not a drop of cum left inside my body.

Spent, her body collapses. I scoop her into my arms bridal style, carrying her to the bed and pulling her so she's snuggled against my side, head resting on my chest.

"I swear it gets better every time we do it," I say once my heart rate returns to normal.

"*Mmm*. You're not going to get an argument from me."

A deep guttural laugh leaves me, her head bouncing on my chest. "That'll be a damn first." She pinches my side.

We lapse into silence, me playing with the hair that fell out of her ponytail, her tracing along the designs inked in the ridges of my abdomen. I'm not sure how long this goes on before she finally speaks.

"Did you really tell the world you're putting off entering the draft to stay at school with me for another year?" Her words are hesitant, like she's nervous to bring it up.

"I doubt it was the world. College football isn't that big overseas."

The hand outlining the individual muscles in my stomach smacks me. "Don't play dumb. You know what I mean." She tilts her head back, resting her chin on my chest to look me in the eye. "Did you mean it?"

It's true, I have a few weeks before the deadline to officially declare passes, but I'm not going to change my mind.

"Every word."

Worry creeps into her eyes. "Brantley seemed pissed."

She doesn't know the half of it. I've been shielding her from the worst of the bullshit he's spewed over the last few months.

"I'll handle him." I press a kiss to her forehead. "It's not his decision to make, it's mine."

The V between her brows makes a reappearance.

"What's on your mind, babe?"

The furrow deepens.

"How do you know something's on my mind?"

I rub a finger over the V. "You get the cutest wrinkle right here when you're thinking too hard about something."

Nothing. She doesn't even blink. "Are you sure? You're risking so much delaying."

"Like?"

She rolls her eyes, knowing I'm being obtuse.

"What if you get hurt?"

"I could get hurt playing in the pros, so it's irrelevant. What else you got?" A smile curls at the corners of my lips.

"Your stock could fall and you might go later in the draft. It would cost you *millions*."

"Pfff." I tug on the piece of hair I'm twirling around my finger. "With another season under my belt, my draft pick can only rise."

Another eye roll. *Ooo I'm really getting to her now.* I know I shouldn't enjoy it so much, but I can't help it.

"*There's* the ego." She pins me with an annoyed but charmed glare. "You had me nervous there for a second."

"It'll be fine, babe, you'll see. It'll all work out how it's supposed to." I roll her beneath me. "For now, let's do this." I slide back inside her.

I'll spend the night losing myself in her; the bullshit will still be there in the morning waiting for us.

#Chapter52

THE SOUND of running water trickles into my consciousness, the soft sheets brushing against my skin as I stretch. I'm not sure what time it is with the heavy drapes blocking out any sunlight; all I know is I'm exhausted, my body sore in the most delicious way thanks to spending most of last night using Mase's body as my personal jungle gym.

Hearing the sound of the water cutting off, I sit up, keeping the sheet tucked around me as I try to get my bearings. My hair is a tangled mess, and I do my best to undo what is left of the low side pony and headband braid I had going on.

A minute or so later, Mase, wrapped only in a white towel tied low enough on his hips to show off his mouth-watering Adonis belt, exits the bathroom, steam billowing out behind him.

"Did I miss an earthquake or something?" His steps falter when he notices I'm up.

"Huh?" I may be awake, but I'm certainly not firing on all cylinders yet.

"I figure it's the only thing capable of waking you up this early." He shrugs, all of his drool-worthy muscles rippling, the residual droplets of water left on his bronzed skin high-lighting the movement.

I stick my tongue out at him, knowing it's a childish move, but I haven't had my coffee yet.

"I've got something you can use that tongue on." Mase grips himself over the terrycloth, always undeterred by my less-than-pleasant morning persona.

"Perv." I screw my mouth to the side, not wanting to encourage him. Still, he chuckles and his dimples flash.

"What can I say?" The mattress dips as he kneels on one knee, reaching out to cup my nape, his fingers spearing into my hair. "You bring it out in me."

I'm pulled into a kiss, the lingering taste of mint a blunt reminder of the morning breath I'm sure I'm sporting. The smirk he gives me when I push him away tells me he knows where my mind went.

Spotting his button-up from last night crumpled on the floor, I swing my legs over the side of the bed and pull it on, giving me a little bit of modesty as I hotfoot it to the bathroom.

After taking care of business and getting rid of the monster breath, I open the door to the bathroom, stepping out to see if Mase wants to pick up where we left off...

Except he's not alone.

"Coach Knight," I screech, my hand slapping against my chest in an effort to keep my heart from leaping out of it.

His expression gives nothing away; I can't tell if he's surprised to see me or not. I'm sure finding a girl inside the room of one of his players early in the morning isn't that uncommon, but it definitely is unorthodox.

"Kayla," Coach Knight greets me, still giving nothing away. "You being here saves me a trip." He gestures for me to come closer.

I'm acutely aware of my half-dressed state, my only saving

grace the fact that Mase is so much larger than me so his dress shirt falls past my knees. He's not any better, but at least he's no longer in a towel and has on a pair of black joggers.

Mase's arm automatically goes around my back, pulling me against his side, his bare skin warm under my touch. I have to make a conscious effort not to nuzzle against him; it wouldn't be appropriate to do so in front of his coach.

"What's up, Coach?" Mase asks.

Coach Knight lifts his Hawks cap, running a hand over his head before replacing it. He seems…nervous? Uncertain? I can't quite put a finger on it. "As you can imagine, your little announcement has caused quite a buzz."

Mase snorts at what I'm sure is a complete understatement.

"I see you anticipated this reaction." Mase nods. "I wanted to suggest skipping breakfast with the team and maybe lying low until the bus leaves for the airport later."

It's my turn to nod when Mase looks my way. Without a doubt, Bette will have ordered enough food to feed an army. Adding one more won't even register.

"Thanks for the heads-up, Coach." Mase lifts his arm from around me to shake his hand. "I apologize for making your job a little harder this morning."

"Are you kidding me?" Coach Knight snorts. "What's a few extra questions from the press? You just gave me an extra year to try to find your replacement. Even then it will be a challenge." I don't realize I'm nodding until Coach Knight calls me out. "See? Your girl knows it too. No wonder you want to hang around for her—she's clearly a keeper."

My face heats at the unexpected compliment.

After seeing Coach Knight out, Mase lifts me and tosses me onto the bed. With my knees bent high on his body, he slides his hands down the backs of my legs, cupping them under my butt for leverage as he grinds his lower body into mine, the material of his sweatpants the only thing keeping him from sliding inside me.

"Mase." I dig my heels into the curve of his ass in an effort to get him to give me what I want and let out a growl of frustration when he pushes up on his arms, holding himself over me like he's doing a pushup.

"Sorry, baby." Yeah, I don't believe his apology for a second, especially when he follows it up with a nip to my inner thigh and a quick swipe of his tongue through my slit on his way off the bed.

"Mason," I warn, pushing up onto my elbows, looking pointedly at the tent in his pants.

"Yes?" He smirks as he openly adjusts himself in front of me.

"Was that it? You're really going to make me think I'm going to get an orgasm and then make me wait?"

The motherfucker only grins harder then winks as he pulls on one of his U of J football tees. "Maybe next time you'll rethink stressing me out about my pregame kiss."

My jaw hinges open. *Sonofabitch.*

"Let's go, Skittles." A hand wraps around my ankle, pulling me down the bed. "I'm hungry."

Under my breath, I mumble about how I have something he could eat, but the teasing jerk still manages to hear me and barks out a laugh. I give him the mother of all eye rolls but quickly dress in my clothes from yesterday. It feels a little walk of shame-y, but I'll change as soon as I get back to the suite I'm sharing with my family.

"Um…" Mase says to Trav when he steps off the other elevator. "Shouldn't you be on the other side of this?" He points to the door I have the keycard poised to open.

I figured the two of them had worked out the same kind of arrangement as they did after the Cotton Bowl where Trav and I flip-flopped beds. Based on his rumpled suit, I take it Trav is the one doing the walk of shame instead of me.

"I helped a lovely lady keep her bed warm instead," Trav says with his lady-killer grin.

"You's a ho, QB1." I can't help but laugh.

"What?" Trav slings an arm around my shoulders as I open the door.

"Eww." Like picking up something soiled, I use only the tips of my forefinger and thumb to remove the offensive limb. "Don't touch me until you've wiped yourself down with Lysol."

"Straight-up savage, sis." The shit-eating grin on Trav's face and the way he joins in with everyone else laughing tells me he's just as amused.

I blow him a kiss and give a mock bow, but there's no stopping the warm fuzzies I get any time he calls me his sis.

"You have no idea," E agrees from the recliner he and Bette occupy while sharing a cup of coffee.

Knowing both my brother and Trav—not to mention B— the commiserating over who gets it worse from me has only begun. I leave them to it and head for the shower. I need food and coffee, not necessarily in that order.

It's a good thing E was too busy canoodling with his wife to get a good look at my appearance, because the sight staring back at me in the mirror as I get undressed is not one an older brother would want to see on his younger sister. There's beard burn on my neck, chest, stomach, and between my thighs, not that the latter few are noticeable with clothes on. The faintest hint of bruising above my right knee and on my hips is the last of the evidence of how thoroughly fucked I was by Mase last night—all four times.

I'm halfway to feeling human by the time I'm done with my shower and start to get dressed. Aside from wearing a scarf—which would be fine if we were back home but weird in Santa Clara—there's not much I can do to hide the beard burn visible on my neck. At least I packed the perfect shirt—a gold crew-neck tee with *Love you to the end zone & back* written in black and a little heart with football lacing—that will help cover the marks most likely to have E lose his mind. I finish off my ensemble with a pair of ripped black skinny jeans and gold sequined Chucks.

"Nice shirt," Mase comments, pulling me onto his lap and passing me a mug of coffee prepared the way I like it.

"Thought you would like it." I give him a quick kiss and settle into his embrace, saying hello to the rest of our friends who have filled the suite while I was showering. I spot the twins at the breakfast bar with T and Em, and Q, Alex, and Kev have joined CK at the dining room table to dig into the buffet Bette ordered.

"Where's Noah?" I ask, noticing he's the only one missing.

"Downstairs doing interviews," Kev mumbles around a mouthful of bacon.

It should come as no surprise that in a room full of athletes, the television is tuned to ESPN, the guys hooting and hollering when the broadcasts recaps the Hawks' victory over the Crimson Tide to become national champs. It takes on a whole other level when they play the clip of Mase's announcement.

I groan and do my best to bury my face against him. Em snorts, and I can already hear her telling me to get used to it because this isn't going to go away any time soon.

"I got it," B calls out when there's a soft knock on the door.

"Well aren't you a tall drink of water," an older feminine voice says once it's open.

"Nan?" Trav asks, rising from the couch.

B steps to the side, confirming Nana McQueen is our unexpected visitor, and I don't miss the way she cops a feel of B's bicep as she passes.

Can we be her when we grow up? My inner cheerleader might be onto something there.

"Travis Joseph McQueen." She scans her grandson from

head to toe and back again, letting out a heavy sigh. "I hope you at least remembered to wrap it up. I don't need you making me a great-grandmother with some jersey girl, or whatever it is you call them"—she waves her hand dismissively—"who's not worthy of being my granddaughter-in-law. Remember…" She steps up to Trav and affectionately pats his cheek. "No glove, no love."

The room erupts in guffaws and Trav blushes, like actually blushes. "Christ, Nan." He runs a hand through his hair, not helping how disheveled it already is.

"Have I ever told you you're my favorite person ever, Nana?" Livi skips over to hug her surrogate grandmother.

"Told you," I whisper as Trav walks past. "*Lysol.*" Mase buries his face in my hair to hide his laughter.

Trav grumbles under his breath but still guides Nana over to one of the open chairs in the living room. "Not that I'm not happy to see you or anything—"

"Yeah, especially with a greeting like that," Olly cuts in.

"—but what are you doing here, Nan?" Trav finishes shooting a glare at the other half of the Roberts twins.

Warm eyes filled with affection scan the room until they land on my boyfriend, all of Mase's muscles going rigid under me. "I came here to warn yo—" Whatever else she was about to say gets cut off by a pounding on the door. Again, B is the closest and plays doorman, except this time there's no pleasant greeting, only an irate Brantley barreling his way into the room.

"About that," Nana says, finishing her earlier statement.

"You can't avoid this conversation forever, Mason."

Stunned silence meets Brantley's booming words.

Calmly, eerily so, Mase stands with me in his arms, carefully setting me down and handing me off to Trav, not once taking his eyes off his stepfather. I remain silent, letting Trav tuck me against his side protectively while also searching out

Bette's gaze. Mase isn't the only powder keg we have to worry about exploding if this takes a bad turn.

"I'm not avoiding it, I just didn't think a bar full of strangers and members of the press was the best place to have it." A chill races down my spine and goose bumps coat my arms at the complete lack of emotion in Mase's voice as he speaks. "I also don't think you want to be having it here." He gestures to their audience.

"I can't believe you want to risk your career all so you can play house with *some girl*." Where Mase's voice was devoid of all emotion, Brantley's is filled with venom, especially the way he says "some girl" like a curse.

I jolt. Trav squeezes my shoulder, in warning or comfort, I'm not sure; maybe it's both. I've long suspected Mase has been shielding me from things when I try to get him to talk to me because I sense he's stressed. I'm sad to realize I was most likely correct in that assumption.

"How many times"—Mase's hands ball into fists at his sides—"do I have to tell you to stop referring to my girlfriend as *some girl*?" he asks through clenched teeth. I take a step to go to him, but Trav only tightens his hold on me, ignoring the glare I send his way.

"Is her pussy so magical you're willing to jeopardize everything we've worked your whole life for?" Brantley's vulgar words make me flinch, and I see Bette jump in front of E as he shouts, "What the fuck?!"

"I'd choose your next words. *Very*. Carefully," Mase warns. His stance shifts, his demeanor hardening in a way that gives me flashbacks to the night Liam showed up at the AK house.

No one speaks.

No one moves. If you asked if our lungs were still breathing and our hearts were still beating, I might even doubt that.

The dead silence filling the room is reminiscent of the eye of a hurricane.

I hate this.

I hate being the cause of all this discontent. The *last* thing I want to do is cause a rift between Mase and his family. For as much as I wasn't looking forward to living in a different state than him when he was drafted, I would have *never* asked him to do what he did. Hell, the reason I did what I did to handle the whole Liam situation was to make sure Mase had the best potential come draft time.

Oh my god, I can't tell Mase about that now—he'll lose his fucking mind for sure.

It isn't until there's another knock on the door that something cuts through the animosity brewing.

Who is it now? It's like Grand Central Station up in here.

Still…

No one moves.

When another knock comes, this one more insistent, Em finally goes to answer it.

"Brantley. Roberts." Grace Nova-Roberts enters the room, taking in the scene in front of her with a clenched jaw. "What the *hell* do you think you are doing?" She sounds more like she's scolding a child than speaking to her husband.

"Mom?" the twins say in unison, breaking Mase from his death-glare stare-down with Brantley.

With grace appropriate only for someone with the name, Mase's mom moves to stand between her son and husband, commanding all their attention. This is not a side of Grace Nova-Roberts I have ever experienced at The Barracks, but if you couldn't tell by her stylish jeans tucked into a pair of gorgeous camel-colored knee-high leather boots and silk blouse, this woman means business.

"When Nana texted me to tell me what was going on here, I didn't believe it. No *way* is my grown-ass husband doing what she says he's doing."

"I think my exact words were something along the lines of if she didn't get up here, she would be planning a funeral," Nana McQueen clarifies.

"Geez, Nan." Trav's body shakes with laughter against mine.

"I came down to try to talk some sense into our son," Brantley explains when Grace starts to tap her foot, waiting for an answer.

"*Step*son," Mase emphasizes the word step, and Grace seems taken aback by the distinction. To be fair, so am I. From everything he's told me, Mase has always considered Brantley more a father than a stepfather since he raised him most of his life. "Until you apologize for your *flagrant* disrespect of the woman I love, I don't want to be connected to you more than I have to."

I suck in a breath, my heart cracking. "*Mase.*" I do my best to convey how much of an overreaction I think this is.

"No, babe." Trav finally releases me, and I automatically go to Mase. "He owes you one *hell* of an apology."

"It's fine." It's not, but keeping the peace is more important at the moment. "He just wants what's best for you." This I do believe is true.

"The *fuck* it is," E bites out, but Bette still has him safely handled.

"No, Kayla." Shit, it's never good when Mase uses my full name. I press back into him when he pulls me in front of him, his hands interlacing themselves over my belly. "It is *never* okay for *anyone* to make you seem like less than you are. I wouldn't stand for it when Parker tried to do it, and I sure as shit won't let my own family do it."

How he can make me swoon like a girl in a rom-com while in the middle of a volatile situation, I'll never know. I crane my neck and stretch to place a kiss to the underside of his jaw. The touch of my lips has some of the tension bleeding out of his body.

"*That's* another one of my points." Brantley waves a hand at me. "What do you think prospective teams are going to think when stories about your girlfriend's court scandals —*again*, I might add—hit the internet."

My breathing hitches and the blood in my veins turns to ice. There's a flash of strawberry blonde as T also puts herself in front of E. This is bad.

Very, very bad.

My eyes go hot as tears burn at the backs of them. This is so not the time or the place for me to tell Mase about what I did, but as I take in the crinkles around Bette's eyes as she gives me a subtle nod, I know this *has* to be when it comes out.

Clearing my throat and rolling my shoulders back in an attempt to project a confidence I don't feel, I say, "There won't be any court scandals." It takes everything in me not to roll my eyes or cower at the reminder of that dark time in my life.

"Don't be silly." The condescension in his tone has me gritting my teeth. "Your school's little Instagram"—Why is it he's making it sound like *I* run the UofJ411 page? Doesn't he realize it's like the bane of my existence?—"made sure the whole world saw the drama that went down—"

"Drama?" Mase barks. "That asshole put *hands* on Kay."

I spin in his hold and smooth my hands down his abdominals. What's done is done. I'm fine now. I don't want him to focus on the bad anymore. I find the waistband of his sweats and grab on. "It's fine," I whisper for only Mase to hear then twist my upper body to face Brantley while leaving my lower half to keep Mase in place. "There won't be any court scandals because we won't be going to court." I inhale deeply, needing to fortify myself for what I'm about to say next, or more accurately, the reactions to it. "I brokered a settlement with the Parkers."

Mase's body jolts, and I tighten my hold. The last thing this situation needs is him flying off the handle. I never expected he would take the news well; it's why I've put actually having this conversation off for weeks. It was hard enough to convince E this was the right plan, the best plan, and I doubt Mase will be any easier to persuade.

I push up onto my toes and reach to cup Mase's scruffy jaw in my hand, rubbing my thumb back and forth over his stubble until I have his full attention. Doing this in front of an audience is far less than ideal, but at the end of the day, it's us, Mase and me, who are what matters.

"I know you're mad." I tighten the hand holding on to his pants when he goes to deny it. "Don't try to lie and say you aren't." The tension around his eyes smooths out when I call him out. "I'm sure you have all sorts of thoughts and feelings on the subject, but I need you to know I made this decision for *you*."

"Kay." The blunt edges of his nails dig into my back as he tightens his hold on me.

"I know he deserves so much more than what he got, but"—I lay the flat of my palm over my heart—"to me"—I move my hand so it now covers his—"*you* are all that matters. I had the lawyers draw up NDAs and what was essentially a combo platter of a gag and a cease and desist order on all the Chrissy/Tina bullshit he tried to drum up."

"You did?" Shock and awe fill his light green eyes.

"Respect, Short Stack." A fist appears above Mase's shoulder, and Trav gives me a wink when I bump it. At least he doesn't seem upset by me essentially airing some of his dirty laundry.

"What does Christina Hale have to do with anything?" Brantley is pretty much seething at this point, and the way his fingers fidget at his sides gives away how much he doesn't like not being the one in control.

"Well you see, *Brantley*..." Tessa attempts to cover her snort with a cough at E using Brantley's first name, but the twitch of Bette's lips tells me I'm not the only one who doesn't think she was successful.

We may be the only ones who know this, but the fact that my brother didn't refer to Mase's stepdad as *Mr. Roberts* is one of the biggest slaps in the face he could give. I think Dad would forgive him for going against the way we were raised since he's doing it as a small way to defend my honor and all that.

"While you come storming in here ruining our breakfast and *insulting* my sister—who, I might add, has only thought of ways to protect Mason's career—"

"*Yeah.*" Brantley puffs out a humorless breath. "Because she sees him as her golden ticket."

"Little D may be short, but she's no Oompa Loompa," B cracks, and Em backhands him in the chest, eliciting an *oof*.

E rolls his eyes, and Mase mumbles to me how I do it better as we watch the testosterone-fueled standoff I feared. If left unchecked, E's overprotectiveness could cause a rift between our two families that might not be able to be fixed once everything calms down.

"I honestly have *no idea* where you've come up with this *ridiculous* notion that my sister is some jersey chaser looking for a payday, but *one* thing"—E thrusts a finger in the air—"she does *not* need from your son is money. From my endorsements alone, I've set her up for life."

E stops and swallows thickly; it's his tell when he's trying to actively rein in his emotions. The way his eyes turn down at the corners when he looks at me tells me he also feels guilty about letting this truth slip. He shouldn't. His net worth is google-able, and anyone who knows the details of him taking over my guardianship would know he would take care of me. What almost no one knows is he did the same for the Taylor siblings too.

"Now"—E stalks to the door and yanks it open—"why

don't you see yourself out before you ruin the *rest* of our morning."

When Brantley doesn't make any effort to do as he's asked, both Grace and Nana McQueen flank him, taking each of his arms in theirs and ushering him out of the room. E slams the door behind them with a sense of finality.

Is it too much to ask for there not to be a lingering sense of drama in our lives?

"I'm sorry." Mase breathes into my hair, resting his cheek on the top of my head.

"You have nothing to apologize for. He only wants what's best for you." Though I believe this to be true, it doesn't help ease the sting.

"It's still not okay."

"Can we please focus on something else, *anything* else, until we have to leave in a few hours?" I request, desperate for a change in subject.

Everyone agrees, but there's a stain on our earlier happiness. The hard set of my brother's jaw tells me this isn't the end of the discussion for him either.

Fabulous.

#Chapte52

UOFJ411: I guess we should all be bowing down to the queen now that we get to keep @CasaNova87 on the team for another year! #GoForTheRepeat #Kaysonova #Football-Royalty

   picture of Kay and Mase kissing after the national championship game

UofJ411: Our boys are really about this whole "cheering for cheerleaders" thing. Congrats on the 1st place for the White Squad and 2nd for the Red Squad @UofJCheerleading #WonderWhatWouldHaveHappenedIfSheCheeredForUs

   picture of the guys and Kay posing with Em and Quinn after the UCA College Cheerleading Nationals

UofJ411: Hanging with the Alphas #HowDoIGetAStandingInvite

   picture of Kay and Em leaving the AK house

#Chapter53

THE WEEKS FOLLOWING the national championship and my announcement to not declare for the draft have been filled with tension. Not necessarily for Kay and me—I still feel solid about us as a couple—but there is this strain that keeps nagging me.

I haven't spoken to Brantley since he came spewing his vile bullshit in front of Kay's family three weeks ago. I've seen Mom at The Barracks on the weekends I've tagged along with Kay when she coaches, but she's been all mum's the word. I'm grateful for it because she is *not* the person I should be taking my frustrations out on.

The person I'm most impressed with is E. Though they still officially call Baltimore their home, he and Bette have split their time between their house there and the Dennings' family home in Blackwell equally now that the season is over for the Crabs. Whenever I've been at the house with Kay, he hasn't once held Brantley's actions against me.

Still…

I haven't been able to let go of how easy Liam Parker is getting off for daring to hurt what's mine. Most people wouldn't consider a six-figure settlement getting off easy, but when he should at the very least be waterboarded for what he did, I do.

I decided to take matters into my own hands and did something that will probably make Kay want to rip my balls off if she finds out…

I pressed JT for more information about Carter King. No one ever went into great detail about the guy, but from the little bits and pieces I've gathered, he controls a lot more than just the street racing scene in Blackwell.

"You sure you wanna do this?" Trav asks from the Shelby's passenger seat as we stare up at the warehouse-looking building JT told me is Carter King's home base.

I look over at my best friend, not at all shocked he insisted on coming; he's my ride or die.

"Yes," I say with conviction. What could potentially happen *after* this is something I'll worry about later, but I figure it's better to ask Kay for forgiveness than permission if it means settling this score.

I pull up the collar of my coat to help protect me from the bitter winter air as I exit the Shelby and approach the three-story building. JT texted that Carter is expecting me, so at least I have that working in my favor.

King answers my knock and leads us through the same garage area Kay and I used the night we fought when I crashed one of his Royal Balls, only this time his Corvette is parked alongside the Camaro. He waves a keycard in front of a sensor at another door, and this time we step into what can only be the residence side of the building.

Unfortunately for me, I'm too lost in my own head to really appreciate how nice it probably is. Instead I blindly let him guide us to a wet bar setup in the corner and settle onto a barstool.

"I gotta ask." King reaches into a mini fridge, pulling out and popping the tops on three beers before sliding two across the bar to Trav and me. "Are you *positive* this is how you wanna play it?"

The fact that anybody I've clued in on regarding my plans has questioned me should give me pause, but I'm too determined to see this through to back down now. It's an eye for an eye—or in Liam's case, at least, one broken bone for another. I nod.

"Okay." Resigned, King folds his arms over his chest and leans back against the wall stocked with liquor bottles. "We can set it up in a way that means Liam doesn't know it's you—"

"I *want* him to know it's me," I say, cutting him off. A gleam of respect enters his gaze, and he pauses, reassessing me. Sure, it would be smarter to keep my identity hidden from Parker, but it would negate the message I want to drive home by doing so.

"Okay then—" Again he's cut off, but this time it's from another door banging open as his sister Savvy comes storming into the room.

"Cart, do you have any butterflies? Charming wasn't watching what he was do—" This time it's Savvy whose words stop abruptly, along with her steps when she notices her brother isn't alone. "Mase?"

"Hi Savvy." I greet her as Carter makes his way to her and lifts the fingers she has wrapped around her forearm.

"It was an accident, man, I swear." Wesley Prince, Carter's number two, is out of breath as he rushes in. "*Ma reine*, I'm sorry."

Carter waves him off, already working on cleaning the long slice cutting across Savvy's arm. "Don't worry about it, Wes. You aren't the first one to knick her during training."

"Why are you hanging with the football brigade?" Savvy bounces a finger between Trav and me. "Is Kay here?"

"No," Carter answers.

"So—*fuck*." Savvy hisses at the antiseptic cleaning her wound. "You race, not play football. What gives?"

I'm surprised by how easy it is to read Carter's thought process on his face as he debates if he should tell her the truth. "Mason wants help dealing with Parker."

"Oh my god!" Savvy rips her arm away from her brother to clap excitedly, reminding me a lot of her best friend with that reaction. "Please, please, *please* let me help."

"No."

"Oh come on, Cart," she whines. "I want to be there when you beat the shit out of him."

"Savvy," King says, retaking her arm to finish placing the butterfly bandages across it to secure the wound.

"Ooo, can we rip his fingernails off too?"

"Savvy." This time her name comes out as more of a warning.

"What?" She shrugs innocently. "That is the *least* of what that douchemonkey deserves."

"Savage," Wes mutters, but Savvy only beams with pride, her shoulders rolling back, her spine lengthening.

"No," King says again.

"Carter." She drags out his name to multiple syllables.

"Samantha." Now his tone brokers no argument, and Savvy huffs. *Samantha?*

"I hate it when you go dropping the legal name." She crosses her arms, looking every bit the sullen teenager.

"If your name is Samantha, how do you get Savvy as a nickname?" Trav asks the question dancing on the tip of my tongue.

"It's short for Savage because of her propensity toward fingernail ripping and such," Wes explains, and now Savvy is back to preening.

In my pocket, my phone vibrates, but I ignore it because we've only just started to get back on topic. Trav's phone goes off seconds later, and all our plans change.

#Chapter54

"UGH." Em groans and drops her phone on her desk with a *clank* as I step inside the doorway to her room and lean against the jamb to see if she's ready to head out and meet G and CK for dinner.

"Your dad again?" I ask, almost afraid of the answer.

"Mom this time." She spears her hands in her hair and tugs on the strands to the point that I see the skin around her hairline blanch.

To say Senator and Mrs. Logan are less than thrilled with the new frequency of their daughter showing up in pictures on UofJ411's Instagram page and the periodic gossip site looking to find out how "top draft pick Mason Nova is really spending his time now that he's not preparing for the NFL draft" would be an understatement.

For the most part, during her year-and-a-half tenure at the U of J, Em has flown under the radar. There was one sorority that tried to rush her our first semester freshman year since she is a legacy from her mother being a member from another chapter, but when she realized they wanted her more because she was a senator's daughter than due to a sisterly connection, she stepped away. It's what led to Em's own distaste for

Greek life. Other than that, most people don't realize the girl with the perfect eyebrows cheering on the sidelines at their football and basketball games comes from a family who rivals the Kennedys.

Unfortunately, that is no longer the case. The drama in my life has spilled over into Em's, making her, and our other roommates, collateral damage.

"What did she have to say?" I straighten up and link my arm with hers after she pulls her cross-body bag over her head.

"Oh you know…" Em waves a hand in the air dismissively. "She just wanted to remind me to be conscious of my image and stuff." She clutches at her metaphorical pearls and mock gasps. "God forbid I actually act like a college student and go to class in yoga pants and a hoodie."

One would think her father, the senator, would be the parent worried about his daughter's image, but no, that honor goes firmly to Mrs. Logan.

"I'm sorry."

"Pfft." She waves me off, and if the arch of her eyebrow is anything to go by, she thinks I'm being ridiculous. So what if I am? I can't help that the guilt is enough to keep me up some nights. "I promised to help 'press the flesh'"—my arm gets tugged up as she makes exaggerated air quotes—"next time I'm home, but remind me to give JT major shit next time you two video-chat. It would have gone a long way for me if I could claim being a national champ again had the Blue Squad not beat us out two weeks ago."

And that right there is why Em has become my best girlfriend. She makes it easy to let us just be us and lets any other bullshit go.

"Q, you ready?" I call out.

"Yup." She comes bouncing out of her room and into the doorway next to hers. "What about you, Bailey?"

I'm still nowhere near as close with my third roommate,

but I've been trying to make an effort when I can. Inviting her to join us for taco night at one of the dining halls on campus was an easy ask.

"Yeah." Bailey is typing something on her phone as she joins us as well, completing our roommate foursome. Whereas the rest of us—Em included, much to what will be Mrs. Logan's dismay—are dressed for comfort in leggings, Uggs, and loose sweaters, mine reading *If you don't like tacos, I'm nacho type*, Bailey is rocking a pair of painted-on jeans and a skin-tight, low-cut, long-sleeved shirt.

We're discussing our plans for attending G's upcoming basketball game as we exit our dorm to flashbulbs and shouts from two paparazzi.

"Ouch," Em shouts as she stumbles back from one of the overzealous photogs, taking me with her since we are still linked.

Once we right ourselves, I gasp at the blood pouring from a gash on her forehead. Q jumps between us and the photographers who shouldn't have been able to get into the building, but who am I kidding? Mase gets in all the time no problem; why wouldn't they?

We shuffle backward as a unit until we are once again behind the safety of our dorm's door. Em has a hand pressed to her forehead to stanch the blood flow, but when she removes it to let me inspect the damage, it's worse than I first thought.

"I think you're gonna need stitches." I gently prod at the line of broken skin, using the sleeve of my shirt to clean the blood away from her eyes.

"Son of a *bitch* this hurts," Em curses.

I lift her hand back to her face and press it over the wound before moving to grab the first aid kit from our bathroom. I doubt I'll be able to fully stop the blood since head wounds bleed a lot, but I can help clean her up, and one of the instant cold packs can help keep the swelling from getting too bad before the doctors at U Gen can take a look.

"How are we supposed to get out of here with them out there?" Q throws an arm at the closed door, the commotion of those who don't belong clearly audible through the wood.

"Call campus security," I suggest.

"Call G too and tell him we'll be missing dinner," Em adds, frowning because we're going to miss out on taco night.

It doesn't take long for campus security to arrive and clear out the paps. Q waits until the three of us—Bailey having stayed behind after all the drama—are in Pinky before calling G. None of us wanted to risk him showing up while the paps were still around and getting himself in trouble because he Hulked out. Our friend may be a gentle giant, but when it comes to someone hurting a woman, all bets are off. Case in point, I can hear him shouting without him being on speakerphone.

Since Em's injuries aren't life-threatening or all that serious in the grand scheme of things, it takes half an hour before we are escorted back to a bay inside the emergency room and another thirty minutes after that before we get to see a familiar plastic surgeon.

"Miss Dennings," Dr. Nikols says with surprise as she pulls back the curtain blocking off Em's patient area from the rest of the ED. "We meet again."

"We do." Unconsciously, I reach up and touch the cheek she helped repair. "Though this time I'm not the patient."

Dr. Nikols greets Em warmly, recognizing her from when she stayed with me after surgery. She steps out to check something outside the curtain, a furrow to her brow after she does.

"What's wrong?" Q asks, all of our emotions run raw after earlier.

"Nothing." Dr. Nikols gives us an easy smile. "I was just looking for the rest of your entourage." Her more than accurate description of our group gets us laughing for the first time in almost two hours.

Q and I each hold one of Em's hands as Dr. Nikols cleans then gets to work suturing Em's wound. When all is said and done, it takes four stitches to close up the damage we can only assume came from the sharp plastic edge of a camera lens.

We're waiting for a nurse to bring Em's discharge papers when loud male voices can be heard shouting seconds before the curtain rips open with enough force to dislodge two of the rings around the metal track, revealing Mase and Carter, both breathing as if they ran a marathon.

"Mase?" I ask, the rest of my question getting lost as my face is smothered into his chest in a crushing embrace.

"Why. The. *Fuck* didn't you call me?" he demands.

"Why are you here?" Em's question reminds me of our other arrival.

I snake my hands between mine and Mase's bodies and push on his hard muscles until he gives me enough room to breathe, and you know, see the others with us.

"Casanova"—there's no missing the smirk Carter makes when using Mase's moniker—"got a call that you were in the hospital."

"I'm not questioning Mason." Em points to where my boyfriend stands still, not having fully released me from his hold. "Honestly I'm surprised it took him this long. But what are *you*"—she pokes a finger toward Carter—"doing here?"

All earlier panic washes away from Carter's expression, replaced by one of frustration. Based on the way I see his hands curling into Cs, I think he wants to strangle Em. Now I'm the one pushing my face against Mase, because laughing is *so* not the appropriate response right now.

"Is it so wrong to want to make sure you're okay?" Carter questions, the bone of his jaw sticking out to the side.

Em shrugs, nonchalant. "I don't see how it's of any consequence to you."

"*God*." Carter rips his beanie from his head and slaps it against his thigh with a growl. "You. Are. *Infuriating*."

"I'm missing something, aren't I?" Mase leans down to whisper in my ear, jolting me out of the sexual-tension-induced haze that comes along any time Em and King spend any prolonged amount of time together.

I'm about to explain this interesting dynamic when his question has *one* specific fact registering. "Hold on." This time when I push for space, I don't stop until I'm able to actually step out of his grasp. "What are *you* doing with King?"

It makes no sense. Carter and I may be friendly because of his friendship with JT, but we aren't close enough for Mase to be driven to form his own friendship with him. If anything, Savvy would make the most sense if he was going to spend time with a King sibling given how much time I spend with her around Tessa.

Like a game of connect the dots, the picture forms in my mind.

Sonofabitch. This is about Liam.

Pissed off and in desperate need of finding somewhere private to rip into him for what can only be described as his Neanderthal thinking, I wrap a hand around his wrist, my fingers not able to touch, and pull us out of the cubicle.

I look left then right, searching for a secluded area. Spotting a janitor's closet, I push him inside and let the door close us both into the small space.

My breathing is erratic, and I pray I'm wrong.

"Please tell me you didn't go to Blackwell to seek King out?" I ask with desperation, hoping I'm jumping to crazy conclusions.

Except with the way he drops his gaze to the left, no longer able to make eye contact with me, my suspicions are confirmed.

I'm going to kill JT.

"Fuck." I kick a bucket, sending it flying into the wall. "I should have *known* when you and JT were being all buddy-buddy in Florida."

Continuing with the *cheering for cheerleaders* campaign, Mase and the guys joined us when we attended the UCA College Cheerleading Nationals the weekend after the football team won their own.

Here I thought it was a good thing, thought it was proof Mase was over whatever lingering jealousy he felt toward my best friend, but what he was really doing was pumping him for information.

I know he—along with everyone else—thinks I shouldn't have let Liam get off as easily as he did, but doesn't he realize I did it for him? Doesn't he know asking about how and why Carter King is considered "powerful" in a town at barely twenty-two years old can't lead to anything good?

"Mason." I clutch at his shirt, tugging until he finally brings his green gaze back to me. "Please, *please* let this go. Don't go searching for your own form of vigilante justice. Liam's not worth it."

Though I can feel him vibrating with restrained anger, the way he cups my face is exceedingly gentle.

"He needs to pay for what he did to you." His voice is gruff.

"I'm not denying it, but it can't be at *your* hands." It's my turn to cup his face, bringing it down until his forehead rests on mine and we're breathing each other in. Breath for breath. Heartbeat for heartbeat. "If you go after him *this* way, he wins. He gets what he was looking for. *Please* don't let him, Mason."

I understand that he wants to put a hurt on Liam, but the possible blowback wouldn't be worth it.

He releases a warm puff of air right into my face, his

fingers tightening until my scalp burns from my hair being tugged at the roots. "I hate it when you call me Mason."

For the first time in minutes, I feel like smiling, and the corners of my mouth start to tip up. "I know." I lightly run my fingertips down the shells of his ears, causing him to hum in the back of his throat. "But it's the only way I know to get you to take me seriously."

"I love you so much, baby."

I don't care how many times he tells me this; the warm feeling in my chest that happens as a result will never get old. I slide my left hand down the side of his face and tap the ring I wear for him to his lips.

"And it's because I love you back that I need you to let this go. Let karma handle Liam Parker." My nose twitches. "I hear she's a bitch."

"You're such a smartass."

The last of the panic I was feeling bleeds away as we fall into this old rhythm.

"Don't act like it's not one of your favorite things about me." I rise up on my toes and cover his mouth with mine, getting lost in our kiss like I always do.

"My rainbow-haired sass queen," he says against my lips before taking my ass in hand and lifting to press me to the wall.

My hands bump against the backward rim of his hat as I hold on for dear life. Through the thin material of my leggings, his erection easily finds where I'm most needy for him, grinding against my clit.

I slip my hands under the hem of his T-shirt, bringing it along with me as I trace over the contours of his delicious lat muscles, about to suggest we play the college version of 7 minutes in heaven when the door to the closet opens and bright light from the hallway illuminates us in all our debauchery.

Our mouths separate with an audible pop, and there

waiting for us to get our shit together is an amused-looking Nurse Vicki and a not-at-all-surprised-to-find-us-in-such-a-precarious-position Em.

"Do you think you could put your *Grey's Anatomy* reenactment on pause so we can go?" Em asks, and I know she's going to tease me about this every time we watch the show for the rest of our lives.

This is not at all how I pictured my night going.

#Chapter55

WHILE KAY and I were working through our differences in the janitor's closet, two very important and potentially life-altering phone calls happened.

The first one was G, and yes, I do realize, like Trav, I've slipped into the habit of calling Grayson G now too.

Turns out while Quinn and Kay were taking Em to the hospital, Bailey made her way over to the AK house, making it possible for G to overhear a very interesting conversation between the girls' fourth roommate and Adam. It seems two of the biggest sources of pictures to both UofJ411 and members of the media were sleeping right down the hall from us. The pair of them were hoping the added attention might trickle down and they would get their own fifteen minutes of fame.

Hold on, time out. My inner coach makes a T with his hands. *Let me take a page out of your girl's playbook and roll my eyes. They wanted to be* Insta*famous. *rolls eyes**

E did *not* take the news well, and Bette had to hide his car keys to keep him from driving up to the U of J. It's too bad because Adam deserved so much more than the right hook G laid him out with.

The second call, and the reason Kay has retreated into the

shower for the last forty-five minutes, was made by Senator Logan. He essentially told Em if she wanted to continue to attend the U of J next year, she would no longer be able to room with Kay.

I can't say I fully fault him given that he was speaking to his daughter while she was in the hospital getting stitches, but it was through no fault of Kay's.

Both these calls led to me driving the girls and me back to Kay's home in Blackwell and Trav driving him, G, and CK to join us.

The last I checked, Em wasn't faring much better than her best friend after her father's bombshell. I left her in the capable hands of our friends to focus on Kay.

I'm slicing fruit like the ninja I am on my phone when Kay enters her room, body wrapped in a hot pink towel while drying her hair with another. Stripping down to my boxer briefs was a calculated move to help her remember she forgave me for my attempted power move with Carter to get payback on Liam. Based on how the tired smile on her face gets replaced with one promising all sorts of dirty things when her eyes track over my nearly naked body, it was a success.

Her gaze never leaves mine as she closes the distance between us until she comes to the foot of the bed. Kneeling, she climbs onto it, not stopping until she straddles my hips, her plump ass settling on top of my thighs.

Vanilla and peppermint invade my senses as her forearms come to rest on my shoulders, hands cupping my nape, fingers extending to play with the hairs on the back of my head. I'm like Herkie when she scratches behind his ears with how much I love it when she does that.

"Hey," Kay says, her gray eyes softening as she stares into my greens.

Gently, I place my hands over the curves of her bent knees. "Hey." I make sure to flash her my dimples.

"I'm so happy you're in my bed right now," she says breathlessly. "I needed it after today."

Her admission hits me in the gut. My strong girl is frayed at the edges, and I love that she turns to me to keep her together. Now's not the time for heavy. It's time to help take her mind off her troubles.

"You know I'll never turn down a chance to be in your bed."

"Perv." She gives me an easy smile, and I feel some of the tension from the day leave her body.

"Only for you, baby."

My hands start a slow glide up her bare thighs, and she sucks in a breath as they disappear under the edge of the towel. I let my thumbs brush across the waxed lips of her pussy in a teasing caress. They continue up her body, following the seam of where the terrycloth overlaps. When I get to where the towel is knotted between her breasts, I continue to push my hands up until the knot comes undone. With the material loosened, I take an end in each hand and peel it apart, unwrapping her like a present on Christmas.

Inch by inch, her naked body is revealed to me, and no matter how many times I've seen it, the sight never gets old. She is a goddess. The perfection before me should be physically impossible. She's tiny and athletic, all toned limbs and killer curves.

The globes on her chest overflow from my hands as I squeeze them, yet they manage to stay perky. She likes to complain about her pale complexion, but I love seeing how the creamy color contrasts against the olive tone my Italian heritage affords me.

Even though she's more compact than average, she manages to have the perfect hourglass figure. Her waist nips in, and thanks to a lifetime of cheerleading, her stomach muscles are nicely defined before flaring out to hips made for grabbing hold of.

Don't get me started on her ass. I mean it—the thing is absolute *perfection*. I thank the lord every day for every, single, squat she has ever done to give it the lift and roundness I can't help but spank and occasionally sink my teeth into. Granted, it's nowhere near the size of J-Lo's or anything, but it bubbles out enough for me to constantly be drawn to touch and smack it whenever she gets close enough for me to do so.

For a person who barely meets the height requirements for rides at Six Flags, she has a killer set of stems. Again, thanks to her conditioning from cheerleading, she has nice thick muscular thighs, nothing chicken-leggy about them. When she wears those leggings she loves so much, I can't stop myself from grabbing on and squeezing them, and the way they grip my body when they wrap around my waist— instant hard-on.

Speaking of hard-ons, the one I'm sporting now is some of my best work, the tip of my cock poking out at the top of my boxer briefs. Telling my dick it needs to chill for now, I focus my attention back to the paragon of beauty literally in my lap.

I brush the errant curls over her shoulder, coasting finger- tips across her collarbone down to her breasts, weighing them, lifting them, giving them a squeeze. Her pink nipples slip between my fingers and I pinch the digits together, giving a gentle tug, causing her to moan.

My mouth joins in on the fun, following the path my hands set for them. First I kiss the soft spot where her neck meets her shoulder, knowing it never fails to send tingles down her spine. My teeth gently scrape against the bump of her collarbone, followed by a soothing lave of my tongue.

Shifting my hands to the undersides of her tits, I lift them, sucking a nipple into my mouth. After teasing the first one long enough to have Kay squirming in my lap, I switch my attention to the other one, giving it equal treatment.

By the way her fingers are latched onto my hair and wetness is soaking through the thin cotton material covering my junk, I know she's not going to let me get away with my teasing much longer.

"Mase." She makes an *mmm* sound so hot I feel precum leak onto my belly. "Stop teasing me."

I smile around her nipple. "No idea what you're talking about, babe." I play dumb.

"Yeah…right." She bites her lip, holding back another moan.

I finally continue my downward trajectory along her body, her stomach muscles jumping as my fingers skate across them.

Cupping her hips, I run my hands back and forth across the silky skin there then dip my fingers to the promised land between her legs.

Holy shit.

She is completely drenched, her clit swollen in a way that tells me it isn't going to take much for her to go off.

Hooking an arm around her middle, I lift her enough to shimmy my boxers off. As I lower her back down, I position myself at her entrance and push inside as I roll her onto her back underneath me. The sound she makes whenever I first enter her is the hottest fucking hybrid of a gasp and a moan, and each time I hear it, it takes every ounce of self-control I possess to not shoot my load.

Slowly, oh so slowly, I sink into her body until I'm pressed inside to the hilt. One arm is under her back, elbow against her side, while the rest is stretched up in the hollow of her shoulder blades to grip her around the trapezoid muscle. My free hand cups the back of her thigh, holding her leg around my hip, keeping her spread open to press *deep* inside her.

Her pussy ripples around me, and then she's coming.

My pace may be unhurried, but it's intense as I continue my slow thrusts through her orgasm.

"Eyes open," I instruct, and they are almost black, only the barest hint of gray visible as they meet mine.

In.

Out.

Push.

Pull.

Her body squeezes my dick, not wanting to let it go when I pull out to the tip before plunging back in.

My fingers uncurl from around her shoulder, tangling in the curls spread around her. I give a tug, angling her head for a devouring kiss, our mouths swallowing each other's moans.

The tingling in my balls alerts me to my own orgasm, but I refuse to come before she has her second. What can I say? I'm an overachiever, at least in an athletic sense. I constantly try to make sure she comes more than I do. It's not like you'll get any complaints from her about it.

I swivel my hips to bump her clit with each pump of my hips, and there it is. Her teeth sink into the top of my shoulder, hard enough to indent the skin, as she comes all over my cock for the second time, milking my own release from me.

Lazily my hips continue to pump as we come down from our orgasms. When the last waves of pleasure subside, I roll us to the side so I'm not crushing her, my still semi-hard dick managing to stay inside her for a few moments longer.

Kay's thumb brushes over the spot she bit. "I think that's going to leave a mark."

"Good." I kiss the little V that's formed between her brows in concern. "I'll make sure to take my shirt off when I meet up with the guys to work out tomorrow."

"Stop." She gives a playful smack to my chest, and I pull her hand to my mouth, kissing the fingertips.

"Hell no. It's proof that even though I'm wifed up, Casanova's still got it."

"Don't be an ass," she scolds.

I place a quick kiss to her pouting lips. With an arm scooped under her back, I lift her and flip us around so our heads are actually on the pillows instead of at the foot of the bed.

"Feeling any better?" I ask, smiling against the crown of her head.

"Mmmhmm." Kay sighs and snuggles into me more.

I cherish moments like this when she's pliant and pliable.

"Can I ask you something?" I curse myself when she tenses and smooth my hand down the length of her spine, tucking her against me tighter. "It's nothing bad, I promise. It's just something I've been curious about for a while."

"Oh-kay." I hate that she still sounds hesitant.

"What's the story behind the hang-loose thing?" Lazily I lift the arm not curled around her and wave my hand in the air like a Y.

"Oh my god." My gaze falls to the way her breasts jiggle with her laughter. "*That's* what you wanna know?"

"Yup." I've sensed there's a story behind the move and have been curious about it ever since.

Kay goes on to explain how the first year she and JT moved up to the Admirals, they were twelve—the youngest age allowed for that level—and were nervous as hell to cheer with the "bigger" kids (her words, not mine). It was hard, *really* hard to not crack a height joke.

"E was the only one able to talk me down when I would get so nervous I thought I would throw up," she explains, going into great detail about how, at their first competition as Admirals, E jumped up and cheered like a loon until they found him in the stands. "When he saw us looking at him, he held his arm out, telling us to remember to *hang loose*."

If I had heard this story before getting to know E on a personal level, I would have never believed it. It's hard to imagine one of the biggest tight ends in the National Football League making a fool of himself at a cheer competition. Now though? I wouldn't expect anything less with how resolute their family is in supporting each other.

"E actually made a comment about how special you must be to use our family tradition without even knowing its history," she says around a yawn. "Can we go to sleep now?"

"Yeah, Skittles." I chuckle and maneuver us under the covers.

"Love you, Caveman," she mumbles with another yawn. She's asleep before I can return the sentiment.

But I do love her. So fucking much. E may think I'm special, but I've known Kay was the special one from the day I saw her that first time in The Nest. With one smile and an eye roll, this little, not-even-five-foot-nothing pixie knocked me on my ass and tackled my heart without even trying.

#Epilogue

COLLAPSING FACE-FIRST ONTO MY BED, I feel it dip as Herkie jumps up beside me, his head resting on my lower back with a contented sigh.

Someone is happy to have his human home.

I'm so tired I want to sleep for a month, but know I need to get up and study. Missing a week of school thanks to traveling to Florida again, this time for Worlds, is no joke when you have to keep up with your course load.

Five minutes, I tell myself, not bothering to shift my face out from being smothered into the pillow. It would take too much effort.

"Damn, this dog is the *worst* cockblock." Mase lies down on my free side, tugging me around to be the little spoon to his big.

"I'm too tired to function, let alone have sex with you," I say, Herkie *harrumphing* when he loses his 'pillow'.

Mase's deep, sexy chuckle vibrates against my back. "All I'm saying is maybe you should rename *him* Caveman. That dog is more possessive of you than me."

"Impossible," I deadpan.

"Smartass." Mase grinds against my ass, the erection

poking me proving I was right about his intentions. What I don't do is deny his assertion. I am proud of that title.

Mase's breath blows across the crown of my head with a sigh when Herkie starts to lick the hand spread over my stomach repeatedly. He may complain about my dog, but we all know the beast loves him too.

The next—let's be honest, more than—five minutes are spent luxuriating in the strong arms holding me and inhaling the fresh smell of soap I love so much. Here with Mase, like this, is my happy place.

In the last two months, things still haven't managed to fully settle, but we have been doing our best to manage what has become our new normal.

Discovering Adam and Bailey were bigger snakes than we could have ever suspected made all of us who live with them uncomfortable in our own homes.

Mase and Brantley are only on the barest of speaking terms. Things have grown so strained between them with Mase refusing to change his mind about entering this year's NFL draft that Mase renounced him as his future agent. I at least hope that by removing the professional side of their relationship, their personal one can start to repair itself. I know better than most how important it is to value one's family.

With a groan, I do my best to extract myself from Mase and push up until I'm sitting up on the bed. I dig the heels of my palms into my eyes before dragging my hands through the riot of curls I'm sure I'm currently sporting. Using the ever-present hair tie on my wrist, I quickly gather my mane into a messy bun, needing it out of my face since I have no patience to deal with it.

The all-star cheer season is technically officially over with the conclusion of Worlds, but it doesn't mean my work at The Barracks is over—far from it. We need to handle all the updates, press releases, and planning for the end-of-year banquet to celebrate our graduating seniors and the ring ceremony for recent World Champions. Yeah, that's right: both my teams—the Admirals and the Marshals—took home the gold yesterday, kicking ass and taking names.

This weekend, instead of practice, all the teams will gather at The Barracks, where we'll make a big presentation of hanging the new banners and placing the new globes (what we call the Worlds trophies) in their place of honor.

After we finish wrapping up the last of the tasks from this season, we shift our focus to the upcoming one. We only have one month to get ready for tryouts. The number of new members (non NJA alums) who have signed up as well as video submissions we have received from those who can't travel for the tryouts is staggering. Given NJA's reputation in the all-star community, it's not uncommon to have people from other states or countries try out for our teams, but Coach Kris thinks the added influx of interest can be credited to my finally allowing her to post real-time footage of mine and JT's clinics.

All these things will be happening while I work to complete the final month of the spring semester. Oh happy happy, joy joy.

"Come on." Mase tugs on my hand, pulling me out of my wandering thoughts. "Let's go get you the biggest coffee Espresso Patronum has to offer, and then…I have something to show you."

"I told you…I'm too tired for sex. I don't care how pretty your cock is—I don't want to see it right now." My feet drag along the floor as I reluctantly let him lead me from my childhood bedroom.

"You know I love it when you say cock," he whispers naughtily in my ear, "but no guy wants to hear his manhood referred to as pretty."

"But it is." I pout because it's true. Dicks in general aren't necessarily pretty, but his certainly is. It's long and straight, so girthy my fingers don't touch when I wrap them around it.

He keeps everything trimmed up nicely, and I get to appreciate the *whole*...package—pun definitely intended—when I'm eye level with the disco stick.

"Still..." He kisses the soft spot behind my ear. "Not pretty."

"Fine," I whine with a huff. I'm tired and cranky—so sue me. "What *should* I call it then?" Sarcasm drips from my words.

"Glorious. Perfect. Hung like a horse. Too much to handle, to name a few."

No surprise, my eyes roll. "God you're full of yourself."

He pulls me in front of him, his arms looping around me. "Only when *you're* not full of me."

I swear he's incorrigible.

"Come on." He nudges the backs of my legs with the fronts of his, guiding me toward the front door. "Let's get you caffeinated so we can go on our field trip."

"Ugh."

"Don't *ugh* me," he playfully scolds. "Hop to it, Skittles."

Unaffected by the major side-eye I'm throwing his way, he places a kiss on the top of my head, effectively rendering me willing to do whatever he wants, and leads me out to the Shelby.

True to his word, a few minutes later, he pulls into a free spot in front of my favorite coffee shop. After indulging in Lyle, the owner's, flagrant flirting, Mase orders me the largest red velvet iced coffee on the menu and a more reasonable medium cold brew for himself.

As we make the familiar trek toward school, I figure whatever he has to show me is on campus. I'm very confused when he pulls into the underground garage of a luxury high-rise only a few miles from the U of J. I send him a questioning look as he shifts the Shelby into park and continues to ignore it as he walks around the hood of the car to open my door.

My confusion only grows as I take in all the familiar cars parked around ours.

No matter how hard I try to get answers out of him, he remains silent, stepping into an elevator, and with a wave of a plastic keycard, the lift starts to rise. His reflection staring back at me in the stainless steel doors gives nothing away.

When the elevator comes to a stop and the doors slide open, it's not a lobby or hallway like I would expect on the other side. No, instead we step right into an apartment—a beautifully decorated one from the looks of it.

When my feet remain rooted where they are, Mase links his hand with mine, his thumb stroking across my knuckles as he leads me out of the elevator and through the small foyer to where the space opens up into a large great room.

A large light gray sectional, with what looks like enough seating for twelve, takes up the majority of the space and faces a wall with an eighty-inch flat-screen and a long rectangular gas fireplace. A plush black and white chevron-patterned area rug fills the floor, and a massive dark wood square coffee table sits atop it. The whole space should come off as staged and cold, but the grayscale throw pillows and a few pops of red help make it feel homey instead.

Beyond the couch, closer to the wall of floor-to-ceiling glass, is a separate seating area made up of black leather club chairs and a small glass-topped table.

I keep expecting someone to come out and greet us, but no one does. Instead, I blindly follow Mase as he pulls me toward that wall of glass and out onto a large balcony through a door I didn't even see a handle for.

When we step outside, I'm stunned speechless, and it's not because of the wide Trex planks that run the entire width of the apartment or the house hunter's dream outdoor space. Nope, the honor goes to the people filling it.

Why are you surprised? You saw their cars downstairs. I don't appreciate the snark from my inner cheerleader when I'm in the middle of trying to figure this out.

"Short Stack!" Trav pauses in flipping burgers on the built-in grill to my right to wave with the spatula, and G holds a cup up in a toast while mixing drinks at the bar next to him.

"Took you guys long enough," Alex comments, Kev agreeing with a nod when I look to my left. They're both stretched out on lounge chairs with tan all-weather cushions surrounding a sunken hot tub.

"Eep," Q squeals, almost dropping the plate she's setting in front of one of the dozen chairs surrounding another massive rectangular table, this one in wrought-iron that matches the chairs around the jacuzzi. A large red umbrella is open to offer shade. "We're all here now."

CK is helping her set the table, placing different serving bowls filled with food in the free space available.

"How can you call yourself my best friend when you didn't bring me one?" Em liberates my coffee from my hand, taking a sip before returning it.

"Uh…" My words putter off. Why does it seem like I'm the only one who doesn't know what's going on?

"You still haven't told her?" Em asks Mase.

"No. Figured it might make more of an impact if I showed her."

I'm at risk of catching flies with how my jaw drops open.

"Well what are you waiting for?" Q makes shooing motions with her hands. "Go, go."

"Food won't be ready for another ten," Trav says, and Mase nods.

"Come on, Skit." He takes my hand in his and leads me back inside.

We pass one of the biggest dining room tables I have ever seen in my life, and I'm obsessed with the gorgeous funky industrial light fixture above it.

The grandeur continues along with the tour: a chef's

dream kitchen, a laundry room, a bathroom, a handful of bedrooms. My confusion over what this all is only grows as I spot one of E's jerseys framed on the wall, as well as an artfully done sepia action shot of Mase and the guys celebrating after the national championship.

Questions churn through my mind with each step we take up a glass-sided staircase. With all the natural light filtering in from the wall of windows, the glassed railings, and the loft-style second floor, the already impressive size of the apartment is amplified.

Befuddled from everything that's happening, my mind doesn't register the contents in the picture collages hanging on the walls as we walk by them. There are more rooms up here, but Mase ignores them, leading me down the long hallway to the opposite side of the apartment, coming to a stop at a closed door.

His chest rises and falls with a deep inhalation. His chin dips as he takes me in with a nervous glance before turning the knob, and then the door swings open to reveal what I assume is the master suite. A California king bed with a tufted smoke-colored headboard and footboard sits dead center, neatly made with black and white animal print bedding.

My head snaps around to where Mase has paused inside the doorway. The way his hands are tucked into the pockets of his shorts, the toe of his shoe worrying a spot on the floor in front of him, he looks...uncomfortable? Almost nervous, maybe. It's a side of him I rarely see.

"I'm fine," he says when I take a step in his direction. "Keep looking around."

Like all the other rooms, the entire far wall is made of glass. A matching glass desk and black leather chair are positioned in the corner facing it with a cool round chair in the same smoke color as the bed a little farther down. I notice there's a large dog bed and remember I also saw one downstairs.

Through the open doors, I can see two different walk-in closets. The curious thing about them, though, is that they are completely empty. The third open door in the room leads to one hell of an en suite bathroom, and I even notice a TV on the wall where the large jacuzzi tub is, perfect for long bubble baths.

Coming out of the bathroom, I stop in front of Mase, placing my hands on his hips and tilting my head back so I can see his striking seafoam green eyes.

"Mase...what is all this?" I wave my arm in a circle, indicating the apartment as a whole. "Why are we here?"

He mimics my stance, his fingertips squeezing, anchoring me to him.

I can feel a slight tremble coursing through his body, and my hand reaches up to cup his cheek. "Mase...talk to me."

"What do you think of our apartment?"

#Epilogue

THE NERVOUSNESS FLOODING my system as I wait for Kay's reaction makes it hard to swallow.

"It's beautiful." The tension releases, my body going almost boneless in relief only to seize again at her "Wait?" I meet her narrowed eyes. "Did you say *our*?"

She caught that did she? I nod, blowing out a breath.

"We needed a place where we could all just...be."

These last few months have been complicated. The football season may have ended, but both the basketball and all-star cheerleading seasons entered their busy times. Add in that none of us felt comfortable hanging around the AK house or Kay's dorm, and it made it difficult to find places large enough to accommodate a group of our size.

CK's dorm room sure as shit couldn't hold us all, and driving to Blackwell every night wasn't feasible with G and the girls' practice and class schedules.

Mom and the twins loved that we started spending more time at the house, but I learned quickly that couldn't be a long-term solution due to the tension still simmering between Brantley and me.

"Come on." I reach for her hand again and take us back

outside, all our friends now seated at the table and ready to eat.

Pulling out a free chair, I help Kay into her seat before taking the open one beside her and draping an arm along the back of hers.

"So?" Quinn bounces in her seat, rattling her drink glass and causing CK to reach out to steady it before it spills.

"What did you think?" Em asks with much more poise than our perky friend.

Kay's gaze darts around the table, taking in the seven sets of expectant eyes turned our way. "I'm confused."

Confused I can handle. There was a part of me that worried she'd be pissed she wasn't involved in the decision, but I didn't want to risk her refusing because of some misguided notion that she'd be seen as a user. She won't say it, but I know Brantley got in her head about her seeing me as a meal ticket.

Em braces her elbows on the table and inclines her head in my direction, waiting to see how I want to handle this. I give her a nod, letting her know I'm okay if she takes the lead.

"Do you remember how my dad reacted after we were ambushed by the paps?"

"When he said you couldn't be my roommate anymore?"

We may have come up with a solution, but the sadness in Kay's voice still makes my heart hurt.

"Well…this building has a doorman, and all visitors have to be on an approved list in order to be allowed access."

"No more leeches waiting outside your door," G says darkly, earning a round of agreements from everyone present.

"The only way into the apartment is through a private elevator, and you need one of these"—Em leans to the left and pulls the plastic keycard that matches the ones we all have from her pocket—"to access it."

Kay is silent as she looks at the small rectangle and back at her friend, a tear falling from her eye. I tuck a finger under her chin and turn her face my way, wiping away the streak of wetness on her cheek. It broke my heart when she admitted how lost she felt thinking about having to navigate her next year of college without the one person who had become her rock at the U of J.

"The Logans' only objection to Em rooming with you was the risk of press and unexpected visitors showing up. This place solves both of those issues." I wipe away another tear that breaks free.

I'm still having a hard time wrapping my head around the fact that Em's father is a senator. It's no wonder she and Kay became friends—the two of them sure know how to keep their identities under wraps.

"But you said this was *our* place?" A wave of snickers goes around the table at Kay's question.

"It is," G answers.

"Why else do you think it looks like *MTV* is doing a revival of *The Real World*?" Trav adds.

I smooth a hand over my hat, rethinking this strategy. I don't know if I'll survive living with him *and* Kay under the same roof. I hope these walls are strong enough to handle the smartassery.

One by one, each person around the table pulls out a matching keycard.

"Could you and Em have gotten a smaller place for just the two of you?" I nod. "Sure. But this"—I circle a finger, gesturing to the penthouse around us—"makes it so I don't have to worry about what could happen if you left to hang with the others."

The Logans aren't the only ones who worry. Before we came up with this plan, E made more than a few passing comments about Kay living at home again.

"Such a caveman." That familiar sassy sparkle enters her gray eyes, and that sense of home that has nothing to do with the apartment and everything to do with this woman hits bone deep.

This…this feeling is why I need another year to bask in it. This person is why I gathered all appropriate parties to make it possible to spend as much time together as allowed.

Like I explained—being here in this place makes it possible for our family to just be.

It lets the girls drink wine and watch their cheesy rom-coms. We even have a room for Tessa and Savvy to stay in should they need to.

CK has his setup to work on his video game, and maybe now that we're roommates, he'll let more than G play it.

The guys and I won't have to battle for time to watch game film at home, and Noah will have a place to chill when he visits when he's not playing for Washington.

"Want to know the best thing about this place?" I lean in, my lips brushing the skin behind her ear while the rest of our friends start to pass the dinner dishes around.

"You mean it's not the king-sized bed in what I assume is our bedroom?"

I growl low in my throat. Oh yes, I very much like that part, but no. What I'm thinking of is a little more Kay specific.

"With all of us living here, Herkie can too." Kay sucks in a breath, pulling back, her eyes wide and showing me a full ring of white around her irises. "And if for some reason one of us can't be around to take care of him, I have a list of dog walkers waiting for you to interview."

Kay hooks a finger in the collar of my shirt, tugging me closer. The tip of her nose skims the line of my jaw, my was-denied-earlier dick starts stirring in my shorts and urging me to drag her back upstairs and christen our new bedroom.

"I'll *never* admit this to him"—soft lips brush the shell of my ear, making that need-to-fuck-her situation grow even more urgent—"but I have a feeling Trav's reality-show-worthy assessment of this isn't going to be far off."

My arms curls around her back and I tuck her in close,

burying my face in her hair to stifle my laughter. She is 100% correct.

And we thought this last year was crazy…

NOTE FROM AUTHOR: Now before you go yelling at me that death and hellfire (or in Savvy's opinion—fingernail ripping)—hasn't occurred I have plans. But first, CK and Quinn have a story to tell sometime in 2021. Add it to your TBR HERE.

Want a place you can talk all things #UofJ without worrying about spoiling things for those who haven't read it yet in The Coven? Join the PFK Spoiler Group HERE.

Are you one of the cool people who writes reviews? *Game Changer can be found on* Goodreads, BookBub, and Amazon.

Dying to know more about the Royals? Well good news. Savvy King has forcefully shoved BTU6 out of the way and will be my first release of 2021. *Savage Queen*: A Royalty Crew U of J Spin-Off Novel will be releasing April 2021 and is available for PREORDER HERE!

Prefer to borrow it for FREE in Kindle Unlimited?

CLICK HERE to sign up for a one-time alert when Savvy King's book goes live. (You will not be subscribed to my regular newsletter.)

Randomness For My Readers

Okay, okay, okay! *holds up hands* Now before you go yelling at me I *need* you to trust me.

Yes…there's *technically* wasn't cliff, but I can hear you… things weren't tied up for Mase and Kay in a neat little bow.

Here's why…

When I first started writing their story over two years ago I knew these two would have *a lot* to say. So yes they have their HEA now…but since these two are **by far** my most talkative characters they have at least another book percolating for a future date. First though, we've got some others in the crew to explore.

Still I can't believe these two are done for now. I held on to them for so long, keeping them close while I launched the BTU Alumni. Then breaking away from my first crazy squad had me reaching for the tequila to calm the nerves. Would people like them? Would they think this new story with a younger group of characters live up enough to take a break from the OGs? The reaction, reception, and overall love for this new series still has me crying the happy tears so **thank you!**

For those of you who have no idea what I'm talking about,

hey good news, there's a whole new group of insanity for you to get to know **AND** they are stand-alones! Plus you got to meet a bunch of them in cameos. Jordan from *Power Play,* and side characters of the series Lyle, Mama Steele, and Skye.

So now for a little bullet style fun facts:

- Mr. Alley and I love watching the CFP Bowl Games and National Championship. In a house divided like ours, where we not only don't like the same sports teams but the rivals of each others, college sports for football and basketball is the one time we get to root for the same team.
- I LIVED for the theories you all came up with in the LTS and GC spoiler rooms, and I'm sure you noticed while reading, I was ALL ABOUT the misdirection in my teasers *evil laugh*—especially when I told you all flat out Kay died and Mase started dating Bailey.
- Most of the IG handles you see in the comments are from my reader Covenettes. So many are great bookstagrammers I would check them out.

If you don't want to miss out on anything new coming or when my crazy characters pop in with extra goodies make sure to sign up for my newsletter! If my rambling hasn't turned you off and you are like "This chick is my kind of crazy," feel free to reach out!

Lots of Love,

Alley

Acknowledgments

This is where I get to say thank you, hopefully I don't miss anyone. If I do I'm sorry and I still love you and blame mommy brain.

I'll start with the Hubs—who I can already hear giving me crap **again** that *this* book also isn't dedicated to him he's still the real MVP—he has to deal with my lack of sleep, putting off laundry *because… laundry* and helping to hold the fort down with our three crazy mini royals. You truly are my best friend. Also, I'm sure he would want me to make sure I say thanks for all the hero inspiration, but it is true (even if he has no ink *winking emoji*)

To Jenny my PA, the other half of my brain, the bestest best friend a girl could ask for. Why the hell do you live across the pond? Mase is yours and **yes** he is the *ONE* hero I will confirm you can claim. I live for every shouty capital message you send me while you read my words 97398479 times.

To Meg for being my first ever beta reader who wasn't related to me. I'm so grateful this series brought you into my life.

To Sierra and Papa and Mama B for answering every,

single one of my 8428376473 questions regarding the hospital and treatment and again I'm sorry—while laughing—that they thought Sierra was actually *in* the hospital and *that* is why she was asking. Sorry not sorry lol.

To my group chats that give me life and help keep me sane: The OG Coven, The MINS, The Tacos, The Book Coven, and Procrastinors & Butt Stuff (hehe—still laugh at this name like a 13 year old boy).

To all my author besties that were okay with me forcing my friendship on them and now are some of my favorite people to talk to on the inter webs. Laura, Maria, Kelsey, Lindsey, Kristy, Stefanie, Becca, Samantha (both of you), Renee, Dana, Lianne, Anna, and Krista.

To Sarah and Julie the most amazing graphics people ever in existence. Yeah I said it lol.

To Jules my cover designer, for going above and beyond, then once more with designing these covers. I can't even handle the epicness of them.

To Jess my editor, who is always pushing me to make the story better, stronger…giving such evil inspiration that leads to shouty capitals from readers that even led to a complete overhaul of these first 3 U of J books.

To Caitlin my other editor who helps clean up the mess I send her while at the same time totally getting my crazy.

To Gemma for going from my proofreader to fangirl and being so invested in my characters' stories to threaten my life *lovingly of course*.

To Dawn for giving my books their final spit shine.

To my street team for being the best pimps ever. Seriously, you guys rock my socks.

To my ARC team for giving my books some early love and getting the word out there.

To Christine and Wildfire PR for taking on my crazy and helping me spread the word of my books and helping to take me to the next level.

To Wander and his team for being beyond amazing to work with and this custom shoot for all of the Mase and Kay books. And Wayne and Megan for being the perfect models! Seriously I think the world can hear my fangirl squee whenever I get to message with you both on IG.

To every blogger and bookstagrammer that takes a chance and reads my words and writes about them.

To my fellow Covenettes for making my reader group one of my happy places. Whenever you guys post things that you know belong there I squeal a little. And for letting me use your IG handles.

And, of course, to you my fabulous reader, for picking up my book and giving me a chance. Without you I wouldn't be able to live my dream of bringing to life the stories the voices in my head tell me.

Lots of Love,

Alley

For A Good Time Call

Do you want to stay up-to-date on releases, be the first to see cover reveals, excerpts from upcoming books, deleted scenes, sales, freebies, and all sorts of insider information you can't get anywhere else?

If you're like "Duh! Come on Alley." Make sure you sign up for my newsletter.

Ask yourself this:

* Are you a Romance Junkie?

* Do you like book boyfriends and book besties? (yes this is a thing)

* Is your GIF game strong?

* Want to get inside the crazy world of Alley Ciz?

If any of your answers are yes, maybe you should join my Facebook reader group, Romance Junkie's Coven

Join The Coven

Stalk Alley

Join The Coven

Get the Newsletter

Like Alley on Facebook

Follow Alley on Instagram
Hang with Alley on Goodreads
Follow Alley on Amazon
Follow Alley on BookBub
Subscribe on YouTube for Book Trailers
Follow Alley's inspiration boards on Pinterest
All the Swag
Book Playlists
All Things Alley

Also by Alley Ciz

#UofJ Series

Looking To Score

Game Changer

Playing For Keeps

Untitled #UofJ4- Add to TBR Releasing end of 2021

Savage Queen: A Royalty Crew U of J Spin-Off Novel- Preorder, Releasing April 2021

BTU Alumni Series

Power Play (Jake and Jordan)

Tap Out (Gage and Rocky)

Sweet Victory (Vince and Holly)

Puck Performance (Jase and Melody)

Writing Dirty (Maddey and Dex)

BTU6- Coming 2021

About the Author

Alley Ciz is an indie author of Contemporary/New Adult, Rom-Com, Sports Romances.

She's a stay at home mom to 3 amazing and crazy mini royals, a 95lb lab, and let's face it on some days her hubby is her 4th kid... But to be fair she totally loves him a a lot.

When she's not corralling her crazy mini royals she can be found writing the stories the voices in her head tell her. Caffeine is a staple in her daily diet since she does most of her writing late at night when the rest of her house is asleep, usually with her trusty dog Buke (short for Beukeboom reluctantly named after a NY Ranger even though she's a NJ Devils fan all the way) Is it any surprise she writes sports romances?

Pizza and mac-n-cheese are major food groups and she is a proud Potterhead and superhero buff.

She is a complete romance junkie and can always be found reading or listening to a book.

facebook.com/AlleyCizAuthor

instagram.com/alley.ciz

pinterest.com/alleyciz

goodreads.com/alleyciz

bookbub.com/profile/alley-ciz

amazon.com/author/alleyciz

Printed in Poland
by Amazon Fulfillment
Poland Sp. z o.o., Wrocław

65678102R00214